About the Author

Sarah Guppy was born in London and moved to Edinburgh in 2002. In both capital cities she undertook a variety of jobs: campaigning, administration and charity work as well as working in the great outdoors. Her first book 'Edinburgh Shorts' a collection of short stories was published in 2014.

To Little People All Over the World

Sarah Guppy

A Dwarf's Tale

A CIP catalogue record for this title is available from the British Library.

ISBN 9781785545016 (Paperback)
ISBN 9781785545023 (Hardback)
ISBN 9781785545030 (E-Book)

www.austinmacauley.com

First Published (2016)
Austin Macauley Publishers Ltd.
25 Canada Square
Canary Wharf
London
E14 5LQ

Acknowledgments

For all those who care and think about the importance and uses of language, you know who you are.

Contents

1

It Begins with Spock

Even from an early age Alison Mode knew she was utterly different. For one thing she refused to kill the spiders that occasionally appeared in her home, she always released the poor wee struggling beasties. *"Dinnae kill them Alison for they are innocent spinners of dreams"* is what her dead ma used to say. A large dream catcher web adorned with beads hung in her front room window with these ideas in mind. And it is not just because she's a left-handed dwarf although *that* can be difficult enough to live with in terms of dealing with people's bias and ignorance. On official forms she often ticked the 'other' box whenever she could get away with it and being labelled 'different' or at least looking different did wield some kind of power it was true. The trick was to hide your differences as much as you could, be discrete. Obviously she couldn't disguise her lack of height but Alison's true but invisible powers were revealed to her slowly through her mother Barbara. Barbara Mode died over twenty years ago in suspicious circumstances at a private care home and it had nearly come to a full scale tribunal but for the huge expenses involved. '*Slipped or fell down the stairs'* said the coroner's report, carefully avoiding the potentially libellous words '*or pushed'*.

Barbara Mode broke her back and legs and was in total agony before she died. But still the care home management weaselled their way out of paying for the installation of sturdy hand rails for the frail. And as for the staff – well – their deceit and the way they closed ranks over witness accounts of cruelty and shoddy care was horror personified. The minutes, the hours, the days and weeks and months and years that followed Barbara's cruel untimely death were pretty much a lived nightmare for Alison most of this time. Indeed, for a couple of initial raw yet numb years, Alison seriously doubted her identity, worth and existence on this planet, for mother and daughter had been so close that when Barbara died Alison felt like she'd lost a part of her legs or heart and she'd practically lost the desire or will to live. Slowly, with the help of two good friends, the Macintyres and a couple of furry guinea pigs Alison began to feel less guilty and angry about her mother's death so much so that she could at last begin to think about reinventing her life and even her very identity. The remembered acts of cooking and caring for others, be they human or animal, took her out of herself she discovered and slowly she'd healed her broken spirit.

Throughout Alison's darkest years of isolation there had been times when she'd thought about taking her own life and she'd so successfully insulated herself from life and other people that she felt invisible. She only half knew she really existed because she left smudged finger prints on glasses and work surfaces. That and the morbid habit of tracing her small hands on walls confirmed for her that she existed physically if not any other way. Only daughter Alison was so profoundly affected by the experience of death that she had become determined to train herself as a carer and domestic home help to try and ensure that such scandalous deficits of quality care did not go undetected. Flora Macintyre and the respective guinea pigs no doubt sensed, on a very deep level, the amount of courage, faith and energy Alison had to summon up from somewhere deep within her just to carry on functioning in the universe if not actively participating in it. And Lord knows, Alison lives in a social inclusion zone where active participation is encouraged in community perhaps as a half-baked consolation prize for being consigned to the bottom of the socio-economic ladder. But the training as a carer was a positive step, a kind of gesture of atonement to make up for her loss after many free floating and drifting lost hours spent in inner chaos and maladjustment and everything in between. It is but a drop in the ocean, as elusive as trying to skelp a live eel in the Leith Docks near to where she lives in a trendy private rent that is completely eating into the savings she'd been left when her mother died. It was getting ever harder to keep the wolf from the door. The converted brick flats used to be nineteenth century warehouses.

She'd managed to move into the flat about five years after Barbara's death but it hadn't been a patch on the top floor housing association flat that she'd effectively grown up in with her mother in Restalrig, a poor relation of Leith. But Alison had to try and do something positive as a free thinking principled individual, she couldnae hope to single handily erase bullying and the abuse of power in the care sector all by herself though she could be a secret witness and maybe even a born again whistle blower. She'd been stuck in a grief cocoon for over a decade; slowly she'd rebuilt her life and in the last two years had built up enough courage and esteem to get herself through college. Alison, who was just twenty-one when Barbra passed away, had lived off her mother's substantial savings for a while until she'd become so socially isolated and depressed that she'd almost forgotten how to hold a half decent two-way conversation.

Alison managed to obtain a series of casual part time jobs but she had no qualifications and she was still full of a righteous rage over the climate of denial and secrecy regarding Barbara's death. She felt betrayed and let down by the managers of the care home, by the police investigating her death, even by the Care Commission itself who she'd single-handedly lobbied to appeal against the official investigation findings.

The combination of utter contempt from disinterested inept authorities, from the self-serving over paid managers of the care home just covering their backs mixed together with Alison's fiery principled character meant that she just couldn't abide fake flaky bosses who misused and abused their positions of power by indulging in or allowing nasty spiteful workplace gossip, intimidation and bullying. And there was so much of this about, Alison noticed – so many well-heeled certificate - and qualification-laden managers and supervisors who called themselves professional this and professional that but who were nevertheless profoundly unhappy, insecure people lacking courage, insight, compassion or integrity when it came to reflecting critically on their own behaviour – never mind the attitudes of underlings. Alison had come to realise with a shock that most human beings were too frightened to own up to their own capacity for evil – let alone to confront cruelty, savagery and injustice in others.

The horrific awful truth was that in these uber times of compressed days and nights most people were too self-interested, stressed or cowardly to feel able to afford to do the 'right thing' and stand up to power and its misuses. If there's a perception that there's not enough honey cake for tea at the Austerity Teddy Bear's Picnic then people tend to clam up even more, casting envious suspicious glances at anyone who encroaches on one's own slice. And that's just basic survival, never mind the bigger pictures or the energy required to spin dreams. Yet once someone has looked evil in the face it is hard to forget its smell, its feel. Banal, every day or glamorous – evil has many face manifestations and Alison had been scarred deeply by her experience.

"My, aren't we des res now," Flora says, teasing her affectionately. Flora Macintyre, maiden name Bundle, owns *Creatures of Habit* a pet shop in Leith Walk with her husband Mac. She peers at Alison now over spectacles, a few strands of hair dangling from her tightly woven bun.

"Are you going to go for a hamster or a budgie my hen? Look, this this little furry fella is giving you the eye over, hammy hamster style. They're hardly any trouble and you could get two to keep each other company Alison."

Kind hearted Flora became curious about Alison who'd been coming into the shop for over two years now. She noticed the short customer who always looked furtive and withdrawn, carefully avoiding eye contact as if she was used to being stared at, as if she couldn't possibly have feelings or opinions of her own. And thank the lucky stars for Flora's natural open curiosity about others: for it was her compassionate interest that broke the awful chain of Alison's isolated grief. Alison's standing in the middle of the shop surrounded by straw, smells, squeals and squeaks.

"I'm not too sure about a hamster or a budgie for that matter. I hate birds in all cages, an abomination. It's a pet hate of mine if you like. I rather like that bugger of a guinea pig over there though – what a load of hair. Guess I'd have to wash him occasionally. Can I take a closer look at him? I'm sure Abacus housing association need never find out about him. I'm calling him a he when actually I dinnae know either. All I do know Flora is that I have got to have *some* living creature in my hoose before Christmas or I swear I'll go tipsy mad as an over laced mince pie. I hate Christmas with a passion; I might just join a Christmas resistance campaign I warn you."

"Aye, but you'll no take an animal to where you are staying now will you? It will get Sinclair's goat and he'll make big trouble for you. I dinnae trust him at all from what you have said. Sounds like he gets up to all sorts with the wrong sort. Excuse the poor joke. Surely it'd be better to wait the two weeks before you move out completely and get a pet. Timing and a clean break and all that."

Flora hands the squirming black-haired beast to Alison who looks enthralled. Sinclair has been Alison's bullying private landlord these last fifteen odd years and has made her life hell by turning up unannounced on several occasions to inspect the flat for no legitimate reason. With ever rising rents, she'd felt under his giant thumb as if forced to dance ever harder and longer to some perverse tune. It really was as if she was a modern heroine in some folk lore tale, one in which she had to take preventative action to stop the very soles of her boots being burnt out. On top of this she thinks he's been spying on her covertly – or at least sending a baseball hatted oik to trail her. And these sordid tactics are still happening in twenty first century Edinburgh, never mind Victorian work houses or press gangs. She'd only trained as a carer in the last eighteen months, it'd been hard graft proving herself and overcoming fresh discrimination but Sinclair clearly didn't like this step to her independence and esteem – he'd somehow found out and wanted her to remain depressed and lonely all her life. Easy pickings then.

For two brief periods Alison had summoned up the courage to apply for state benefits but the experience had been so fraught and humiliating she'd given up. Society's propaganda had worked very well, instilling deep guilt about dependency, need and poverty, genuine though these were. But it's Sinclair that feels like a kind of draining social parasite to Alison Mode and she'd had to act. Thank goodness for Flora and Mac, they'd helped plot Alison's escape.

"You know you're welcome to come on over on Christmas Eve, Alison. Mac wouldnae mind, we've got that many tatties to cook up. And Christine and her girls all know you; you are practically Auntie Alison to them so please dinnae feel all alone. It doesnae have to be this way. Think about it if it all gets too much. A bit sad sitting on your tod with the tinsel and the telly. So you'll come back for this wee one will you? You'll be needing a hutch too so while you're here go and look at the hutch range at the back."

Walking back in darkness to the Leith waterfront, Alison feels more cheerful. Someone likes her and accepts her for who she is – another human being. A full moon is reflected in the water, a solitary thing of beauty in a world that's grown cold, harsh and damp. Soggy dead leaves litter the ground, bearing ominous black spots of dis-ease. Late night bar drinkers gather along the harbour under designer lighting to review the day and drink wine but nobody notices the small huddled woman in a green duffle coat and hidden headdress walking by, holding her own against the first drifting snow flakes of the season. Alison had gotten used to it: either she was invisible as folk politely looked away or she is a freak in a circus. For Edinburgh often seemed a perverse, contradictory place where great play was made of progressive toleration despite an entrenched social conservatism. When she was a wee girl, buying shoes with Barbara Mode had sometimes been awkward, her unusual shaped feet attracting morbid fascination. Climbing the steps to her door, she recalls with a start that today is the first of December; she'll move out to her new housing association home in nearby Restalrig in two weeks.

Restalrig, a poor relation of Leith with no gentrification as yet, was worth the wait and gentler on her pocket. Some of her precious savings are spent on maintaining Barbara's grave in Seafield Road cemetery; she liked to go there sometimes to be at peace and to pick the wild brambles that grew there. The dead didn't judge her or ask her to endlessly account for herself; the dead just were and they were far less frightening than what the likes of the living could do. For it'd been only last year that the muddy and scratched body of a month old baby had been found near to the cemetery, as if some mother was truly desperate to avoid admitting she couldn't cope, as if the very vulnerability itself had to be hidden away and fronted out.

You just had to just pretend things didnae affect you when really they did deeply; you couldnae let some bastards see the pain and fear they cause. Otherwise, as Alison had discovered to her cost, polite Edinburgh society called you someone suffering from "mental health issues" – whereas rougher Old Reekie just dismissed you as a *wee daftie.* Either way you were ruthlessly judged. You had to throw the fiery sarcasm and acidic verbal abuse back and quickly as well to avoid being the victim of malicious gossip. And even that wasnae enough sometimes. Alison still recalled the pain of being bullied in the playground by ignorant children who knew absolutely nothing about dwarfism or what caused it. *Are your mum and dad the same size as you then? Why doesnae your da ever pick you up at home time, pal? Don't you have a da or did he die of shock when he saw you?* The kids at school always looked surprised when they saw Barbara Mode as she looked average height, but they knew exactly which questions to use to torment and humiliate.

Sighing with tiredness, Alison makes beans on toast and looks at her tiny pairs of shoes laid out so neatly in the hallway. Yes, her shoes *were* doll small; she'd gotten sick too of hearing the jokes about missing her six other brother dwarves and was she grumpy or dopey today and where was her red riding hood jacket? It'd become so tedious but she'd dealt with her tormentors the best way she could: with wit, guts and humour as she'd have no chance physically. She'd gotten good at the art of mental withdrawal, with the re-using of the very same words and definitions that were used against her.

And now Christmas is fast approaching like some paper chain rattling consumer phantom, driving many families mad with the pressure to buy or be damned, to present a happy confident front. The collective frenzy and melt down only a few weeks away! She'd given up having to present any kind of front to the world, it is exhausting and it'd be living out a lie and Alison's never really been good at outright lying. She is what she is and the last year has flown by. She has nothing against Christmas you understand, it'd just been the fact that Barbara had died around this time and she never found the transition from one year to the next easy. She'd need another kind of saviour in the straw to tide her through and keep her right. She'd had a premonition that next year, in mid-January, she'd re-join the human race and the world of work but it'd been a strange long incubation healing period mending her broken but fighting spirit. She'd signed up to a care agency, *Help Is At Hand* as the demand for care work had surged. Okay, the pay wasnae great, but low pay was better than no pay and it's just the feeling of belonging and independence that she craved, a sense of purpose. And for so many years she'd been an unpaid unrecognised carer; one of a largely silent army caring for relatives and now she's about to become a paid one.

Barbara Mode had been her best friend of all and her source of strength, the one who had stood by her and taught her what she knew. She'd call him Spock she then decides, switching her single bar heater on in her front room, noticing through the gap in the curtains that earlier snow flurries are now mutating into mini blizzards in the orange street lighting, temporarily coating everything in a kind of translucent wonder. She'd been a *Star Trek* fan and had always liked logic and deduction as well as imagination. She'd owned guinea pigs twice before, but had appreciated Flora carting her off to Gorgie City Farm to meet some potential animal candidates to coax and snap her out of her gloom. The hutch could be in the front room; she'd let him run about.

*

"Stop that, Spock, at once! I'll not tell ye again, pal. I dunno, you give an animal a break and a good home and how do they reward you? Did you really have to climb on to the coffee table and scoff all four cheese scones in one sitting? The other day you attacked the jellied fruits and then looked not quite right. You'll become as fat as a restless Buddha and you'll no fit into your hutch."

Alison tries in vain to scoop the circling beast in her hands but he's gotten canny over the last ten days. He's hiding under an antiquated looking stool by the window, ready to make a fresh move. Relenting to him prematurely, she'd been unable to resist his charms or company and had gone back to *Creatures of Habit* and hired an impromptu taxi to drive her, Spock and the hutch back in one go. Stuff Sinclair frankly, she'll be crafty and throw a duvet cover over the hutch if he paid a surprise visit or she'll cook up a story about a bad headache. She is getting tired of being intimidated and afraid; she's lived under his shadow long enough.

There will be a way to beat these *wumps*, the word she's invented to describe folk who condemn themselves through their own dealings and words and are weak, unattractive, morally dubious posturing slime balls. For ever since Barbara's death, she's been keeping a wee journal--dictionary-hyphen-encyclopaedia of her own to somehow document, record and identify potential threats, cures, thoughts and ailments and different kinds of slime heads. She could quibble away existing cultural definitions in her own secret tome, a brown and gold embossed leather-bound book world that she'd named *The Quibblon,* her very own private language having the same name.

They could try and define you and label you all they like, using black-spell words to plant fearful gossip and smears but at least in *The Quibblon* she had the final say, the last words. So many people did not see the depths of their own poison in their choice of words and attitudes. There were advices and queries in the good book too, a principled guide for general living gleaned from insights and whispered messages from the universe's living and the dead. For not only does Alison Mode have visionary powers of the mind, she also hears messages from another parallel universe. Her vision always seemed to enter some slow motion film whenever she received some message: taps dripped more slowly, thoughts and time were suspended, and it was as if she became a semi-limp conductor or receptacle for others. And it could take a while to fall back into and possess her usual sense of self when her mind travelled or she was spoken to in this way.

It was a peculiarly modern blindness, the widespread idea that people always were in control of their minds and destinies, that life and experience were just about what could be immediately perceived or weighed. She, Alison Mode, was only half present as such in those moments or conscious states – anybody who didn't know her well might well assume she was just day dreaming away.

Giving up on catching Spock for this evening, Alison murmurs herself to sleep. Tomorrow and the next day she'll tell Spock the things she'd learnt that weren't fit for human ears – about the way some folk looked alive but were actually dead and unfeeling inside, about the use and mis-use of objects and thoughts. And she or he would sit on the old oak stool, the one she'd christened *The Sneeezewood* which she'd used to slowly re-cover and develop her ability to concentrate. Sitting on *The Sneezewood* was a favourite contemplative activity of hers, but this intense ability to focus concentration had all really started when Alison was just a girl when she discovered by accident that her mind had infinite unusual properties. She could make warts disappear from her fingers by simply concentrating her mind completely.

And it didn't just stop there with this early talent for wart removal – for she also healed her ailing mother's frequent arthritic aches the same way. Emerging from a long depressive slumber she now saw that she must somehow amend her mother's agonising death and confront the many evils in the world, social and otherwise that she'd seen and felt. She will and must become a protector and advocate of the weak. Rising above it all was always one option of course but sometimes it wasn't satisfactory and didn't feel just. Turning a blind eye or a deaf ear was not enough either, *something just had to be done but how and what exactly* thinks Alison Mode who, unknown to her, had been born in the twilight zone, an inbetwix and in-between place of perpetual transformation.

Quibblon Alternative Dictionary

Wumps, *n.* Weak, unattractive, morally dubious and posturing individuals

2

Sticks and Stones

It had been a complete white blanket of a Christmas after all despite widespread scepticism and betting shops in Edinburgh hedging the chances against. The snow had begun in earnest three days before, even driving beggars off the streets with *their* blankets but not dulling entirely the delicate grace of the golden lit trees in Princes Street which looked as if they really had been touched by some faery hand. Alison loved the big wheel and tasting a sample of German Christmas cake but after a while the festive crowds got a bit much, she couldn't hear herself think. Flakes of all sizes and designs fell on buildings and on thick coats hurrying by in dark streets, they dusted Arthur's Seat with seasonal icing and whirled excitedly about before crowning a-new infinite numbers of the city's citizens with fleeting jewels of gossamer ice. A kind of mass shoring up and stock making and taking occurs in hundreds and thousands of kitchens, a sorting of the odds, the ends and the sods of things in anticipation of up and coming plenty.
On the big day itself Alison played cards and bluff with the Macintyres, feasting on good crispy stuff. She'd danced liberating jigs, not giving two figs. And on New Year's Eve she journeyed to Jenner's to gape and stare at the luxury wares, all lit up like some elusive treasure trove. Drinking a wee dram of whiskey while she waited in a queue however at some freebie cosmetics counter with the tantalising offer

of *making your wishes come true with our free glittering make over;* Alison overheard a woman full of decidedly unseasonal spirit.

"Look at *her.* Let's face it no amount of pan stick is going to disguise her skin. She looks so dark and wrinkly already. Who'd be interested in her, do you think she's one of those Romanian illegal immigrants?"

The woman uttering this glanced in Alison's direction; giving the game away but not before several of the other women in the queue heard this very public put down. Some women looked sympathetic but were obviously afraid of saying anything as folk often are. And this is all it takes for one kind of all too prevalent malicious gossip to prosper and fester: enough people who are paralysed by cowardice, prejudice or fear. A ball of pure black fury began to build steadily within Alison and as soon as the woman and her friend had received their glossing over and goody bags and were beginning to walk away, she'd tested her skills.

Recently she'd been sitting on *The Sneezewood* a lot, meditating. *You want to give me the snake look lady; I'll give you some real ladders s*he whispered, directing a thought to the back of the woman's rather plump calves. And lo and behold, wonder of wonders two rather nasty looking ladders exploded unravelling in the woman's lacy tights, a case of nylon self-combustion if ever there was one. The woman shrieked causing heads to turn alright, but for all the wrong reasons. Nobody detected foul play or even any kind of cold turkey so that was that; it seemed she'd not lost her powers.

Walking up to George Street though after this practical demonstration of the just powers of redistributive thought, Alison considered what she already knew. A delicious smell of roast chestnuts wafted at her nose, how anyone could stand selling in the snow she didnae know – but still it was a livelihood. Could she now take this revived ability to some whole as yet unknown new level? In the late nineteen seventies, when she'd been a teenager, she'd had some early success with moving objects but she'd doubted herself for a long time, caught up as she was in survival and raw grief. Huddling her coat close to herself to keep out the freezing blasts, she felt as if she could try and master her mind even more – but that some thing or *things* in the plural were still missing, she didnae know what yet but she'd know it and feel it when she saw it right enough. A small tingling excitement thrilled within her at the possibilities before her, replacing the burning indignation at the rudeness of the customer in Jenners.

These things usually come in threes, Barbara Mode had said and Alison sensed she now had one power object, true enough in *The Sneezewood.* Yet she still had to classify and discover what the old oak stool could really do. What were its true properties? Alison recalled the odd circumstances surrounding her ma finding the stool over twenty years ago now in a charity shop on the corner of Junction Street near an imposing statue of a mature Queen Victoria. *Good sturdy stool for hire or sale: enquire within* is what the clumsily hand-written sign had said in the shop window. Intrigued by the choices given and by the unusual option of 'hiring a good stool' Barbara had promptly bought it outright.

And then walking by The Assembly Rooms Alison had been attracted by the magnificence of the vast Georgian chandelier hanging fully visible from the icy street. The hall looked warm and inviting, she'd stepped inside on lush carpet but quickly realised that there was a private function on and that she had to produce a ticket to be properly allowed in at the inn. She'd been desperate to use a lavatory and the doorman waved his gloved hand and his discretion and on this occasion let her through, handing her an evening programme to "*celebrate the philanthropic achievements of a Hester Nestle, well known stationary card heiress and entrepreneur*" although quite why Alison didn't know as clearly she wasn't a smartly dressed guest. Perhaps it was just protocol, the done thing. Walking out, she'd caught the critical eyes of a male guest this time who was trying to hide his bemusement at her presence. *What the deuce is she doing here?* is what she'd heard the man thinking but not saying of course. Because on top of being able to transmit focused thought and move inanimate objects, Alison Mode could also hear the thoughts of others, including, somewhat awkwardly, the voices of the Establishments which could make for a very noisy world indeed. And it seemed to her, walking home towards the top of Leith Walk and glancing back to see unfolding fireworks, that the *Assembly Rooms* was a misleading name for such a building which she suspected these days hardly ever hosted a true representative assembly of the city's people.

*

Still the snow lingered on, covering streets and branches and The Links where Alison Mode is walking, taking in the first dull still two weeks of January. Stricken bare trees, some of them very old, are true survivors. She's sure she doesn't suffer from seasonal affective disorder but overhanging cloudy damp gloom is enough to drag some people down into life sapping depression. Everything is morose, quiet and wet including people's spirits as post-Christmas blues and greys refuse to budge. There's not many people daring to venture out. *That awful woman customer in Jenners – what a cheeky midge!* As if dwarves or little people didn't also have a right to look nice, as if they didnae have a sexuality of their own. Surreal and sometimes dream-like images of the always youthful and eternally sculptured appeared relentlessly on city billboards, in magazines, on television cruelly reminding Alison of her abject failure, of her complete and total 'otherness' which in a competitive and individualistic culture is deemed just *too* individual. Not that she watched much telly these days, though it did seem to have a calming hypnotic effect on Spock.

Her first Christmas in her new flat had gone okay, Flora and Mac helped her move her things and there had been no nasty surprise visit from Sinclair, who she'd given plenty of notice to. The Macintyres bought her a moving in money plant for a house warming gift which she'd placed in the front room and today she needs to buy some bed linen as her existing sheets are threadbare. Maybe she can hunt out a January sale or two. Crunching across The Links in fur lined winter boots; she gazes at one of the tall Georgian houses overlooking The Links where next week she's to start a six-week-long contract with an elderly English couple. The Polish receptionist woman from the agency *Help Is At Hand* wasn't that clear over the phone about the precise requirements of the booking but Alison gathered it was ironing, cooking and general personal care.

Then horrors! Out of the corner of her eye she thinks she spots a lurking person hiding behind a clump of trees she passes by. A tense moment as she considers it may well be one of Sinclair's small but intimidating army of city wide *wumps.* Surely his motivations for trailing and harassing her were gone now, now that her tenure with him was over? But his interests and tentacles spread deep and wide across the city, she knew that much. But no, it's an elderly man innocently walking his dog, in perhaps the first walk of the New Year. Relieved, she walks on, watching her breath form little clouds in the icy air.

In November she'd signed with a private care agency but there'd been no work to actually go *to* up until now so she'd unwittingly joined the unclassified and officially invisible yet highly visible folk, the endlessly drifting randie down-and-outs, some in glad ripped rags and some carrying lumbering bags who just mill aimlessly about in Leith – gaping at buses, rummaging through bins, rolling and re-rolling tobacco, whistling at anything in a skirt, loitering with and without intentions to do all sorts. A human tragedy really, yet permanent fixtures in many of Britain's city scapes – irrespective of how 'the economy' is perceived as doing. Visible yet invisible, formally berated and scapegoated, yet conveniently forgotten and tolerated in the alley ways of the informal shadow economy. And it really was hard to tell from the outer appearance as to whether they truly were deserving of their lot or were in fact misunderstood uprights or just morally ambiguous upstarts. Just then, as she's lifting her head to the skies, a low flying magpie appears, dropping a twig upon her head and giving her a start. Another early unseasonal nest builder. *Kwik Stix, quick fix, pick me for which trick!* a mysterious whispering voice says as she looks at the innocuous twig lying on the frozen ground.

She feels it's a sort of sign, a second missing power object that she's been hoping for. Picking it up she knew instantly that it must be held in the left hand for maximum effect. And later that day, bargains bought and sitting on *The Sneezewood* again, Alison holds the *Kwik Stix* in her hand whilst visualising the Assembly Room's mighty chandelier swinging ominously on its ornate chain. That snobby staff member at the Assembly Rooms, maybe he'd been hired and drafted in for an exclusive event. He'd looked at Alison like she was a piece of dirt who didn't belong there and it stung.

And lo and behold in The Assembly Rooms and also in a vast house in Stockbridge, other less opulent lights and chandeliers sway simultaneously and shed glass tears and pieces plopping, in an ever so sophisticated manner, into the assembled chinking champagne glasses of Hester Nestle's ever increasing social circles. The footman at The Assembly Rooms had almost fainted with fright at the rocking chandelier. Faithful thoughts really could move glass mountains. She wasn't allowed entrance to that ball, but she was determined to attend another ceremony at some point. *Kwik Stixs, quick fix, pick me for which trick!*

3

The Wipers

The Wipers are an unusual retired English couple in that Mr. Simon Wiper is extremely tall and thin with a fancy moustache whilst his wife Miranda is quite rotund and though not as small as Alison Mode she still has to labour hard to reach certain higher kitchen cupboards; often standing on a chair. Not that Miranda Wiper often visits *that* particular room anyway for she has, for the most part, decided to wear but not iron the proverbial trousers in her marriage. Having tasted financial independence and power in their former cleaning business, she's now reluctant to relinquish either and the quality Alison notices straight away in the house she's to work in is a certain cutting frostiness which is as sharp as the deadly looking icicles she's seen hanging from the property's front guttering. *The Wipers.* What a name, and to have owned a cleaning business too! What's in a name, hmm? But Alison suppresses a smirk, remembering the snickers over her very un-Scottish sounding surname *Mode.* The freeze has deepened and lengthened its grip across Edinburgh, lethal ice is now replacing snow and true grit whether literal and metaphorical is in short supply.

Alison's not had much contact with "the English" in Edinburgh; there had been a few Sassenach children in her primary school but knowing herself the pain of being labelled odd, she's now trying to avoid the same trap.

People in glass conservatories should not throw stones is the code Alison tries to live her life by as far as possible – but admittedly one's own judgement and tolerance could be tested in this glass house if one of your clients for the next six weeks insists upon wearing a fluffy baby blue dressing gown both day and night, as well as serving guests tea in a make shift drawing room-cum-bedroom haphazardly assembled in, as Mrs. Wiper put it, "one's very own conserve-a-tory." And this said with a degree of self-mocking but also a watchful curiosity about her new home carer. To add to this, Mrs. Wiper's hyper-arched and pencilled eyebrows gave her a perpetually wry and lopsided expression. They are almost as startling as the contrast between her louche devil may care appearance and her clipped commanding tones.

However, neither of them had appeared shocked at Alison's dwarfdom or doubtful of her personal capabilities; Mrs. Wiper hadn't batted an eye when opening the door in fluffy blue. Her lack of height and unusual head wear attracted no doubtful questioning looks, and it was to their great credit really, but nonetheless Alison finds it endlessly fascinating the way folk could be both tolerant and compassionate in some respects but harsh and narrow minded in others. This seemed to be true in all walks of life and she'd given up on politics precisely because she's sick to the heart of these inconsistencies. Ultimately it was all about lining your own pocket and self-interest no matter how you dressed it up she'd realised after the tragedy surrounding her mother's death. The glass conservatory area where all three sit now drinking tea on wicker chairs is not that large admittedly and it looks like it's been added to the house at a later period. A drawing room, bedroom and conservatory all in one. A makeshift sofa and bed is to Alison's left, it was certainly economical if not unusual. And from the moment she stepped into the house on The Links Alison's second hand on her watch has speeded around way too fast as if the whole house existed in some strange magnetic black hole, a speeded up time warp. Something's clearly out of sync and it's not just the lady's eyebrows.

"I do hope you don't mind caring and attending to people who have perhaps very different backgrounds to your own, Ms. Mode? I gather from the agency you've not had that much experience but that you're a recently qualified hard worker with plenty of initiative. No doubt you are thinking that Simon and I are completely eccentric ex-pats. Well, you won't be the first. I suffer from anxiety attacks Ms. Mode which you may find hard to believe I know. I fear I'll be attacked by seagulls and being an economical kind of person as well as a pragmatist why wear lots of clothes which only have to be washed and dried? The fact is, I have no one to impress with my dress. Yes, we are die hard traditionalists; we're sceptical of Europe, an independent Scotland and wary of change aren't we Si?"

"Mrs. Wiper or may I call you Miranda – let me assure you that I'm very open minded, I was brought up to be tolerant as far as is possible. Frankly, I've had to be a bit feisty but fair to survive being called a midget and all kinds of things. And I still get verbal abuse believe me. To answer your question, yes I'm recently qualified but I had to provide references from college to be properly registered with *Help Is At Hand.* It's probably best not to discuss religion or politics as folk will never agree – but I'd be grateful if you could clarify what you need from me and when."

Alison's mother and tutors at college had taught her to always take a quiet pride in who she was and how she was and not to make grovelling apologies. She refuses to be intimidated by the Wipers' wealth or their southern English accents. Without being arrogant, she considers herself as good as anyone else. Using her silent but advanced telepathic skills, she can actually hear Mrs. Wiper's cynicism. The woman has a very noisy head, full of disruptive and condescending thoughts, which are ultimately helpful to nobody Alison imagines. All that misused intellect going to rot. Simon Wiper coughs politely into a handkerchief.

"Well I can't speak for Miranda as she won't like it but I'll need some help with polishing, ironing, picking up prescriptions and climbing in and out of the bath. And a hand with my tomato plants would be appreciated as I don't get out as much as I'd like. You have seen an old boy's dangly bits before I take it?"

Mr Wiper offers Alison a weak smile, clearly delighted at being able to get some kind of brief snatched word in edgeways. Miranda Wiper formally nods at her husband who appears to be present in body only as his mind is obviously elsewhere. And maybe given the amount Mrs. Wiper dominates proceedings it's hardly surprising. She doesn't seem to notice his boredom and disengagement at all, maybe because she's too involved with herself or perhaps she's just exceptionally good at not recognising the huge gulf that's grown between husband and wife.

Separate sleeping arrangements, separate meals by all accounts, a recipe for two blind marauding elephants in some bespoke china shop if ever there was one. Miranda's beginning to sound suspiciously like some opinionated or highly strung *waffle-lopocus,* another nick name Alison's invented and entered under 'w' alongside *wumps* in the faithful *Quibblon* back home. It took the term chattering classes to a whole new level but it was entirely possible to qualify for both entries. There seemed to be a lot of it about after all. Glancing at her manic watch, she hopes this first meeting won't go on for too long as Spock'll need his scoff and run.

Returning at a punctual hour the following morning to the Wipers' house overlooking The Links, Alison notices that her watch is now ticking at a pace it should be: there really *must* be something about the Wiper's house that they live in or is it her weird and wonderful mind playing tricks on her? Last night, over a TV dinner for two (she'd treated Spock to a wee smidgen of diced cod in cheese sauce) she couldn't get the image of Miranda Wiper's blue dressing gown out of her mind. Mr. Wiper opens the door this time; at least he changes *his* clothes though Alison's getting the distinct impression from them both that they haven't ventured out into the world for many months, if not whole years. Now that state of mind Alison could relate to. Always try and find an area of shared experience if you could, maybe they were the last overarching unpoliticised threads that held society's fabric together. There is an unruly funk of a smell about them both and about the house.

"Ah, Alison. Good to see you. I did enjoy our little tête a tête yesterday. Breath of fresh air, what. Miranda's upstairs attempting some polishing and she'd like some help. Quite often though she doesn't make it upstairs to do anything. After this, I'm afraid I'll need help bathing and applying lotions for some troublesome bed sores on my back. And the shopping and laundry situation urgently needs addressing. Uprisings and boxer rebellions in the laundry basket and in the kitchen. So back up action required on a number of fronts stop, not possible to tackle everything in one day, what. Please excuse the military talk, Ms. Mode. Before I became a business man I was in the army."

Simon Wiper gestures up some steep elegant stairs. He's sweating profusely even in the winter chill as if from some unspoken burning inner conflict too embarrassing to articulate. Alison notices the way he's more forthcoming when he's not around his wife but then people married and lived together for all kinds of reasons, sometimes known consciously to couples, but often not. Some married for status or sex; some had outgrown the original fit. Others never fitted but just used the other partner to express some forbidden part of themselves. Yet others yearned to be free and went searching or hunting for the missing jigsaw piece that they imagined they saw in the beloved desired other. And all of this Alison knew and had observed even though she had no formal degree in psychology. She'd had her school girl attractions, declarations and crushes too for at least love and lusts didnae discriminate against the short, there is at least the *appearance* of equality in this respect.

Following Mr. Wiper carefully up the carpeted stairs, she's startled on the way up by some mounted glass display cases seemingly exhibiting a mini history of cleaning equipment and cloths from A-Z. Flattened dusters, sprayers, ancient bottles of cleaning fluid, sponges and brushes. It took the humble J cloth to whole new dimensions. Opening a door on the first floor Mr. Wiper reveals a large cabinet of a room, resplendent with military regalia and marble fireplace. Miranda Wiper's sitting on a chaise longue surrounded by iron crosses, cups and medals.

"Alison! You came back. I'm jolly glad. I didn't frighten you off with my dressing gown, then? As you can see I'm attempting to polish the dear hubby's medal collection and let's face it there's quite a few of them. Please park yourself over here. Your timing's excellent by the way; I feel a headache coming on from all the metal polish. Si dear, will you please open a window and bring us some coffee? The best silver pot please we have for guests."

A flash of some hidden emotion scuds by on Simon Wiper's face but then he's all simpering smiles, sweaty moustache and *yes, dears* again and off he scurries to his housebound husband duties but not before giving Alison a grateful look as she offers to open the window.

"I'll get the window, Mrs. Wiper. It is a bit whiffy in here and you really do need to be using softer cloths for polishing metals. These are scouring pads and way too abrasive, you'll scratch everything. Do you have any others anywhere?"

Sighing loudly then as if decades of polishing relics and portraits had taken its earthly toll, Miranda Wiper removes a frighteningly large nail file from her dressing gown pocket and begins to file her talons which have been honed to sharp little points. It looks like this is a little ritual that's repeated often. Alison averts her eyes quickly, concluding that the file is actually a kind of warning weapon. Her arrival in the Wiper's home seems somehow timely and yet untimely given the state of the many clocks which all state different times and it's as if both are starved of any other human contact.

"Well we do have some other cloths I believe in the kitchen if you're brave enough to go down there. Who knows what you'll discover. I'm sorry not to be more enthusiastic but there it is. As you can probably see I'm afraid housework has become an unofficial battleground for unarmed conflict. I resent doing it all."

The grimy kitchen sink cupboards are practically bare and devoid of any modern known cleaning and polishing agents – an irony in a home which has built its money from precisely such products. To clean or not to clean. And the food cupboards! It's as if the tooth fairy was the last person to have cooked in this home and an excursion to a supermarket is in order. There's homogenised milk, lots of dried fruit, mouldy old bread but not a lot else. No butter, flour or the basic stuffs of life. Quite what they live on is a mystery but the marriage seemed to be all about presenting various displays Alison realises, padding back up stairs to assist Mr. Wiper with potion- lotions. She's confronted by him on the second landing, wild eyed and quietly desperate. He snatches at her small hand pressing it with dramatic emphasis.

"Ms. Mode perhaps you can help me hatch some kind of coup d'état, a domestic escape hatch from all this. *Please*. I'm going ever so quietly mad you see. Stir crazy one might say. You'd never believe it, but once Miranda used to really love cooking and being sociable. We had such parties here in the early days but she's been so withdrawn since her sister died down in England who is the only remaining family member left. Have you ever experienced grief or loss I wonder? She's bright you know – a real blue stocking. You should see the books in the attic. Look, I'm not anti-women getting an education or being independent and while we had the business it was our kind of shared baby if you like. We never had children you see – there were complications but isn't everything complicated really if you scratch beneath the surface? But I never saw this in my younger army days. The fact is I must *get out regularly* as I'm growing leaves here. I'm turning into a human hot house tomato plant and it's not pretty. I can't recall the last time I had an ordinary pint. I'm not allowed out as she starts hyper ventilating and angsting out about me being attacked by seagulls of all things. It's just an excuse. Ms. Mode, is there *any* little thing you could think of to remedy this situation?"

"Mr. Wiper, it's really not my business to say how you can rescue a marriage is it? Your wife will not appreciate it, folk rarely do. But I will think about it and yes, I will keep mum so to speak about this wee chat. One thing's for sure you need a major trip to some supermarket. What do you live on man?"

"Stale air, classical music, caffeine and stewed prunes. My bed linen's not changed nearly often enough, I'm sure it's not helping the bed sores. But it's difficult for me to bend as I'm sure I have lurking arthritis as well."

His outburst is interrupted by a loud thumping noise reverberating on some ceiling.

"That's her reminding me to make the coffee damn it. Sometimes it's the only way we communicate."

Washing herself later at home after that first eventful day, Alison notices some newsprint has somehow made a ghostly looking impression on her arm. She doesnae know quite how the words have rubbed on to her skin but somehow the newspaper she bought earlier has left a mark and message. *Don't fake it, bake it* and she knows the words have it again, that they might provide an answer to Mr. Wiper's plea for help. For perhaps ordinary butter and powders may have other uses after all too she muses, submerging herself in bath water and holding the portentous *Kwik Stix* in the left hand. *Great this isn't it.* And there she was thinking she's just trained to be a practical carer dishing out her very own brand of practical magic in the mix only now and then if needed. *Fruit cake, ginger cake, double take.* Cook yourself into intimacy and out of grief. Bring it on blighty in the old nightie. Now it seems she's blending into a kind of make shift carer and cake counsellor all in one package. Well, one needed to diversify these days and be flexible and use resources as necessary.

And playing cards with the Wipers the following evening by a roaring fire, Alison winks discretely at the fireplace. *White flour, re-flower, I call upon your high white power!* But just one bag of pure white flour sent down a chimney and through a fire only to explode all over a lady's well-worn dressing gown isn't going to be enough to cure this domestic stasis. *Pucker and large it up then white power and times this by five.* Five bags of self-raising flour were duly posted then down all available chimneys, affectionately bombing The Wipers into more open communication, active submission and participative housework. It is practically the first time that Alison Mode, all three foot six of her that is, told a white lie to cover her tracks over the spilt flour that is now decorating all the rooms. She wasnae particularly comfortable doing it but The Wipers seemed to accept the explanation that it really was the ghost of Miranda's dead sister come to nag and remind them both to at least attempt *some* kind of maintenance work on this modern Marriage á la Mode. Perhaps they were both really at their wits' end about it all, and to live without any humour is surely a kind of joyless existence.

"Good heavens! Do you really mean to say that you think some kind of entity or paranormal *thing* has caused all of this, Ms. Mode? I have to say that as a former military man my credibility is a tad stretched here. And yet I too cannot explain it. Miranda, are you alright?"

A shell shocked Mr. Wiper had escaped the domestic dusting with just a few brushings of white on his moustache. Mrs. Wiper however looks a bit of a wide-eyed spook and seems to have momentarily lost the power of speech.

"I really wouldnae be alarmed you two about this kind of thing. I've heard of long dead relatives going on strike and causing havoc as well as living relatives mind you. All manner of things happen on western domestic fronts. My money's on Miranda's sister and I think it's some kind of message for you both to not take yourselves quite so seriously all the time, to do a bit of shared housework. After all you cannae take your period antiques or your medals with you when you go too now can you? Mrs. Wiper, I gather you used to make great cakes hen and really delight in cooking up the unexpected. Can I suggest you get cracking on the cleaning for a bit while Mr. Wiper and I go out shopping? Your cupboards are scarily bare."

Alison phrases and steers her comments carefully, aware of her powers of suggestion but not wanting to lecture her clients. With a bit of stealthy timing her Plan B could come into fruition and she might help to preserve more than just the food supply in this barren stale home. Both she and Mr. Wiper sneak glances at Mrs. Wiper but thankfully no panic attack ensues over even the idea of being alone in the house for a mere hour or two. *Frankly the woman needs to eat and think a bit of humble pie*, Alison thinks as they march out with big shopping bags.

She'd noticed a very old Ford Cortina parked outside the house on her first few visits, you could still decipher it under heavy frost and ice. Somehow it, too, needed to rumble back into life.

The warm sweet smells of cakes and biscuits filled the house over the next few weeks and together Alison Mode and Miranda Wiper turned out upside down cakes, right side up honey cakes, kiss-my-cherries quite quickly cookies and roly-polies galore. At last the kitchen began to resemble a proper working living space again and every egg that was beaten there seemed to somehow restore a heartbeat of hope in turn. Mrs Wiper hadnae laughed so much for years and cared less about the baking mess. She'd just needed something; some add with spice activity to take herself out of herself. *Life is very messy, hen, not everything runs to an exact recipe but that's okay, I'm sure you can handle it* is what Alison had said in a kindly way. And Mr Wiper even had a crack at Bread and Butter Pudding and Spotted Dick; he looked quite romantic in an apron. Gradually he ventured out of the house out more and more, each time returning home intact and unharmed by any errant seagull which was in itself a kind of faith preserver.

He'd take himself off to the cheap but cheerful *Jolly Old Codger* drinking hall full of colourful weathered Leithers, coming home full of stories and wetting Mrs. Wiper's appetites. And thinking of romance and a possible late re-flowering of relations; Alison realised with a start that St. Valentine's Day was just next week. The last January weeks have whizzed by, her contract with them would soon stop, her Jill-of-all-trades needed elsewhere. So far there hadnae been any message on her phone from Evelina, the receptionist at *Help Is At Hand* advising her of more work in the foreseeable future. But this could change in an instant; it was the nature of casual labour. Mr. Wiper's bed sores and apparent mobility problems had improved remarkably, very probably down to regular doses of conversation, clean bedding and fresh air exercise but they'd have to find someone else to help them with the laundry in the future. Mrs Wiper re-discovered her wardrobe in turn, wearing a balance of skirt and shirt. And stranger than any impromptu marriage guidance and home care Alison offered was the fact the second hand on her watch seemed to move at a normal rate as soon as these changes were implemented.

Clocks functioned as they should in the house, it was as if the whole energy field of the building had been cleared but perhaps a slow release Valentines Cake might help finally seal the deal on the day. Slow release referred to Alison's potent bottle of bubbly *Twilight Dew* she'd carefully collected from select plants and flowers in Seafield Cemetery which when sprinkled or consumed compelled a person to either confess the truth or hear the secret wishes of another. Alison was yet to discover what a very strong dose from the little blue bottle would unleash, but experiments to date proved it could be smuggled and cooked into a sponge cake's air pockets; revealing after digestion hundreds and thousands of forgotten half-baked desires.

Quibblon Alternative Dictionary

Pucker and Large It, v. Colloquial, informal slang meaning to polish or spruce something or someone and to then exaggerate, emphasize or buff up that object or person. Add a *pal* or a *mate* at the end of it for added emphasis depending upon which side of the border you live on.

4

Mayhem and Humbug

Underneath the old Rowan Tree,
I see you but you don't see me

Alison had a strange premonition about Geraldine McEwan when Barbara Mode tested her on words beginning with 'g' like good parents should. Withdrawing from the present moment, her eyes usually went into a kind of trance and sometimes an image or two would flash into her mind. She had no control over such moments or impressions; both mother and daughter had come to accept young Alison's growing gifts and abilities. Cash-strapped Barbara Mode had taken wee Alison into the pawn shop, eager to obtain something for her engagement ring. She'd kept it for a few years after Rick, the man, had left without warning. *Don't sell to that man, ma. He'll no give you a fair price. Try the other shop, too,* is what Alison had said. And she'd been right about that as she'd been spot on with many other things. Shortly after that episode she'd begun to take an interest in metals, copper wiring and gazing at candle flames: she'd discovered she could increase the intensity of the light somehow by simultaneously rubbing the wire and looking. And it was round about then that Alison discovered the hidden powers of the moon's movements: thought-wishes cast on specific nights held even more power. But all these kinds of knowing in advance were still not enough it seemed to protect a person from the worst aspects of human nature. 1975 in Edinburgh. They'd been methodically working their way through the alphabet on the teacher's suggestion but Alison had inexplicably come to a mental standstill at the letter g. *Gumption is what you have my wee lass* is what Barbara had said.

Maybe so, but that particular spring night back in the mid-seventies had been a restless, sleep-deprived one. A full moon had glared behind ten-year-old Alison's curtains and she knew that Geraldine, playground pack leader, would stop at nothing. Blood, tears, flesh. Girls excel at inflicting subtle psychological torture. It's all done in the whispered coded innuendo, the knowing hidden looks they give each other. A quick kill or a protracted drawn out campaign, designed to wear out and exhaust the chosen victim's nerves. Geraldine already sensed, the way some girls do, that Alison had a soft spot for a boy called Kelvin, who was of average height. Kelvin was not disgusted or frightened by Alison's dwarfdom, he had better manners than that, but he was embarrassed to be associated with Alison Mode. He had his own boyish reputation to consider after all and there were whispers in the playground, rumours about Alison having some kind of strange hypnotic power. In the desperation of the hunted she'd quickly scribbled it, the potential life saver code, down on paper. *Would words be enough to save the human bacon?*

Y M U C R Y 4 E B I

"What's that supposed to be, Alison? Is that your *special code*, the one you use when you do your hocus pocus tricks. We all know you fancy Kelvin, there's no use hiding. My ma says there's no such things as witches anyway and that you oughtn't to bring cooking herbs into school. Miss doesn't really like it. The school has its own dinner ladies."

"Yeah, that's right, Geraldine. I reckon it's a bit weird eating fresh mint, you're supposed to *cook* herbs, stupid. And why do you always smell of rabbits? You smell just like the hutch in the classroom. Can't you afford to buy soap what with your mum being the only one at home?"

Nicola, another spitfire of a little girl, backs Geraldine up in front of the baying gang of girls. A couple of days ago they'd blindfolded Alison, turned her around twice in the middle of the playground which had left the victim disorientated and afraid. *Blind dwarf's bluff* had been great fun for about half an hour before a staff member spotted what was happening. Now they are standing in the shadow of the school's adopted Rowan Tree in a corner of the playground. Alison's ma had said Rowan Trees were supposed to ward off evil, but looking at the girls now, who seemed possessed by a kind of frenzy, Alison wasn't so sure. Ever since she'd started at the Leith primary, her love of rodents and small furry beasties had been further enforced by the customary class room pets. Barbara had bought her daughter a first gerbil on her ninth birthday, after they'd visited an animal sanctuary and saw a young pine marten being bottle fed. A few weeks back some boys had joined in with the name calling and jibes but had got bored, preferring a football to kick around.

I saw her talking to the tree, she was casting a spell.

Her clothes look like charity shop clothes.

She said she saves spiders and her mum lets the webs grow in the house, imagine that.

Nicola said Alison gave her another dirty evil look and Nicola hadn't done anything.

Alison fancies Kelvin but she should find a boy dwarf really. Who'd fancy her?

Her mum never talks to my mum or even says hello in the morning, who does she think she is?

Then May Day came, a day for oppressed downtrodden workers and young hopeful lovers tying the knot maybe. Spring has sprung up in school tubs and in surrounding gardens and the Edinburgh playground looks blossom covered and deceptively peaceful. For maybe it's actually a different kind of personal mayday featuring an anguished but unheard call for help. After all, it's been going on for months now, this unholy terror war waged by kids. Who ever said children were or are little angels? Only a simplistic fool would say that. She'd concocted *The Formula* for them over a month ago, hoping it would satisfy and appease them and for a while it had worked and kept the baying nasty little pack off her. She'd fed them artfully paced chunks at a time; it had taken their minds on to something different.

Y Y U R

Bay City Roller mania has hit the City of Edinburgh with extra dollops of outsized tartan, braces and spiky haircuts, but Alison's fanzine cotton socks and T shirt had not been enough either, in fact these items seem to have somehow further fuelled a kind of infantile envy. Then in PE Geraldine noticed for the first time that Alison's feet were slightly different sizes, an enormous corn on the left foot fuelled further fascination, repulsion and persecution. So they stole a shoe. The names and the spiteful calling of them had almost followed her home in her one remaining shoe making her feel doubly odd and disfigured. *Bye, Bye Baby*. People had stared at her as she hobbled unevenly home but luckily Barbara had come to pick her up at home time. She'd done this ever since her only daughter had plucked up the courage to show and tell all. The sores on her legs caused by stinging nettles being rubbed on skin, the bruises. Unfortunately stinging nettles grew in abundance along a strip of wild open ground alongside the playground, but leaves made their way through the railings. Geraldine had stolen one of her shoes for weeks on end, hiding it under a girl's toilet. *Now you see me, now you don't.* Alison's class teacher, a mild tempered man, had just underplayed it and dismissed it as harmless fun but when said shoe disappeared permanently things felt more malicious and the Head had finally been informed. And predictable too were the denials proffered by both girls and parents alike. *Not in our back yard, nothing to do with me. Our daughter wouldn't do something like that.*

Y Y U B

Mister Collywobbles's Kitchen Kids Magic Show had begun to be broadcast on Saturday mornings at around that time, Alison would later recall fondly. Offering mainly magic entertainment, the shows however also included a small element of very basic cooking recipes for children to try at home with the aid of a parent or two. Evidently some TV Executive had decided that mothers might appreciate a hand or at least a nod in their direction, acknowledging all the time they usually spend in kitchens. And at 10 am ish every Saturday, Alison would sit enthralled in front of the black and white TV, watching as the larger than life funny man in a hat and a green cauliflower costume would cook, performing great delicious feats of illusion with the simplest of cooking utensils: colanders, cucumbers, rubber balls, spoons, and marbles. Objects disappeared, appeared, doubled in size, and mutated. Children could impress their mummy and daddy with simple dishes. The best thing of all was that Barbara Mode and many other adult viewers couldn't work out how the tricks were done. Once Mister Collywobbles escaped, Houdini like, from a tightly bound orange crate, causing mini uproars from concerned viewers thinking that some kids might try this at home too. Escape + transformation = joy + freedom. To Alison, this equation seemed to offer the best lesson and she made it her early business to master the arts of basic juggling and baking. Not long after this she'd discovered she could remove warts from her fingers, she'd then moved on to the irritating corn on her toe. That was a blight that she could deal with privately; the bullies at school had to be shown up for what they really were even though some still would not see it.

The formula, fed to the tormentors on a weekly basis, managed to defer the taunts for a few weeks but it was never going to be a real and lasting solution. Looking back, Alison realised she'd been stringing them along, not biding her time exactly but at least trying to plan calmly what to do, who to tell and how. *Would she be believed?* She was fiercely independent; she didn't like admitting she needed help with something. And it would be her alone who would have to deal with any nasty aftermath in the playground. Seeing the big top circus one bank holiday on The Links had been the final hook for Alison, she'd seen other juggling dwarves getting all the laughs.

Much to the crowds' delight, one plucky dwarf had even ridden an elephant, unperturbed by the disparity in size. Their learnt moves were perfectly co-ordinated. But then world events, of a grown up dramatic kind soon encroached a bit on the world of the playground and TV magic shows. The Lebanese were fighting for their freedom too, in a faraway land called, ironically enough, the Holy Land. Alison had seen the grainy images on TV, enough to make out the cloth turbans some wore on their heads. From then on she'd pretty much adopted the full time wearing of some kind of make shift headdress, in recognition of minority and persecuted groups everywhere who were fighting for respect and dignity.

I C U R YY 4 ME

5

Sinclair

At dusk, the industrial chimney visible at the end of Wardlaw Place in Gorgie pokes an ambiguous brick finger into the ether. By day it is magnificent, a hymn to Victorian forward thinking engineering but by night fall what seemed like earlier forward thinking now regresses into something symbolising the ever more efficient modes of proletariat oppression and production. Like a lot of things, it depended upon your outlook or frame of mind and the quality of the light at the time. Some said they've seen bats flitting about at the peak and maybe the chimney was and is an achievement as well as an instrument to be used for good or ill. Munching on a superb oily fish supper, Sinclair lips his thin lips satisfied with the day and his belly. Shadowy Gorgie, forged and built in dark stone with hard uncompromising labour. Yet it isn't far from the airy New Town, you could walk between the two mini worlds in twenty minutes or so. Samantha, his current convenient squeeze, lies next door in scanty underwear in the tenement flat's small box-like bedroom. His upbeat mobile ring tone blasts the room with sound. He may be well over fifty, but he's still nifty with technology and females.

"Hello, hello? Ah, Davie my lad how are you feeling? How's takings at Junction Street – did you get to speak to Ahmed? Dinnae worry aboot him, Davie – his boss knows we rent out the back rooms on the cheap, like. We're back rooms boys, Davie after all but it's all hunky dory. It will all come out in the wash if you ken what I mean. Whaasaat, you say? Three decent bookings for flats in February, that's alright isn't it. Dinnae ask aboot the Gorgie office, I have not been in. Dealing with other little affairs."

Pause. Sinclair glances knowingly at the bedroom door. A bored Samantha, tired of waiting for the wee bald man's attentions, resorts to washing up the dishes cursing under her breath.

"Where are you now, pal? Ah, right. At the snooker hall right enough. Make sure nobody can hear you, daftie. I dinnae want to be laying you off. Did you get the juice on her, *the dwarf* I mean? Great, so we know where she lives and you got the flat number. Good, text it to me will you tonight. Just make sure she doesn't see you when you trail her, she's quite sharp even though she's a midget like. I'll try a letter and see what happens but ah'm sure she keeps an animal now. I found some straw or was it hay lying aboot like just after she moved out and there was a pet kind of smell in the place. Could be useful. Keep on her, Davie and let me know her movements. Got to go now, duty calls, eh?"

Sinclair hangs up with a smirk on his face. He's matured well and the shaved bald head hides the fact that the hair line had been receding. Davey's alright and can be trusted with tip offs, ready cash, pickups and information; he's been working for him for many years now. There are certain advantages to running a letting agency behind the covering shop fronts of two sympathetic launderette and dry cleaner owners. It has no official name, no books, no tax, existing for the chosen few by word of mouth referral only. At Leith's *Squeaky Kleen* it's liquid cash 'n' flash and no deposits required, the naïve are often dazzled by the deal. The business rent for the letting agency also is literally dirt cheap and there's a good supply of young students and immigrants coming into use the launderettes anyway and people washing and dry cleaning clothes in such places often needed somewhere to live or knew someone else who did. Supplies of more affluent western students are also a certainty; everyone was chasing qualifications these days. Sinclair's the second in command of this outfit, the rarely seen big boss man dabbles in all sorts but his speciality is in real estate.

"Is that you finished blethering away then finally? You and your grubby little pals. I thought you said you'd come over to visit me, you bastard. Spend time and make a lassie feel wanted. Plenty of men are dying to go out with me you know, William. Dinnae think you're that good looking with your shiny baldy heid, pal. A lot of women won't go for the Kojak look right enough."

Samantha's getting hacked off, he'd better watch his step. They'd actually met in the Gorgie Road premises as she works with the dry cleaners, the sods and the soap suds were all there. *William* What a raw nerve that lassie has Sinclair thinks, unrobing himself and lying back, Caesar like, on the pile of cushions. Nobody ever calls him by his first name but then nobody knew his first name or his Fife family history and that's the way he likes it, pal. His estranged father of the same name lives in Dunfermline and runs a funeral business, as his grandfather had done but Sinclair prefers to deal with living flesh instead.

"Are you staying over tomorrow night as well then? Ah'm not sure whether to cook especially or not. You get through the meat right enough when you're here. Can you answer me please when I'm talking to you?"

Samantha lies down beside him. No amount of nagging, prodding or ribbing gets Sinclair responding, he moves and talks only when he wants to, living in a moral empire seemingly of his own making. He's from the Kingdom; he always was an independent thinker with a shrewd bloody eye on survival. An acquired taste. Recently, Samantha's been talking about wanting a baby like a lot of women do. He might have to then design an escape hatch as nothing must stand in his way. If only he could turn into some kind of bat himself, just disappear like and hang around strategically in the City's old crevices, attracting new tenant-payers from dank beams with the power of magnetic red eyes. *Tush man,* he tells himself secretly, *it's to be got through graft and thrift. Don't let anybody tell you* is what the tattoo says on his arm.

He'd got it done in Leith after he'd been booted out of his da's house at sixteen and never gone back. He hadnae fancied the wood cutting and joinery apprenticeship and didnae want to be at his da's beck and call either. He'd had a feral childhood, mutilating flies by removing their wings and smoking at the age of nine. Consumed with envy and bitterness, he couldn't stand things that flew or moved freely or easily, even strangling a gosling on one occasion. Once, his God-fearing da had locked him in a morgue overnight out of fury to teach him a lesson in Presbyterian respect. He'd looked the dead in the face underneath the clinical plastic covers; he'd smelled them and survived. *Come on, Sammy lass, give your man a wee massage*, he whispers seductively in Samantha's ear. Lassies are so easy to manipulate and fool, their vanity knows no bounds.

*

Waking in the small hours, Sinclair switches on his laptop and begins typing. Samantha snores on, oblivious to his interests and methods. *Ah but the end justifies the means.* The trick when laundering is to never give too much away, don't give a specific address or clear line of accountability. Be soluble in water, dissolve and simply crumble away in the hand with no trace if the police or the tax office or anybody comes sniffing around asking direct questions. Coffee and breakfast will have to wait until later; he must get the letter done today. That midget Alison, she'd become too confident, she'd showed him up with her too prompt rent paying and made him look like an imbecile in front of his pals. And that was one thing naebody in their right mind should do. He's sure she's hiding something, too, but what? He must know, it could be a potential lever. Hunt it out, show no mercy. That uppity freak is too goody two shoes for her own good, she must be shown not to mess with Sinclair. Keep the tone touchy-feely, professional, and concerned.

Edinburgh Lettings Ltd,
20th February, 2014
0808 300 200

Re: Flat 2F2, Harbour Front, Leith EH6

Dear Ms. Mode,

I am delighted to inform you that you have in fact over paid Edinburgh Lettings Ltd, by some £178.32p, a sum included in the total last quarterly invoice for the rent you paid for the above named property which you resided in until December 17th, 2013 I must apologise as this was due to miscalculation on my part as you had in fact come into the Junction Road office some two weeks prior to the date the last quarterly bill was due. Unfortunately, no record of your visit or receipt was issued to me at the time as I was absent; the error was noted only once the payment had been actually processed.

It would be appreciated if you could please call the above number to make an appointment with my colleague to come into the office to see either myself or Mr. David MacPherson who is available during office hours. I am keen to refund you the monies due as soon as is convenient to yourself and would like to take this opportunity to thank you for your custom and tenancy. Here at Edinburgh Lettings Ltd we pride ourselves in delivering value and quality in service. In order to obtain your current address my colleague had to contact your current housing provider, I emphasize that this is not usual practice but given the funds owed we felt we were justified and reasonable in our actions.

I await your further instructions.

Sincerely

Mr. W. Sinclair Esq
Manager

It is about the words you used after all. Saving the document on a memory stick, Sinclair makes himself a pot of hot sweet coffee. He must visit Dalry Appliances again today, he knows the man who works there and can get a good supply of white goods delivered free across Edinburgh. Not washing machines though, that would be taking business away from *Squeaky Kleen,* but fridges, cookers, freezers, yes. Rubbing a port hole on the frosted window glass, he sees an early morning wag tail bird pecking delicately below in the kerb side. Spring is nearly visible, the sun is returning to the world slowly and closing his eyes then, Sinclair sees red, orange and gold spots. And that's without any dried seeds, pipes or magic mushrooms, like. His da hated druggie culture so that's precisely why it had appealed to him. *I'm a visionary, me. Advanced for my time.* Seeing the bird had made him hungry. Stepping stealthily out of the flat he descends the stairs to the street in his full length black leather coat. Fresh flesh. He must have it, now. Only Davey really knew about his road kill habit, about his cravings for wood pigeon or maybe a squirrel if he's lucky. Dinnae bother yourself with any cooking, we've been eating raw meat since the Celts and Picts lived in caves. Finish off what the crows and ravens left. Still early mornings are the best time to get the score, the too slow creatures that never quite made it across the city's roads and paving. Parks could be good too, you just need to know where to look and watch. You never know, The Meadows might offer up yields.

The city bypasses, the arteries like, now they were rich pickings with a good sack once a month. Just don't get caught, watch the timing. It wasn't illegal though was it, just offensive to some. Rabbits are prolific across the city; their meat is versatile too. Pop one in a pie, dinnae bother with the skinning. Once he'd left a few hedgehog guts in

Samantha's fridge for a laugh, fobbing her off with lame lamb claims. She'd shrieked hysterically and, he'd pissed himself laughing almost. All good sport. Turning out of Wardlaw Place he grins, picking out a toothpick and coughing abruptly. A dry, crackling cough full of the burnt out fires of the damned. *Must stop smoking the Cuban cigars though* he silently notes, he's getting awful catarrh and cannae taste anything.

6

Bad Egg

Late winter is the most magical time of year and though Alison Mode is most definitely not a snob she does find it profoundly depressing to see so many young Edinburgh laddies walking bull terriers on the estate she lives on. It was a herd or pack mentality, one lad had one so they all had to have the same kind of dog. *Gladiator dogs for gladiator gang boys* is what her ma Barbara always used to say. She'd grown up in an identical looking flat just one block away and at least Abacus housing association bothered with things like planting bulbs and snowdrops even though some let their litter, bad language and dog mess drop with abandon. But an all-encompassing transformation is in the air, the city's citizens and bird populations wait with baited breath for the first green tender buds and up on Arthur's Seat the intense yellowness of the gorse signals the future months' shades to come. *Help is At Hand* had not called for over a week, and Alison had traipsed furtively back to The Assembly Rooms in George Street curious to assess her powers to move inanimate objects through the power of intense directed thought.

Yes, said what looked like the young manageress in a silky waistcoat, *we have had trouble with the chandelier rocking adversely for no apparent reason. Funny you should mention that. The odd tinkling sounds too as the glass pieces seem to ripple together without warning. We have never had this kind of thing happen before and given that the whole building is listed and potentially vulnerable we are wondering if it's overly sensitive to traffic vibrations. That certainly seems the most sensible explanation we can think of; we have no resident spook that we are aware of. But the whole glass appliance has been insured to be on the safe side. Strangely, it's only been swaying over the last few weeks and seems to respond to the presence of large after-dinner crowds.*

Then the woman had paused, looking at Alison and her suspect turban-headdress suspiciously. Terror insurgents could take many shapes and forms after all so the do *fear the other syndrome was very topical,* more so perhaps in times of scarcity. It was a question of how much tolerance you could afford. Alison arrived home satisfied with herself. So it was really true, she *did* have advanced proven powers and maybe they could be developed further. The chandelier, the white flour bombing acts at The Wipers, why, she'd just grown rusty what with her grief and depression. But first, she said to herself, she must classify and consolidate what she already knew. Take stock and form a strategy for the good will of all.

For if she had gifts of some sort, then really what right had she to exercise them without a kind of accompanying responsibility? Like a good scientist or clinician, she must do a knowledge audit and reflect upon and hone her existing skills. Spock was fed earlier and has now fallen asleep on a blanket by a radiator. She didn't like to be too strict with him, he needed his run-a-round and anyway, he looked as cute as a wee furry ball and she hadn't got the heart to always insist he slept in his hutch.

But how to structure, reference and describe on paper what she knew? Sitting on the old but trusty *Sneezewood* stool by the front room windows, Alison closes her eyes with the *Quibblon* upon her lap. She must enquire within from a still place of trance. She'll have a few sacred minutes with closed eyes to prepare for open eyed clear vision or clairvoyance. The answers and guidance could come from that still point at the back of the mind, from the deep depths of underworld unconsciousness, from the timeless universal source – it didnae really matter but it took great patience and practise to master these realms successfully. The mobile phone which Alison's finally mastered sits switched off on the living room table for now. A present from Flora at Christmas, her friend said she must have it for her own safety and sanity, as going into all these unknown people's homes could be potentially dodgy.

It was her only concession to technology so far. *It won't kill the agency if you get murdered Alison by some nutter but yes, they have a legal responsibility or duty of care to police check all the people you'll be caring for. Still, some do slip through the net don't they and are lots of funny folk about*, Flora had laughingly said with worry in her eyes nevertheless. But both women had been uneasy, it's an issue this employee safety as well as resident safety and Alison vowed to herself that she'd ask the management at *Help Is at Hand* about health and safety policy, about emergencies and whether some work related calls and expenses could be claimed for. In fairness, she had been given a pile of documentation from the agency covering some of these issues but just hadn't as yet got round to deciphering the policy talk.

And she'd already called the agency about the too-good-to-be-true sugary letter she'd received yesterday from Sinclair at Edinburgh Lettings Ltd. She'd become wary and wanted to check to see if this mysterious David MacPherson character, a colleague of Sinclair's apparently, or indeed anybody else, had actually rung or visited *Help Is At Hand* as the letter claimed, to obtain her new address.

But she'd discovered that no such call or visit was made from Edinburgh Lettings Ltd which pricked Alison's antennae still further. Some funny business was a foot and she's uneasy. That early January walk across The Links when she thought she was being followed or 'stalked' proved to be a false alarm, but over the last few weeks she'd had the odd sensation she was being watched and tracked like some animal prey. She'd gone ahead and rung the number provided on the letter from her mobile, making an appointment to see Sinclair tomorrow morning at the Junction Road premises. She couldn't really use the word 'office' as truthfully it was just a room at the back of the launderette, but it might be possible she'd over paid. Better safe than sorry; be upfront in all your dealings.

A huge, black, new moon hangs suspended in solitary isolation in the February night sky behind the heavily embroidered curtains. Although the curtains are pulled as she mustn't have any visual distractions, Alison can still feel and sense the magnetic power. And as every true initiate of the moon knows, new moons and full moons are times of new beginnings, of enhanced empathetic magic. It's a matter of being receptive to the rays of wisdom and insight which casts subtle illumination upon all that is hidden and denied by day. For the sun casts shadows as well as light and some matters are revealed and truly known and seen only in darkness. No, it's not speedy direction and emergency guidance in specific spells that she needed right now, the *Kwik Stix* she felt sure would be useful in identifying the precise and best future courses of action in that department.

She'd put the stick on her bedside table, she's not used the stick just yet but saw it more as an on-the-spot-get-out-of-a-tight-corner instant remedy fixer, whereas *The Sneezewood* seemed a great overall strategic thought conductor and facilitated fine meditative states. Opening her eyes then, in a kind of cathartic outburst, she begins to write an entry in the *Advices and Queries* section in the *Quibblon's* back section for miscellaneous notes

What do I now know?

Domain I = my inner world, which I access through awareness. I tune into my thoughts, make no judgement but simply observe and try to harness especially the power of positive, creative thoughts though regular atonement and reflection.

Domain II = the inner world of others: I am blessed with the fortunate (or unfortunate) ability to hear another's thoughts, not all of them pleasant, polite or nice – instead a lot of them are dark, morbid, covetous, cruel and selfish. Yet that is the partial reality of how people really are, whether they like it or not. You have to start from where you're actually at. You cannot deny the darkness or destructiveness and maybe the best we can hope for is the 'Peter Pan syndrome' – namely, being very aware of the shadow self that we all carry around. Peter Pan had his shadow nailed to him – food for thought. Being aware of the darkness within and without and acknowledging the shadow's potential does not make one evil or bad – indeed the *well-integrated shadow*, if used wisely, can provide instigators for change and is courageous and pioneering. If denied though the shadow will creep up on you, play a trick and catch you unawares. So be aware, be whole, and fear not. Reflect regularly and own the shadow.

Domain III = the shared transpersonal world, a space without in which shared objects can be moved, transported. A kind of 'neutral' eternal space, existing both within measured time as we know it and yet with no time and 'timeless' as with the respective inner worlds described. Now is it possible for me to 'implant' ideas into the minds of others through the power of transmitted thought? If light, sounds and thoughts travel in waves how to suggest thoughts to others in such a way as to leave them still with their own choice and free will as to whether or not to accept and act on that suggestion? *I don't want to be a mere brain washer, that's just cheap and manipulative.* Clearly the technique does work with objects, but I'd like to experiment more.

NB: Is it possible to transplant a piece of past time (i.e. a record of people and their actions and feelings) and cut and paste it into 'the now' or the present? Can one 're-run' events and consciousness like a film? Is it true that some events 'imprint' themselves with energy on to specific geographical places only to be re-seen and felt by receptive people over and over? This could explain the phenomena some called 'ghosts'. For logically if Domain III exists both within measured time in the modern western sense as well as without then surely it might be possible to mix 'n' match the 'tapes' or tap into simultaneous times using different states of consciousness?

There must be different states of consciousness which allow or facilitate such inter-dimensional communications – a kind of neural interface if you like to use a computing term. We are all separate atoms, beings, creatures, it is one truth. There are geographical, physical and psychological boundaries, and yes, we can split atoms, particles, light and bend light, too. This is one collection of 'truths' as developed by western modern man, usually white western men in fairness who tend to see things (arguably) always in isolation to each other.

Reductionist, atomistic and perfect for dividing and measuring light waves into different colour vibrational frequencies, all true – but also perfect for dividing, measuring and conquering people and setting one human against another in blinded splendid isolation. But there is something else which is also true at the same time: we are also interconnected; there is cause and effect, there is proven telepathy and out-of-body-experiences. Clearly, consciousness and 'the mind' can travel beyond the actual physical space of the brain and if consciousness exists outside or beyond the physical brain as well as within the brain then maybe it is itself eternal and maybe experiences that exist both in time and in consciousness can be spliced and re-run. And maybe in this shared transpersonal, tran-physical realm or mode, thoughts can be transmitted to another and be 'received' just as in radio transmitters or TV aerials. It's just a frequency one could become more attuned to if you felt or heard the calling or the need. And what is a co-incidence anyway – but two things 'co-

inciding' in the universe. If water could 'remember' traces of elements left in it previously then maybe time could 'remember' also. The question was: did time 'contain' consciousness or does consciousness contain time?

Alison *Mode. What a weird Scottish sounding name*, some of her teachers had said along with her class. What's in a name? A whole history and identity, that's what. She didnae quite know where her da came from in Scotland but it had been a parental marriage á la mode evidently. It was good to get the troubling thoughts off her chest and reading the scribblings to herself, Alison concluded that it didn't really matter if the *Quibblon* had a dictionary feel at times and a journal or diary approach at another. *It's my way of making sense of the world, it's a method of differentiating between the madness, chaos and order within and beyond in the external world. Contradictory forces are my speciality. And anyway the quality of discernment is sometimes in short supply.*

Let folk think what they like should they stumble across this tome after I die, she mutters deep frying herself a fine egg sandwich with bite the way she always liked it. It's late and she had nothing else to raid from her fridge, sod the world's judgements about eating at odd hours and comfort eating. And nobody could say she didn't have an inquiring mind. Spock's run out of his gripo nuts which help him to pass wind, she must stock up over the weekend as well as do a food shop. So far Alison's resisted the lure of having an Internet connection installed citing sensory overload to Flora. *For a sensitive soul like me I cannae be doing with too many colours, sensational news stories and images all at once,* she'd ranted to Flora who was really raving about Flatter, the latest social networking site vying for global domination in an apparently relentless thirst for trivial gossip, mindless updates and 'exclusive' exposés turning millions of people into self-absorbed status freaks as she saw it. She didn't know when and where this frantic screen watching would end, the TV and the mobile was enough for her and she couldn't see this changing.

Flora had hinted at Alison's 'quality of life' without the Internet – as if it was on a par with fine clothes and food, decent pay and holidays but Alison has always liked to live simply needing quiet grotto like time for silent contemplation and re-newal. She's never been a great chatter either – a waste of energy in her mind. Pulling blankets snugly around herself she drifts off to sleep. The knitted patchwork creations roughly sewn together with wool were made by Barbara Mode throughout her adult life time – both when she was living with her daughter and later when residing in a private care home.

And that episode and experience had been criminal really, another kind of silent social crime and cultural impoverishment and deficit. Her mother had worked all her life as a dinner lady in a primary school and had paid taxes and NI contributions faithfully yet there were no affordable and long term places for her in state run homes for the elderly and though Alison had struggled honourably with the care of her mother; after several years it had completely exhausted her. Someone was needed to care for Barbara all day really and Alison had to work. On top of this a formal carer's allowance, a benefit which Alison qualified for punished her for working longer hours. It didn't pay to be female or to care is what Alison had concluded. And lying awake and thinking about her mother again, she remembered hearing what sounded like Barbara Mode's voice in Seafield Cemetery back in January when she'd paid her first visit of the year to her grave. It was just as she'd been walking out of the graveyard, pushed along a path by a gentle but icy breeze, that she'd heard a voice whispering behind her telling her not to worry. *Collect the early dew from these hallowed grounds* is what she then thought she heard passing through wrought iron gates and heaped dead leaves.

*

The washing machines spin loudly, nearly drowning out all conversation and road traffic so Sinclair shuts the back room door so as he and Alison Mode could have a *nice wee chat* as he called it. He stands behind a shabby looking desk shuffling papers. A single filing cabinet stands in a corner under dim strip lighting which flickers like an ailing pulse. Cheap dodgy wiring. *Life's a clean breeze with Squeaky Kleen* proclaims a dog eared business calendar sitting on the desk.

"Ms. Mode or should I say Alison now that you are no longer a tenant of Edinburgh Lettings – it's good of you to arrange to meet me. How are things with you? I gather that you are a qualified carer now; all that hard work at college must have paid off. Congratulations, you must feel very proud. You got my letter no doubt about rent arrears, then?"

Sinclair smiles and eyes her testily, sussing Alison out and reading her body language. He'll have to wing this one carefully he thinks, she's got some kind of power or secret he's sure of it. Maybe both. She's different somehow from all the other tenants he'd known and he doesn't just mean her dwarfdom. No, there's something else. In her fifteen odd years as tenant, Sinclair always thought her a bit of a closed book, a dark, wee horse in big boots who kept her cards close to her chest. She's certainly sitting in a chair that's too big and high for her now as her munchkin feet hang some distance from the ground.

"Rent *arrears* you say? I thought you said that I was owed a payment due to paying too much rent in fact. This is a bit of a shock you know. I bought the letter you sent along in my bag. Can you please explain to me how you calculated this? I'm devastated as I'm usually very careful about paying the right amount on time. I have never been in debt in my life."

Hot coils of angry steel are beginning to burn in Alison's dark brown eyes, but she holds her head high ignoring his smarmy fake questions and stained yellow teeth. Sinclair's bald shining head looks misshapen and somehow alien in the room. How on earth did he know about her college qualifications? Perhaps she'd mentioned it in conversation. Muted rumblings and churnings of dryers and washing machines from next door fill the silence. Out in the front shop a telephone rings several times before being answered. Should she directly confront him about the lie in the letter? Possibly not – now's not a good time. Choose your battles, save your energy.

"Yes, I must apologise again, Ms. Mode. All very embarrassing but we have recently taken on two new staff members who are actively undergoing training. The letter you received was actually supposed to be for another former tenant. I'd had a whole great pile of them to sign and they'd been typed up by my *new assistant* who's currently mastering a couple of software packages. Samantha mixed up the addresses and file contact details so the letter that you should have received went out to someone else. And vice versa as I said. So in actual fact you owe Edinburgh Lettings Ltd the sum quoted in the letter which was I believe was around the £170 mark or there about. And I have a detailed breakdown of accounts just here to confirm this which clearly shows moneys paid and dates paid."

Sinclair spins round in his chair to reach a drawer in the filing cabinet. So smooth. He loved these moments, this watching the cornered trapped victim struggle to understand. Bamboozle then club with polite factualness, knock away any arguments or points methodically, like kicking away stool legs one by one. Or picking the wings off flies. And thinking of stools, he'd always had his eye on that weird antique-y Eastern looking stool she'd kept in her flat for all those years. It looked like it would be great for rolling and splitting tobacco, dice and mice on. Sinclair always thought Alison Mode a bit weird, not a hippy exactly but maybe she was into crystals, tarot cards and reading tea leaves.

“Surely there must be some mistake here, Mr. Sinclair. Can I please see the accounts you have?”

Alison pours over the papers in the dim light trying to make sense of it. A terrible gassy smell has seeped from underneath the closed door, something like rotten eggs or even flesh. She hides a small shudder, wondering what she’ll say next without this whole thing becoming really nasty. She just wants to get this sorted quickly and painlessly. She’s got a huge shopping trip due next; she can’t be here all day haggling.

“I should say at this point, Ms. Mode that I’m prepared to waiver this last outstanding payment due in return for the antique stool you own and your possible employment in Edinburgh Lettings Ltd. Let’s face it, care work is not well paid and I’m sure I can offer you more attractive remuneration and benefits. We need a receptionist and office administrator urgently and I’m wondering if this position may interest you, Ms. Mode? A plucky resourceful and hard working person like yourself *and an animal lover, too*, I gather.”

Sinclair artfully placed emphasis on those last words, watching her face carefully for a reaction. If this sweetener didnae work, he might have to up the ante. He’s allowed her a few minutes to take this all in but he must have an answer, he’s a busy man. At a recent Christmas fancy dress party, he’d been invited to he’d turned up as a quasi-Dickensian *Heartfelt Scrounger,* as this hat fitted better than Artful Dodger. He’d thought about turning up and announcing himself instead as the *Hardworking Scrounger* but he wasn’t sure that those present would grasp his line in dry satire as instant quick fix techno-hedonism seems all the rage. Tapping info in his lap top, Sinclair then glances quickly at his tablet for a tip off from Davey. He too had succumbed to the power of ‘the tablet’ but he drew the line at sending pictures of himself doing leisure activities. Sending endless ‘selfies’ for visual consumption to people he hardly knew never mind to the wider world was not good for a man who lives in the business underworld. Don't be too visible. Some habits we keep to ourselves.

Maybe in some odd way that was what he had in common with Ms. Mode: they were both strong-willed outsiders and ultimately private people, thinks Sinclair wondering when Alison will say something. But the Christmas party costume and trumped up name had been testament to his money laundering and cash collecting skills and a kind of double whammy joke at the expense of both the hated dependent poor and the affluent politico-chattering classes, both of which he despises with a passion. He'd turned up resplendent in hired top hat, his pale-skinned sheen blinding the drunken party goers still further.

"Mr. Sinclair this is all very sudden, this proposition of yours. And I thank you for the offer of employment, it being very hard to find any kind of work these days. But I trained as a carer because that's what I care to do, it's what I enjoy. As for animals and the stool – well, the stool I cannae part with. It brings me great comfort, *The Sneezewwod* does. Now if you will excuse me, I didnae bring any cash or cheque book with as I was under the impression that I was the one owed something. I will send a payment in the next week and that will have to do."

She got up, nodding formally to Sinclair to keep things polite as far as she could, and then pushed the door to the front launderette firmly open. Escaping out into the street, she cussed herself for her stupidity for naming the stool in front of him. *Dinnae be foolish* Alison, she says to herself. Dinnae give away your private language for language is power and a different kind of currency or code. Having no name, no way of identifying something, and living the life of the excluded eccentric outsider was a way of evading the relentless surveillance and accounting one had to do for oneself these days. She walks up Leith Walk slowly to do some shopping, suddenly very aware of the traffic cameras watching every move.

Though she's been living at her new flat for a while now she still needs a few knick knacks like a wash tub and a bathroom mat. And she's run out of supplies of fresh herbs which she needs for cooking and various ailments. Crossing the road, she's nearly run over by a speeding car and it reminds her of the awful stories from Flora and Mac about people, usually women and children, being trafficked in modern day Edinburgh. She must call Flora soon and tell her how she's settling in and to get a fresh supply of free straw for Spock's hutch. It was hard to believe this kind of casual trade went on looking at the imposing houses around Gayfield Square and beyond, but one day when the time was right the world could know Alison's language and her story too. She refused to let Sinclair's antics get her down as she'd received a voice message on her mobile earlier that morning from *Help is at Hand* telling her about a client in the New Town who needed her services at short notice. If possible Alison should report for work tomorrow morning at no 38 India Street EH1.

7

Good Egg

Being a practical person at heart, Alison Mode had invested early on in an A-Z, for though Edinburgh is a small city in comparison to vast amoeba like conurbations such as London, New York and Beijing, it's still possible to live your entire life in one specific zone or neighbourhood and to not really have a clue as to how other city inhabitants actually live. *India Street.* Consulting the page carefully by a burnt out rubbish bin, the charred remains of somebody's Saturday night entertainment perhaps, she sees her destination is in the New Town. It must be one of those big Georgian houses again, maybe even grander than The Wipers. She'd seen the Wipers about town in their car, they'd hooted at her enthusiastically. It looked as if their relationship had turned some kind of corner and she was glad.

With another start Alison realises today is the first of March. Judging by the clocks at The Wipers it seemed time could really fly on occasion. *White rabbits* she says to herself believing in the power of this uttered mantra, although Sinclair's eyes yesterday in that awful launderette encounter really did have the slightly possessed intense look of a mad March hare. What a nerve that man had – but there's nothing she can do about it. Although she's not a coward she knows that if she reports this to the police she may never see an end to his tactics. He knows where she lives and she doesn't trust him. His reference to her as an animal lover had also unnerved her as she'd been careful to hide Spock's existence from him in her last few weeks as his tenant. She'll pay him reluctantly, still not really convinced that she owes anything, but choosing her battles. Breathing in blustery air under cotton wool clouds, she walks down Princes Street, passing a kilted busker playing an electric guitar and wearing a pig's mask. Brave man, for though it's milder, Alison's still not cast off her sturdy winter boots.

Ringing on an imposing polished brass door bell, Alison admires the understated but elegant mauve and yellow crocuses that sprout from two flower pots. Less is more. There's a long five-minute wait during which Alison thinks she may have made a mistake in writing down the number, but finally the grand old door is swung open to the sight of a stately looking elderly woman with silvery hair and a walking stick. She's not much taller than Alison and wears round gold spectacles on a chain.

"Ah, you must be the carer cum home help from *Help is at Hand.* Please do come in. It's very good of you to agree to assist me *Mrs. Mode*, very good indeed. My husband's away in London so much with his work and this will continue until the summer really. He tries to fly up every weekend that's if he's not too tired. Let's go in and I'll show you the ropes."

Walking and hobbling down the hall was like walking back in time by two hundred years or so, the walls and ceilings are adorned with gold leaf painted lines and elaborate plaster decorations of Greek Goddesses, fruit and urns. *Mrs.* Mode. Alison didnae really mind the assumption that she was married; there were far worse irritants than that. The unmistakable sounds of Baroque music fill the front drawing room which features a long sash window overlooking a similarly narrow but lengthy back garden full of fruit trees. The music's coming from a stereo towards the back of the room.

"Please sit down, *Mrs. Mode* and I'll ring for some tea. I have a charming Asian lady who comes to assist me with my shopping and cooking but nobody to attend to my dressings and exercise for my poor strained feet. This is because the other lady I have, a trained nurse, is on pregnancy leave and there's not much I can do about Mother Nature. But I do get the most awful pains in my legs as well and the GP, the homeopath and the acupuncturist all said I have bad drainage and poor circulation of blood and fluids which can lead to awkward puffiness and redness. I'd really like to be far more mobile than I am right now but it's hard."

The woman rings a small silver bell, which made the pince- nez quiver slightly on her nose. Alison soaks up the room around her; it's almost like a museum: two chaise longues, an inlaid rosewood writing desk, book cases, and a card table. The tarts' knickers curtains bring the tone of the décor down slightly, but then again they are in tasteful shades of shell pink and pastel blue. They sit round an oval dining table just by the window. A huge mirror hangs over a marble fire place which is very different from her own artificial log gas fire back at the flat in Restalrig.

"No doubt *you know who I am*, Mrs. Mode. I'm sure your agency filled you in with the details which must of course be kept in the strictest of confidence you understand given the nature of my husband's office and more importantly, my title and estate."

"It's *Ms*. Mode, actually, and no, I'm sorry, but nobody said anything about your husband's job or who you are. I was told the nature of your ailments, what was required and how long you may need someone for. And that is it."

A petite smiling Asian woman comes in carrying the tea on a tray which she sets down on the table. Alison's having a hard time trying to place the woman's accent, she concludes it's upper class old school Edinburgh which actually sounds quite English. A hybrid, heaven forbid. Surprised, the woman gazes at Alison across the table and the glass lenses and over the great social divides. Her blue eyes and their distanced expression emanate centuries of quiet elite power. Alison gets the feeling she's being assessed, surveyed, considered.

"*Ms*. Mode, I am Lady Katherine Hyde, formally of the Hyde Estates, my family having owned land in Scotland since the sixteenth century. My great great grandfather made his fortune importing tea and sugar from the West Indies but in truth, the estate was bequeathed to one of my ancestors back to 1145. So don't let anyone tell you it was just the greedy or entrepreneurial English who owned slaves and plantations. My husband Lord Edward Hyde, is chairman of *Interferax* a pharmaceutical and chemical engineering company now heavily embroiled in controversial tests of pesticides for genetically modified crops. He also happens to be chairman of the Parliamentary Cross Party Committee on Ethics and Standards in Public Life."

Lady Hyde pours tea, offering milk, biscuits and sugar from a sophisticated pewter sugar boat, quite possibly modelled on a ship owned by her great great grandfather. Alison's sure it's Vivaldi's *Four Seasons* that she can hear.

"Ms. Mode, do you take milk and sugar? I'd like you to start this afternoon as soon as Neesha leaves at 2pm promptly. I'll show you the dressings I have to apply to my feet and leg every other day on the doctor's orders. It's most tiresome but there it is. I'll need a good breakfast when you come in the mornings as I stated to the agency, that's three mornings a week and Neesha can't do all the mornings. She'll do the shopping though. I want to see if I can gain more mobility in my legs and feet as at the moment I do feel bed-ridden and house-bound but it's not of my choice, this lifestyle. And frankly after my dressings need changing I may need a wee blether or two. That, the radio and monthly editions of *Farming Life* keep me going. It's immensely tiresome being my husband's ad hoc secretary and dealing with zillions of emails."

*

A whole shock of daffodils sway gracefully in the long garden at number 38 India Street. But Lady Hyde has to be content with looking at them from a distance and only imagining their fresh smell. The last few weeks have gone well and both she and Alison have developed a rapport, becoming unlikely comrade-companions in arms over the plight of carers, the animal and natural world generally and the "poor wee bairns" who regularly go to school with no hot breakfast down them. Alison's been recounting her Leith childhood and the way her mother used to buy second hand clothes and old bread to make ends meet; having had an absent husband who vanished as soon as he found out his other half had given birth to a dwarf. *Numpty freak and scabby loser* is what had been hurled at Barbara Mode at a time when she needed more support, not less. And this abuse had been face to face not via some anonymous virtual online forum, those at first harmless masquerades which mutate in an instant to sinister bloodletting arenas.

This in turn led on to other lively topics about the UK's widespread culture of abuse, inequality and bullying in all its shapes and forms. *Was this a worldwide phenomenon and how much had technology contributed to the casualization and brutalisation* of *language?* Sobering stuff indeed but now Lady Katherine sits bolt upright in her four poster bead, two pillows behind her and a whole pile of cushions under one leg to encourage its circulation. The bedroom, which overlooks the back garden, has one window slightly open to air the place out. And all these searching questions and conversations invariably conducted over splendid Baroque notes which seem to fill the entire house as the good Lady said it calms her nerves and allows her to forget. She'd had a morning administering to angry repetitive emails from people who argued that her husband's position in *Inteferax* compromised his neutrality and objectivity when it came to discussing matters of pesticide use and genetic engineering.

"I get such terrible pins and needles Alison in my left leg particularly. That's something we do have in common though isn't it – we are both left-handed and are acutely aware of the all prevailing care deficit which may or may not be related to budget deficits. A lot of people feel more generous and understanding to the less well off when there's no recession after all – there's a perception that there is enough to provide for all. But when money and credit becomes tighter there's often a tightening of suspicious hearts. What ever happened to the concept of the soul or the sacred, hmm? For I think this relentless emphasis on costs, audits and measurement itself is a kind of depressive if not a deceitful distraction. Now please can I first have the daily pill and then the cold cream applied slowly? And if you could massage the puffiness in the ankle that seems to ease it slightly. It's a good idea of yours to raise the leg this high in relation to my body, I hadn't realised it should be quite so high. Can you also please pass the hot lemon with honey and ginger?"

Alison massages the leg which looks red and bloated. She'd questioned the way Lady Katherine's GP insisted upon wrapping up the leg most of the time, somehow treating the disorder as a self-fulfilling prophecy and not looking at posture, fluid, acidic intake and attitude both physical and mental. *Attitude* – or how one sees and holds one's predicament. Now there's a trick. Stealing a glance at Lady Katherine who has closed her eyes, Alison realises she'd never met a member of the aristocracy before, having only glimpsed these elite rarities on TV or in magazines when stories ran about weddings, garden parties or horse racing. *Yes, it is strange the way us hens get on – Lady Katherine being a blue blood and me a working class Leither lassie; yet we are both free independent spirits who admire people who fight back and think for themselves. Her blood is red, too; she has feelings which are genuine. She may be one of the privileged minority but she does at least know this and she's not fake, deceitful, cruel or judgemental. She's a real slow thinking and moving gentlewoman in a world that's often brutal and instant and yet where there are often no easy quick-fix answers. A kind of rare old fashioned species in fact in a very nice way. It's please this, Alison and what do you think about that Ms. Mode all the time.*

Privately Lady Katherine raged against those who plundered the arctic for cheap oil, at those who decimated ancient fields and their wild fragile flowers in the dubious names of efficiency and progress, at those who used technology to invade the privacy and decency of human souls. But she couldn't say this *publicly* precisely because of her husband's visibility and position as well as her own status. Reputation and privilege could be much prized and hard fought for but could ultimately restrict too.

"Isn't this ironic, Alison? To most people *I look and seem* rich, powerful and influential from the outside no doubt, but *inwardly* I often feel power-less in the apparent tides of prevailing opinions. I wonder how many of these sweeping waves of social opinion are manufactured, frankly. And how many others feel the same way do you think? Many I suspect; people right across the political spectrum. We only appear to have consensus, empowerment, consultation and democracy. We have things at a push of a button and sensory overload, in fact. And we have thousands of packets of unsold and uneaten bagged supermarket salads and chicken meat thrown casually away. Yet at the very same time there's begging and impoverishment at the centre of this excess, 'choice' and waste. We cannot have 'it all', know it all or control everything. There are limits which are sometimes mysterious. Something doesn't add up, does it?"

At this fiery outburst, Lady Hyde, who'd spent years being a decorative but largely silent political accessory, relapsed into an exhausted coughing fit which was only assuaged by yet more lemon and honey and another diverting game of whist.

Back at her home later that evening Alison Mode wondered how she could possibly help her client's low mood as she's concerned for *her* welfare. Bags of dried lavender placed on the pillow to calm the nerves would just not be enough and she couldn't exactly tell Lady Hyde to *pucker up her apron and just do more cooking*. No, Lady Hyde was not ball-breakingly strident and in fact she could do with a bit of fire and shaking up in an entirely different way from Mrs. Wiper. After all, some women had expensive handbags, bathroom appliances, and husbands as lifestyle accessory options – and it increasingly seemed that questions of faith or politics were equally trivialised. She'd spoken briefly to the quiet sounding Lord Edward Hyde a couple of times on the phone and he'd seemed nice enough down there in London, vaguely saying that he'd be able to next fly up in a fortnight but that there were "a lot of matters to attend to," which could be a euphemism for anything.

Cooking up a big bubbling cauldron of pasta *al dente* or with bite, Alison thinks Lady Hyde also has a bit more substance than her husband perhaps gives her credit for. There must be some trick she can pull, some motivational life nudge as with The Wipers. Maybe a wee focused think on *The Sneezewood* would help. For contrary to what a lot may think about women like her, Lady Hyde didn't actually spend her days grooming a solitary inbred eyebrow over caviar. Now, *those* days must surely be over for the majority, but Ignorance, Squalor, Idleness and Want were still rampant everywhere.

Outside on the Restalrig estate a wind has picked up which hasn't deterred some crazed teens from riding wildly around on cobbled together motorised bikes unfit for human roads. But no matter, eh, there's fresh garlic and basil to be sprinkled and enjoyed and there's a job she's needed for and it was hard to put just a price on that. And that was another thing, Lady Hyde stoically endured so many absences and excuses from her husband when many with less wouldn't and couldn't. Biting into her fresh pasta feast, it had unnerved Alison that there had been two silent voice messages on her landline answerphone and one on her mobile too.

One of Sinclair's underworld henchmen perhaps, she knew there was a whole network of them. An intimidating warning to pay up quickly maybe. Thank the lucky stars she'd not yet succumbed to the lure of the Internet which, for her, was another portal or channel through which her sacred grotto like private time and peace of mind could be invaded and commodified. *No way.* Alison saw her mind as a last bastion or frontier, it was her possession and she controlled the off switch and imagery.

"What's it all about then, Spock my lad?" she asks, throwing him a small fresh piece of penne regatta with pesto, somehow convinced that he may have Italian blood in him somewhere. Spock's on his daily mad hour or so when Alison lets him run his wee hind legs off round the flat. But Spock's found his miraculous guinea pig way to *The Quibblon* which is lying open on top of *The Sneezewood*, having leaped on to it from the coffee table. Extreme times call for extreme acts of faith, and the courage to be different and true to yourself even when you know you may be judged. Pausing in his snuffles, Spock appears to be reading an entry and then looks up at her enquiringly with his small black eyes.

"My wee little furry genius, what are you trying to show me?" rushing over, Alison almost squeals with excitement herself. She loves these eureka moments, with or without a power object. Somehow, she didn't know how, but maybe in honesty she didn't want to know how or why as that would kill off the mystery and magic – somehow Spock's directing her to an entry under 'T' entitled '*Thought Transference*'. Spock had been tuning into his owner's thoughts no doubt, it was catching. And she would be prepared to swear on her dear mother's grave that, before cooking, the good book had been lying open on 'A' not 'T'. 'A' was for the uses of Arrowroot, amongst other things, Arrowroot being the roots of a South American plant *Maranta Arundinaceous.*

At that moment Spock jumped off *The Sneezewood* in a little cloud of dust clearly wanting to play *catch me if you can hen* and Alison knew in that moment that she must try and direct a thought to Lady Hyde. She'd already proved she could move an object, now it was time to try a thought. It wasn't brain washing it was suggesting or absent healing. And sleep, or a pre-sleep state may just be a good receptive time to try and reach her client. Who knows, maybe she's actually restoring her client's fundamental faith in herself and her abilities never mind this learnt identity Lady Hyde had acquired, polished and inherited like some plush gem.

*

Holding the herbs in rubber gloves some distance away from herself, Lady Katherine Hyde sprinkles some powdered arrowroot in the four corners of her bedroom which has fleshy dimpled cherubs and rosebuds on its pink and cream wallpaper. Cussing quietly under her breath, she needs her walking stick to make the distance satisfactorily. Her legs have been massaged but are bandage free and are slightly less puffy and blotchy. Something seems to be working for Lady Hyde. Watching her now, Alison tries to suppress a giggle. She feels for the *Kwik Stix* in her overall pocket which she'd bought just in case anything goes wrong.

"Do you think I'm going a bit mad, Alison? Tell me truthfully. I woke at seven this morning and a little voice in my head said *sprinkle some dried arrowroot to heal your heart*. Can you believe this? I have never had any, what you might call, brushings with the paranormal before and I'm not even sure I believe in that kind of thing. But there it is. I had a restless sleepless last night, waking several times but not needing the bathroom just waking. It was most odd. I had the strangest feeling someone was thinking about me, too, I couldn't put my finger on it. Then I had a dream and you were in it Alison! You invited me back to your home, cooked me an arrowroot omelette, sat me down and very earnestly said '*that other people tend to see you as they see themselves, Lady Hyde. People see you as they are not as you are'* so you said I was not to worry about what people thought about me and that I should go down to London. But for what purpose I do not know as yet. It's all very mysterious.

Then, on waking and purely on some instinct I went down to the kitchen and asked Neesha if we had any arrowroot. She arrives early mid-week you see, she's very efficient. The poor woman looked startled but I knew I had to sprinkle in the bedroom particularly as it's the room I do most of my worrying in. Then before you arrived and after Edward phoned at his usual time, I heard another little voice saying that I should *sprinkle my entire body with arrowroot to change my life destiny!* Needless to say I drew the line there as things were getting a bit too weird. Well, Alison? You are keeping very quiet. What do you make of it? Has this old gal finally lost the plot?"

Lady Katherine peers anxiously at her through her glasses as Neesha brings in a laden breakfast tray.

Hesitating, Alison Mode's in a real dilemma. Should she risk telling Lady Katherine about her white powers? Even if she were to tell her client some of what she knew she may not be believed. It's a gamble. And even Flora and Mac didn't yet know the full extent of her abilities, thinking that she's just an eccentric lonely dwarf who reads tea leaves, keeps a guinea pig, and bends coat hangers out of shape whilst gazing at the galaxy. Lady Hyde's already proved she's a good keeper of her husband's secrets but what about hers? Perhaps she could reveal a bit seeing as her client's virtually chomping at the bit with boredom. She's been working at number 38 India Street for about six weeks and has begun to feel a bit at home, so much so that Lady Hyde's requested that both Alison and Spock stay the night for Easter and once or twice a month until the summer months. She's made the normally reserved and cynical Lady Katherine laugh out loud with tales of Spock's acrobatic shenanigans. Feeling bold, Alison takes the plunge. She knows private suffering when she sees it. She'd not said anything about the very strong smells of exotic spices emanating from the house's basement, as it seemed Neesha was cooking up some delight.

"Lady Hyde, I must make an intimate confession which must remain as confidential as the matters you have shared with me. It was me, last night, who was trying to speak with you and *send you a message on the ether waves* if you like. Not through hypnosis but through thought transference, by focusing a thought directly to you, a bit like telepathy but I'm not reading your thoughts, I'm trying to suggest things to you subliminally. Clearly it works, you picked up things well. And yes, I visualised me sitting you down at my home and giving you a bit of a life coach speech. Katherine, if I may call you this, I can also move objects at will through time and space. Some may call me a healer, some a white witch, others a sensitive. But I can see and hear things which a lot can't and I'm still discovering my abilities. I have been praying for your legs in a way to get better every night. I visualise your blotchiness going and you being able to walk freely and seeing you powdering just now gives me a glimmer of hope."

Munching liberally buttered crumpets, Alison then tells Lady Hyde about the death of her mother Barbara and how this had profoundly affected her, leading her to care deeply for the sick, the vulnerable, isolated and depressed no matter who they were. It was a pity, she said, that she'd not sprinkled the arrowroot all over her body, but would she like to try this now after breakfast? She need not be afraid as she's bought along a special divining stick if you like or power object which would make the magic work. It is all about the power of self-belief, about staying true to your universe's purpose. Lady Hyde could change her destiny through applying her mind. Life is what you make it and Alison suggested she really break the repetitive mould and go and visit London for a change of scene. Stuff the emails;

she's not just her husband's secretary. Was there some unspoken rule that said she could not enjoy a modicum of freedom? And all the while she's saying this tears begin to fill her client's eyes – moisture which somehow evaporates into tiny sparks, lighting up Lady Hyde's eyes which are becoming rounder by the minute.

"But if *we* are to go to London on some kind of SOS ad hoc mercy mission, Alison, we simply must have a decent supply of cherry brandy. I insist. I can't go alone you see; you must accompany me. Hold on, I'll ring Neesha and ask her about it."

Lady Hyde looks assured and confident behind the old Bentley's steering wheel as they set off. Her oversized herring bone coat lends a dapper look to her bony frame and when she turns corners or speeds up little beads of sweat appear on her forehead as she wrestles with the big leather steering wheel. They're driving through Lothian countryside, following the East Coast railway line and catching spectacular picture post card views. Woolly lambs jump around in April sunshine and farm land looks lush and new. The unusual combined therapies of thought, herb powder, massage, fluids and laughter had restored mobility in Lady Hyde's legs. Getting out of Edinburgh had been quite easy but they've got several hours ahead of them before they hit London's sprawling outskirts. Alison didn't quite know how she'd got talked into this and she's only ventured out of Edinburgh three times in her life, day trips to Glasgow were usually all her ma could afford.

"Don't worry about Spock, Alison. He'll be in safe enough hands with Flora and Mac. It sounds like they animal sit a lot as well as dog walk on the side. Besides, it's only for a few days up until Easter isn't it? Do you know, it's been over fifteen years since I drove this guzzling beast? Edward always used to say that it was a job for our former chauffeur, Thomas and not for me. The man at the private garage where it's kept said he thought its owners had died as it had been that long since it's seen daylight.

Well I declare. I'm very much alive, thank you. Now we must decide the rationale for this visit, I for one am reluctant just to 'do the sights'. What will Edward say should I turn up announced at our Pall Mall pad do you think? Or maybe I could just stay at Annabel's in South Ken."

"Lady Hyde, Katherine – I'm not very good at long car journeys or being in enclosed spaces for too long a time. I went to London once as a wee girl with ma but I cannae really remember much except for seeing the London Bridge gates open and what I thought was a porpoise fin in the Thames. Oh, and I remember the red buses and the vastness of it all. Could we stop along the way to eat something?"

"Of course, my dear, we can stop if you need hot food or a loo. Should have asked Neesha to whip up a portable chicken Korma or two. She's an excellent cook, only fresh ingredients. You probably smelt the curry powder, huh? It was she, bless her, who told me not to, and I quote here, get myself into a "massive Raj" over husbands and housework. This was all tongue in cheek you understand. Up until then I'd always used the word tizzy myself but she said that I shouldn't be too accommodating of Lord Edward, that I should withdraw to rediscover my feminine mystique. *Shakti*, I think they call it but then she's from Delhi and they still have divine females there. Not like here, where most people's conception of God or the divine invariably conjures an image of a wizened white old man with a beard. But you have the map, thermos and packed sarnies there by your lap don't you? I have always been partial to a really good chunky cheese and pickle doorstep sandwich. That and a bowl of cornflakes grated with cheese but without milk. War time foods what oh, on our little austerity drive here excuse the pun. All unleaded petrol of course. I'll have you know I drove *very* large tractors and even combine harvesters on my father's farm in Aberdeenshire. Started driving 'em at fourteen and never looked back. It's always been my dream to saddle up and try a big HGV lorry sometime."

Lady Hyde is on some kind of roll here and having tasted a smidgen of emancipation and rebellion she now seems determined to make the most of it. They'd bought along her supply of leg ointments to be on the safe side though and she's switched her paging device off so nobody can reach her for a while. They stop a few times before they reach Birmingham and a cheap eats where they drink orange coloured cups of tea in plastic cups to loud piped musak.

Whilst driving Alison had insisted upon a window being open and she'd gone on to tell Lady Hyde about the refreshingly straightforward but not rude language of *The Quibblon* and the Twilight Dew with its potential mind reading uses. *Sometimes what appears as fairness, correctness and politeness hides a multitude of sins and hypocrisy*, Alison said. And sitting now in the Americanised eatery her client looks as if she's hatching a plot. Thank the moon beams, for the staff at *Help is at Hand* do not realise the full range of Alison's unusual on-the-job-skills and Lady Hyde is treating this little trip as paid consultative work.

"We must genteelly storm parliament Alison, and confront these uses and misuses of trust, public money and language. I know so many people in The House who say one thing publicly and claim morality yet do the opposite privately. And hypocrisy is what most people cannot stand. Yes, I know my husband could be accused of the same thing and believe me what I'm suggesting is not easy. What I propose may well mean the end of my marriage and a grisly tabloid mess but I've been doing some serious thinking you know. I don't think I can stand the toothless sly words any longer. I'm that concerned about the degradation and under valuing of both humans and nature and corny though it may sound, your own personal story has inspired me very much, Alison, and I want you to know that you have a loyal friend in me.

Your discoveries are safe with me too and you are forcing me to re-consider the workings of the human mind for I don't take *you* to be a dishonourable liar in any shape or form. I must draft a speech, Alison, and we must hatch a cunning plan. Let them call us mad, sad or eccentric hags. They probably will as well but no matter, we press on. For what is a life if not lived truthfully to one's essence and principles, eh? Security is tight in The House but I think I know how to smuggle us both in."

"You're a good egg, Lady Hyde."

"Why thank you, Alison, or should I now say *pucker and large it, pal*. The same to you even though you are an influential white witch sorceress. And now that you mention eggs, you've given me a wonderful idea we absolutely must act on."

And if the old Bentley's steering wheel was difficult to wrestle with when turning the odd corner then the Royal Borough of Kensington & Chelsea's mighty rubbish collector was three times as hard. But sod the special license that might have been required, for Lady Hyde had a moment of inspiration last night talking over plans at her friend Annabel's. Over crêpes and coffee old school chums Annabel and Katherine had systematically done a search on all the politicos both online and on paper, searching out known politicians of all tribes and colours who they strongly suspected had told lies about interests and fingers in pies and who were known to take liberties with expenses while visiting both duck houses and fuck houses.

The Bentley's safely parked by Annabel's flat but right now Lady Hyde cuts an odd dash sitting undaunted in the dumpster's driving seat in greasy workman's overalls, with grey wiry hair tied, blighty style, in a polka dot domestic front scarf. She may be over seventy but she has stoked fire in her belly. For someone has got to make these people really listen to the little people. Her two friends stand by the kerb and open driver's door; they are in a quiet little side street somewhere in Westminster trying to keep their voices down. Light April showers aren't enough though to dampen the ladies' spirits which have already been slightly lifted by Lady Hyde's supply of cherry brandy.

"Good thinking Annabel and Alison for distracting that Council garage foreman, you kept him busy on the phone then nutted him hard in his manhood. He'll live. Both of you are my witnesses when I say I'm not planning to murder anyone, steal or damage irreparably. This is polite civil unrest, a noble tradition born of exasperation, alienation and chronic frustration. Is our cargo ready, ladies?"

"I'll say, Kat. You look like the *true mother of swag* in all that get up. You'll probably get the London fashionata pulses racing if this reaches the press. Stranger things have happened in the thirst for street cred and authenticity. You do know a sympathetic lawyer don't you – in case things get hairy? And yes, everything's packed and ready."

Annabel's the latest recruit to this private war, enacted publicly.

"Away we go then ladies and up you both climb. It's just after three in the morning and we have Plan A's selected list and directions. We must have this vehicle returned by day break so we'll press on; we are not stealing, only borrowing for a just cause. Toodle peep. The politicos and lobbyists are not the only ones who can conjure rot and spin rubbish. It's not just *Inteferax* that I'm angry and disappointed with you know ladies, there's quite a few companies, quangos and other fandangos who either studiously avoid paying a fair share of tax and or support practises or products which harm the environment which we share. Plus, I'm absolutely tired of cross party political impotence when it comes to poverty and inequality and I argue passionately that female carers in our society – be they paid or unpaid – should be better paid and listened to. I understand all the underlying philosophical, economic and historical reasons why the British have always been ambivalent about the poor and needy – but there's been enough waffle uttered, usually by the well paid. I have done my research; I have got the newspaper articles and cuttings.

Also, I don't believe people should be spied on if they are a trade union member – in fact I'm alarmed by the levels of Government surveillance and spying done sometimes."

And they drive off to the rallying cries of *wumps deserve dumps,* driving to a list of ten addresses or so within central London where rubbish and rotten eggs are dumped ceremoniously on driveways, doorsteps and footpaths.

There had been a frightening moment when they almost collided with a bunch of men working on the sewers who were trying to blow torch and melt down huge retrieved slabs of congealed fat by the roadside which had silently accumulated down below in the cities' vast Victorian underground network. Maybe both rot and excess *was* everywhere after all. As above, so below. And driving back to the Council's depot at the beginning of day break, Lady Hyde had recounted a frightening fact about whole drifting plastic islands of packaging in the middle of oceans, testament to another awful deficit of care. But at last it's mission over and on to Plan B. They'd been careful to not dump packaging on doorsteps; instead they'd concentrated on food waste and things that biodegraded safely in order to avoid being called hypocrites by some who wanted to undermine them. Not content with dumping disposable waste they'd also put polite anonymous letters through letterboxes pointing out misuse of public funds, hypocrisy and greed, conflict of interests – in short the many ways power and influence can be abused and misused.

It *was* extreme and slightly comical, and maybe their action would be called futile or eccentric given the scale and influence of big money and lobbying, Lady Hyde acknowledged all of this, but equally it was outrageous and infuriating hearing the politicos ranting on about taking personal responsibility when some were frankly taking none. And then of course the excessive focus on individual responsibility put collective or shared responsibility neatly on the back backburner. Which suited the interests of some, of course, when convenient. Plan B's logistics however are proving to be far trickier to pull off and Lord Hyde had to be approached for authorising a formal Parliamentary pass, which meant Lady Hyde had to spill some beans and announce her surprise visit to London. If Lord Edward had been displeased to see his wife so unexpectedly then he hid his real feelings with great aplomb. Citing an interest in hearing a commons debate, Lady Hyde had secured her means of entry but Alison took the trades and services entrance, smuggled in with ID papers as the Hyde's tea making personal P.A.

The House of Commons debating chamber is sometimes open to select invited members of the public where they can sit on old wooden musty seats and take in centuries of law making, and if the laws weren't asses then quite often those who made them could be. Sitting next to Lady Hyde quite high up in one gallery like structure, Alison wonders how many spiders and their webs survived in this place as the chamber has high wooden beams and plenty of Gothic looking nooks and crannies. Hard to just brush off with a duster. The thought occurs to her that what she's looking at is in fact another kind of circus stage set with performers merely enacting mostly scripted parts. The jammy dodgers' buffoon performance art club where great play and political capital was to be made in *appearing* to be more morally upright than 'the other lot' – so much so that continuing injustices and wrongs actually continued.

The loud cynical jeers reverberating in this Mother of All Parliaments do actually sound a bit bray like today, so much so that Mr. Speaker calls for order. There's a bill being debated right now about the safety or otherwise of a particular pesticide, some MPs are getting concerned that not enough tests have been done and that insects have developed ever greater immunity to crop sprays. On top of this, the accumulated effect of spraying seems to decimate wild bee populations and their pollinating habits. People, including some farmers, often forgot about the plight of the bees.

Prior to this session starting Lady Hyde and Alison had circulated in the bar and restaurant areas amongst the big wigs, MPs, committee members and pressure group campaigners managing successfully to spike cups of tea with so much Twilight Dew that drinkers would be blessed or cursed with the ability to actually read and see one another's private thoughts. Fun and games. In fact, Alison said, heated dew mixed with caffeine could in theory result in even more extraordinary behaviour and so they were sitting now in great trepidation.

"Would the Right Honourable members for Scunthorpe East and Leicester Central and indeed the others on this signed letter accept these second findings as they stand though – namely, that a renowned independent team of scientists and micro biologists have tested the *Factorus Detritax* compound spray on animals and crops over an extended period and have found no adverse effects?"

It is a London MP speaking who happens to be a personal friend of Lord Edward Hyde. Thankfully, Lord Edward was not able to be present at this debate and Lady Hyde is well aware of possible fallout. *I know that man from somewhere* Lady Hyde whispers to Alison. Spiders are not the only creatures that spin webs it seems.

"I appreciate the Honourable Member taking the trouble to inform the signatories of the letter the result of these vigorous sounding tests. The *quality* of the testing was never in question but the claim of being an independent scientific team is, as, speaking on behalf of the signatories; we identified two members on that team who work for large agro-chemical companies. We are also highly concerned about said private companies applying to the EU for licenses and grants to further develop other products. This at the best of times is a highly contentious use of tax payers' money, but at a time of severe recession and great concern over the loss of flora and fauna such corporate behaviour could justify being called obscene."

The MP for Scunthorpe East has a florid determined look about him. He isn't about to quit. But then nor is the London MP.

"I can assure the Honourable Member for Leicester Central that the two scientists you have identified as working for agro-chemical companies only worked on a consultative basis and were never permanent staff members – in addition they were transparent about other freelance work they undertook."

There's a slight pause then in the house when the only thing that can be heard is a rustling of papers, perhaps the ones in Lady Hyde's hands. Somewhere a peer or MP yawns. The London MP is getting visibly irritated.

"In addition to our concerns about transparency of said scientists I also have to say that we were dismayed to see that your right own Honourable Member chose to commission this research when you also sit on a governing board for a similar corporation, *Interferax,* whose practises, in accounting, tax paying and test trials have all been shown to be questionable."

"How dare the Right Honourable Member infer too that I am somehow, in on this, this for want of a better word, *shit.* I fear his party and indeed his co-signatories are merely bitter and twisted because we are actually getting the subsidies and investment needed and we are actively creating jobs."

A gasp and a mini shock wave ripples through the members at hearing the s word. Wigs and toupees wobble, glasses and Liberals twitch. The s word, though commonly known and used was deemed to be improper, for it was private vocabulary to be used only with informal economy behind closed doors. Perhaps said member had been drinking, it was not unknown. The atmosphere turns nasty; contempt is in the air. And maybe the Twilight Dew was adding to the acid and bile.

"Further, might I draw the House's attention to the conflicting interests of a number of the signatories?" The

London MP waves a copy of the letter provocatively for effect.

"You bastard, you'd stoop that low would you? Yes, you have. My apologies to the assembled house for the foul language but we also have reason to believe that our homes have been bugged."

"Ah! Now we have it! The cat's out of the bag at last. Let the whole House be a witness, we are now being accused of spying. What a joke. May I ask the gentleman concerned to substantiate these unruly claims by immediately providing hard evidence or that he and said counter signatories apologise publicly? I can only feel grateful that this sordid affair is not being filmed."

"Sordid affair you say? You hypocritical bugger. Even your wife knows you are bonking your secretary at *Interferax*. I will not take a lecture on deceit and morality from you."

"Piss orff you rancid toad."

The MP for London lunges at the MP for Scunthorpe East, provoking yells and shouts of "shame" and "order in this house" and Lady Hyde knows her cue when she hears it. She stands quickly in her makeshift pulpit, speaking in a loud shrill voice. Though short in stature, her fine intelligence shines through her voice. This is no aristocratic airhead. Talk quickly, seize the opportunity and airtime.

"Shame on all of you, gentlemen. I would also say honourable gentlemen but I'm not sure many of you actually are. It's just protocol after all, isn't it – the powerful rhetorical language of political correctness and tradition which often deceives and distorts, however unintentionally, and doesn't honestly reflect ambiguous lived reality. And I still don't see nearly enough women in this house – surprise, surprise, so I cannot say as yet Honourable Gentlewomen can I? More's the pity, it's taken this long. We are allowed to be powerful domestically and sexually however- but political power's to be curbed. I call it pig's ear politics. And this in the famous Mother of Parliaments! Pontificate, equivocate, deviate, obfuscate is

all I and I suspect millions of voters across this Island actually hear way too often – in other simple words I hear a tremendous clash of egos, greed, self-interest and point scoring which sounds like a load of waffle-op-ocus as my fiend Ms. Mode here would say, worthy of translation and entry in her no nonsense straight forward book The Quibblon, recommended reading members for who those who spin, lie, manipulate, deceive, bully or torment then claim innocence standing on the moral high ground. Well, poppycock. And there are loads of different types of abuse, misuse and bullying aren't there, members?

From dodgy accounting to name calling amongst grown up children in workplaces to bullying by grand Government targets in The Star Chamber. It's a refreshing rarity to know and meet someone who says what they mean and means what they say. Looking around, I am reminded of a vast hall of mirrors in which people see something of their secret self-reflected in others and then attack what's reflected. But this is of no use to real voters or their lives is it, members? Now, how come it is, members, that so many profess they care about specific issues and so many voters place their cross, believing also that their small act of interest and care will somehow make a difference?

In actual fact, people of very different political tribes do care about many similar issues but just have different ways of going about it. But this broad area of shared concerns over, for example, deprivation, the environment, inequality, tax evasion, lack of jobs for example gets scuppered, hijacked and watered down by the competitive two horse electoral race system we still call our modern 'voting' system. But in my view, horse racing and trading and point scoring is for Ascot, Appleby and Countdown but has no decent place in modern politics. I guess you could say, members, before I'm bundled off by some security guard, and no doubt labelled unpatriotic or worse a suspicious deviant – that this is an impassioned plea for consensual politics, for focusing on building shared ground and respect and not on endless one up man ship and pseudo efficiency in the name of short term markets and profits – no matter the cost in blighted lives or decimated species. No wonder many say 'frack off'– politely and otherwise.

This narrow unimaginative kind of thinking is so destructive. Too much emphasis on competition anywhere, including in politics, is damaging as it weakens shared trust – how about the flip sister side of it which is co-operation? There could be more vested interest in cooperation couldn't there? How about a healthier balance between these two principles? I fail to see how seeking consensus is weak or unmanly or is about copping out; I see broad tolerance and the ability to compromise as a sign of maturity. And I cannot believe I'm the only one who thinks this way, I refuse to believe it.

This redundant political system has a terrible smell of rot about it, it's a kind of terrible tragedy of the commons that ordinary Britons, whoever they vote for, seem always to be left feeling enraged, disappointed, and saddened by the continued failure, impotence and cowardice when it comes to making real lasting change to specific issues. I don't claim to know all the answers, it isn't easy. I have met caring, altruistic, honest Conservatives, and I've known greedy, self-interested Socialists – so I'm not playing that old tired game of assigning specific qualities and attributes to political camps when the fact is we are all inter dependent individuals.

We admire expressive entrepreneurs but want to retain traditions. And these two deeply underlying rivalrous political philosophies, one focusing on freely choosing individuals, the other on the needs of the collective, underpin everything whether people see this or not. And the lack of consensual politics or PR alongside the two dualistic philosophies explains I think the ongoing antagonism between capital and labour. As a nation we invent great things and at times show great diplomacy to the rest of the world yet still we cannot sort industrial relations or true democracy! However, people are both self-interested choosers as well as dependent social animals – it is not just one or the other. Both houses are dominated by a particular elite group which concerns me as it's not representative and I'd say exactly the same, mark me well here, if both houses were dominated by working class Asian engineers from Liverpool.

And this has nothing whatsoever to do with the so called politics of envy – what a lazy and arrogant intellectual argument that can be to assume a person's envy and anyway I'm a member of the elite so I'm hardly going to envy the less well off. Besides, people actually envy many attributes and qualities not just wealth. No, this is about the politics of fairness, balance and decency but our politics has become trivialised and seems about random pick 'n' mix issues whilst systemic processes and core issues are continually unaddressed. I argue that savage inequality and social immobility is as cancerous and toxic as raw unknown chemicals sprayed on crops. And so it is that millions of good intentions and crosses shown by those in the ballot boxes who are willing to engage get gradually disillusioned and dissipated in our highly fragmented, divisive and adversarial political culture. Why shouldn't the act of speculation and trading of currency which often benefits money traders more than citizens – why shouldn't this be taxed and used for the abandoned common good. How else can the common good be defended and valued if religion is losing its moral weight? Tobin had the right idea. Good intentions and the common good are continuously undone and are scuppered by the wonky political two horse race.

Ah yes, here is my security guard. Please be gentle with me, I'm going willingly aren't I? Well, members just a last outburst from this posh old biddy about the plight of the poor's children in Glasgow- some of whom have rotten teeth due to poor diet, poor education, lack of NHS dentists ... and this lack amidst mountains of food waste ... now, my good carer friend here who has more integrity and real guts in her left toe than many of you, could tell you a thing or two about hardship, discrimination, taking personal pride and initiative and courage under fire. You have all heard the expression silly money, haven't you and yet there's nothing silly or frivolous about excessive pay or grinding poverty.

No, I'm not some raging Marxist; you need not fear me – though if I were I'd sincerely hope you'd defend my right to be one. Is this truly a free and fair country really? I think not. And if you want somebody to blame for my behaviour you can pin it on my husband, my upbringing, my wonderful pioneering home help and my savvy Asian cook whose nous, curries and common sense keep me smiling and happy in a mad dark world. So there we are gentlemen, my sordid outburst is over. But now it seems we are being marched off politely."

They are taken first to a locked room in the building's basement and then escorted to the nearest police station where Lady Hyde has a hell of a job trying to persuade a disbelieving copper that her husband is Lord Hyde and that he can bail them out. So much for freedom of speech. They are charged formally with several counts of sedition, breach of the peace, anti- social behaviour and disorderly conduct. But there *had* been both cheers, jeers and claps when they'd been lead out of the house, it seemed they'd touched some buried nerve in the body politic. A dour faced and furious Lord Edward finally clears them with the aid of an expensive and well connected lawyer who manages to dredge up extra phantom medication as the cause of her erratic behaviour. Damage limitation. Lady Hyde can tell her husband's saving his real fire power until they are safely back in Scotland.

They return to separate flats and riding back in Annabel's gas guzzling jeep, Lady Hyde recalls that one journalist had been present at the debate so they might get a bit of newspaper exposure. Somehow, she concludes, a bit of Twilight Dew had slipped into her own tea, too; she'd been on full flow capacity back there. There'd been no need for the *Kwik Stix* on this occasion, but she felt sure there would be sometime. Still, the trusty stick had enjoyed its first change of scene travelling in the inside pocket of Alison's jacket. The three of them down liquor-filled Easter eggs and cherry brandy, getting pleasantly tipsy dancing round Annabel's front room into the early hours and stomping out the blues, grumps and wumps in one fell swoop. Three birds exorcising and trying to kill off three social evils without getting stoned.

Quibblon Alternative Dictionary

Waffle-lopocus, *n.* Highly Strung and/or opinionated persons, tendency to drone on and repeat, as distinct from mere '*moaners and groaners'* who are more indulgent and pessimistic.

8

French Fondant Fancy

The fallout from the two confirmed friends' DIY parliamentary antics was, not surprisingly, two pronged. *Political* fallout and coverage was reduced to a brief article in *The Daily Splurge* and the hack who'd been sitting in the debating chamber, though sympathetic, had been unable to identify or trace Lady Hyde's recommended publication called *The Quibblon* or indeed the identity or whereabouts of the mystery two ladies seen in the public gallery that fateful afternoon. The article, titled *Is Bizarre Personal Protest Legitimate When All Else Fails?* launched into a debate about democracy, representation, single issue politics and whether the Brits really do become eccentric or apathetic as a result of her culture's unresolvable contradictions. It was all heady stuff but Lord Edward Hyde had a job and a half containing the story from further leakage. Telephone calls to several offices within a few square golden miles had been quickly made, the timing all important to try and slide the bill through.

The *emotional* fall out was more severe though as Lord Hyde had no problem containing his fury at his wife's unhinged outburst. Lady Katherine's hiding under cover back in Edinburgh, having been stuffed first class with Alison on to a plane back. The Bentley would follow later. There'd been a screaming match in front of Annabel's flat, Lady Katherine hadn't realised the power of her elderly lungs. Resting up, Alison's in her own front room with Flora and Spock, who's nestling up on her lap, as her mobile shudders into life. It's a text from the good Lady herself, true to her word. *May Day, all is not over yet. I'm still alive and he's thinking about what I said, there are ripples of unrest. Thank you.*

"You know you ought to consider getting a smart phone with all these apps now that you are going up in the world and becoming influential and famous. The smart sets need to be contactable twenty-four hours, day and night. What a laugh, though London, eh. You should get your mobile encrusted like mine, look. It's the centre of my world, a vital organ and I cannae operate a business without it."

Flora flashes her touch screen model at Alison, showing her the back which has got mock silver and diamanté animal heads on it. Tablets, slabs, screens, pads, pods, apps, ithis, ithat. It was difficult enough deciphering subtexts and motivations within normal face to face language without this extra layer and aesthetic embellishment. A fancy phone is not really Alison's cup of tea. She's more concerned right now about the threatening letter from *Edinburgh Lettings Ltd* demanding she pay up within the next week. In the thrills and spills of civil unrest she'd forgotten about the smelly encounter in the launderette the other week.

"You know it's funny Alison but while you were away in London I noticed this funny looking fella skulking around in your block's lobby area, someone must have buzzed him in unwittingly. This happened a couple of times and he seemed interested in the bags of straw I was carrying, asking me if I lived in the flats and if I keep a pet. He was too friendly so I just fobbed him off. But you say you've already had another offer of work you busy bee you. Where is it this time? You do realise I'm getting a free supply of gossip here. I never realised there were quite so many characters in Edinburgh".

Alison laughs it off uneasily as the two chat away, catching up with each other. She's sufficiently aware of the fact that there had been many who had likewise dismissed her as a 'character' in her forty-eight years of living in Edinburgh. Flora's like an older sister to her and one day she'll spill the complete jar of beans to her too. But only when it's safe enough to do so and she doesn't know when that will be. Early May warmth beckons Alison outside more, she's been thinking about buying a small dog lead for Spock which might work well on The Links.

*

Bruntsfield is home to vast numbers of academics and intellectuals living in sturdy Victorian houses and flats and being near to Nicholson Street and Edinburgh's cosmopolitan Southside it boasts a good range of arty bohemians too. Alison knocks loudly at the door of Number 23 Spottiswoode Street with a clean and new pack of leg splints which had been requested in the rather garbled message left on her mobile. The message was left by a Noel MacArthur, self-employed art dealer, artist and critic who had broken a leg falling from a ladder whilst trying to paint on an enormous canvas. His partner was away and he needed temporary assistance changing splints and doing basic housework. It had been interesting walking past the day dreaming students sunning themselves on rugs by blooming cherry trees that line pathways on the Meadows. Late spring in Edinburgh, city of not just one mind but many with great open panoramas of the skies.

Today it's cloudless and a bearded Noel, resplendent in oversized painting smock, shows Alison into the kitchen area where a large ginger tom cat sits, Zen like, on a cushion watching the conversation. It's a struggle for both of them getting down the tiled hall as great stacks of portraits, wooden frames and and paintings lie against the walls. Noel is flustered; he's got an urgent art review for a magazine to be completed by tomorrow.

"Alison am I glad to see you, my dear. Excuse this old woolly woofter having a bit of a melt down over housework. The girl at *Help Is At Hand* highly recommended you. I hope you managed to find the address alright and thank you for coming at short notice. A bit pathetic really isn't it. The thing is Laurence, my soon to be living in partner, is away on an urgent family matter in Paris and my plaster's due off quite soon. I have run out of things like bread and milk and I don't like to keep asking the neighbours. Can I get you a cup of coffee or something stronger like wine? I'm not a day time drinker really but dating a Frenchman has got me drinking lots more red wine."

Alison didn't usually drink in the day either, in fact the last alcohol she'd drunk was at the Macintyre's Christmas party when she wisely stuck just to wine. Noel pours her out a glass for both of them, obviously thinking that it may lubricate the flow of conversation. Underneath his camp rather theatrical manner he is actually quite shy Alison thinks. The kitchen and drawing room furnishings are all very kitsch and 1960s looking and they sit down in one of those round bubble or space pod like chairs which completely encase you all around. A lap top lies open on a spotty black and white Formica coffee table, but the real centre of attention and focal point of the room is a giant crude plaster cast of an erect penis which is mounted on three metal legs.

"The rate of pay is not great and I'll only need you for two weeks I'm afraid. Shopping, light housework. My cast finally comes off next week so my leg will see daylight again and no doubt I'll need light bandaging at first. What a fragile lily I am. The Polish receptionist lady at *Help Is At Hand* said you were not squeamish. Oh and Walter needs feeding, he has a special tuna and sardine diet, lucky thing. It's been bloody difficult getting up and down the stairs to feed him and deal with the post as I'm sure you can imagine. Never again will I attempt such a large canvas I have said to myself."

Alison guessed Walter meant the contemplative ginger tom. After she'd discovered the lie Sinclair had told in that first letter about visiting the *Help Is At Hand* office in Leith Walk to obtain her new address, Alison felt ultra-wary and had personally gone into speak to the manageress there about the passing of personal information to any third party. And she didn't know exactly how some London journo had managed to weasel out the fact that she worked for the agency but the agency's owner, a woman called Doreen, had received a call only in the last few days. How Lady Hyde was getting on now in the aftermath was anybody's guess. She was also concerned over the safety and security issues inherent in visiting clients' homes and on her visit to the agency office before going down to London she'd obtained an emergency bleeper which provided 24-hour access to Doreen's work mobile.

Hearing Flora mention the man loitering around in her block's lobby area while she was away made her doubly grateful. Over the last five months Doreen Brogan had received highly favourable feedback from satisfied clients and was therefore happy to invest in a bleeper for this new-ish staff member. Alison had yet to suss it out though and hoped she'd never have to use it. Apparently the down side of the bleeper was that it made a loud piercing sound, giving the game away and warning away any potential threat. If only it could operate through echo location, like some softly squeaking dolphin. Noel's phone rings, interrupting her rapid flow of thoughts.

"Noel MacArthur, hello? Oh hello, Dan. Yes, I can email the copy to you in the next two hours for definite. Sorry for the delay, slow Internet connection. Oh, yes please. Another review in two weeks? Great stuff. I get to visit a gallery, have an arty mingle and enjoy free nibbles. How could I complain? Thanks again, Dan. Yes, the plaster's coming off next week and I've got someone to help me out a bit here just for the next fortnight. Ciao."

Walter jumps up on to Alison's lap leaving a trail of cat fur all over her. Maybe he can smell guinea pig, animals are sensitive in that way. His brown and gold eyes are like two opaque marbles.

"Apologies, Alison. Very rude taking calls in front of strangers, but you know how work can get. Now, where were we? I have written out a shopping list for today and things that need to be done round the house. Sorry, I know you are a trained carer rather than a cleaner or home help as such but I guess we all need to be flexible these days."

Alison smiled, wondering at the huge plaster phallus in the room which was so obvious a conversation starter yet was thus far attracting no comment from its owner. It looked unfinished, as if it needed further sculpting. If she needed further evidence of people's quirks, tolerances and intolerances she need look no further. For only the other day on TV she'd seen a news report describing how most Britons tolerated gay marriages and partnerships more than they did infidelity and adultery. Again, arguably an odd mix of expressive free-thinking liberalism and sentimental social conservatism. And Noel's phone ringing unexpectedly was deemed impolite and intrusive yet the edgy cut and thrust art could potentially disarm some people more. Taking her spare key and shopping bag from the coffee table, Alison ventures out to the local shops. Noel also hadn't batted an eye at her lack of height but sooner or later she felt some client would.

If art imitates life then it must also imitate different kinds of love because love, of course, is part of life. And, as Alison rapidly discovered, Noel's affection for his partner is as operatic in its intensity and scale as many of the paintings stacked against the hall and upstairs in his studio are of his Byron-esque beau. Oil paintings and charcoal sketches of Laurence, pensive and thoughtful in some, naked and reclining with strategically placed grapes in others revealed his lustrous eyes and fine physique. Alison caught her new client singing songs of unrequited love at all hours; making her wonder if Noel had ever trod the proverbial boards. One morning, about ten days after her first day working for Noel, a postcard arrived announcing the immanent return of his love in two days. Alison had just helped Noel finally remove the plaster for good after many months. It'd been a tense moment but the pale looking skin would gain its colour soon. Noel prodded his thigh, sighing and saying he'd be glad to stop taking quite so many pain relievers.

"Yes, my dear Ms. Mode. I must say I feel like a snake that's just shed its skin but not lost my acid rattle and tongue I hope. Maybe I should keep the plaster for posterity. And in answer to your question, yes, I trained originally as an actor, a musical theatre one to be precise. I'm a baritone by inclination, training and tone though I can swing it higher if you push me. Debut 1963 in *Picasso, The Musical* which played briefly at The Hackney Empire in London. Good enough reviews, enough to get me noticed and cast as a dancer and chorus member in *Fiddler On The Roof*. If you watch the movie in slow motion, there are certain crowd scenes you can spot me in. I was once a lean dancing machine, hard to believe I know looking at me now."

"Do you want to cook something special for Laurence when he returns? I don't mind staying on later if you want and giving you a hand. It sounds very romantic you two meeting anyway – on a set for *An American in Paris*, you doing the set design by this point and he a young dancer. Have you really been having an on off affair for over ten years?"

"My dear girl, I know some people who have been carrying on like this for longer, even swinging both ways if you take my meaning. What about you, Alison? Is there nobody special in your life apart from Spock?"

Alison agrees to help cook up a little number with tomatoes, puff pastry, pesto and basil leaves. She looked at a recipe book at home for ideas about deserts but found none. On the day of Laurence's arrival and with Noel's approval, she instead placed trails of love heart sweets round the house, even one leading to the toilet where Noel had cello taped a little sign to the toilet's ball chain flush: *Please be gentle with me, don't pull hard, I'm fragile.* It made her laugh out loud. *Viva eccentrics, viva la différence.* Laurence was as handsome as he had been portrayed by his lover and thankfully was fluent in English as Alison's French was a joke. They kindly invited her to stay for a candlelit supper in the true spirit of liberty, equality, fraternity and Laurence, it turned out, had originally trained in the circus. What a rich varied canvas of people was to be discovered behind Edinburgh's closed doors.

"We had many little people like you Alison in our team in the touring *Cirque Fantastique*, they were very good flame throwers and rode ponies bare backed even though they were often heckled by the ignorant. Are you scared of heights or are you quite acrobatic?" Laurence asked politely.

"Not as far as I know. I used to do cart wheels and handstands when I was a bairn. That's Scottish for a child. And generally speaking I prefer my feet on the ground but who knows? But you have got me thinking; maybe I'll see what I can do. I can juggle three or four fruits or eggs at one time though."

This challenge was too much for Laurence who snatched up five lemons and began throwing them rhythmically in the air. He then held a headstand before his rapt captive audience for a full five minutes, growing pink in the face whilst reciting Baudelaire. After this excitement and the eating was over, they reminisced about productions and auditions they'd attended whilst trying to throw home made string rings around the enormous plaster phallus. An unusual evening's entertainment, a bit chaotic and cock-a-hoop. The lovers began to make eyes at each other and it became late so Noel ordered and paid for a taxi for Alison. But walking up her block's steps to her flat she was confronted with a shocking, awful sight. For if politics was deemed a necessary evil, then other kinds of violating evil were completely unnecessary. Her front door had been violently kicked in, her flat vandalised and trashed. The single word *freak* was scrawled on one wall, plates had been smashed, pillows slashed with a knife spilling out feathers.

A small lake of pasta sauce and cereals covered the kitchen floor. Crying quietly, Alison walked from room to room shocked at the display of hatred and malevolent spite. It was in stark contrast to the acceptance and good cheer shown her at Noel's. Her privacy had been invaded and brutalised but the insulting word had given the possible perpetrator away. Stupid. And maybe there might be fingerprints she thought, trying to remain steady. The older Polish man who lives in the upstairs flat and who Alison sometimes sees passing on the stairs calls out to her from the warped wreckage of the door.

"I am feeling so sorry for you, Mrs. Mode. I called the police when I saw your door and what had happened and they came around a few hours ago. I saw them dust for prints and they asked for your details. I said I didn't know but they will call around again tomorrow morning. Here, this is the number they left for you to call. It's been a funny night as first there was a fire alarm in the whole block and everybody left their flats and ran outside. A fire engine visited and stormed the block but could find nothing so we think it was a false alarm. Or maybe a stupid joke. Then somebody saw that the alarm system in the lobby area looked like it had been smashed deliberately. Bad luck, huh? Some people have no shame. Have you got somewhere you can stay for tonight? I'd offer myself but I'm a bad smoker and my sofa is very uncomfortable."

His accent is thick but he has kind honest eyes. Alison puts on a brave face and thanks him anyway. She didn't like the sound of the false fire alarm at all; it's too much of a co-incidence. But worse than all this, much more gut wrenching than any damage to her mere and meagrely acquired *things* was the vacant hell hole of Spock's hutch. It sat empty and broken in jagged splints on the carpet. He'd been taken along with some cash Alison kept stashed in a kitchen jam jar. The front door is completely defunct; it's nearly off its hinges. No point in staying here, unsafe. She calls Flora, trying to control her voice but completely breaking down over Spock. To have already lost one pet and of course her mother in sinister circumstances and now this. *Is there any end to the inhumanity, Flora?* She'd cried down the phone, recalling the way she'd slowly rebuilt her life and well-being despite many adversities. Spock's only small, he didn't take up much space but he looked after her in a funny kind of way too.

Her small child like shoes had been flung everywhere; she nearly trips over a shoe as she's talking. For so long it had taken real courage and faith to just keep going. At Flora's the following morning, Alison received a similarly tearful call on her mobile from a distraught Noel saying Laurence had upped and finally left him in the dead of night without reason or warning and that all he now had to remember his best beloved by was the plaster penis, modelled as it had been on Laurence's fine upstanding organ. The poor man sounded as if he had the beginnings of a cold too. Talk about over baked and blown emotion; she couldn't just put the absurdity all down to a hangover or any puffed up pastry they'd cooked. But then Love has its own fallacies which are not always logical.

He'd said he was a mere husk of the man he once was, his vital love juices depleted. In any other circumstance Alison Mode might have laughed out loud.

9

Lawless

Slaters, 1853. Chimney Sweepers. On the brick wall are the ghostly painted traces of Edinburgh's commercial past. The city is full of them, tucked away above windows, on the corners of side streets. It's turned out to be a good little earner today, the basement flat by *Chuckie Pend* and the swish wine bar, that is. The tenant, a naïve Hungarian student, had coughed up rent and cash for some good quality dried seeds as supplies of dried mushrooms have run out for now. But it's always good business to get them doubly reliant on you and if they mess you around with late rent payments you can threaten them with blackmail over drug use. One way or other he'd screw them over and in his time he'd heard some pretty lame excuses over arrears. Sinclair's standing under the wide archway of this name just round the corner from Lothian Road; it must have once accommodated horse drawn coaches and servants. He's counting out the notes in the shadows and entering the payment in his book. So far, so good and the morning's gone well apart from that fucking irritating rodent hamster thing squirming around in the potato sack.

Sensing danger, it had bitten him in the struggle last night in the flat. It'd had been easy pickings though and the ruse about the fire alarm just came to him spontaneously as all his evil genius ideas did. He'd hidden in a stairwell and watched the block's residents scurry downstairs wide eyed, like lemmings to the cliff edge. Waiting until all was quiet, he knew he'd have to act quickly before someone like a fireman made an entrance. Lucky he studied judo once; he can kick ass and wood hard with fine footballer legs. He'd have to work quickly, then time things well in the confusion and slip amongst the waiting crowd. If questioned, just say he'd been asleep in a top floor flat. Staying over at a pal's place, like. Shame about that unusual antique wooden stool, he'd had half a mind to nick that, too, but it was just too conspicuous: Another time maybe.

"Aw, shut your squealing you overgrown rat. Carry on like this and I will bung you in the microwave. You're lucky to be alive, pal. The Romans had the right idea eating hamsters and guinea pigs with apricots and wine in their togas, man."

Walking out through the archway, Sinclair gives the sack a violent little jolt. Just enough to shock, mind, though actually the wee beast is far more useful to him alive than dead in some sandwich. He's tempted though. It's coming up to lunch time as well, might stop with Davey somewhere to eat something. Maybe get a cheap kebab on the way back to the lass. Having already tried horse, badger and squirrel meat though – he's keen to push the frontiers of his stomach's bravado. Another notch in his culinary cred.

"Where to now, Guvnor? Gorgie Road is it to see the Missus and get a freebie cooked lunch or do you want to do a launderette swoop for fresh leads. Leith has been heaving with young student things these last ten days, all of them wanting to learn English and go to college, stupid sods. Chances are Gorgie's numbers are up, too."

Davey sits waiting in the driver's seat of the Vauxhall Cavalier parked nearby. It'd been a gamble but no warden had swooped. Shouldn't push it though. The car radio is on; the constant background noise helps him to relax. A slightly built man with huge ponderous saucers for eyes, he's forever staring inanely at nothing and nobody. He's been Sinclair's right hand man for years; they go way back through gang fights, turf disputes, girlfriends, drug busts, recessions, laundry cycles. Davey used to be a cabbie in Edinburgh; he knows the city like the back of his scabby hand. July and August especially are their best months, though spring can be good. And during the festival, the city's population practically doubles up with potential. They'd often worked until the early hours every night chatting up, priming and booking out new tenants. Get the patter juices going, go with the flows. Always alert of course and on the lookout for Council officials or the police. And getting by with a little help from their friends who appreciate the beauty of the informal franchise relationship. He who dares wins at the spins.

"I'm tempted by that Chinese place in Bread Street where you pick out your live lobster then they clobber it, boil it, and serve it with a bit of lemon. But Samantha won't like it as I said I'd be over there for two. That said, there's those two newbie Africans down Easter Road that do need checking on. They settled in alright last week, deposit's been paid okay but one was still looking for a cash in hand job so one of us should check their dosh situation. They looked very clean though, said they were Seventh Day Adventists or something, so part of the God squad. Maybe just see they have all the basics. Shouldn't be a problem unlike those posho English pals a couple of weeks back, eh. Can you imagine, threatening me what with his father being a solicitor. Would you mind just checking on them after you drop me off at Samantha's? I think his name's Toby Nedembe or something. His dad's a Nigerian oil trader – or so he says. They plan on staying a while I think. Just send me a two-line text update."

They drive off in heavy traffic towards Gorgie Road, the sack with its live contents lurching from left to right on the back seat along with boxes of cutlery and hand towels.

*

He knows Samantha's still hacked off with him the moment he walks into the flat. It's always in her tone; women can never hide their real feelings for long. They say brightly "oh I'm fine" in such a screamingly mock polite way that it's a giveaway. The TV is on and smells of bacon and fried onions fill the sitting room and glancing down at the shag pile carpet, Sinclair sees the remains of some fry up on a plate. These days she gets odd cravings at all hours what with being two months pregnant. And shag pile was a good apt name for it, pal, as it was where he'd done the business and spread the good seed and now, as a result she's sprawled out on the sofa like some small grounded whale. She studiously avoids looking at him but the sounds emanating from the sack he's carrying rouse her curiosity.

"What the hell have you got in there, William? It sounds like a piglet or rat. It better bloody not be some animal you want to kill and eat here on the spot. No way, not in my flat. The animal parts in my fridge were bad enough. Oh, do let it have some air. It's cruel. Just tell me what it is first though."

"It's a neglected guinea pig that one of our former tenants didnae want as they're going back to Bulgaria. Said they'd just leave it out in the streets to run wild so I thought I'd do a good deed and take it to Gorgie City Farm seeing as we are so near to it. They're bound to have rabbits and other guinea pigs and he'll get a good home."

Sinclair places the sack on the carpet and goes to the kitchen to chop carrots. He pours tap water into a saucer returning just in time to see Spock tentatively poke his head out of the sack and sniffing at the air. Samantha resorted to calling him William when she was particularly annoyed with him. It reminded him of his father.

"Since when have the likes of you been an animal lover, eh? That's a turn out for the books. And why are you late? I spent ages peeling onions alone waiting for you to turn up. Is this how it's going to be when the bairn is born? You might as well tell me now."

"I have always been an animal lover, that's why I go for mad daft cows like you. Sorry about the bacon and all that but just to remind you again that I'm the one who actually brings home most of it, like. The bacon I mean, hen and you know my work involves all hours sometimes. Now if it's alright with you I'll fix myself some bridies, tatty skirlies and beans and you can just put up with the guinea pig for a couple of days. And if you can't be civil to the father of your future child then I'll just take myself oot for a wee while."

Sinclair loves laying down the law and drawing the line. Stupid bitch Samantha, getting pregnant and thinking that will keep him, Underworld Landlord of the Launderettes, tethered and committed. No, *his* pinky tail was ever active and resourceful. He never said that he was interested in becoming a father, she'd slyly come off the pill without telling him. And he'd been good to her so far hadn't he? Showing an interest, soothing her anxieties, like. He must have his freedom at all times, operating in his own moral sphere where he makes the rules. Heating a couple of meat and tattie pies up and putting them in a paper bag, he walks out the flat slamming the door as a warning behind him. Let her stew in her own bile for a few hours until she can be grateful.

The strip clubs near the Grassmarket provide an interesting evening of entertainment, it's good to be reminded of his virility and desirability. Sinclair's shiny, bald head and smooth line in patter held the male patrons and dancers in perverse thrall, as over vodkas and orange he recounted tales of drug busts, exotic dancers and several politicians who'd not paid rent but had an appetite for expensive underage flesh. Dirty laundry alright. He knew the juice on lots of people, that's why nobody had ever blown him out. Oh yes, people loved filth, cruelty and perversion – there's always been a market for it in all walks of life. As he walks out the club in the early hours he wraps his long leather coat around the young lass on his shoulder who is a dancer at one of the clubs. It's a fake gesture of the fallen gentleman, and she wobbles and giggles on the pavement, a feather boa bird wearing huge plastic platform shoes held on by precarious looking straps. *Both Africans have got jobs so no probs with rent* said the text from Davey.

That was a relief as baby clothes were expensive. *I should have asked him to bring the motor back though* Sinclair thinks, wondering how far away the girl lives. He couldn't hold on for much longer. That was the beauty of cars; you could get your end away on the spot but out of sight, like. Leith was always a good patch for that kind of cheap instant bang. But then she's opening her front stair door in a block just round the corner and clumping up the stairs. His calculation's paid off. She's got interesting dark eyes but he's forgotten her name already. Once inside he snatches off her feathery sequinned costume and pushes her down on the bed. No point in small talk really, she knows the deal and they've drunk enough.

She laughs out loud, calling him Kojak, asking if his other head is just as shiny. Pure Edinburgh, the hen can't be more than nineteen or twenty but the language is fruity. Maybe she's a graduate or day time student; this was what many students resorted to in order to survive. They get sophisticated at ever younger ages these days and it's quite a warm June night, the small bedroom windows open allowing the sound of late night drinkers and revellers in. She waves an orange flavoured condom at him but he throws it away, unzipping his dick and plunging it into her. This is no time for smooth build ups or establishing rapport, no, sometimes people just needed a good dog work out. She's given up protesting, just as well. Samantha would kill him if she ever found out but she won't of course. They never do. But condoms kill off the risk and danger element and that was the whole point, they were for numpties and this lass pumps and grinds well, panting on queue. Well trained, she's done it before probably.

Come to think of it, this one that's under him now might be a good one to prime and hire for his other developing business interests. Prime meat, he knew plenty of men and women who'd pay good money for this human tail in the posh swingers club he's thinking of. Amazing what secrets lay contained within the city's architecture. Picking a perfect looking strawberry from an idyllic pack of six that Sinclair bought earlier, she pops one into her mouth. The tourists just saw the safe tartans and shortbread as they were supposed to. Afterwards they share a reefer and a bowl of peanuts and she writes out her contact details. She lights candles which throw distorted ghoulish shadows on the walls. The encounter didn't seem to have dampened her interest in him and smiling in the flickering half-light, Sinclair recalls his brief time at secondary school in Fife when he'd been nicknamed *Ruff Muff.*

Returning stealthily to Samantha's flat at dawn, he unlocks then relocks the front door and steps across the dark front room to the bedroom. Be careful; don't trip on the cowering beastie. He'll answer her possible questions later. Put it off as long as you can, but maybe she's got the message. Samantha snores slightly as he tosses off his clothes and rolls himself up in the king size duvet. She smells of chocolate and rolls over, turning to face him. Let that smart arse midget suffer and go grey with worry over her precious pet. He knew all along she was hiding something. In a few days' time, he'll pass a final ultimatum to her. Maybe in somewhere hidden away, maybe underground when no one else is around. Deliver the killer blow then, show no mercy. Somewhere where there is growing mould, wearing one of his kilts with a stuffed animal head for a sporran. Nice touch that. He'd seen big mould growing in various properties, pink, yellow and black like big starfish. Deadly and corrosive and sometimes invisible like a type of social cancer. Back at his pad in Leith he had a whole collection of stuffed heads going back years, the lassies liked it. A human animal wearing another animal, all part of the big food chain of life. Gorge on the entrails, leave the heads for last.

Why not, it's a fucking free country isn't it? I can gob where I like, I can spit and shit. After all everything is *to go* these days, he likes live in live out relationships. Easy come, easy go. Fuck it, he's considering growing an online avatar if the business takes off, like. He could become Mr. Toby Flux Esquire and search out new flesh. There's whole new markets sprouting up in all sorts of places. He'd heard of this really wild club in the New Town where mature lassies do their stuff in front of gold designer curtains. The Age of the Affluent Cougar.

And they were another funny kind of animal weren't they, a growing breed harking on about women's rights when it suits them but give them an inch sometimes and they'll manipulate a mile. Cut throat. And all done deftly with a soft touch, a hint of perfume. Because make up both entices and seduces but sometimes is also a kind of domestic war paint, designed to keep people at a distance. Funny that, eh. Some things look ever so pretty and inviting but really they are full of poison and cruelty. And incredible really what some of the affluent did with their tucked away leisure time, no accounting for taste. Some of them got away with all kinds of behaviour, behind closed doors. Discretion always assured. And that Alison Mode, she won't want anything to happen to the beast will she? Talk of the devil, wonder where it is now, probably hiding under the sofa. Maybe it's terrified. But then a lot of life is about terror, pain and humiliation. Attack or go under. People like strength, they like winners. Drifting off to sleep then he dreams he owns a giant golden cuckoo clock which when chiming every hour reveals one of a whole carved parade of his victims, both two legged and four legged. And there have been many. An eternal merry-go-round of the damned. On the clock's ever rotating conveyor belt is a wooden figurine of Alison Mode in a clown's costume, her face frozen in perpetual shock. Sinclair delights in winding and re-winding the clock up, forcing the maniacal appearance and disappearance of the figures. You could hire and buy coffins for both the dead and the living, shame his old man hadnae cottoned on to that one. *Bind your time my son and control your own destiny.* He'd engineered some actual vanishing acts too but that was another story. Guffawing in dreamland delight he unwittingly kicks Samantha hard in the abdomen waking her with an anguished cry.

10

Scraps and The Waters

"You is drifting off again Alison, you total dream time girl. I can tell, it's that far away boat song look. You sure you not been smoking Mary Jane or turning into one of those ugly punky rockers. I prefer a roots girl rocker myself. Babe-girls who wear Joseph coats of many colours like a sweet rainbow."

Leonard's large afro is dotted with silver beads of rain as they, Alison and Leonard, sit together on the back of the rag and bone cart. He glances towards an intense rainbow which has magically appeared just in front of them after the brief sprinkling of rain. June showers. It's 1979, year of ominous change. They are parked along Ferry Road as rounds extend to here. Meg, a small brown and white pony has to have blinkers on as she gets jumpy with sudden movements. Piles of scrap metal lie on the back of the wooden cart, a throwback to an earlier time. Irons, metal pipes, grills, parts of ovens, fencing. Metal wiring, wool and big piles of cheap bendy metal coat hangers which are regularly thrown out by a big tailor's shop in Constitution Street.

"You haven't done any homework have you for over a month now. How do you get away with it you skiver? And so what if I like to collect metal coat hangers for magical experiments. They conduct electricity, pal. A bit like me. Maybe I could be a steel engineer when I'm older and really work the metal. I like punk by the way, I find it refreshing."

Leonard says nothing but looks at her with sneaking admiration. A punky dwarf. She calls him a tyke, he calls her a clype-dyke but both have taken their fair share of aggro and grief from teachers and pupils. It's the lot of the outsider. Recently she's got into the habit of wearing black lace, bovver boots, donkey jacket and gelling her hair back in a unique way which she hoped would give a loud *begger off and dinnae mess with me* message to some in the school. Earlier Leonard reminded her of the importance of bands like The Stylistics and The Wailers in raising tolerance levels, in developing understanding of different skin colours and takes on life. He says before he mutated into raga-reggae he'd been a funkaholic with heavy duty super fly flares. They were kind of dating in secret as friends and he'd fumbled under her tea shirt, kissing her clumsily in an alley after eating crisps.

But it had been an awful sex education module in the biology class that made Alison want to prove a point about diversity and budding boobs of many different contours in front of the hissing spiteful row of girls who'd given Leonard and herself knowing looks. How dare they insinuate and assume that dwarves or any disabled person did not have a sexuality or needs. I have *a* sexuality not an asexuality she'd felt like screaming at her tormentors. Most of the image obsessed boys in her class wouldn't be seen dead with Alison but Leonard's cottoned on early to the fact that Alison collects, hoards and bends metal coat hangers. He'd suffered a few jibes about the colour of his skin, blacks were rare in Edinburgh. On the first few scrap rounds he noticed her slyly packing coat hangers away in her school bag and it made him curious. Saturday jobs were way more interesting than school. Mr. Johnston, the scrap metal dealer and proprietor, hadn't noticed anything unusual and she must be a bit brave and intelligent to do what she does, not caring what others thought. He'd lightly quizzed her one afternoon. *Sticky gum, oh stick right on the lying ex-chum's bum* is what he thought he'd overheard Alison saying once, when he'd caught her staring intensely at a girl's back in one of the school's long corridors.

"Did you really stick chewing gum on chairs using your mind and not your hands, Al? How is that possible? Don't tell me you're one of those druid types that goes dousing for water? And what do you mean 'all is one and one is all'. How is it possible to make objects travel? You must prove it to me before I believe it. Next thing you are going to tell me is that you've had out of body experiences. I knew you were different, Alison but not that far out."

He'd grinned at her but she'd not risen to the bait. Instead she'd dared to invite him round for tea, having given out a loud skirl sound on the estate to signal when to him when it might be safe to walk to the front door. She'd shown him the large pile of bendy twisty shapes, insisting that she too was a kind of mini conductor just like them and that she'd discovered the power of concentrated thought. It's all about vibrational thought energy silly, she'd giggled whispering for him to keep his voice down but his trousers up.

She'd waited over two months before telling him about the chewing gum or marbles she'd sent through space, to unhinge her bullying tormentors, some of whom lived, unfortunately, on the very same schemie and so could closely observe Alison's every move. To be bullied at primary school was bad enough but to be targeted again at secondary was devastating. *A dwarf going out with a black boy, a dwollywog* is what the sweet little boys and girls shouted, consumed with an odd mixture of fury, envious resentment and insatiable curiosity. At school, they'd not dared sit next to each other.

And Alison shuddered in ancient history class when the teacher, one of the better ones, had described the fine line between idolatry and sacrifice in ancient Greek religious ritual and the way certain chosen individuals were surrendered and rendered to bits as some kind of offering to the Gods or cosmos. Ancient scapegoats in distant lands, too, a seemingly eternal need for bloodletting in order to cleanse a people or tribe of all evil or unpleasant elements. A never ending process of course as shadows follow folk where ever they are, magnetic black holes or destructive force fields if denied.

They'd heard about a huge awesome statue of Athena that stood in the Parthenon, this was followed by a more interesting physics lesson in which the bumbling teacher spoke about radio waves and something weird and wonderful called *gyroscopic introjects* which made Alison, who saw herself in essence as a dryly funny introvert, feel suddenly very hungry. She'd gone home that day, locking herself in the bathroom as many teenagers do, only to examine her belly button and developing bosom in full detail. *No, I'm not weird. My body is as good as any other. If it's a witch I'm called, then that's what I'll become on my own terms as a tool for survival. I'll spell things out for people; let them know what's what.*

This was years before Barbara Mode had slipped and drowned in that awful private care home of course, at a time when soaking in waters had a good association. One revelatory thought had whirled round her heid again under the soapy suds: incredibly the physics teacher said that radio programmes which had been recorded ten, twenty or more years ago were still retained in the atmosphere's 'memory' and that many radio boffins and enthusiasts had accidentally tuned into and 'received' an old recording which had been floating around in the universe's atmosphere. This was possible because newer radio listeners had by chance set a radio on the same wave length and this got young white witch Alison thinking about the nature of electrical impulses. Sound, light and thoughts all travelled in waves she'd realised. She needed to do this often, this immersing her body in water just to calm her thoughts, relax her mind. Could it really be that there was another parallel universe in which there was no time as we knew it? How come the universe's atmosphere retained the ‘knowledge’ of the initial radio recording? How come something broadcast ages ago didnae just disappear dissipated off into space? She knew waves could bounce and was the human brain a bit like a TV or radio transmitter and receiver in that it was possible for some to ‘re-hear’ or ‘re-see’ events, people, conversations from the past in the here and now?

This would suggest that today’s events and people could be super imposed on earlier happenings, that both times could exist in one geographical space and in this sense the current reality suspended temporarily. Being a bright lassie, she’d quivered with excitement at the implications of all this. Maybe ghosts could be explained using hard physics; maybe the human mind could be in two different places in time at once! She hadnae wanted to completely unnerve her mither with all this. A few times Barbara had not got back in from work and neighbours watched Leonard’s comings and goings with avid unhealthy interest, an alternative neighbourhood watch.

Old iron and old ore is what Mr. Johnston Esquire cries out in the streets of seventies Leith. He’s been faithfully doing the rounds on his patch for over twenty years now; people leave good bits of scrap. He’ll retire soon but he’s had a good innings. He’s given Meg a horse bag to munch through, keep her busy while he partakes of a quick greasy fry up breakfast. She stomps a bit with her front hooves and sometimes snorts but she’s got a sweet nature. Leonard and Mr. Johnston get on very well, they met in the very same café over six months ago, and the elderly Scotsman took a liking to the energetic fourteen year old West Indian boy who is flunking school and getting into trouble. Leonard thinks Alison’s pretty in a different kind of way; he likes her dark brown eyes and has been with quite a few girls in the school already. Late 1970s Scotland. Political stasis, years of strikes. Bungled hopes, economy in recession, and a different kind of retrograde or waning. DSS claimants soaring and this on top of the other DSS, *Dour Scot*

Syndrome – a deep melancholic wistfulness incorporating grim quiet stoicism. Glasgow gutted, unemployed youth hang about in Scotland's main two cities in two tone rude boy suits or trawling around on scooters causing mayhem. Mods, rockers, dreads, punks, goths. Though savagely unequal, the Brits have always excelled in creating eccentric sub cultural identities. You might well be poor but you could always dress to impress. Dress up if you're hard up.

Globalisation yet to occur, the Internet confined to American security forces. Bankers at this time still existing in the same moral orbit as the humble masses. Predatory venture capitalism, take overs, speculation not as frenzied and unregulated as now, when those who work in finance sit at the top of the food chain, daily over seeing fresh kills, spoils and hunts – only to laugh, hyena like ever louder to the banks. And the tones of laughter drowning out the roars of growing fury from the general public who time and again are too seduced, intimidated or powerless to do anything about the new elite. The importance of capital's and credit's unmitigated freedom of circulation even if this has costs and implications which inhibit and diminish the freedoms and choices of whole nations and peoples.

The world not yet grown mad with policed rights talk, which serves the rights of some more efficiently than others and the mass production of things not yet intensified and blown up, that cruel endless conveyor belt – treadmill always offering people some glittering unattainable object or prize, forever a shimmering mirage on some imagined horizon. Identities and human bodies somewhere in the middle of often contradictory forces both within and without – perhaps even identities up for sale too. Some people were finding the new leader, the Iron Lady, refreshing with her steely determination but not Alison's ma who thinks Mrs. Milk Snatcher is out to clobber the poor and vulnerable with words, dodgy deals and deeds. But the sun's out again now and Mr. Johnston's returned wiping the grease away from his mouth and geeing up old Meg who clops the young steely nerved friends home.

*

The sandwiches have become dry in the intense heat. Luke warm fizzy bottles of cola and a flask of tea. An August bank holiday in 1986 and Barbara and Alison Mode are lying on Portobello beach, listening to the sound of the waves and the call of the wheeling gulls. They'd slapped on some sun tan lotion as the TV weather man earlier that morning had mentioned high temperatures. The beach is crowded but not packed, the sea warm to swim in. Earlier, Alison had been cloud busting as a form of relaxation to take her mind off the horrors of the job in the bakery. She'd been close to walking out today she really had – just about ready to tell the overbearing boss to go and butter up his own arse if she didnae like the way Alison applied 'too much of everything' in the rolls.

And thinking about buttering up and flattering people, Alison Mode's never been good at either, she had a generous heart her mither kept telling her, so she did. Barbara's wading though some pseudo-Regency bodice ripper, they kept her going. Alison's not been in the bakery job long, it was the only one she'd been able to find where the other employees didnae wretch inwardly at the sight of her, repulsed by her dwarf body. Repeated applications for jobs and a series of terrible interviews had nearly pushed her over some edge. For years she'd had a whole series of low paid jobs, restless at trying to find her niche. And then the awful thoughts that she'd not fit in anywhere, that she wouldn't enjoy any job, that nobody would just accept her for who she was. School had scarred her badly and she'd left at sixteen, desperate to get out and away from the bullies that stripped her of dignity and esteem. At first Barbara had tolerated her daughter living though a kind of psychological hibernation-recuperation period but then she'd drawn the line, insisting that her daughter earn her keep and get some kind of life purpose back.

"Look, Al. Unemployment is very high at the moment and it's nothing to be ashamed of, it's not your fault, though I do wish you'd stayed on at school. If you'd just gone on a typing course and learnt some secretarial skills, but no, my hen, you wouldn't hear of it. You cannae say I didn't warn you. Try to make a go of the bakery job and stick at it. Stand up to the boss if you have to, don't exactly answer back but show that you have some self-respect. Nobody else will blow your trumpet, Alison."

Barbara, in her mid-forties, had made up the sandwiches before they'd got the bus out here together. Her pretty polka dot shirt ripples gently in the slight breeze. Alison's inherited her dark eyes and sharp features. Yesterday Alison managed to reign in her tongue at work but only just. Tempers had nearly flared by the big ovens as she'd had loaded the umpteenth batch of macaroni pies, trying not to complain about her burnt fingers ensconced in big linen catering gloves. Gazing out to sea, Alison wondered again at its existence. Maybe thoughtful cookery could be used to liberate and inspire instead, it was an idea. They'd gotten there early in the morning and had been delighted to see a single swan floating gracefully along, perhaps drifting or flying in from Crammond, further along the coast. Far from looking lonely, it seemed very serene in its solitude.

They'd had ice creams and tackled magazine crosswords and Alison drew an image of some fecund primeval woman in the sand, using shells for her hair and surrounding her with mystical spirals. Okay, it would be washed away in the blinking of an eye but seeing the image, albeit briefly, validated her in some way, it reminded her that she even existed, that she too could be a maker of marks in a transient fickle world where things and people were very often not quite what they appear to be. She'd learnt about the healing powers of spirals from a book she'd borrowed from Leith public library – if she was to become a fully-fledged seer and white witch then she had to perfect the tools of the trade. She knew she could move objects, read and hear people's thoughts but she wasnae about to don a long black cape and buy a crystal ball.

No, that would be way too obvious. And swimming in the sea in the morning, mother and daughter both stepped over the pink broken carcasses of crabs, half eaten by gulls. Barbara had looked so happy floating on her lilo and swimming underwater, only to emerge with a big scrap of seaweed tendrils on her hair which made her daughter laugh. Queen Kelpie. And for a moment, Alison flew with the gulls in her mind's eye and she looked down at herself and her wonderful unique one off mither who'd had it real rough raising a lassie bairn by herself on a shoestring budget and who tried to be tolerant and understanding of her fiercely independent daughter who had to learn the hard way sometimes about keeping her opinions to herself sometimes and choosing her moments wisely revealing real feelings only to those tried, tested and trusted.

She saw two remarkable women struggling to survive in an often hostile unsympathetic climate prone to over work and insidious trivial gossip – two real life heroines reduced to mere human scraps in the waters, drifting endlessly in forces beyond their control, drained and worn of resistance but not shorn of decency or a sense of integrity. She'd heard of these extraordinary stories of survival in the news – people stuck for days, weeks or months on shoddy boats or rafts or on Islands with nothing to drink but salt water. You find out very quickly who you really are in these circumstances where no masks or role playing is required and nobody is watching. You are forced to confront yourself, virtues and weaknesses alike.

And sea waters were great conductors for purifying the soul and washing away your troubles. The walk down to the shore had been made easier for Alison because of Barbara's company. Let the wagging tongues say what they will. The critical judgements and assessments made quickly and clinically by the other people on the beach who were also subject to this same crippling social ritual of looking at others' bodies and also being looked at – this everyday commodification and objectification that all were induced and seduced into – both men and women – obscuring sometimes the ability to see the human behind the object. Why the hell should they not enjoy a wee sea bath, they had same right to exist as others warts and all. Was it a crime to be poor and plain in a world that prized youth, wealth and physical perfection?

Then Barbara had to use the ladies' loo and Alison had drifted off in a reverie again gazing at the passing clouds, oblivious to two leering lads who, seeing she was small and alone thought they'd try their luck. *Excuse me love, can you spare any change? Fancy a bit of small broom handle action after, mind you might be a tight fit.* She'd ignored them and their casual everyday obscenities but they'd thrown two stones at her before sauntering off, arrogant cocks-of-the-walks that they were. Good grief, couldn't a female lie on a beach, unharrassed? Evidently the two men thought her still fuckable or maybe not – perhaps any proposed sex was their sick way of *saying cheers hen for allowing us to take what measly money you have and now as an act of pity because no other human in their right mind would want to 'do' you we will give you a good rodgering, a good going over.*

It seemed to Alison that British culture particularly excelled in these mundane put downs and public humiliations – some women joined in too, happy in the mocking, smearing and degradations of other women as a kind of sick sport. Violence in the language, savagery in the money distribution, sickness in the whole system. Screw the oiks, she'd get a tea shirt printed up and wear it loud and proud. *Dwarves get their ends away every week. Get over it.* Both political correctness and its close relation anti correctness were tailor made for hiding cruelties, injustice and prejudice as well as highlighting them. Maybe it brightened up the sheer plodding empty boredom of the lives of many; it was a different kind of bloodletting and hounding out given that hangings, torture, witch burnings and hunting with dogs had stopped. It kept the Brits perpetually enraged, blinded, confused as to 'who was to blame' for the way things were.

Because there had to be someone to blame, someone to shame, smudge, humiliate. It was all about individuals taking responsibility, but never whole communities or societies and certainly not bankers and large companies. Given the already rigid class divides and yawning gaps between the haves and have nots and on top of this the nervous strains of recession, was it any wonder that many suffered in the mind as well as in the pocket? *Witch, weirdo, muppet, slut, goddess, daftie, angel, bitch.* Women have always been much easier to shift loads on to, carrying the true costs and the contradictory and particularly unresolvable burdens of archetype and advanced Capitalism.

Growing up as a poor female dwarf with a single mum near rough and ready post ship building Leith, Alison knew early on about fear and rage in the street language, about the conflicted judgements made about all females. As a girl she'd seen prostitutes who were beaten up yet gloated about, she'd seen the effects of drugs and joblessness and like many others no doubt before her, she raged against the system and the unequal status quo. Was Britain and Scotland within Britain ever less savage and hypocritical? But being a canny lass even at the age of eight or so and having learnt the crass cultural lingo well, she realised the only way to survive both bullying and the stark market system was to capitalise on the mythology of archetypes. If the world saw females as either ors, as conniving avaricious bitches or cunning tricky witches then so be it – maybe she could profit from the double standards!

The undercurrents of brute force machismo money and potent sexual language and behaviour which ran together alongside the cheap lines in empathy in pseudo feminised service capitalism like two mismatched cables ready to explode at any moment blowing the whole world's system apart. For increasingly everyone 'did' instant empathy and sugary sweet sympathy these days seeing as they at least were usually still free at the point of access. Yet others 'did God' as if both were expendable life style choices. Or was it touchy feely American psycho- expressionism, expansionist and 'spiritual' in its thinking with remembered elements of the halcyon quasi mythical days of the 1960s – and this combined with the remnants of stark nineteenth century accounting language. Welcome to Britain, late 1980s style. The early beginning of psycho-spirit language, maybe to counter or even bolster the efficient zeal of the markets.

Let the world wait while she perfected her skills. Alison would shout loudly, ask questions, define her own language, be awkward, climb walls and roofs risking condemnation in her fight for her right to be who she was and to live how she chose. Later they will go and find a nearby pub, one which is female friendly and they will drink beer maybe or even lager, craving a quiet dark anonymous space. Yes, these places and spaces still existed but they had to be fought over and defended like prize virgin rainforests, wilderness generally and all that is good, humane and kind in this world if not the next.

*

A dark June full moon hangs in the sky above Arthur's Seat as Alison Mode slips into the cool fresh water pool. New moon, new beginnings. Try to forget Sinclair's savage campaign, the crude violence of the break in. Spock *will* be re-found, she'll use all her powers to find him. She hadn't swum for years – not since that day out with ma on Portobello beach back in 1986. Well, that was nearly true for she had dipped herself into Portobello indoor swim centre briefly but had been put off by seeing a large pieces of red nail polish floating around in the water like some ominous shells of artifice, reminding her of Barbara who, when she had the time, would paint on some colour to treat herself.

But she hadn't been able to fully face the water, any waters in fact for, let alone submerge herself or even go swimming for even though Barbara hadn't exactly drowned in the bath – it was an all too painful association. Nobody in their right mind could complain or even legally insist she see a doctor. Leaving her clothes on the water's edge she tentatively swims out naked into the middle of the small pond hoping that no fish would take a nip at her toes thinking her food. She really didn't want to end her life as fish food.

Maybe she'd forgotten how to swim. But the physical movements came back to her, like some long lost friend accidentally rediscovered. She just had to prove it to herself, had to know and feel that she was still alive and slightly wild at heart despite it all, that she could take control of her life and destiny once again – despite all adversity and Sinclair's campaign of intimidation. She had courage, raw guts and hope and was willing to take risks.

How many other people in the city, in the world were being subjected to bullying, malice, slander, contempt, violence, blackmail, extortion if not worse? She allowed herself to think this terrible thought as a necessary kind of quiet motivator which made her more determined than ever to use her talents and the rest of her life to confront evils full on either within or without. *Look first not last for the hidden shadow and secret motivations Alison* she caught herself thinking. A nearby frog croaks then, reminding her of the pleasant aloneness at that moment. She hoped she hadnae disturbed some mating ritual recalling then her precious mither reading her a Red Indian tale about salamanders and geckos defeating dark things through camouflage and quiet observation, learning the art of seeing light and many shades of grey even in pitch blackness. And sometimes she wanted to disappear into dark waters herself and live the life of some unrecorded free moving amphibian. What a welcome underground existence that would be, a quietly examined life but one that still remained full of soulful primeval mystery and depth.

A world you could safely disappear in anonymously and nobody begrudging you for that part time disappearing act. An area of your life reserved for your own viewing only and not offered up for shared surveillance, measurement, accountability, consumption, comparison. Paradise might be found in this happy compromise but not in some ideological utopia which promised impossible standards. Alison thought that this hidden private aspect of human existence was worth fighting for, it was a last modern sacred frontier and right: the right to define yourself and be your whole self safely in your own space, in other words the right to sole ownership of your identity.

Yesterday she'd had a moment in the afternoon in the city centre when she just thought she couldn't go on with the daily mechanics of her life any longer – all the cards seemed totally stacked against her and she doubted whether she'd have the strength to survive financially or spiritually. Perhaps someone, the kind Polish neighbour maybe whose name she still didnae know, might find her rotting body by a pile of small white pills. There were plenty of these real life stories of neighbours realising something was wrong after months or years, of not having heard that weird old codger next door shuffle around. The recent break in had shocked her again, it felt as if the very earth's tectonic plates had cracked making her doubt her sanity, existence, worth. She felt broken beyond repair and despaired as to what might help. She'd walked to the world famous Frankenstein's Bar on George Fourth Bridge and found herself unhealthily glued to the continuously playing horror films from the 1930s and 40s which were screened just outside the gothic looking former church. She'd identified with the pain, sorrow and isolation of the disowned monsters and misfit creeps meeting misunderstandings and tragic brutal deaths.

Then it came to her out of the blue of the sky. *Seek out the waters to find your inner peace again.* She'd bought some dried lavender tea and managed to get home in one piece after all. *Empower yourself at home if you cannae do so politically.* Use the psycho-spirito talk for your benefit. *Go with the flow* seemed to have some kind of real value. She resolved to re- visit the geese pond in Holyrood Park, she'd not visited it for years but she had a feeling that's what she'd need. A dark kind of medicine, a shot of wild waters. She could hear herself and feel herself again there, God knows she needed to re-discover her sense of self and worth.

If only more people actually thought, considered and cared enough – if only life hadn't become this cruel grinding process of soul extraction in the name of abstract disputed concepts like efficiency. Whole human heart beats reduced to a series of invisible electronic financial pulses, mere robotic automans to the big cash machine in the sky. But hey, even if the whole of mankind was in moral, ecological and financial turbulence – we could always still say we have markets. That was one mantra thing people could always be sure of if all else crumbled, failed and deceived them. Trust markets instead to solve the world's ills.

But earlier this evening, after eating, she'd done the deed and ventured out alone at night instantly refreshed by seeing what she thought was a shooting star in the night sky. Maybe even these awful encounters with Sinclair served some purpose; she was being tested for some as yet unknown reason. In physics positively charged protons and negatively charged neutrons somehow needed each other – the two governing contradictory laws somehow holding matter or mass together in some kind of finely tuned balancing act. And humans, being atoms in some sense too must succumb to these opposing charges too if unaware. How arrogant to presume humans are immune and distinct to the laws of physics.

Approaching the pond, she'd disturbed some sleeping Canada geese that honked their dismay. But she just knew she had to immerse herself once more, the shock of last month's violent break in had affected her deeply and had led to quite a few teary sleepless nights raging at just how awful and evil humans could be to each other. Fuck what the world thinks about her or her neighbours who might well have spotted her slipping furtively out of her stair door at a late hour, she'd already spent way too much of her early adult life worrying about what she had no control over ultimately – that being other people's judgements and perceptions. Five years from now and would it all really matter?

Maybe she'd be buried like her mother in Seafield Cemetery and her body's atoms would be released into the soil or atmosphere and she'd be re-born as an earthworm or another soul or she'd make it her life mission in the next re-incarnation to wipe out the likes of Sinclair and his ilk in this world. Perhaps somebody, fifty years from now – that is if the world hadn't been nuked or burnt out in the big current carve up for resources and global dominance, somebody would be breathing in atoms in the air which had once made up her physical body. If she didnae like the person in question she could always lecture them from on high – a disembodied voice speaking from an unknown source. And maybe science could really then prove that there is a place, a space in which science and religion meet, somehow containing all these different charges and wave lengths into one big eternal *Now* which was located in different dimensions and places in time simultaneously. *Aye, right.* The sum total of human world consciousness compressed into a small grain of rice lending new meaning to the expression all is one and one is all. Swimming herself back to sanity and connectedness, Alison thought again of that day out on Portobello Beach, a rare day off for her working mother. It hadn't been that long before that very same day that Alison had heard via the Leith grapevine that Leonard, her first and only boyfriend, had fled to the West Indies in search of a new life and maybe a wife.

11

It Comes in Threes

July 18th, 2014

Grey rain falling, perhaps forever, providing a *dreicht* kind of symphony. Yes, even in July Edinburgh endures rain – that is why the parks and gardens are generally so lush and moist. But Alison Mode no longer knew the time of year, indeed no longer knew time generally for day was night and night day. Intense despair and grief had returned since the midnight Arthur's Seat swim, depression hung again in her shoe box of a flat rather like some toxic chemical residue that Lady Hyde had protested about. She missed Spock terribly. But that wasn't the only horror for the good lady herself had left a slurred message on Alison's answerphone saying that she deeply appreciated Alison being in her life, that she wanted to keep in touch somehow and that Lord Hyde had beaten her black and blue so she had escaped to her family estate in Aberdeenshire. She didn't know whether she would go back to him, it was all left in limbo and there were the ugly but necessary questions about the potential carve up of properties in Edinburgh and London. Maybe a cooling off period was needed but the terrifying savagery of his attack had nearly hospitalised her and it had to remain strictly hush and under wraps. She was calling to let Alison know that she was deeply moved and inspired by everything and that she hoped life for her in Edinburgh, on a very different kind of estate, was tolerable.

The impeccably clipped voice wobbled and quivered in a watery kind of emotional quaver and then she'd rung off abruptly. So savagery and cruelty didn't discriminate among the social classes either. Flora too had called a few times, leaving anxious messages, asking if everything was alright with her and imploring Alison to please call her back when she could but saying she understood if work was tiring her out. *Work, ah yes.* The wonderful world of work, or rather the lack of it, for in contrast to the rain which had plagued the city non-stop for three whole days, work had dried up. No calls had come in from *Help Is At Hand* and perhaps this was a temporary blessing not a curse for right now she really didn't' want to be around other people and their problems. For she was a woman who'd fallen to earth and who now wished this same element would swallow her up completely. And to top it all off, she's sure she's caught some kind of severe bug from swimming in wild open waters as her nose streams constantly.

Days had drifted by in this silent state of mourning for Spock and she had resorted to writing in *The Quibblon* as it was the only way she could cope with the loss. The good book was many fine things to her: guide, confessional, dictionary, journal, sounding board. A few weeks back she'd pinned notices on trees near where she lived in a desperate attempt to assuage her guilt over him but of course it was futile. She was dealing with malicious spite and evil, phenomena which unfortunately never completely goes away, potentially lurking as it does in every human mind. The police also had been unable to shed any light or real help over the vandalism of her flat and property as they confirmed what she somehow first sensed – that no finger prints had been left. She'd got the lock fixed quickly, she'd had to, but the re-wall papering had yet to be done. Mail lay abandoned in an unopened pile by the door, the curtains had hung unopened in the bedroom and front room for days on end in a kind of silted make shift morgue.

And maybe someone had noticed this draped inertia from the street outside; perhaps even the friendly Polish neighbour but so many were afraid to speak out let alone truly reach out and connect to another. Probably enough troubles of their own in all reality, different kinds of shit plastered beneath different kinds of coverings. Some of the shit was visible and new, some old and invisible. Barbara Mode had been a good mother like that to her, teaching her early that life was not about endless roses at the door, that you had to deal with mess and disappointment somehow, that you couldn't always confront it head on but sometimes had to choose your battles, duck and cover. In a sudden fit of rage she'd stripped off the existing wallpaper, tearing down the foul desecrating word *freak* that hurt so deeply and disinfecting the entire flat.

Thank something that the precious *Sneezewood* and *Quibblon* had been left untouched though. She felt violated, invaded, robbed and stripped of her dignity. And now stuff it all; fuck the whole miserable world and its inhabitants. How she could even have thought about caring for others or being a cultural pioneer she didn't know. She couldn't be bothered to draw back the curtains in her bedroom or front room, let people think what they like. In the silence of the kitchen she manages to find the fridge and some milk, butter and purple cabbage in it. But not a lot else. Not enough food for a lounge lizard let alone a bloody couch potato. Outside it is actually the twilight zone again, but this time it's a night of crescent moon and she's lost track of the day – she thinks it's the 18th of July. Enough scoff for a wee bowl of porridge though, she'd have to go the way of the Wipers and other Sassenachs and commit an act of sacrilege and have it with sugar not salt. But the salty tepid porridge can't shift her mood either; she can't be bothered to finish it.

Lady Hyde's shocking message had got beneath her skin, another tale of domestic abuse going on behind closed doors. Such a violent cruel and intolerant culture really. So much for British tolerance and fairness – they seemed distant ideals from a gentler age. No, dysfunction didn't discriminate across social divides –some behaviours were very socially mobile though not always visible. Blowing her nose yet again in a sodden tissue, she again feels silently enraged, determined to fight back, protest, rebel, and question. *But what fucking use are personal passion, creativity and compassion without reason? And what good reason even when confronted by the evil in people?* She didn't know what the answer was either to all these forms of abuse, bullying, intimidation and harassment. It went on and on – dumped from people who were insecure, afraid, cruel, jealous or unhappy in some shape or form. Yeah, yeah, yeah. She knows all about the psychological theories as to why some behave terribly but that doesn't make it any easier dealing with it sometimes. What the hell is she supposed to do – wear garlic, carry a dagger and crucifix and stab the likes of Sinclair who she's rapidly realising is a kind of ghoul who uses and preys upon endless flesh?

Surely not in modern day Edinburgh, dare she tell Flora this insight? It might well be the final stigma and taboo mightn't it – the dread of being labelled as having "mental health issues" when really Alison's thinks she's as sane as the next person. Maybe Flora would listen with an open mind. Leaving the half eaten bowl of porridge on the kitchen table, she creeps back into her bedroom thinking about taking her own life. She'd seen a baby's coffin once, a shocking sight, but they could come in small sizes. Is life about endless struggle, battles and pain? She didn't choose to be born a dwarf, sometimes you cannot really choose your feelings either but she had chosen the fateful care home Barbara Mode was admitted to. And the guilt still returns about this, years later. The tormenting thought that she could have done more to prevent her death.

Perhaps she really is going mad right now. Lying on the bed in darkness scenes of horror return again to her mind. Her nightmare of a Leith primary school when the calling of the names started, her very real terror about going into school some days which she'd thankfully been able to share with Barbara. If you are physically smaller and more receptive than your tormentors what the hell do you do? Then there was the forsaken awful care home manageress, Ann Hogg a gloomy deceptive *wump* if ever there was one. Alison couldn't prove it, her lawyer couldn't prove it, but she just knew Ann Hogg lied. Lies about the cleaning rotas, about the staff on duty the day of Barbara's death.

Yes, said Ann Hogg. *She could tell the police exactly who was on duty that day. All her staff were trained to very high standards and were checked for records. She always insisted two carers assisted residents both in and out of baths. She couldn't explain why a lot of baby oil was present that day in one bath: An oversight. They did have a problem sometimes with leaking liquid soap dispensers.* Ms. Hogg's manner had been seemingly smooth, polite, and professional. Yet the coroner's report said there were odd bruises on Barbara's body which were not conducive to a mere slip. But nothing could be proven ultimately in a court of law, nobody had seen Barbara slip or cry out for help. All the staff witness statements backed each other up meticulously; there was nothing you could put your finger on.

Yet the question marks lingered, the ambivalence unresolved. The police had carefully pieced together Barbara's movements that day. She'd had scrambled eggs for breakfast, done some knitting in the afternoon and watched TV. Seven of the twenty-five residents had baths that night, taking turns. Alison had fought to get at the truth, asking question after question but coming up against a damp brick institutional wall: and no witnesses apparently. Perhaps writing might give her some peace right now, she thinks switching on a side light and snatching up *The Quibblon.*

Dearest Spock,

Are you alive somewhere still? People reading this may think I'm mad going on about experiments, magic, other worlds, states of consciousness, the human condition, the meaning of life, the nature of good and evil, street every day philosophy, life in modern Scotland and the world as we know it. Well, stuff that. These are my private thoughts to be shared with who I choose. At least I ask the questions, still care and take risks. I don't claim to have all the answers, Spock. All I do know right now is that I'm wondering if that bastard Sinclair has taken you, tortured you and roasted you alive in some oven in one of his properties? It's July now Spock and I swear I miss you. I haven't worked for over a month and a deep sucking vortex of depressive grief is sucking the life out of me. No, this is not indulgence dear wee beastie. I honestly don't know if I ever will work again or when and if I can cope with going on with my life without you. Does anyone need me to wipe their arse, hear their woes, bake cakes, offer convoluted counselling, dispense medication and generally be invisible yet visible Jill-Of-All-Trades?

Give me a sign, Spock that you are still alive. I'm trying so hard not to feel sorry for myself I really am but being burgled, bullied, humiliated, and threatened and now without work have shattered me to the core. Being poor and struggling doesn't really help a lot either. Why is it no surprise Spock that women always suffer more in times of recession in terms of cuts to benefits, carrying the main burden of child rearing and in any case putting up with lower pay? Enduring one ambiguous loss never really leaves you in life Spock and you going too is just about killing me off my little furry saviour.

For all the adages and sayings are true as I realise that little things do mean a lot, that people worry far too much about non-living things and that it's important to give love and honesty where ever you can even if you have not been given it yourself and are tested. I'm being tested right now Spock perhaps in my darkest hour ever. But I have a gift, Spock I am a seer and visionary and though I'm short I see the capacity for kindness and its exact opposite in humanity and it's hard to remain true to yourself, to remain principled and do what is right and just. I didnae sleep last night, Spock for my own truly dark forces tempted me over an edge and it was a sweaty struggle to say 'no' – I will not sell my soul for any price. It was the noble sweat of an urban shaman but I cast the devil-doubt off, I dismissed the thoughts. Looking at your empty hutch helped me Spock, it reminded me of my responsibility to you as your carer (or maybe you are my carer) as I felt humbled again, needed and grounded. Maybe I need to be protected from myself, huh? And I will remain true to who I am no matter what and I will defend my principles though I'm often finding myself defending myself against hostility and aggression and criticism from some other women too.

I could visit a sex shop, Spock, and buy feathers and a huge dildo and threaten Sinclair with fist, fake phallus and feisty feathers, easily mocking his version of man hood. But it would backfire on me; I'd be named and blamed somewhere. Then maybe burnt or beaten. You think I joke? And all this played out in a harsh punitive climate which doesn't like difference, wildness or being challenged. Can I deny my feral warrior nature? Should I don the wolf's mask and clothing and become a predator myself, become the thing that trails you and hunts you? I saw a wolf like husky dog the other day slinking low on the Links Spock, and I had a weak moment when I imagined wearing its fur and marking out ground by night. I'd be arrested soon If I tried such a thing but believe me I feel your loss and hanker after the primordial, the wild elf-self.

The dog-wolf sniffed the air like you used to do and I sniffed too in recognition. Then the owner yanked the beast a bit too hard I thought but at least there had been a run around. Sometimes I can forgive dear friend, but at other times I must stand up and say something, yes all three foot six inches of me. I have always believed that animals feel pain and fear the way we do and so, with this thought in mind know that I'm thinking of you even now with tears and great undying love. I doubt myself Spock; I question my powers of mind and wonder whether I have a right to use them.

Before I started writing this letter I stood stock still for several hours with a glass of water on ma heid to teach myself the discipline of balance and concentration. No, I refuse to believe that I'm a dangerous deviant. I will trust myself to do what's right. I just have always done things my own way and sometimes have paid a heavy price for that. I am learning the art of compromise; I believe in that too but only if I'm treated reasonably and fairly too. It works both ways in the human jungle. Yes, I had that thought too and this was all in my front room Spock and I had to draw the curtains in case anybody saw me. You know what it's like. Matters of the private soul are just that.

Yours forever
Alison
NB

I still clean your hutch out; I can't help it. The price of a bunch of carrots has gone way up you know round here.

She had to stop writing then as the tears flowed again. She no longer knows anything it seems, she's as rootless and route less in life as the shrivelled cabbage in her fridge. Redundant, useless, hopeless. Groundless and meaningless. Without warning the doorbell went and Alison forced herself to peer though the spy hole. It's the Polish neighbour again bearing rye bread, bless him. Feeling too wobbly to open the door but touched by his thoughtfulness, she shouts out through the wood. They shared the very same block and in the winter, cold sudden blasts still managed to climb their way up the stairs like unwanted inhabitants. And sometimes the gusts were wilder than a pack of wolves, the sounds echoing down the block like some eerie cry of those beasts.

"I have a terrible cold, a bug and it's just not safe to open the door. Thank you for the bread, it's very kind of you and funnily enough I have run out. Just leave it by the door please. I'm alright, really I am, it's just a shock being burgled and losing my pet. I can't really come out right now; I look like a zombie in a dressing gown. I wouldn't want to alarm you. Thank you for thinking of me though."

"Are you sure everything is OK? I have not seen you for a while and usually I bump into you a couple of times a week. I am so sorry about what happened, the burglary I mean. It is terrible I agree. Just forget it now, if you can. If you would like me to get some shopping for you, please just leave a note through my door and I will help you."

Alison smiled sadly though the key hole, watching him place the bread on her mat then climb the stairs. What a damn good neighbour. She must thank him personally, find out his name. So many strangers to each other and all living in one block. Make the effort. Finding one of her bent coat hangers in the front room, she sits on *The Sneezewood* for some peace of mind. The TV just didn't work for her at such moments, it was sensory overload. Right now Alison's brain is like one of those high speed telephone switches – thousands of lit sparks and rubbing the metal in her left hand acts as a kind of surrogate conductor by proxy. She can focus her mind with the feel of it, bending it into unexpected shapes. Fond memories of her mother reading her wondrous tales of fairy tale dwarves returned again, they who outwitted giants and evil with stealth, courage, compassion and persistence. Right now it's not a spell she needs to find quickly, it's not the *Kwik Stix* which lies safely beneath her bed but a divining direction, an overall structure and strategy for coping.

Maybe later she'd mix up some dried mint and rosemary to ease her runny nose. She keeps a few key herbs for emergencies. She wondered if Lady Hyde would be alright up in Aberdeenshire, thankfully no ugly stories had leaked out about her political outburst or her private life. She had a mental picture of Lady Hyde sitting in a vast hall sipping soup with a silver spoon – whether this was actually how it was being an aristocrat she had no idea. The fact is they liked and respected each other, but then life can be stranger than any fiction. Lord Hyde was both well connected and influential but was shrewd enough to remain largely invisible to the gaping eyes of the ever hungry hoards enthral to the media.

High profiles but still low key – an artful form of social engineering akin to eighteenth century cameo silhouettes. Then there had been the odd dry laugh she'd heard in the hall a couple of times over the last two weeks – now where had she heard that laugh before, she badly needed her powers of recall. A very modern goblin chuckle. It seemed to be emanating from some vent in the hall ceiling but whenever she walked directly into the hall it stopped suddenly. Was there really an afterlife, some other realm of existence? The rational part of her still refused to believe it, yet she could not deny she'd heard what sounded like her mother sighing in Seafield Cemetery. Again it was the ambiguity that was difficult to accept, the never knowing like the overhanging care home legal case, suspended forever. No closure for the dead.

Then with a shudder she recalled the encounter with Sinclair in the launderette. *Of course, that was it.* The dry corrosive laughter, she'd blocked it out. But quite why and how she was hearing what sounded like his laughter in the hall she also didnae know. Was the vent acting as some kind of portal or gateway? A kind of vortex into space, into another dimension? Maybe he is practising some continuing dark art on her, not content with stealing, bullying and extortion. She'd heard of such phenomena before. But then thinking about Sinclair again there had been a kind of empty vortex in his eyes, too. The crescent moon is very beautiful in its distant allure even through great steamy sheets of summer rain.

Peeking furtively behind the front room curtains, Alison heads off for bed, sinking her head on the pillow. It's all too much, life. The coat hanger and *The Sneezewood* had calmed her though and she feels her mind drifting off in some kind of cerebral sea. In the early hours she is woken by a soft tapping sound, again seemingly coming from the hallway. At first Alison thinks it's rain dripping in from somewhere but, listening closely the sound isn't quite right. It's not water, rhythmically seeping in, but something else entirely. Afraid but curious she rolls out of bed and walks towards the hall. Her heart is racing, her hands sweating. *Spock's in the cave sweet heart* whispers the transparent white apparition of Barbara Mode. *Have no fear, my darling.*

12

The Cave

Sitting round the table in Flora and Mac's kitchen above their shop *Creatures of Habit,* Alison sits in a profound state of shock. She'd been sitting like that, for hours in her flat before Flora had arrived and whisked her away. It was purely by chance that Alison had left her mobile on earlier that morning. Plates of baked beans on toast lie on the table and Mac's pale blue eyes had welled with tears when he'd heard what Alison had seen. Despite his gruff stoical manner, he is deeply but privately emotional, as a lot of Scottish men are. Sometimes these deep feelings and affinities with the land, with ancestors and the nature of the human animal only came out in the relative safety of rugged vistas crammed full of rolling heathers and rocky challenging peaks formed in a gradual process of thousands of years ago, a kind of visible testament to the Scottish soul and psyche.

One had to dig away long and hard to get at the molten feelings buried and encased in the hearts of Scottish men long ago. *Bravehearts?* Sometimes maybe, but perhaps also dead repressive hearts in a culture which could feel at times, to both Alison and Flora at least, oppressively macho. Fire and brimstone outwardly but often buggery, balderdash, blind men's bluff within. That or a debilitating melancholy. Flora's always loved brown fruity sauce with everything, even with chips and fish suppers which were abundant down in Leith. Shaking out dollops on her food, she eyes Alison sympathetically. Bright sunlight shines through the window, the rays highlighting the drained shadows under Alison's eyes.

"Is this the first time something like this has happened to you, Alison? Maybe you are a bit of a spirit magnet, if not a full blown medium. I do believe you though – but I have to say I haven't had any experiences like this myself. It must feel weird and frightening."

Alison catches Mac's eye and smiles sadly. The baked beans are getting progressively colder by degrees; Flora gently taps her fork on the table indicating that she should eat up. But she'd not been able to sleep a wink last night, not after seeing something as devastating as the ghost of her mother. She's so not in the mood for food. Right now the only thing she can be sure of is the ground beneath her feet but maybe now not even this as her legs don't reach the linoleum floor but hang in limbo. And below the floorboards, the faint sounds of cats mewing and puppies yelping can be heard. The kitchen looks and feels homey, a large basket of fruit lies on the nearby pine dresser.

"Maybe it's a gift, Alison and you need not fear it but you need to know how to use it or it could maybe destroy you like any misused tool. You told me about the voices in Seafield Cemetery but after the chandelier episode in the Assembly Rooms you kind of convinced me. In fact, to tell you the sordid truth, I've been trying to bend some spoons and entice more customers using the power of thought like you said but I'm just not having any luck at all."

Alison laughs loudly at herself, never taking anything too seriously as this also could drive you quite mad. She'd re-discovered her ability to laugh when living with a pet and learning magic tricks. A few slightly misshapen spoons are on the window sill. Mac looks at his wife as if she's lost some plot but what the heck he loves her anyway. Nobody's perfect after all in this life or maybe the next. But there is no hidden jealousy or deceit in Flora and that's what Alison and Mac love about her. True friendship and earned trust is in itself a small every day kind of miracle after all. Alison had wisely not told anyone yet about the necessity of the repeated mantras or the different kinds of power objects but had shared the secrets of *The Quibblon*, knowing that both of them also despised hypocrisy and savage injustice dressed up in that two faced voodoo doll of rhetorical political correctness.

Dependent upon prevalent political and economic winds, the doll always showed one of two faces. Flora clears the table, not having the heart to force feed Alison. Conversation moved on to Lady Hyde's brave rant in the House of Commons but Alison had to edit other more recent news on that front, fending her tried and tested friends off with vague accounts of the good Lady and Lord having settled their differences and all being well. She hated lying of all kinds, but a white lie to save the honour and proven integrity of a friend – whether rich or poor – this kind of principled lie she would tell.

Conversation moved on to Sinclair and what could be done to catch him and stop him for the burglary and hounding of Alison was as appalling and awful, in their eyes, as the hunting and goading of animals for sport not food. Maybe there would always be the Sinclairs of this world and quite possibly the next inflicting direct psychological taxation which is just as devastating as the other life sapping direct and indirect financial kinds. They would do anything to try and help her they said, any little thing at all. She was to just ask, that's all. She should just call if she feels afraid or lonely, they would be there for her. Given the circumstances, she could stay over there if she wanted until things were better. Alison manages a little laugh, moved as she is by their loyalty and compassion in her hour of need. What a precious and priceless thing true friendship is, she reflects again watching Mac shift some Battenberg cake out of the fridge and making sly jokes about the great carve up of the Scottish economy and who would get the most advantageous slice of the cake – England or Scotland? Speculation aside, one thing was for sure Scotland would continue to be served that other German cake, Hapsburg-Hanover.

Walking back home in the early evening past the famous statue of good old Queen Vic, Alison studiously avoids a couple of infamous alley ways with massive overflowing rubbish bins which sometimes spelled danger. She carefully avoids stepping on the paving's cracks – *step on the pavement cracks and break your mother's back* was a horrible folk lore. It is July now and quite where the time had gone she didnae know. Perhaps it too was susceptible to being sucked up into different kinds of black holes irrespective of whether the hole was in one's air vent or attic or not.

People had been stabbed, raped, robbed, harassed and stalked down some of the city's alleys but both affluent city dwellers and tourists alike didn't always want to know about the violent, the mentally ill, the desperate or the poor. And this truth never universally acknowledged all over for its cost implications in the former empire as well as now in the *common* wealth, whose wealth the common good did not always get. Guns and drugs are sometimes present in Leith's side streets and not just air guns either. Edinburgh had its fly tipping hot spots just like everywhere else, old mattresses just dumped – once Alison had even seen a TV dumped outside her block with a fuzzy live green screen despite not being plugged into anything so tangible as a plug.

She heads off in the direction of *Small Fry, Big Fish* a renowned Leith chip shop near the bottom of Easter Road. *I'll be damned if I can find the energy to cook right now back at the flat, and why the hell should I frankly? I spend most of my life caring for others, supporting them in many ways – if it's not that, then I'm doing housework, tending to Spock's needs or my mother's grave. Well, sod it; I've earned the right to a wee dish o' fish. My impact and footprint on this earth has been and will always be modest compared to some. And you can't put a price on real friendship though* Alison reflects, waiting in the chippy for the rather large fish tea to be packaged up. So, the universe is immensely complicated at any one time, it is teeming with vibrational energy and many truths and this is just the collective thoughts and states of mind of billions of people which must be impacting somehow on the atmosphere alongside the continuing horror of burning oil on mass.

On top of all these cosmic layers was the seemingly infinite numbers of technological gadgets and gizmos, alongside noise and light pollution which meant that it was becoming ever harder to hear oneself think and be true to one's whole self, let alone to keep calm and continue eating various kinds of cupcakes which apparently had become the nation's latest feel good factor food. Space in all its meanings was becoming a scarce resource like fresh water, to be fought and competed over ruthlessly. But comfort food and endless TV shows about cooking, conspicuous consumption and lifestyle choices couldn't completely cover up inner blight, crisis of faiths and rot could it. *No, give me a real Edinburghian whopping fish supper and a whole pint of finest Edinburgh tap water for me any day pal. I haven't dropped down dead yet from it.*

Maybe there really was an underground sage like man in the city, under the castle rock or Arthur's Seat even who operated some mystical tapping of the elixir of life from a subterranean tavern. Frankly, these days anything goes in the moral and economic whirl pools each of which could suck a victim dry, vampire like, leaving in their wake walking human zombies petrified in a kind of free-for-all political stasis. Afraid, divorced, addicted, distracted, anxious, poor, struggling, redundant, isolated, depressed. It seemed to be the all prevailing spirit of the times, the zeitgeist indeed all over the world since the bankers and politicians ganged up. But that message from her mother's ghost! It defied the part of the brain that ruled logic and reason but then human consciousness has always been fluid and multi layered. *Spock's in the cave sweet heart, have no fear my darling.* Alison hadn't mentioned the message she'd heard Barbara say to Flora or Mac, she didn't want to burden them further as their small business was already struggling with the strain of increased rates. Besides, some things were still sacred and personal.

At home listening to folk music and eating her fine Scottish fish tea supper doused in vinegar, the realisation finally hits Alison. She'd been going over and over it in her mind. *Caves.* As far as she knew there were no caves as such in Edinburgh were there? She knew Edinburgh had one underground city called Mary King's Close along the Royal Mile but where else could be called a cave? Of course, *Niddry Street.* The little whispered message wafted past her ear, floating feather like on some invisible ether. The vaults or the caves there had existed since the eighteenth century; they once housed great barrels of whiskey and accommodated the poor and unsavoury. Out of sight, out of mind.

Perhaps not much had really changed since the great South Sea Bubble bust when slaves worked, shackled on great coffee plantations. The proliferation of mass farming and new style coffee houses in Edinburgh within Alison's life time with socially lubricating syrups and powders made her wonder if this was a new kind of oil to ease and stimulate toil where once opium, pot or a pint might have done the jobbie. But could Spock really be there in the caves in Niddry Street? And how on earth did he get there – as far as Alison knew some objects might be capable of tele transportation but guinea pigs and even humans were firsts for the books, even for the likes of *The Quibblon*.

She'd heard of one particular cave called the Banshee Labyrinth which was visited by a female spirit foretelling a death but she didn't like to venture out into places of the dead for gratuitous reasons or for mere titillation only, instead believing in honouring and listening to the deceased instead. There was enough unjust exploitation going on amongst the land of the living never mind amongst the living dead and she didn't want to contribute to any of it further. Alison goes to the kitchen taking her greasy but empty plate with her and as she does so she's startled to see a white hand shove a note through her letter box. *What the hell is this now* she thinks – infuriated at this latest intrusion and demand. Can't a woman be left in the peace and safety of her own home for a day without being hounded in some shape or form? She's scared to move, routed to the spot. Walking tentatively over to her goody one shoe doormat, woven faithfully in the Highlands, no doubt by some small modern day crofter-farmer, she picks up the note. SiX o' CloCK ToMorrow MoRnING, NIdDry StReet CaVes, No. 30. YoUr PiG AwAiTS. NoW BuRN ThIS Or ElSE.

Alison sneezes again and cusses herself for not having a handy tissue available. She could do with a gin and tonic or something stronger like a fine whiskey but realises she hasn't anything alcoholic in the flat, more's the pity. She's managed to disinfect and clean the whole flat and spent ages scrubbing off the nasty abusive words from her sitting room wall with a sponge, resorting finally to a scouring pad. Though the awful daubed word '*freak*' had been erased there were still marks left and it was impossible not to see the word again and again on the wall like some awful scratchings left by a tortured ghost. Just after Barbara died she'd had a brief period where she couldn't get through the day without a drink to numb the pain but she'd managed to wean herself off with Flora's and a friendly GP's help who hadn't patronised or pathologised her, but just listened to her. But this latest message, delivered by a small but real white hand and not by a ghostly apparition really took the proverbial biscuit. It can't just be a simple handing over of Spock to her can it? Oh no. Life's never that simple. But she's no longer convinced it's just the invented rent Sinclair wants either. How did the ghost of her mother know about the cave though? It was all too weird. Maybe departed loved ones did still linger and travel with the living at times of need particularly. And Alison *had* just been thinking about caves, coffee pots and water supplies and then this note. She'd been too scared to look through the spy hole to see, perhaps, a disappearing back stabber. She slumps down on the sofa in her front room, burnt out and exhausted.

Behind every great man or woman is sometimes another man or woman but sometimes it is just a wee pet, maybe even a guinea pig. Spock *must* be being held captive by Sinclair or one of his henchmen in one of the caves in Niddry Street! She knew where the street was, she could picture it in her mind's eye for the eye in the mind as well as the thoughts in the mind could visualise good or bad. She'd heard of kidnapping but guinea pig napping was also a first. And her mother always did say some things come in threes – first the robbery, then the cold caught from swimming, then the ghost. Should she burn the note now as requested? But why the hell should she be intimidated by bullying and threats in her own home? The rebel in her, the freedom fighter who valued justice, honesty and courage above anything else refused to be ordered about. She never was a shilpit lassie. It had gone on for too long as it was, Sinclair's micro reign of terror. And she couldn't be the only victim in the city now could she? Far from it.

But at least there'd been no more coughing she'd heard in the flat only hers which is now completely doing her nut in. Alison pours herself a glass of juice from a carton which she'd left hurriedly on the coffee table. Bloody colds and germs even in July, she had no cough syrup either. Useless. She tries to fight of feelings of self-loathing but the luring under current is strong. The nasty niggling little voices in her head start up, right on cue the way they always did. *No paid work currently and now a failed housewife and lousy pet owner who couldn't see what was coming. Stupid self-absorbed Alison Mode, just when you thought you were really getting it together as a modern day white witch on a mission. Not good enough really is it?* Now what on earth would *The Quibblon* say about sadness, depression, spirits that cough and trying to rise above it all in adversity, possible danger and doubt? Closing her eyes, she thumbs through the pages at random. *F,* Flour Bombs and Possible

Uses of Flour and Fox gloves (extracts of), flushing out your opponent's true motives, *O*, the divining uses of oil and oracles. *R,* rosemary and medicinal uses of rhubarb. *D*, depression and down hearted ness, dandelion leaves and dark forces either from within or without. Or both at once. She reads on.

D, for depression and down hearted ness, dandelion leaves and dark forces either from within or without.

The answers to these very common ailments are to start by first looking thoroughly at the source of the anxiety. Is it something that somebody said to you or did to you or is it self-manufactured? Dark chocolate is one option, toadstools a no no and stay away from spotted mushrooms. Sitting with it but not feeding it more food, as it were, is another. All things pass after all and sadness or anger are not to be feared or denied. A life that's too sweet or all sweet will offer no challenge, grit or opportunity for growth. Artificial and temporary lifters of mood are doomed to fail also, for what goes up suddenly and quickly must come down. Cracking a salty joke and making someone smile, doing something for another is usually a winner. Doing what makes you happy. Dandelion and rosehip tea are great but salt circles and salt throwing are also beneficial. Turn around twice and sprinkle a bit today.

Of course, protective salt circles. Healer of woes and sore toes in water. Alison needed something to ward off a looming pit of despair and fast. Quick, get the *Kwix Stix* also from under the bed. Might as well grab the duvet too, could do with being wrapped up now. Sprinkling the salt on the carpet with the *Kwik Stix* in her left hand, Alison again closes her eyes searching for some kind of cure or answer. Turn around twice with a clear question, breathe deeply. *Kwik Stix pick me a trick please do.* Was it something that I myself said? *What goes up, must come down*. Of course, that's it. Now if my mother came and dropped in for a visit from somewhere and through a vortex or time portal, then maybe it might be possible to travel back *up* through it. Logical.

A kind of cosmic lift in a sense though who knows how many floors there were in the universe's architecture? Guffawing at her own joke, Alison pours herself another juice; she loves the pithy type's substance. A small idea is growing slowly in her mind like a seed. Try it tomorrow, maybe. But before this try uttering some words, see if you can suspend things in space and in that very act maybe suspend time. You can't run before you can walk, hen. A sudden fit of curiosity seizes Alison and placing a pen on the coffee table in her front room she stares intently. *White power, word power raise this pen at this very hour – show me how uplifting a mere pen's work can be!* Alison slowly repeats the words and incredibly the pen starts to rock from side to side and then *whoosh!* It's right there in front of her suspended in mid-air. But if a humble levitating pen could be physically raised through the power of thought, how about a live earth worm?

Alison digs up a worm from a flower pot and places it on the table too, staring so intensely her eyes begin to water up. *Power of my mind I conjure you, raise this wee beastie a foot or two.* Well, Alison knew she had a way with nice words but this hidden ability took her breath away for there the wee bugger is hovering mid-air by the pen. The worm wriggles awkwardly; it's a sight for sore eyes alright. Well, I may as well go for a heavier object still, she thinks knowing in advance what her next step will be. Focusing on *The Sneezewood* on the other side of the room, she once again focuses on the object in question. *If the higher mind can really meditate then oh, my clear mind make this stool now levitate.* Talk about the right words at the right time, used with good intentions for now Alison really surprises herself. *The Sneezewood* wibble-wobbles, tilting from side to side before slowly making an ascent joining the pen and worm – a motley collection of objects, none acquired through higher purchase.

Alison drinks in the moment, realising the implications of what she sees before her. If she can raise *The Sneezewood* in Domain III using Domain I then who knows what else the stool could do. Prepare in advance, an early start. Sometimes preparation and the right frame of mind is enough if not more than enough. Radio waves provide comfort well into the night wrapped in a duvet on the sofa. And thinking about seeds she's been so busy this year what with the move, her home visits and now all of this palaver that she had forgotten about the simple happiness that growing flowers in boxes gives her.

*

Sitting on *The Sneezewood* under the hall air vent early the following morning, Alison swears colourfully under her breath like any self-respecting practioner would who resented rising at a punishing hour to confront a sadistic bald shit head with some shady agenda. She'd risen extra early and removed the plastic air vent covering. It's a gamble this, a risk. But she has to try; she has a hunch that came to her last night. She's always been a trier, a fighter. Fight the good fight; bring on the tulyie with Sinclair. What will be, will be. And with the right words it might just be possible. She'd do anything for Spock; she never could bear any massacre of the innocent. Only the other day she saved another worm in front of the block of flats knowing that each one processes and farms lots of soil every day. Another underground worker, often taken for granted.

A gang of children, no more than eight or nine in age had laughed, mocked and spat on a nearby bus stop not quite daring to spit at her but given half a chance, eh? Maybe black holes could be harnessed and there could be eyes in the very air. Silence in the early morning; sleep for most but not for some who worked shifts. *White power, white power I now call upon you even in this early hour take me to the creature that I love!* Just as true wishing upon a star can fulfil a dream so calling upon your higher self can. Try it at home and see for yourself. It's free; no tax is imposed upon it. The *Sneezewood* begins to rock and sway, creaking in noble tradition. For some traditions are worth preserving, providing stability as they do. *Whooosh!* Alison throws away the coat hanger and closes her eyes. Slowly and incredibly she is being drawn up, sucked up, up through the air vent and through an opening in the roof and she is rising and flying on the stool through the city's atmosphere, feeling her headdress wobble and holding on to the stool for dear life as really she should have thought about a kind of seat belt.

Edinburgh's famous sky line is unmistakable in the rosy pinks and golds of that clear July early morning. Alison's often wondered how seagulls see things and now she knows. Such limitless space and freedom. There are no aeroplanes as it's not high up enough for that but there are wispy clouds floating by like some shared downy eiderdown and looking down there are just a few cars on the road and the odd person walking down roads and there's a strange kind of calm Zen up there, a putting one's own lot into perspective in the greater scheme of things. Though it's summer there's still dampness in the air which may evolve into dry heat in several hours' time. A kind of hands on practical remote viewing experience this. Small houses, rows upon rows. Order and grace and lives seen from afar. Roofs and low flying birds. *Talk about a night out on the tiles and high flying birds!* She'd read once that mice can squeeze themselves through a hole as wide as a pencil and feeling bold she whispers instructions to *The Sneezewood* sensing that it's taken on a life of its own. *Take me to India Street; let's see what the fallen lord is doing!* She is taken up Leith Walk in a blink of an eye and streets and roads widen out into Regency squares and crescents as *The Sneezewood* whooshes over the New Town towards the Hyde's home. So far, nobody on earth, certainly no early riser has spotted this strange fly-by-day creature who now lands gracefully on the roof of Number 38. *Pure, breathless, wondrous magic! As valuable, precious and life affirming as the silver threads of the common money spider for we are all inter connected in the vast web of life and, knowing this, each affects the other whether they know or like this or not.*

And using her powers Alison looks through the roof and sees Lord Edward Hyde alone and asleep and wonders about his real state of affairs, away from the public gaze and behind closed doors. He's an aristocrat it is true, he has a title and reputation which is sometimes a hindrance and not a privilege for he too is restricted by expectations and the past. For money can't buy some kinds of choice in life though it can bring independence. Yet this man also uses a flushing toilet and has down moments and doubts himself like the rest of the human race – hard to believe so convincing, seductive and imposing is the engrained veneer of class and all its 'trappings'.

Trappings is the right word too, for all human kind that walk this earth are bounded and defined by *some* label. The Internet or inter-national net can never erode this truth as on the earth plane at least there is no unlimited moral freedom. Lord Hyde's blood is blue in one sense but also red not blue. And red and blue each have many subtle shades and components; they *can,* do and must mix. Such is the value of tolerance and being broad minded. And all of the above is what Alison Mode thinks, up there upon the exact pinnacle of the roof rocking slightly between left and right on her stool this July morning noticing that some unkind local residents have placed vicious looking metal spikes on their properties to defer nesting seagulls and no doubt pigeons, too. Nobody wanted to be crapped on and investing in land and property were always dead certs.

So Alison Mode, a single carer from a poor working class part of the city, a woman berated, mocked and bullied for her skills, looks and appearance over which she had and has no 'choice', a much lauded word but a word open to misuse, abuse and manipulation like anything else – sees and feels The Great Divides and yawning gaps between rich and poor, men and women, East and West from her stool on high yet still sees the inherent vulnerability and dependency even in this powerful man of the elite. Time passes by up there, for Alison is trying to get the spell-medicine right. Cut your suit according to your cloth, reap as you sew. Just deserts maybe? She despises Lord Hyde for beating his wife, for being a moral coward but what good is hatred to a man who is emotionally crippled if not crude despite being plausible and articulate?

A passing early postman stops and stares up at her, it's nearly 6.30 am as the crow flies. Can't hang around too long, Sinclair's not patient. The postie doesn't point and laugh but you can see the assumptions whirring round: *is she mad? Maybe she's mad. Could it be the menopause? He'd heard that women do strange things in cycles. Should he call the police? But it doesn't look as if she's about to do a break in. Ah, she's an out of work actress, that's it. It's nearly the silly August season and she's doing some do-ally rehearsing for an experimental play – a one-woman show. Don't shout at her, humour her if you are unsure though pal. She might just be a psycho instead.*

Time to summon some bravado and a covering line, for one must always account for oneself, give reasons, justify. Alison winks and waves to at the postie who's decided he must call *someone* about her. For one thing, the lass doesn't look safe rocking from one side to another on that stool thing. Never in all his rounds as he seen something like this on a roof before. He whips out his mobile, pressing buttons, staring in amazement at her. A smartly dressed woman parks her car on the opposite side of the road, shutting and locking the doors. She watches the free street entertainment for a few moments, clicks her teeth and walks on, *so* not impressed. For speculation it seems goes on everywhere these days – on the side lines, in hedge funds, in the gutter press and now on roof tops.

"I know it looks funny to you pal, but I'm a woman on an unusual mission if not in an unusual position. Between you and me I'm here to help out a friend in need. I'm fixing their roof and checking out the cracks and I think I have found something wrong. Could you do us a favour? If you go to the house's front door, you'll see a key under the mat. Look, I'm not a nut job, okay? The guy who lives here is a friend of a friend. He's in a crisis but you'd never know it. There's no need to call the coppers, pal."

Alison may be short but she sure can yell out when she needs to. She can see the postie hesitating, not sure if she's taking the piss. *Is she having a kind of laugh, what's she like, eh.* But he stops his call mid-way and gives her the benefit of the doubt, walking up the grand steps and flicking up the mat during which time Alison's already sent the thought direct to Lord Hyde through the tiles. *Beware the shoulder pads, pal. Watch for the hair! Pucker and large it right up up and away to the cave on a higher plane please!* No sooner said then done and Alison's speeding down Princes Street, up North Bridge and down Niddry Street faster than the speed of light. This is travel in a new kind of fast lane, that of the third interpersonal shared Domain, one can access it through a mind of one's own. More cars on the road now and people walking to work. 6.50 am, still time. *Catch the bastard unawares. Stealth tactics; thought I'd just drop by 'early' see.* Hovering above the spot, Alison closes her eyes transporting herself in her mind's eye to the interior of the Banshee Cave, now home to new kinds of brew. *Phhoosh,* she's done it again and finds herself sitting on the stool a few yards away from a bored staring Sinclair wearing a kilt, whose bald head catches the light like some faulty explosive light bulb. Poor Spock's squirming with shock, tightly grasped as he is in Sinclair's hands. The air's damp and dense in here. In the shadowy lighting Alison can dimly make out the silver sporran on the front of his kilt and what looks like a badger head attached to it. *Fresh kill maybe.* Be careful.

On seeing Alison's sudden, late, fantastical appearance out of the blue, Sinclair's mouth drops open in shocked disbelief. Out of this world, this. Crazier than drugs. He's standing by an enormous barrel which must have once housed gin or whiskey. He's been carefully rehearsing what he would say to her before she arrived, perfecting the tone and now this. *It's that bloody stool she's sitting on! So that's the secret of her powers. She's a bloody witch, this woman. A genie who must be stopped for I am the only true King of The Underworld. Too clever by half and she's only half the size of me which makes it all the more infuriating. I must have the chair and her knowledge which I can extract. Everyone has a price; what's Alison Mode's I wonder?*

Sinclair cannot afford to have an enemy or adversary in the city with these kinds of mobile talents and influence. No way. *Careful now, my son. Be too hasty and you'll frighten her off or she''ll see through you and you will have gained no knowledge. She could be an ally or colleague to begin with. Prime her first. Prey upon her fears.* He works to control his face which is consumed with envy, hatred and the cursed fires of the damned. He gently releases his grip on Spock but not too much. Make it as difficult as possible for her. Watch her squirm. Covet, appropriate, lust, consume, use, discard, exploit, intimidate, terrorise, deceive. If it's not one mode, it's another and Sinclair will try some, or all, of these tactics with Ms. Mode. He cannot let her get away this time, not again. Not now he knows she has a magical chair. Who knows what else she's got in that pissy little flat of hers, too? But time for that later.

Alison's eyes are adjusting to the interior of the Banshee Cave and she doesn't like what she sees, it sends a shiver down her spine. In a strange neat row in a corner behind Sinclair lie the regurgitated remains of several animals in pellet form. The lumps are big enough to be large mammals, or at least parts of mammals. Eerie furry middens, right enough. As a child Alison had visited the National Museum of Scotland several times and had seen, behind glass, the mushed reconstructed bodies and skeletons of rodents, insects, small birds all of which had been prey for some owl. But these were larger remains and Alison wondered how often Sinclair came here to feast on raw flesh. Was it some kind of ritual he engaged in? She didn't want to think too deeply about it.

Just deal with what's in front of you, the best way you can. Move too quickly and suddenly and she knows full well Sinclair's capable of killing her pet in front of her. It's in his cavernous empty looking eyes she can see it, and now the dry mocking laugh again. Dusty ancient arched bricks form an atmospheric background to a modern day bar area with chrome and leather seats and an area where bands screech their hell-for-leather souls out. Who knows how many people were dispatched here, the victims of dodgy deals in their day hundreds of years ago? No wonder some say the aggrieved and grieving still haunt the place, hoping for justice or a hearing this time round to make amends for some past atrocity. Sinclair wants more than the imaginary rent but what?

"So, Ms. Mode I take it you got my message. The post is not very efficient these days so I had to use my initiative. Just as well, isn't it? This bugger here is beginning to get on my *tits*, not that I have any of those though. Now I'm a generous understanding kind of man, Ms. Mode, you know this. I called this friendly little impromptu meeting just to say that I'm prepared to overlook the little matter of the unpaid rent if you in turn might like to come and work for me? You are a bright resourceful woman, Ms. Mode, a true fighter and some men appreciate this in the *hospitality business*. Hard working businessmen, politicians. A lot of them are actually very lonely, they just cover it up. Of course I'm not suggesting you become a fully-fledged prostitute or lady of the night, far from it. But as it happens I'm setting up a hospitality wing to my existing interests and I believe there's a niche market for dwarves. The earnings are very good, if I say so myself and, whoops, didn't mean to crush you there Spock, so consider this an offer.

Oh and I'm also interested in your *funny little stool,* Ms. Mode it's ever so quaint knowing someone who has mastered the art of the appearing and disappearing acts. So, I'll waiver the rent that's owed and return Spock safely to you if you give me the stool and work as a dinner escort for my company. Plenty of men prefer a shorter assertive woman, some of them are so busy hustling and dominating in the day that all they want is a good whipping into shape in whatever form that should take. They find it oddly reassuring; to be reminded they're not in control of everything."

Spock lurches around so wildly at this proposition that Sinclair tightens his grip still further. Alison's heart is racing, if it could scream out then it would be yelling by now but she sticks to her guns and holds her ground upon the stool. She's a lady who has loved, lost and suffered a lot after all but out of this has grown a fierce dignity and moral courage and she's not about to lie down and die just now. Oh no. You have to fight the good fight and stand up to power whoever you are, where ever you are.

"I'd be so relieved and happy to accept your job offer, Mr. Sinclair. How did you know that I'm struggling with money? Well, that bit's true. Caring is not really a lucrative profession yet we carers hold folk up we do, we are the hidden push pins of society as valuable as the bankers but just not really appreciated in the same way in a world that wants quick fixes and credit and is in thrall to those kinds of value only. My concern is for Spock; please can you bring him over to me? Have you at least fed him and treated him decently?"

Sinclair is so vain and egomaniacal that he isn't wary of Ms. Mode's instant acceptance. He walks over, handing her the long lost beast. He nuzzles up to her straight away, a comforting surrogate big mama. But at his point Alison Mode's eyes harden in defiance and contempt. Never give in to bullies. Hold your head high in self-respect and humility but never arrogance. *Pucker and large it, pal.* A few uttered words to *The Sneezwood*, words of command and direction and it's *I'm not a celebrity and I never want to be but I want to be right out of here, pal.* And whoosh! *The Sneezwood* is transported far away into the third dimension, leaving Sinclair to stew in his own juice. Talk about winging it on-the-fly.

13

A Friend In Need

Salt, butter, flour, sugar, eggs, porridge oats, lemon juice, cooking oil, bagged salads, baked beans, mouldy looking potatoes, onions, a round of soya sausages and olive oil. And that's not including the fresh herbs that pretty much fill the cupboards most of the time: ginger, nutmeg, mint, cucumbers for astringency, other more acidic things plus witch hazel tonic of course. Running a finger along the sticky bottom of the cupboards, Alison Mode sighs at the amount of grime and dust that seems to be never ending. Gazooky oatcakes, there'd always be housework on top of paid work with all the hidden emotional labour that can go into maintaining good healthy relations with colleagues, let alone families. *Celery, bread, cheese, pizzas, green pesto, pine nuts, sultanas, carrots, more food for Spock.* A good caring white witch-philosopher must be stocked with the essentials and the basics for cures, spells and treatments especially if she worked a lot in domestic settings. It is all part of the stock in trade; she just knows she'd have a need to use all of them at some point.

Some of these uber women she'd read about in the media – the ultra-glamorous career orientated women who wore shoulder pads and power suits and hired others to clean and cook, these types of women relied on others to help them acquire necessary ingredients. Unspoken inequality between women, too. And speaking of shoulder pads, well! Alison had used her time on the Hydes' roof wisely and had sent an animating thought to a pair of shoulder pads stitched into one of Lady Hyde's elegant dinner jackets which was hanging in the couple's wardrobe in the bedroom. Poor Lord Hyde had two speaking shoulder pads nagging, tormenting and whispering to him all night giving him no real peace of mind. For the pads came alive, they developed mouths and speaking tongues that spoke unpleasant but necessary truths to the high-and–not-so-mighty Lord who, though bright as a button, was still a stubborn cloth eared bigot and brute. True pride after a fall? Perhaps, but to cap this whole sorry episode off, Alison placed one of Lady Hyde's silvery long hairs on the pillow next to him the following morning to add salt to his wounded but inflated pride still further. It seemed a fitting lesson. The shining strand of hair tormented him.

Shopping list finished, Alison walks to her front room where Spock is having his usual run around hour. After they'd safely got back the other night, courtesy of the third dimension where there aren't any awkward wrong kinds of leaves clogging up transportation, Spock had jumped instantly behind a chair, traumatised by the whole experience. He'd sat there quietly hunched up, nervously twitching his whiskers as if Sinclair would appear at any moment and strangle the living day lights out of him. There seemed to be 24-hour stress related telephone lines for most things these days but nothing for frightened pets unfortunately. She'd have to gradually coax him out and back into his old ways. Right now she is cooking up new ways in her mind to teach Sinclair a lesson he'll never forget aware that fury, violence and relentless lusts for acquisition, status and possessions of various sorts will now be the all-consuming feelings he'll most probably be feeling. It was all so bloody predictable, here she was, a single woman trying her hardest to do the right thing and be brave, self-reliant, thrifty, kind and as honest as she could – yet all these personal qualities and more were not enough to extinguish evil and cruelty and the abuse of power in all its forms. Yet she is the epitome, all three foot six of her, of hard work and five vegetables a day, she ought to be lauded as an everyday heroine and applauded by the Government as a model citizen-subject. *Was she really empowered as an individual woman?* She didn't really feel that way as at this particular moment.

Sinclair's cruelty and tyranny infuriated her and consumed her in turn but it's rarely a good idea to fight fire with fire when another element could do as well. Perhaps her feelings of being over whelmed by hatred for Sinclair's behaviour was another individual symptom point wasn't it – one kind of net result of aggressive hyper capitalism-globalisation which commodifies, consumes and costs up everything under the sun, even human emotions and nature. Yes, there had always been sadistic bullying men and women but living in such a fiercely competitive and hypocritical society that didnae want to look at or confront things didn't help.

Despite trumpeting fairness, decency and land-of-opportunity speak, Britain remained highly intolerant and in denial. Sinclair's dubious offer of 'hospitality work' as well, who knows if this meant *escorting* men, too. And she certainly didn't suffer from lazy-itus and didn't have the gene for rudeness either; no one could accuse her of that. She's wondering what on earth to cook for her supper and whether Spock's had enough of skulking around when her mobile buzzes into life. It's Flora, who has texted over a smiley and a few pearls of wisdom. *How was ur flight home? Wot a palaver. R U Ok? Call me.*

"Flora, keeper of the fauna, how are you? Thanks for your text. I'm okay-ish I guess. Trying to take my mind off caves and dark underground places right now but it's not easy you know. Have you sold any of those rabbits I saw the last time I came in? Poor things, hope they go to a good home. Do you want to meet for a coffee later today; I could come round to your place for three and help you out with the animals and customers if you're on your own until you shut up shop. No, I haven't heard from Lady Hyde for a while though I have a feeling I may do soon. Dunno. Flora, *please please please* don't talk about her or Lord Hyde to anyone else apart from Mac. As it is I shouldn't really have told you but what happened shocked me so much I had to tell someone about it. On the surface their lives looked perfect and privileged but I think this stuff's been going on for years."

The call is cut off accidentally by one of them and on a sudden whim Alison thinks about dying her hair blonde as she examines her face in the bathroom mirror. One of Alison's ears sticks out more than the other but it's only slight. It's taken her years to learn to like and accept herself as she is and as she looks. After Barbara's death her self-loathing, anger and guilt was so deep she'd thought also about cutting herself as a form of release less permanent than death. But she'd changed her mind then and isn't sure about the hair now. Creating *The Quibblon* was a step forward, it was a book that truly helped save her life. But it could be too potent, the dual action power of a woman's prerogative and peroxide combined. Spock runs into the kitchen, the cute thing. He's sniffing the kitchen floor by the oven checking out the crumbs.

A child of the late 1960s, Alison had been an addicted Trekkie ever since the shows were beamed down to Barbara Mode's black and white television. And in a dangerous inter galactic world, Vulcan cool reasoning often saved the day or helped to steer a middle course, useful qualities to have in today's extreme reactive turbulence. From an early age Alison wanted to pin her hopes and aspirations on more than just a kitchen apron, those star travel shows were about moral choices, tolerance and shared teamwork not just alien invasions and other life forms. *Okay, wee man. I get the message, you're hungry. Me, too. I'm so hungry I could eat my own hand and I'm a vegetarian.* A large bottle of cooking oil is going to be useful she thinks, beginning to peel onions.

*

Later that day, after the shopping and cooking had been done and Spock fed, Alison's mobile rang again. This time it was Evelina, the Polish receptionist lady from *Help Is at Hand* calling again about work and about time too for it was over three weeks since she'd last worked. She'd not heard again from Noel and she hoped he wasn't drowning his sorrows in wine. A witty but sensitive soul, Noel.

"Alison? I'm so glad to have caught you today as I wanted to allocate this work to you as a priority seeing as we are getting such great comments from your clients so far. I'm not really supposed to be doing this but you can keep a secret, hmm? Are you available to work tomorrow for again an indefinite period? Sorry not to be more concrete but the client says he doesn't know how long he'll need specific care in the evening for. It could be for a whole term or even an academic year. He's an American university student living in Edinburgh and his sister's flown back to the states. She used to attend to her brother in the evenings you see. He's got some strange allergy to light so he goes around in these thick bandages, he says he needs help with changing them and general housework three evenings a week. Brett Gribble's his name. Lives up at Marchmont in one of those big houses divided into flats."

Alison hurriedly writes down the address and telephone number. Evelina said that the client would appreciate a call to just confirm tomorrow and times she could work. July had become August and the city's population risen along with the temperature. Expansive fresco blue skies beckon residents and visitors to the great Scottish outdoors, and Alison, walking up towards Leith Walk and Flora's shop is just one of many out this sunny Thursday afternoon. She's still thinking about getting some kind of lead for Spock as she's keen to let him get some fresh air. As far as she knew Edinburgh Council did not prohibit the public walking of guinea pigs and rodent shit as yet was not a big issue. The fight isn't over yet she knew, but would it ever really be?

She wondered if she'd ever be able to sleep peacefully at night. Her courage and independent fighting spirit seemed to attract a never ending flow of evil. But what, really was the alternative? And if one didn't fight the good fight head on both within and without, surely many would shrivel away in cowardice and pay a different kind of price ultimately. As Alison walks into *Creatures of Comfort* she's greeted with a cacophony of animal sounds. Flora's looking flustered as she cleans out a rabbit hutch.

"Alison! Please come and sit down for some tea. Mac's left me all alone with this glorious menagerie of beasties and boy can you hear them protesting! I have had the shop door open all day just to let some air in. So tell me is *The Sneezewood* safe and sound and locked away? Now that Sinclair knows what it can do – well, you'd better watch out Alison. That postie who saw you on the roof of the Hyde's –will he report you? Sit down, do. Now, Earl Grey, Lady Grey, Golden Handshake, or just plain old British Builders' Breakfast Tea? Alison, what the hell is happening to you anyway, hen? I'm worried frankly I really am. About your mental health, sanity and stress I mean and not in a patronising or pathologising way either. Can I help you in any way? What can you do about *him*? That's the question."

Just then a parrot squawks loudly as Flora's pouring hot water into a teapot. In times of strife and turmoil, teapots are very comforting and given the right kind of tilting may even produce predictions or subtle indicators of things that are, things that were and things that are yet to be. In addition to the flat above the shop, there's a small back room with kettle and chair just to give one of the Macintyres a breather in the middle of the day. Flora keeps an eye on the shop area from where she's standing but then realises she's forgotten to move a couple of tortoises to a larger cage as she was supposed to. Dealing with this, she leaves Alison to choose a tea. Alison's tearful again what with everything she's been through. At times like this she really misses her mother and being an only child somehow intensifies the loneliness.

Oh is it a crime to feel useless again or a failure? Why is it always me who is the brave one, forever in torment and struggling endlessly with money, bullying cruel landlords and painful memories? One must work hard to perpetually maintain appearances of sanity and calmness. Show any vulnerability whatsoever to some and they will show no mercy to you only contempt. That is a hard truth I have discovered living in this elegant but rocky fortress city. Battles of all kinds are enacted here.

The two friends sip *Golden Handshake,* a fine Chinese blended tea from Chelsea and chat about this and that and everyday bits and bobs, avoiding heavy topics like ghosts, death, loss, stress, depression, landlords and the nature of evil. Somehow the bright August sun lends itself to little doses of whimsy, day dream and nonsense which are a daily must for all people, where ever they are. Just then a customer walks in looking out-of-it and as daft as a skewed brush, asking if Flora stocks chickens of all things. But the customer, a young ladette, begins to look longingly at some hamsters and Alison knows her cue to leave right enough. The mellow afternoon is ruptured suddenly and without warning by Sinclair who jostles her aggressively as she walks towards home in a quiet side street away from prying eyes. No witnesses, your word against mine. This time maybe she won't join the list of the vanished without trace but next time? *You sick freak of a bitch, you made my girlfriend lose a baby,* he hisses menacingly in her ear spitting on her face then and kicking her crying to the paving.

14

The American

The imposing Victorian house in Marchmont is testament to another rarefied age, an age of private indiscretions contained effectively within elegant facades. Unlike the current vogue for expressing and sharing personal emotions and experiences publicly on mass for instant consumption. Show and tell. Tall well established plane trees line the avenue; it's a world away from Restalrig yet accessible via a thirty-minute bus ride. Strange but true. Damage limitation was so much more effective back then in the nineteenth century, there was no Internet and over hanging fears about God, the noose and the workhouse which were so strong that most usual suspects could be dealt with easily. After all, good gentlemen of the city bought stocks, enjoyed private fucks and then returned home safe to the family who accepted all in that world without question. Also unlike now of course, these current times when debates rage about the philosophy and uses of information, about what the public should have a right to know and what not.

Standing on the specified doorstep the following morning, Alison notices the antique looking lace curtains hanging in the bottom bay window. She'd rung Brett Gribble last night, he'd sounded pleasant enough as he'd given directions and indicated that he was not attending a lecture if she wanted to call around. She'd applied thick foundation make up to cover up the bruises on the face and legs from the attack yesterday. The saliva and bruising were cosmetic matters, but in truth she'd been terrified and had not really slept a wink. She didn't want the assault on her to be visible to the public, let alone a new client. Yet it's a hot day, she hopes nothing will crack and run. She's got a smart summer skirt on which she hopes doesn't look too business like. The burgundy coloured door is cautiously opened on a brass chain; part of a pale squinting face appears moments later.

"Ms. Alison Mode? You're very early. Please do come on in."

A sound of a chain being pulled back and the door is opened onto an impressive looking tiled floor. Mr. Brett Gribble's appearance impresses too, but in a very odd way. He's a young man, not more than twenty-three or so with short very shiny dark hair which looks like it's been lacquered down with gel. But it's the top to toe bandages covering and wrapping his entire body that really takes Alison's breath away. And she tries not to be a woman easily swayed by instant presumptions. There are a few social recluses and hermits on the Restalrig estate she lives on; she's seen one bag lady hobbling out of the block opposite who likes to spend whole days sitting on benches staring into space.

There's another who has a very long beard who gobs spit on the pavement and on bus stops in front of people. Then again, who is *she* to label others eccentric when some invariably will tar her with the same brush seeing her dwarfdom and the Eastern looking headdress she wears on and off even in the summer. To date, none of her clients have said anything about the headdress either – they may even have thought it a manifestation of the latest British obsession with health & safety. In this way Alison Mode, carer extraordinaire, was doubly unfashionable and unusual in that she didn't 'follow fashion' and neither did she think only of herself which seemed to her to be another all prevailing Way of the World. And there must always be some outcasts or precariats if not proletarians in the underclass it seems, those who bear and carry the sins of others. Society, particularly polite society, will tolerate only so much difference before you are purged from the system and left to drift. Mr. Gribble gestures for her to come on in; his arms are bandaged right up to his hands.

"I'm sure you can see why I was kind of reluctant to open the door fully open like this. There are so many gossiping tongues round here who gape and stare at anything or anyone different. And I thought I'd get more civilised treatment in the UK compared to the US. Lucky no Americans around to hear this, eh or I'm liable to be sued or pursued. To be honest with you Ms. Mode, and I sure do try my darndest to be as honest as I can, I have had it up to here with dressings and academia if you will kindly excuse the pun. It's not a good combination that's working for me right now."

Mr. Brett Gribble is frighteningly clever, his wit as smooth and slick as his hair. Alison is shown into the front room with the olde worlde looking lace curtains. On a table in the bay window is a chess set, it looks like he's been playing himself and imagining he's both black and white. Pieces lie scattered across the board; maybe the man is a strategist of a kind, an odd kind of player in a life that's seen only as a game. It's a possibility that certainly occurs to Alison who sits on a chair near the table, all the while trying not to look alarmed at Mr. Gribble's bizarre appearance. There's a nervy restless energy about the man despite the intellectual vigour and the restricting bondage of the bandages. His eyes blink and glance nervously at the windows and his fingers twitch and the entire head, hands and feet are the only parts of him which are not covered.

The feet are clothed in thick cotton socks and as he speaks not only do the fingers twitch but he tries to scrounge his hands into tight exclusive balls. Alison doesn't know what she's looking at here, another case of extreme social anxiety, a life style choice or a man recovering from a kind of trauma. Somehow he manages to lower himself slowly down into an armchair which is in a far corner of the room. Large piles of academic papers litter the floor near the chair. Clearly Mr. Gribble is an avid reader.

"Ms. Mode, I'm sitting as far away as possible from the window as my skin is super sensitive to light which is why as you'll see I've got lace curtains as well as long drapes. I've been studying here at Edinburgh for over two years and my condition has deteriorated dramatically over this time. Before, when I was living in Boston I could cope with brief exposure to light but I think academic rigours have left their mark on me. I would offer you something to drink but it's a struggle getting up and down. It's good of you to call around this morning ahead of this evening I mean just so I can show you what's involved. I hope you haven't had to travel far? Will you go out and get some lunch somewhere after – if you want recommendations for local eateries I can give you several.

After we finish meeting and greeting I will need to pop out to see my Director of Studies but as I say I should be back for five. Basically, I need help changing my bandages and applying calamine lotion and other things when I get in from college at around five pm three days a week, on Tuesdays, Thursdays and Fridays as I said to the lady at *Help is at Hand.* I do hope you're not squeamish? The thing is my skin sometimes looks very white as if I have no blood circulating. I will also need a full body massage to stimulate circulatory flow. Are you experienced in this area? The girl at the agency said you have a range of certificates some of which I gather are in lifting clients, complimentary medicines and acupuncture- is that right?"

"Aye, that's right Mr. Gribble. I'm interested in Chinese medicine and herbs too and I know my basic biology and am also familiar with a lot of common medications and ailments including arthritis, hay fever, eczema, irritable bowel syndrome, incontinence, and various allergies. I know how to lift and bathe safely, I can operate a range of wheelchairs, and I know all the latest devices one can install in the home – be this residential or private. These days I find conventional knowledge of medications and ailments, all the stock in trade tools of a home carer, are just not enough anymore. One has to be flexible and innovate in one's own way."

"I'm glad to hear this, Ms. Mode, I really am. You sound like an honest worker with a conscience and initiative. Flexible too. My flatmate Stephanie went back to the states quite recently; she'd been my informal in house carer if you like. She and Grandma Gribble are the only folks I have left now."

There's an awful heavy silence in the room then and somehow Alison doesn't want to be the one to fill it. And yet the silence has a manic-exhaustive quality to it, full of unarticulated rage, grief and sorrow maybe, or as if Mr. Gribble was quietly collapsing inside under the constant weight of trying to be interesting and intelligent. And to get constant straight 'A' grades of course from Uni, there must be that added pressure layered in there Alison realises, maintaining a respectful reserve. Clearly he's very bright, almost luminescent in his brilliance she thinks, noting also the titles of books piled on the carpet.

Being And Reality, Am I Who You Say I Am, Captive State, Bedlam & Bentham: The Age of Surveillance And Anxiety, What Price Freedom, Justice And Freedom In Late Twenty First Century Hyper Capitalism, The Appropriation of Language And Its Uses, Is This It Then, The Word Thieves, Hell Is Other People, My Mind's A Rubik Cube. It's a heady mix, enough to give an ordinary Joe or Jane a headache even without the bandages. Looking at the walls around her she spots a series of flying ducks and a cheap reproduction of a Turner.

She knew the painting was a Turner as she recognised the brush strokes and the subject but more to the point Barbara Mode had a small series of Turners in her hallway before she became so incapacitated she had to be uprooted to a care home.

"My parents worked in finance Ms. Mode before the markets crashed and they died in September 2001. They worked in one of the twin towers in NY. They were some of the many victims and it's still with me, the scars, pain and emptiness of that time. It never leaves you completely; you just have better days and worse days you know. I had a fear of flying before and I was nervous of great heights but that polished me off. Okay, I had a kind of breakdown. It was difficult flying over here to study; I had to be anaesthetised practically to cope. But cope somehow I do and I was and am lucky to get a scholarship to study what I wanted. That, and a diamond of a carer-friend, Stephanie. Not that I'm convinced that a second college degree is going to get me where I want to go any quicker, but there it is. Maybe the idea of progress as such is an illusion too.

In my part of the world, back home, hundreds of college graduates compete for jobs in check out supermarkets. It's meltdown madness just like it is here. But please do go and look next door in my bedroom as this'll be where I'll need to be changing and hopefully getting muscle relief. Those college lecturers sure make you crane and strain your neck, what with all those slick power point presentations. My sheets need to be changed, too, but I do have access to a washing machine next to the wash room, sorry *bath* room. My landlady looks fierce but she's actually a kind woman. She's the owner of the house, her second home's the flat upstairs but she's only here a couple of times a year. Go see for yourself. I rang for a taxi to pick me up in half an hour as bus travel is unpredictable as they watch my punctuality with a microscope. Lucky me, huh?"

Ignoring this last question, Alison walks into the bedroom and is startled for a second time this morning. For on the back bedroom's floor which overlooks a decent sized garden with a rockery are dozens and dozens of empty mega sized coffee jars, testament to late night caffeine habits and prolific essay writing. Or then again, to perhaps something else entirely. A flat modern pine bed is parked up against one wall but in another corner near the

French windows opening on to the garden is a huge flat computer screen, quite possibly the biggest technical screen Alison has ever seen – apart from cinema screens. On the modern estate where she lives of course she's glimpsed generous sized TV screens – but this screen with all its silver and black controls and substantial motherboard to boot seems to Alison the Big Daddy of all computers.

Why did Brett's screen have to be quite so large? is what she thinks but doesn't say out loud. And half hidden behind the screen itself, on two shelves built into an alcove are more coffee jars yet to be opened, fresh off some hyper market shelf no doubt. Strangely, for a man who says he's allergic to lengthy exposure to light – there's an office lamp screwed on to the unit the PC sits on. Presumably at night then Brett just sits in the spotlight for hours, peering at the screen under the lamp's rays, no doubt fuelled by caffeine and anxiety over essay deadlines.

Rolls of bandages, bottles and jars of medication and creams are stacked on a dressing room table. Alison sincerely hopes she'd find *other* food and drink items in the kitchen to put her mind at rest over Brett's dietary habits. Was his twitching just the simple coffee shake she'd seen just a few minutes ago? Again, Alison didn't like to pry too soon. No doubt motivations and hidden rationales would unravel themselves if they were ready to face the light of day – literally or metaphorically. Glancing down to her wounds on her shins as she walks back to the waiting Brett, Alison praises the different wonder of women's thick pan stick make up. It covered a multitude of shins and sins and luckily Brett seems so self-absorbed in his own life and condition that his eyes had not wandered casually down to Alison's skirt, legs or shoes. That bastard Sinclair, what on earth would he try next? Sitting down to face Brett again, she offers to make them both tea but he politely declines, saying the taxi will be here soon but thanks. He offers her the weak but slightly wary smile of a man who's weary in battle. Quite which way the struggle would go Alison couldn't say as she shyly makes her excuses, promising to return later for five pm sharp.

And walking away from the talented but fretful Brett, the flat's tasteful antique lace curtains and the copious supplies of coffee jars, Alison pauses for a moment to consider the very real possibility that she is as self-absorbed as Brett Gribble appears to be to her. It did seem to be everywhere, this vain enacted condition but perhaps it was the product or outcome of sheer utter bloody necessity. Beggers or the low paid's range of choices in buying were not as varied as the more affluent – but they *could* choose behaviour sometimes just like the rich. The poor could take personal responsibility it was true – but they didn't get to choose, often unlike the rich, which lawyer represented them in court should they, in a moment of pressure or stress, say something untoward and condemning.

To be too self-centred could not be right or healthy – nor was it happiness inducing ultimately – but Alison had also learnt the hard way about compassion fatigue, about the way some would milk you dry and take advantage of your basic kind heartedness. And this kind of taking advantage, in fairness, also happened to the poor and rich – in this at least they were equals. *Incubus Succubus.* Both groups lived under the same sky, both were vulnerable to the corrosive, sucking and draining effects of big money and its movements. Nobody in the end was completely immune though risks were not equally carried.

The steady exploitative erosion of human dignity, undermining the common interdependent thread of lives, let alone the natural commons of all living life forms. Yet many of the very rich were privately and discreetly charitable – choosing to give to those less fortunate. Individual acts of re-distribution seemed less contested than state ones. And these acts were often very generous indeed, given by individuals who you might personally like. There were no easy answers to what remained true. Thinking of common ground, Alison finds a patch of grass with a wooden bench. Not exactly a square, but in this rising baking heat any seat will do frankly. The heat has been so insistent the last week or so the grass now looks positively African, stark and bleached. No matter, the gulls are ever busy, tapping their pink webbed feet upon the barren grass, hoping for scraps. Or a worm that turned. And Alison Mode is a model citizen-subject, she's self-reliant, deserving and doesn't cost much to anyone – she's even had the foresight to bring her own packed lunch and flask of tea.

Munching into tomato rolls in front of the gulls, Alison soon catches the eyes of some self-conscious teenage girls who are basking nearby in the rays. They start to whisper about Alison's odd coloured legs, trying to catch her eye and infect her somehow with their hang ups. *Just ignore them,* Alison says to herself steeling up within again to the utter thoughtlessness of some. There's no sport or wind up to be had with Alison so they lose interest finally and slap on oil and lotions on pink burning skin, trying to get their kicks and gratification with some instant iPhone and pad interaction instead. Little clusters of people, perhaps nearby residents, sit and talk on rugs on the green. She falls into a day dream, forgetting the time for the moment as she reads the words inscribed on the bench.

In Loving Memory of Gerald Jones who used to sit here contemplating his naval. 1943-2013. "Don't worry about what the other Jones's are doing, this is your life, remember who you are."

There *were* real life vampires and trolls after all, people of various means and variable assets, who would seek to undermine you, slur and mock you for sport either behind your back, in front of you or on some instant too convenient social media site. Those flows of unregulated bile and abuse could corrode trust and honour just like excessive flows of capital and credit. It was going on everywhere endlessly, this naming, shaming, purging and blaming. Scary. All that had happened since January had just re-enforced what she'd already known and experienced before. *Don't panic whatever you do.*

It's a game of psychological spiritual and financial warfare that Sinclair's playing with her, fucked up as he really is. *Just deal with today the best way you can. The answers will come.* Two canny herring gulls had watched her carefully whilst she'd been eating the rolls; they'd flown in circles around her. Waiting for an opportunity. But then, *gazook*s! Glancing down to her calves, Alison sees the heat's been interacting with the thick foundation – what must her face look like? A pink shiny lobster on legs. Quick, get out of the rays as the skin looks troubled and flaky. Walking on and keeping a careful eye on her watch she realises she's still hungry.

At the green's other end is a clutch of small shops, she'll take her chance in *Just A Crust* though she resented paying over three pounds for a measly and greasy looking cheese sandwich. *Surely Brett Gribble's in no position to be firing me on a whim because he dislikes my appearance?* Barbara Mode once said when she was a girl that the ancient Greeks used to go and watch statues to try and learn the art of patience. *I can't really spare the time for that though and anyway, there are no notable statues of females in Edinburgh to watch apart from Queen Victoria* she realises, vainly fighting off a gull which had swooped suddenly and without warning, snatching the sandwich clean out of her hand. No wonder Mrs. Wiper was wary of their moves. But more shocking than this unprovoked attack is the headless gerbil Alison finds on her doormat when she's finished the first shift at Brett's. That and Flora's hysterical message on her landline saying her shop has been ransacked, no animals left alive.

15

Hell Hath No Fury

Sinclair stands in the Banshee Cave, his fury building slowly within him. Candles and subdued bar lighting cast eerie shadows that flicker on the ancient white painted brick walls. Lucky he's in with the proprietor who's been good enough to scratch his proverbial back and direct good supplies of fresh young tenants in his direction. It's fortunate that there were no witnesses to the brief exchange between him and Ms. Mode that had occurred just now but then he'd asked for total privacy for 30 minutes and had got it. And he's been able to reciprocate in a fashionable, retro, gentleman-like way and make broke young students' bodies available to the guvnor of the cave and trusted others in the circle. Bodies have many kinds of uses as products, canvasses, trophies in magical circles of influence and otherwise. Sinclair always prefers words like 'facilitating meet ups', 'enabling social networking' and of course the catch all phrase *leisure buddies.* Touchy feely feminine psychology kind of language with lashings of pseudo empathy designed to cover up the ugly economic transaction.

Strip, quick screw then duck for cover in a hideaway den. It's hot out on Edinburgh's streets but right here in this subterranean brick hub, he's feeling cool in his kilt and strange perverse fantasies are brewing. How was it possible for that midget freak and her kiddy's high chair to just vanish in thin air? How dare she make a fool of *him.*

He leans against the bar, plotting. He's not a man who's easily intimidated or spooked as he's the one who lays the screws and tactics on targets but the faint sound of what sounded like a female scream as the dwarfess had disappeared had been disconcerting even he had to admit. Joe, the proprietor, had said it was just an old fish wife's tale; Edinburgh was full of them and to pay no attention. Just superstition. Still alone, he helps himself to a whiskey behind the bar but one of Scotland's finest fails to water down an intense rage. The dwarf must be stopped at all costs and that stool, that alternative seat of learning, must be his. She'd dared to change a ducking stool in to a high flying bird's ace card. Think of the extra influence, the shock, awe and power he could wield in the city if he could only get Alison Mode to give up her secrets before she gave up the ghost. Hurling the empty glass against a wall, he stomps out, raging and oblivious to two staff members as he passes. *This is no fockin' time for social niceties pal* he practically growls at Davey as they lurch off in heavy traffic towards Dalry.

"Before you say anything, Samantha, about me being late for my tea, remember who it is like who feeds you and pays your bills. As it happens I had an important business meeting in town which I couldn't miss and I'm not in the mood for your nagging tongue."

Sinclair leans against a sitting room wall, eyeing her suspiciously. Grumplestiltzken. Faint traces of hair stubble tarnish his otherwise bald shiny head. He's recently acquired a flashy ipad, iPhone gizmo device which he likes to interact with as he's talking to people to make them feel like he's not really that interested in them. *Not bothered, pal.* He taps away texting a contact down in Leith, glancing across at her every few minutes. Keep people on their toes. She's varnishing her nails on the sofa but seems anxious. It's so warm and light that she's kept a sitting room window open and the remains of a microwaved ready meal sits in a plastic tray. He and Davey had sneaked in tepid pints in a boozer round the corner within the shadow of the ominous chimney but now he's feelin' crabbit and bitter. Samantha stinks of cheap perfume and he thinks he can see a hint of eyes shadow and blusher on her. *Fucking tart, can't turn my back for five minutes and she's eyeing other fellas up.* She's not paying *him* enough attention however and it's pushing his already overheated button. A woman must serve a man and put his needs first and make an effort with her appearance, yes, but she mustn't play around. That's solely a man's privilege and right, comes with the territory of being a breadwinner.

"Can't you even bother to at least look at me when I'm talking to you? I did call didn't I to say sorry I'd be late. So what have you done with my tea then? Is that it – on the sofa? I don't know why I bothered to be honest. Could have had a decent lamb curry with Davey my boy. Mid-week I like hot food to keep me going. You ought to know that. *I take it you scoffed all the mince and tatties as well then?"*

He's provoking her now, he knows it but he doesnae care, it's a kind of instant free sport this, tormenting people and giving them no rest. Degree in Bastardhood. Play to their insecurities, psyche them out. *Gobbledy spook.* Do it on line, adopt an anonymous avatar name, do it in person. Tease, bait, frame, decimate. Wear them down, hound them. His contacts in the city keep tabs on identified targets, emails and mobile numbers could be easily obtained then used. Hundreds of recruits, bots, tenants, two suicides over the last eight or nine years. One drug related. Thinking about tabs and poppers, well of course all of those were coming back with a vengeance ever since the glorious rip roaring 1980s. The glories of the ever shifting black market, specialising in the forbidden, the denied and the desperate. Stupid fat cunt, she's put on a lot of weight just sitting around the flat. She never goes anywhere, apart from the laundry, her mother's and the local chippy. She's gradually turning into an insecure human dough ball. Life on the emotional bread line. Looking at her now, he wondered why he ever wanted to fuck her over.

"Don't you focking give me a hard time aboot not cooking your dinner. Why the hell should I be your unpaid servant? I cooked already this week and I'm tired. And I really don't appreciate another lecture from you as to my cooking. Since when did you bother to cook and clean for that matter?"

He snaps at this daring to speak back at him impudence and quickly packs his phone in a jacket pocket, grabbing her by her shirt collars, wrenching her up. Forcing her to stand up and abandon her half-finished nails. Fear enters her eyes; she's suddenly doubting herself and her worth. He shoves her forcefully against a wall, his face only inches from hers. In the past, these rough house fights were a prelude to hot sex but not now. Now he just wanted to frighten her, remind her of her place. Too bad if she's pregnant.

"Don't you dare talk to me like that again. I'm getting a bit sick of your attitude, Samantha. Who rescued you from a crummy job in a café and that overfed bitch of a mother of yours? Like mother, like daughter, huh. Using fancy words like *appreciate* now are we? This'll teach you."

He slaps her repeatedly on the face and shakes her violently, suddenly out of control and in an unknown zone. Terrified, she starts to cry trying to babble out words about earlier that evening, but it's all too late now, she's been through enough.

"You never wanted it anyway, did you? Did you, you bastard? You thought I got pregnant on purpose, well you were wrong there. Anyway, it's all too late now. Are you happy now, then? Now that you'll not be a father after all?"

She struggles away from him, sobbing loudly and clutching her abdomen in doubled up agony. Startled, he watches her unable to understand but then realising slowly what it must mean.

"You had to pick another fight with me today didn't you, just because. Oh I can't bear it anymore. I want to go back to my ma's. That's right you jerk you get it now don't you? About an hour before you came back in this evening from 'your terribly important meeting' I miscarried. Awful it was. Didnae know what to do with it, like. So I flushed it down the pan. Just leave me alone, Sinclair."

Looking uncertain, she walks to the bedroom door and slams it shut. *Mum, oh Mum. Where are you? Somebody help me, please.* The loud sobs continue, somehow disabling Sinclair and further cementing the huge gulf between them. For although he understands the emotion, he's alienated by the raw expression of it. He stands numb with shock for several minutes, processing what she's said. *I flushed it down the pan.* Then, without really knowing why, he leaves the flat and heads off for Leith.

*

The radio's on very early this Thursday morning and there's a semi-serious report about deep cracks appearing in roads running up to the Forth Bridge. The wrong kind of tarmac had apparently been used by the contracting firm; it was buckling up in this intense August heat wave. An impatient reporter, broadcasting from a new pirate station *Forthright FM* sounds full of contempt for yet another bungled and expensive public-private project. Edinburgh, the Lothians and Scotland's entire central belt has been swallowed up in a heat wave warping metal, whipping up latent intolerances but boosting the livelihoods of whole fleets of ice cream van drivers who toured Edinburgh's estates or schemes with relentless precision. The world and Scotland may indeed be warming or even boiling over but there must be time for ice cream, it's a child's right. Sinclair's lying in bed alone in his main HQ and centre of operations in Leith.

Rolling up a fag, he flicks a large winged beetle-like insect back on to its back on the nearby carpet but it's all too late. It had obviously flown in through the open window during the sultry night but had died at some point, perhaps landing on the bed. It looked foreign, an alien invader from overseas. That *Banshee Cave* female wail that Sinclair had heard last night while dealing with that shrunken flying witch-freak, it's only this morning that he'd put two and two together and come up with an unknown answer.

Last night he'd walked for a long time, around Dalry and towards Haymarket trying to come to terms with Samantha and an all-consuming jealous rage. He's lost a son or daughter in the making, he's owed rent. Humiliated by the confrontation in the Cave, he's been reminded of his own insignificant powers compared to the powers of the female dwarf. Still, at least now he hard evidence of the freak's powers – she really had made Samantha miscarry. And there he was, thinking he was a kind of somebody who could hold their own with trolls both in the flesh and online. Samantha's become a burden, an expensive inconvenience but he'd been half toying with the idea of being a father. He could have passed on his tricks of the trade to a Sinclair Junior maybe.

Scottish Bridies and raw sausages are what a working man needs to get himself through the day, sometimes a big fry up. Old Leith Dockers piled hot food down them as a necessity, Newhaven fish wives made do with caller herrin', fried tatties, boiled, peeled and baked – chuck vegetables in if you could find them. Scrounge, grow, steal, swap, and rummage in odd places. Sinclair never said no to sea food either – cooked or raw he was fair game. Chewing his way through this make shift breakfast, he's formulating a wee plan. Drastic times call for drastic extreme action. He knew the dwarf was friendly with a plump pet shop owner in Leith Walk. Maybe that would provide a way in. He had to have that friggin' wooden stool by hook or by crook but he dare not try another break in and entry as she's bound to have had extra locks and precautions installed. But terror and clever tactics could make people do all kinds of adverse things. He smiles slowly to himself, glancing at the cheap plastic kitchen clock on the table. No doubt that was fockin' made in China too. He didn't like to think about what had happened to Scottish industry and manufacturing over the last forty years. If it wasn't the effin' chinks then it was that bloody lot down South, issuing diktat.

Timing is all, is da had said. It'd been over twenty years that he'd last seen his old man in Fife. That, and if you really want something bad enough and you work at it you will usually get it. Ma was such a mouse of a woman; she knew what da got up to in Edinburgh once the business took an upturn. Money and hard cash were always a turn on for some lassies and women could be expensive to keep, up there polished and dusted like, next to the good old footie regalia. And thinking about footie, that other Scottish staple diet, he sticks on the TV, hoping for some highlights of a game last night at Murrayfield but no such luck.

Once, as a treat, when his ma and pa had been getting on better they had taken him to the footie stand down Gorgie Road and he'd balled his happy little heart out and jeered and chanted with the rest. Chuck an insult, roll with the punches then bevvies all round, dissecting the good game, analysing the moves, placing the bets. *No sign of Scotland's heat wave abating* says the sexy news caster cougar woman, surveying a satellite map. *Sprinklers and hose pipes are banned in some areas. Yeah right,* mutters Sinclair. *You cannae police folk from watering their lawns if they had one.* But he'd noticed the dead and dying plants in Princes Street Gardens yesterday when he'd walked up from Haymarket. The Council was struggling to keep it all fresh looking for the tourists who wanted to see abundance and colour not blighted dearth and earth

Seize the day, my son. Don't let the bitches or the bastards for that matter grind you down, he reminds himself, putting on his khaki combat-style cap and leaving the converted flat and walking away from the harbour front towards Constitution Street. He lives not far from his old tenant Alison Mode; it'd been a job keeping this hush hush. Both his folks had gotten lucky on the horses at

Musselburgh, there had been a few big good wins. They'd gone cruising on the Agave; he'd bought her a poodle with a gold dog chain. And talking about good wins, what about that *Good Win* banker pal who disappeared off the face of the planet. Now that was an admirable art that, the phenomena of unaccountable distant yet present money. He admired that he did and practised in the same way though on a smaller scale. Wheeler-dealers. But what if the accountants themselves were accountable to no one – aye, right. What then? Maybe the earth really was flat and cash could just fall off the end of it, like a lorry pal.

It's after a quick brew or two along with a fry up that he sees her. *Good timing,* he smiles again to himself, checking his iPhone for the time. Maybe Alison Mode is walking to a client but there's only one way to find out. He must be careful and move with stealth at a distance, taking the utmost care not to be seen. Hunt the prey. The really great thing about stalking, fishing and phishing on line is that's all anonymous but here on the streets where things are visible – well; the stakes are higher of course. She's wearing a green canvas jacket, easy to spot and track and she seems to be heading towards the bottom of Leith Walk. She's carrying a sizable bag, too, perhaps full of shopping. For a woman of a compromised height she sure moves quickly, he'd give her that all said and done. He crosses the road following her unseen past shops. Looks like she's been walking from her Restalrig home alright. Maybe she's going for tea with her pet shop friend; it seems to be about the only friend she's got.

A little frisson of secret excitement pulses through Sinclair's veins as he realises that it's likely that he's just one of a select few who are in on the secret life and powers of Alison Mode. He can hardly contain the triumphant glee. Who would have known it, eh? Never a real believer in fairy tale ghosties, ghoulies and long leggedy beasties, he is now a convicted convert in real life. He doubted the existence of Nessie, broomsticks and UFOs but this accidental discovery; it's not one that he'd been expecting or planning in the big scheme of things. Objects and people that can actually fly and travel, not just virtually or in the mind. But he knows an opportunity when he sees one, these days you have to capitalise on every little thing you can lay your hands on.

From the other side of the road, Sinclair watches Alison Mode walk briskly into *Creatures of Habit*. So, that was it after all. Who knows how long she'd be there as well. Maybe all afternoon, might be a long wait but it would be worth it. As it happens, a pal of Davey's lives practically opposite and he can keep an eye on things from there. Bored games for catchin' flies. Chances are the fella would be in this time of day; they could smoke and play cards. He needs to speak to Davey anyway about a little forthcoming business in hand. Could be time well spent.

*

She finally emerges smiling from *Creatures of Habit* after several hours, without the bag. Sinclair's killer hunch was right; the fella was in and recognised him as a pal of Davey's so that was alright. Turned out he and Davey were at school together, Edinburgh being such an aloof yet intimate city where some pretended not to know you even when they really did. Sinclair sits bolt upright gazing out the window overlooking the street, ready for action. No Cuban cigars here but the steady stream of roll ups fill the room. That smile on her ugly face. And that headdress! Maybe she kept dead shampooed mice in there. He wants to wipe the smile off and inflict pain. The pint-sized bitch-witch must be punished, tortured and humiliated for sport and gain. Britain's a free country, after all isn't it? It takes all sorts of private pleasures to make it tick. And if you can get away with it, do it. Maybe this final dose of Sinclair's special treatment will make her submit the secrets of the stool. But even he knew that just owning it, possessing the stool wouldnae be enough. If she's a proper working witch then she's bound to have mantras, spells, codes isn't she?

That's common knowledge. No, he had to know what she called it, its special name and how it operated. No good just having the tools of the trade without the instructions, words or know how. And Alison Mode would need to be alive most certainly for this process of mastery. When he'd hurriedly done the break in, he'd noticed a large old dusty book lying on a bedside cabinet. He'd opened it but couldnae decipher the ornate handwriting. Perhaps it was the source of her knowledge, a technical manual of a kind. But somehow it also had to be obtained through force, trade or trickery.

He could bump her off later, maybe. A quick, silent death – then dump the body when he could afford to do so. *Now let's not jump the gun my son, these things are for the future,* he utters to himself running down the stairs and through the stair door, careful to trail her at a distance. With agility he follows her down Leith Walk and up a couple of quiet little side streets, prime locations. He waits until she turns down a third street before he pounces on her, kicking and hitting her to the ground. Twice bitten isn't she? But not shy. And the bruises from the first attack not yet healed. *The Sneezewood is what it's called* she gasps, lying broken on the pavement. *Really it is. Please don't kick me anymore. You can have it, just leave me be.* Satisfied for the moment with this admission he gobs on her in triumph. Some lassies liked a bit of spit on their privates. A calling card. Ownership of territory. Would she play ball now? He hoped so. She knows he knows and he'll steal and strip her knowledge slowly.

Women must never have that much power after all, it could spell the end of the world. But just to be extra sure he walks back to *Creatures of Habit,* gambling on just making it to the shop within opening hours. And of course Flora doesn't know what Sinclair actually looks like does she? She's never actually seen him, only heard a description no doubt. It's plain sailing then, feigning interest in buying a rabbit while overhearing Flora inadvertently mentioning to another customer that tomorrow, Friday, the shop will be shut all day.

It takes a real effort of self-control not to just pop off the wee bunny Flora's handed him right there and then in the shop, feeling the animal squirming around in his hands and sensing its fear. Maybe a few more heavy duty calling cards are needed to reinforce the message. He'd broken the necks of one or two animals in his time and teeth were always good for instant decapitation. Neck bones are easy to snap in rodents and birds. Another tingle runs through Sinclair's veins, this time the anticipated primitive forces of revenge and blood lust. *Heads will roll.*

16

Grandmother Gribble

"Yo, It's wonderful to speak to you again, Alison. Being straight up with you. I feel we have forged a most unlikely friendship in the different faces of adversity. What's going down? I've moved back down to Edinburgh for a while though I'm staying with a dear friend in Dean Village, volunteering at *Extra Rib* and avoiding India Street like the plague."

Lady Hyde's voice and precise pronunciation carries well on the mobile as the two pals talk away. *Yo. Being straight up with you.* But there's something different in her voice now, too, like she's allowed a bit of L.A street life or more daringly still, a bit of rap phraseology to colour her pure blue blood. When Alison was unemployed and grieving, both officially and unofficially, she'd become addicted to pulp daytime TV with heavy American and Australian inputs of Secret Bosses, Relationship Makeovers, Dish the Dirt on Your Neighbours and relentless music video clips. *Yo, bitch. Big mama this and that. Give me a high five, ma brother.* Not mockney exactly, but perhaps creating the happy illusion that life is an endless aspirational party, an orgy of imagined camaraderie. It sat strangely alongside a pseudo Dickensian nineteenth century accountancy-market language and techno speak. But then again maybe Lady Hyde really had undergone some life changing epiphany moment meeting real city immigrants or down-and-outs.

It was possible an encounter had rubbed off on Lady Hyde temporarily or while she was checking out stodge TV in the refuge she's volunteering at. Alison didn't want to pry into her friend's marriage or state of mind, Lady Katherine would tell what she wanted when she wanted. Though it was becoming ever harder to preserve emotional privacy and drink in an odd dram of silence these days, there had to be some areas of human existence which remained private, unknowable, and mysterious. It was another kind of anonymous human right. A given that just existed without the need for justification. Alison's walking on her way to work again in the heat, it being a Tuesday Brett Gribble night.

The bruises from the second attack have subsided a bit but the psychological shock of the headless rodent left at her door and hearing her best friend's devastation over a wrecked livelihood has certainly been another nemesis or turning point. She *has* to deal with Sinclair once and for all. His behaviour is taking harassment and bullying to new zones. Better not mention these latest events to Lady Katherine yet though, she's been through enough herself and too many cooks spoil the broth. Alison listens to her friend with kind interest, walking along to Brett's.

"That's good. I'm glad nothing leaked out into the press or Internet by the sounds of things. I mean about your rant in the House of Commons or the fall out at home. And we *were* very careful that night in London, driving down quiet little back streets like furtive creatures of the night in the council dumpster. It was only after, in your pal's pad, that we got totally trashed on vodkas and cocktails. Lady Katherine, this may sound like an odd question but then you know my powers by now. Has Lord Edward said anything to you about hearing voices, doubting his sanity, hairs, or consulting his conscience? The only reason I say this is, well, I said a few little casting words on your roof while rocking up on my stool. A postie saw me right enough but I humoured him before any police arrived. Aye, that's right, this wee hen really rocks in every sense of the word don't I just. Well, I know you have an ample supply of power suits with shoulder pads and the way he treated you so infuriated and repulsed me I felt I had to help a good pal out."

"Funny you should mention this now, Alison, as dear hubby's just been prescribed a course of anti-depressants and has actually been 'off sick' from work for quite some time. But what do you mean *on our roof, Alison?* How on earth did you get there? I'm getting the feeling, Alison, that you have only told me about half of your powers and naturally enough I'm keen to know more. Are you trying to say that you *animated* some shoulders pads? And what's this about hairs, I can't keep up. I'd much prefer to catch up with you face to face, Alison. I'm not sure if my phone is being bugged and anyway I've just read a disturbing article about Internet providers and mobile providers hacking into zillions of private conversations! Oh, what the heck, Alison – I need to get this stuff off my chest. He's been trying to call me but I'm afraid I have nothing to say to him just now.

One message he left on my landline up in Aberdeen was positively delusional in tone and I thought that he might have been smoking pot. He used to you know back in the early glory years of our marriage. And we women are supposed to be the emotional illogical sex. He was saying my clothes *spoke* to him, that he was hearing voices from the wardrobe in our bedroom. I humoured him along but said nothing about you, instead politely asking what the voices were saying. *Coward, fop, procrastinator, hypocrite, boy-man* were apparently what the voices were hounding him with. Another time he said he saw a pair of lips mouthing words in one of the corners of my Jean Muir jackets! *Serves you right, you bugger* I secretly thought. Is that really dreadful, Alison? That I had that thought about a man I'm supposed to love, honour and obey? Maybe when I met you I embodied an entirely new entry into your funny little *Quibblon* – an *UFF.* Unhappy, flighty female. An Uff in a huff. I don't know what's happening to me but just recently I've come to care less about what people think and keeping up appearances. I've had my nose pierced and I'm helping a friend out at *Extra Rib,* a worthy homeless shelter. Learning a wee bit of street patter – fascinating. It makes me happy you know and I like their perspective frankly. Privilege can be a different kind of manacle, strange but true. So my pal, our protector of the innocents, what's going down with you in this heat?"

"Look, I'm nearly at my client's now and I need your opinion on something a bit, er, delicate. Are you on your way to the homeless shelter right now? Maybe I could call you later if that's okay when I get back later this evening. You could come round to mine of course, you'd be welcome. I can't offer champagne but I can read extracts from *The Quibblon* and I've got cheapo beer. Always good for a laugh, eh? It's just something playing on my mind, a puzzle. Alright?"

"By all means give me a tinkle later; I'll be wrapped up in my perennial duvet sheet waiting to hear from you. I could come round tomorrow night, Wednesday. You sure everything is okay with you Alison, you sound flustered. Well, I love puzzles so count me in. And I'd love to meet Spock, I've heard so much about the dear chap."

Alison's been working with Brett Gribble now for two weeks and has noticed the way her client breaks out into fresh anxiety attacks after Grandma Gribble calls him from the States every Thursday and Friday at six. It's disconcerting to witness and it being a family matter, Alison has to be judicious with her tongue. Brett's looking tired, anxious and drained in his customary bandages as he opens the door slowly again, déja vu like, to Alison. It's as if the wrappings have soaked up most of his energy. Last week it'd taken over an hour and a half to get him gently washed with water and changed. Trials by bandage.

"Gee, Alison; I'm glad to see you. Whatever you do, don't study philosophy and politics at university; you may never hear the end of it. And what with all these security cameras you have here in Scotland and concerns about what you call 'the database state' I'm beginning to think that a version of *The Panoptican* has finally arrived. A giant enclosed concentration camp of a jail, housing society's undesirables and suspects. Don't smile, Alison. Bentham's eighteenth century dream invention is already a reality in some parts of the world. Maybe I, too, will get my body preserved in bandages and pickles, not quite like Mr. Bentham though. Apologies, you probably don't have a clue as to what I'm talking about. It's something we're studying right now at college – in a nutshell, it's just the way societies have become very self-conscious and introspective what with the way people often police and monitor each other and now even themselves. Every area of life seems to be offered up for surveillance, dissection, regulation, consumption.

There's less and less need for heavy policing and arguably prisons too if so many are living in fear of being spied on by some other. And if the 'other' is not some neighbour or alien, then the other is the state, a terror group or even an alienated cut off part of the self, scarily enough. Of course some say that all this watch tower stuff attacking and surveillance is a great way of controlling the masses, keeping them afraid and docile. No surprise, a lot of these geometric government spy stations on earth and defence GCHQs are installed with cameras, mirrors and curved white symmetrical walls. White walls reflect good white wash, if you'll excuse my cynicism. Watching them, watching us, watching you. It's no wonder that a lot invariably make enemies though they don't mean to. Even friends, family, that kinda thing might become foes and you might end up going loopy as a bonus."

He smiles weakly at her, semi-hobbling down the corridor and alone in his intellectual brilliance. He had a world vision and perspective on human nature worthy of

Nietzsche. Or was a victim of his own success, maybe. They were both isolated, they had that in common and it was an irony in this over information age, too. You tried to be the best you could be, you started out with good and honest intentions but some people twisted what you said and used it for ammunition. It was going on over the pond, it was going on here, people capitalising on what another's said and choosing to react and maybe misinterpret words for hidden agendas. Mass plagiarism and a cheapening of shared language.

"Can I get you coffee or tea, Alison or maybe you'd like some pasta. I'd sure love to sit and down talk with you. You have an unpretentious air which is truly refreshing seeing as most of the human race have become *word thieves.* It's the last shared commodity or currency up for grabs you know. Language and its appropriation, that is."

Flopping down on to one of the chair's by the front room window, Brett's eyes fall upon the chess game which seems to be an ongoing game for him.

"You know I had the strangest sensation when I first saw you. I had the gut feeling that you either play chess now or that you were really good at it in the past. You have to tell me, am I right?

Alison looks on, bemused. Though curious about the game, she's never lifted a finger to play it.

"I'm trying really hard to get grandma back home interested in it, anything to encourage her interest in a hobby, a game, activity. She's one stubborn lady. I have even thought about getting someone to install *Hype* in her home but I don't think she'd use it. Way too freaky and intrusive for her but a way of me keeping an eye on her. I mean well, too, you see, though she doesn't always see it that way. She finds mobiles difficult enough. But as I say anything to get this grandmother Hubbard right out of the cupboard and engaging with some little thing, I don't care what."

"Does your grandma suffer from a form of *social anxiety* then?"

Alison carefully asks, feeling ridiculous as she's saying it for who doesn't ever get anxious and down about things. But her curiosity's been pricked, she cannae help herself. Labelling and diagnosing could be a power trap, too, a way of controlling and scapegoating targeted people under a deceptive guise of care and empathy. God, how she knew that. She liked Brett's suggestion of the pasta though.

"Look, Alison. I trust you here not to share this with anyone. It's sensitive. My grandmother back home in Boston hasn't left the sanctuary of her walk in closet for over ten years now. We have a home help like you, a Filipino lady who flushes out her whoopy-doobrey bucket, takes food and water in and out for her, makes conversation and changes bedding. She refuses any other help of any kind saying she's not mad and that it's just not safe outside the closet any more. She says things home in on her and that there will be a takeover or an invasion of the homeland any time soon. And that she's entirely happy with having her very own private Boston Tea Party for one going on day and night, right there in her own walk in closet."

*

The river Charles cuts through the old American city of Boston like a life giving artery. Fine old houses line it and other smaller networks of rivers, testament to past wealth and commerce. And it was in this city, fought over and occupied by Red Indians, sons and daughters of liberty and the colonial English alike, that Grandmother Betsy Gribble was born. *We live by a river where we wash our cotton out, so thank the Lord thy giver* is what Betsy Gribble was taught by her ma and pa back in the 1930s when a terrible recession had gripped the nation by its neck. Frederick Gribble said he could trace his ancestors way back to the seventeenth century Puritan pioneers and both his wife and daughter believed him, knowing him to be a fine upstanding man of both industry and integrity. He'd gone into clothing manufacture just like his grandfather before him and as a little girl Betsy chewed liquorice bootlaces while watching effluent and discarded dye swirl tantalisingly downstream only to be sucked out into the Atlantic.

Things were clear cut then and livelihoods hard earned. Betsy turned her hand to tailoring and machine stitching in her daddy's factory winning the respect of her fellow immigrant workers from Russia, Italy and Ireland. It was true that output was down with some jobs and factories falling by the wayside but the good folk of the city and the nation still needed Boston cotton and calico overalls, pinafores and shirts no matter what the weather. Basic necessities and the self-reliant work ethic were the shared fabric that held people together in relative tolerance and respect then, there was a sense that all and sundry were in a unified struggle to survive and raise families.

Folks admired thrift and freedom, fair competition and independence of thought, free from either state or commercial monopolies. For any dominating entity or force, inflicting high taxes or punitive policy restrictions could be seen as an affront to individual liberty. In Frederick Gribble's particular factory, trade unions were heard of and tolerated but there was a wide spread feeling that there was no need for representation or organisation despite the unrest and destitution in the rest of the nation.

Betsy had met Alfred Maloney helping out in a Catholic soup kitchen for workless families and the jobless for though minding one's own business was prized so too was looking out for the other fellow who maybe was not so fortunate. They talked, tea danced, served soup and kindness to the fearful destitute, the angry, the ashamed and the grateful and he proposed to her by the Old State House so any self-respecting father couldn't refuse his daughter's hand on any reasonable pretext. They married young, bought chickens and set up home together with the help of folks from both sides of the family and listened with admiration to Theodore Roosevelt's uplifting broadcasts to the nation talking about New Deals and brave new public works. But she liked to keep two names, it reminded her of independence. Though money was scarce for most, there was time enough for care and thought for one's fellow human being. One could *afford* a certain level of practical compassion and decency, mostly of a non-financial kind but even these subtle delicate threads of community understanding could be snapped easily over the thumb given a test that's just too severe.

And this is true in times of scarcity and plenty, maybe even tolerance has a price that's constantly negotiated and haggled over. The couple, who had a son born in the late 1950s, didn't really think about things too deeply but if you'd asked them at the time if some areas of the human soul and life were above mere earthly judgement, they'd have both maybe said 'yes' quite cheerfully. Besides, they liked Roosevelt; he was a man with thoroughly good intentions. But Betsy Gribble- Maloney's world was fire bombed and trashed completely when she discovered that her darling husband had polio which rendered Alfred crippled and semi lame, as vulnerable as any true Lamb of God. Things and tasks which had been easy and quick now became difficult, and Alfred took it real bad, lying down bedridden a lot yet being a proud man and father. But who could she blame for this, apart from cruel random chance? Nobody.

They did not like taking help from family, but accept it they had to. Complete surrender to some unknown hand of fate was frightening enough, but mother Betsy bore it all with stoical grace and wit, rising above the pitying looks of the females in her neighbourhood. *Your ancestors would have been real proud of you, my Betsy*, is what her own ma and pa had said, still adoring their only daughter and grandson no matter her stubborn wilfulness which ran in the family, insistent as any river you care to mention. Then it happened, the terrible act. For, no matter how hard up you are, there's no excuse for robbing and killing others. He was a desperate man, the South American man who stole into their house one day when Betsy was out and Alfred upstairs.

He took food and savings and didn't mean to use the gun, he really didn't, he told the court later but he became afraid when he saw the boy standing there in a doorway. Little Johnnie boy who was only seven at the time hadn't realised what was going on so he'd played on happily outside until he'd heard the gun and started screaming The Colombian panicked and fired at Alfred, a quick death. It was an accident but they hung him anyway and Betsy's never been the same lady since that day. At first she carried on as if nothing had happened, as if Alfred had just slipped out for some groceries but then one day, she burst her own banks bawling and cussing near the Mystic River, only to be rescued and driven home by a passing African American in a bashed up Ford.

But if her husband's sudden death had been traumatic for Betsy, then the horrifying death of her now grown up son, Johnnie, and his wife in the Twin Towers scarred her permanently. Ten-year-old Brett had been adopted back in 1997 as Johnnie and his wife couldn't conceive but the Boston Social Services Dept. had been impressed by the Gribble-Maloney's financial prowess which had overruled any concerns they'd had about older parents adopting later on in life. After the tragedy of 2001, Betsy had singlehandedly cared for Brett with the aid of a small trust fund, putting him both through college and making sure he had the best start possible in life. It wasn't easy for all parties concerned, being as they were an unconventional family in a city and nation that appreciated moral and financial stability above freedom of expression. Once Brett was old enough to fly the nest that's what he did but the young teenage man's life had been again thrown into orbit a second time by the stock market collapse of 2008. Gradually, Betsy withdrew from life, work and friends until the very thing she was trying to forget swallowed her whole and she fled alone to the walk in closet, afraid of everything, maybe even herself too. It is torture to feel angry and yet guilty for loved lost ones when you are supposed to only feel grief.

Blame and bitterness brought a kind of ambiguous closure from behind shut furniture doors. And sorrowful righteousness, born of a broken heart and spirit bred new intolerances and hates in a world that seemed so unjust. For years Betsy's only companions were a rifle she'd acquired, visits from an elderly neighbour and Maria the Filipino home help. Everyone else was prohibited as was laughter, curiosity and alcohol. Life continued in a way in that house largely thanks to Maria, who made it her business to air, wash, clean, fetch shopping, paint and generally keep Grandmother Gribble as comfortable as possible back behind the walk in closet's doors.

Betsy tolerated a weekly sheet change and daily emptying of pot pans. Maria tapped on the doors to signal the arrival of food – but there was no guarantee it would be eaten. Other than force feeding the elderly lady, there really was not much Maria could do about any of this except to keep on trying to get through to the old lady who she considered to be a friend. For Maria ran on raw faith, that invisible yet refined thing. She'd foreseen and then recounted the true life story of President Obama through the plywood and glass which had gotten a mixed reception from Betsy, whose tolerance levels had been severely tested beyond repair.

"Free this, give away that, great; do we open doors to all, Maria – is that what you're saying? Does America have a permanent open doors policy, Maria honey? Like, does the nation look like it has a bottomless purse? Conservatives believe in conserving what's good about this nation and earth, we believe in the value of traditions. Look what happens when you forget to lock your doors and look after your own. I'm still paying that price let me tell you. Now there may be some of who say this lady's not got a generous heart but you give to some folks and you trust too much and that's misused and taken advantage of all too

often. That's what I say. That's my final word. So be discriminating about who you give to, charity begins at home. No such thing as a really free lunch box deal. Maria be a good girl and please read out the seventy-third Psalm again for me just like you did last week so magnificently.

You have such a fine singing voice. Now, those words I do trust not the lying words that come out of politicians' mouths. Endless dirty tricks they play misleading people over what's really going on. And the arrogance with which some of them behave, presuming and assuming they know folks' every wish and fear thinking they know no best how to spend our money. Well, some things are just unknowable and that's part of the great mystery of life and all creation. And thank the Lord above for that. No wonder some folks have a notion to just not bother voting anymore when they get to hear such a grandiose cacophony of money spinners and con job merchants. Get to it my girl and bring me up some more warm milk and those peanut butter cookies. When you get back up I'd love to hear about any river cranes you may have seen recently, now those innocent creatures I can honestly say I do miss dearly."

*

They make an odd threesome, Lady Katherine Hyde, Alison Mode and *The Sneezewood,* perched precariously as they are on Brett Gribble's Marchmont roof under a canopy of bright August stars. *Talk about another late night out on the tiles!* It'd been a last resort this outing and they kept their voices down as much as possible. A few party revellers had sung along on the pavements a few minutes ago, but otherwise the street was quiet. Luckily the sloping angle of the roof hid most of them from street level sight. Fumbling with the string, cabling and microphone, Alison's reminded of the nightmarish Panoptican society that Brett had gone on to explain the other night, in response to her confused questions.

Still, it couldn't really be helped. Lady Katherine had been deeply moved hearing the tale of Grandma Betsy Gribble through Alison who'd in turn heard about the extraordinary lady from her adopted grandson. Alison hated the idea of poking her nose into Brett's private business but really his symptoms and sanity had been taking a turn for the worse and Alison felt, as humanitarian carer and home visitor extraordinaire, that an extreme act could be justified on this occasion. She knew it was hypocritical of her in a way, considering how she valued her privacy – but equally, she reflected, she appreciated Flora's kind intervention in her own dark years.

And it had been the drastic but logical conclusion that both she and Lady Katherine had come to both after the protracted chin wag the other night and the spying that went on last night, here on this very same roof. At any rate, Alison knew Lady Katherine was dying to try a fly on *The Sneezewood*, especially after hearing all about the previous ducking, diving and *whoooshing,* vacuum like, up through the weird ventilation hatch in Alison's hallway. The good lady had stood quietly cussing under the innocuous looking air vent, beer in one hand, *Quibblon* in the other while Spock looked on impassively.

My goodness me, Alison you have your very own high powered astral portal in your own home, a kind of in flight gateway or terminal to unlimited destinations. Who would have thought it possible, on just a simple command? I can see how the metal rubbing focuses the mind too. Would The Sneezewood respond to my voice commands also? There would be only one way to find out right enough. But Lady Hyde had been so completely revolted and incensed when she'd heard about Sinclair's behaviour – his savage beatings of Alison in the street and his brutal killing of Flora's entire stock of animal pets in the shop, that Alison had to practically implore her not to instantly hire a private marksman or detective to just snuff Sinclair out once and for all. She'd seen the still visible bruises on Alison's shins and the look of re-lived terror and pain in her friend's eyes, and it made this normally well-bred elegant lady feel really quite violent in response.

But somehow they both knew that revenge fighting was not really going to be a solution at this point, satisfying though it might feel at first. Try to teach by example and only strike as a last resort. Last night they'd talked about Lord Hyde and Brett in Alison's kitchen, their eyes falling upon a block of butter and Lady Hyde's make up compact. Simple props to grease the string, a mirror might come in handy. *Of course, eureka!* It was worth a shot. *Pucker and Large it well up, pal.* Run and snuck a mirror, a mobile phone camera and a mic down the chimney, see what happens. And anyway, Lady Katherine said that the worst thing that could possibly happen was that they'd both get charged with the 1824 Vagrancy Act or nicked for flying an unregistered piece of furniture on an attempted break in. Then it really could be a case of an UFF flying another UFF, *Unidentified Flying Furniture*. One way or other, the authorities that are could always find something to pin on you. But if they were careful, they'd need not get seen or caught.

And last night the trial roof top experiment paid off, the string *had* been long enough and the evening offered up many surprises. They'd discovered, with the mobile and mirror's aid, that Brett Gribble was addicted to Internet chat rooms in a big way. The mobile phone's camera told no lies, small though it was. He'd sat, tapping away his life story sharing intimate details of his life and feelings with people using chatrooms and Hype, offloading to those who most probably didn't actually give a damn about him. Alison saw a small adopted boy again in her mind's eye, someone struggling to be noticed and heard. After dear grandmamma Gribble had called at her customary time, Brett had descended into a frenzy of electronic getting-it-off-your-chest beating, slurping through super human amounts of coffee and offering rich expletives up to the big hungry black hole of a screen whose appetite for banal trivia and snide malicious gossip was terrifying.

From the safety of the roof above they'd seen it all, the metamorphosis from cool-headed academic to raging living mummy. Or maybe it was a lost mummy's boy. It was like witnessing conversational quick sand in that the more Brett offered up, the more the hungry and anonymous hoards from the voids demanded. A bottomless pit. *You want me to get the crazy right out, don't you?* Brett had screamed at one point, shaking his head at the PC. *Well, no way. I have got some self-respect.* Lady Hyde had again packed the extra-large ball of string into a pocket and she unrolls it now, checking the length.

On both nights, the friends' flight here had been hassle free, the hardworking and versatile stool responding well to the good lady's *up, up and away; let's free the two Gribbles of bonds today!* Bonds seemed an apt word that Lady Katherine had conjured on the spot sitting on *The Sneezewood* as she had, in that Brett and his Boston based Grandma seemed to have too close an emotional bond. On top of this, both were stuck and in bondage in their respective ways – bound by their pasts and conditions. They had lofty ambitions to be sure but they 'had to try, didn't they' is what Alison said, winking at her pal and holding her hand bravely as the two friends were sucked up through the air vent in the hall way and transported in style. *Whoooshing* up Leith Walk, Lady Katherine quipped that it beat travelling air business class or even, joking aside, by prospective tram as at least they could avoid crowds and congestion with a flying stool.

They'd set off very early on both fine evenings, after a fortifying glug from Lady Katherine's wee flask of malt whiskey, a fine old Estate brand called the *Grouchy Pheasant* which she'd placed in her apron pocket. Aprons could be useful outside kitchens too as they had deep pockets and long strings.

And having friends in high places both literally and metaphorically meant that Lady Hyde had gotten access to a pentacle shaped quality listening in device complete with ear plugs which could intercept calls undetected and allow one to clip on, to clothing and collars. They were equipped with mobile phone camera, very long pieces of cabling and string plus a flashlight. Like Alison Mode she passionately believed in standing up for the vulnerable and down trodden, she'd been reluctant to eavesdrop too but had heard enough about the Gribbles' wasted potential for life. Lady Katherine slowly lowered the cable down the chimney, having first attached the mobile camera and torchlight to one end. She then clipped the fluffy ear plugs into place and had adjusted the apron strings as Alison unfolded the buttered and oiled cabling and string down the chimney. As an educated and independent woman, Lady Hyde had, rather like Miranda Wiper, long wrestled with the regular dilemmas of unknotting apron strings, but sometimes they came in handy as grease busting hold all work overalls.

Alison had never known butter to come in quite so handy, it was a funny old mixed business all of this: high tech, Mrs. Beeton's revenge of the Victorian savvy housewives and pantomime dames. All this hobnobbing around on the home fronts. And all in the name of a justice, *substantive* or restorative justice in the aimed for outcome, if not *procedural* justice in the process of getting to the aim. For sometimes ends can justify means if the ends are honourable. It was a terribly dangerous risk what they were both doing they knew, but lives without bold adventures and good risks was too awful to contemplate. They identified with other stifled souls, it made them keen to act and both friends knew what happened to many who were starved of their instincts.

Frighteningly, maybe there were hundreds of others like poor Brett and his isolated Grandma, let alone the Wipers who were restricted and shut off in their thoughts if not in their bodies. And this in a time of superficial over 'connectedness' in the iClouds above. Virtual excess and actual starvation. Yet it really didn't have to be like this both friends knew, each having had their own personal battles and obstacles to overcome which were not exactly of their choosing either. They were just circumstances, like the situations and scenarios folk find themselves in every day and yet have to find a courage, imagination and even compassionate humour to be and give of their very best.

"Do you think we've become different kinds of freedom fighter, Alison? Your turban headdress is wobbling ominously; I thought I really ought to mention it. *But shh now!* Microphone and mirror are in place and I think 'I'm picking something up' as they say. The listening device is in place; the cable was just long enough. Lucky we gave the chimney a clean and brush first yesterday though. And the mobile's okay with the wee light. We're all set! And the moon right now a waning old Gibbous, at least that's what you said. A Gibbous for the Gribbles indeed. Brett's fiddling about on his PC again, every inch the dutiful student. My goodness me, he appears to be taking photographs of himself in his bandages! Don't do it, Brett. Draw the line here … wait for it. Now, what? Of course. It's nearly time for the infamous call from Grandma. Here we go…"

And Grandma Gribble berated, nagged and encouraged her grandson down the telephone line asking after his studies, his dressings and diet. Brett joked and laughed as best he could but the questions were getting repetitive and intrusive and Lady Hyde's cut in right on cue. There had been a stunned silence on the line but some things just had to be said after all. Lady Hyde's getting good at rants she realises.

"*Now my dear Grandmother Gribble, you cheeky little midge you! This is the voice of a friend of your grandson's well meaning Scottish carer. I'm tuning in with my humble but wise little penny's worth of kind good sense. Is it not a fair thing to say that we are all biased human beings to an extent? In that each of us follows our own self-interests first and foremost, this is no crime or sin. And yet each of us is also dependent whether we know it or like it or not;*

dependent on one another's labour, services, respect, capital, tolerance and goodwill. Now some do forget this most basic truth about the human condition and try to kid themselves they're a special case and that there's a particular glory in being poor or rich or self-indulgent when there's not. Mrs. Gribble Senior – if you don't mind me calling you this – how do you know what you know?

To paraphrase another famous American politician 'there are known knowns but also unknown knowns' so that although much of life seems predictable and logical, there are still lots of things which are still mysterious and maybe unknowable. But rather than freak out over this we could stop still in wonder more often, be still and listen to that quiet little inner voice, contemplate the beauty of nature and the miracle of love. Some call this the divine, others the sacred within the self. Many have forgotten how to breathe properly, ma'am, some simply don't think about how what they say and do affects others ... as if some folk think they live in a self-imposed vacuum. Gated mind syndrome I call it or G.M.S – I should really enter this into my friend's life saver book. Iv'e heard all about your remarkable bravery, tenacity and grace Betsy Gribble, and though I'm across the pond so to speak I want you to know that I think you have so much more life to live and things to give. Don't hide yourself away in anger and fear; step out into the light. I'm not a religious woman as such, Mrs. Gribble, but I'm 'spiritual' I guess in another way.

And the strands that join us, the whole web of life itself, must be strong enough to tolerate surely a range of views and beliefs in the collective overcoming and wrestling with shadows that we all do as humans, Mrs. Gribble Senior, irrespective of nation, class, gender, religious or political inclinations. How do you know that you'll be attacked and mocked or taken advantage of if you step outside the closet, Mrs. Gribble? You really cannot allow your whole life, all your talents and abilities and future hopes and aspirations to be blighted by a series of tragic past events because to think like this is to really deny any potential for good to come or even, dare I say, it denies the stuff of God or good to flower in you.

It's also so self-defeatist because this attitude robs you of your joy in the here and now. Don't give the doubting little monsters in you any airspace whatsoever, Mrs.G. You have suffered enough, but you are not the only one to endure terrible loss and great sadness. One way to heal a broken heart or spirit is to give selflessly to others, be of good service to some greater cause and lose yourself. Here in Scotland my friend and I are daily confronted with the worst excesses of our shared economic system, it's hard to remain honourable and kind when, on the face of things, so much seems to divide and oppress folk. But who says you cannot enjoy your life and find peace? Does the good book say this? It certainly doesn't say this in my friend's book called The Quibblon which I dearly hope you'll read some day as it may cheer you up and make you laugh. Have you any idea as to how your grandson really loves you, how he'd do anything to make you happy again? And to doubt your ability to cope with whatever life chucks at you is to actually doubt yourself as a person and any possibility of any divine working out or any good karma that might evolve in your own lifetime! There is no glory in hiding your light under a bushel, Mrs. Gribble Senior and nothing's to be gained from not taking any risks. Please accept this hand of friendship and suspend judgement. I mean only good.

Your 'knowing' is based upon what's gone before, we know by experience but as soon as you are prepared to admit to the possibility of not knowing something and not being afraid of this then life once again becomes an adventure, full of learning, discovery and meaning. The problem is that sometimes we think we know something in advance but actually we're presuming. If you choose to spend the rest of your life hiding away in a closet then you will never get to test your faith or convictions in action, nobody gets to enjoy your personal qualities or gifts including you too and you don't allow anyone to reach you emotionally let alone teach you anything in return and how presumptuous is that, really, to be that convinced that we know all the answers and can never be wrong?

Pain and loss are awful things it is true, but more awful still is the way these things can rob a soul of living fully. Take back your life, Mrs. G for somebody somewhere will really appreciate what you have to offer. Nelson Mandela said something about being born to make the most of ourselves and to make manifest the glory that is within us and frankly, Mrs G you're playing at this endless one-woman tea party behind closed doors doesn't ultimately serve you well. It is the wise and mature man or woman who tolerates a range of views and opinions, even if they differ at times from our own. And you haven't actually gotten rid of the fear living this way have you? Face the fear full on, step by gentle step. So step up to the mark, step right outside of yourself, for your whole life is just whooshing past."

Later that evening, when safely back at the Restalrig flat, Alison Mode again pondered Lady Hyde's extraordinary way with words. She'd lit a large candle, staring into the flame in a trance like state so much so that one end of the *Kwik Stix* she held in one hand got burnt and she'd had to quickly retrieve it. That's what can happen when you lost your plot and focus. Spock also got a bit too close for comfort, sniffing at the air as if deciphering some rodent omen. But he'd been extra twitchy over the last few days anyway, jumping whenever post came through the letter box and running for cover when the phone rang which was unusual.

Thankfully though, Alison hadn't heard any more dry coughing in the flat which was unnerving. Is Sinclair astrally projecting his voice somehow? If she could experience the embodied spirit of Barbara Mode, then why not a disembodied voice? Alison sensed that it wouldnae be too long before she got sent another message from one of Sinclair's sidekicks or mules – maybe there would be another encounter in some dark alley or side street, Edinburgh was full of them – full of the sordid muffled voices of the oppressors and the hunted, both the living, the dead and living dead.

Tourists took photographs of these dark old abysses and spaces wanting ghoulish atmospheric hints in their holiday tints – but only to imagine the horrors of diseases, child prostitution, slavery, destitution, beatings, witch burnings, hangings and murders safely from afar. As if these things, these very human evils which have always existed, ever really were glamorous or glorious. Unfortunately, there was and is no accounting for dark demands and thirsts for cheap grisly kicks – for if there is profit to be made and livelihoods at stake then aesthetics and niceties fly quickly out of one of these shadowy tenement windows screaming madly: *Decency is all very well but it doesnae exactly put bread on your table!* She feels another philosophical entry coming on for *The Quibblon* and begins to write.

F is for freedom. What is it though and how can I experience it? Was freedom a kind of *natural justice* – that being the balancing law of equilibrium, moderation, mediation, co-operation. Maybe. But some would say gross inequality *is* naturally just because some are more talented and hardworking than others. Others say this argument may have some truth sometimes but that it's exploited and still doesnae justify the sheer differentials. But what of the now? Bonfire of the vanities, the planet itself and all in the name of cheap instant credit flows. But then these days, who knows who really holds the reins of power – maybe even those who reign by blood or those mysterious entities called 'states' don't call that many shots in the new international geopolitical hypermarket which enforces and regulates some flowing bits and bytes but not others. And, being a prudent street thinker both at heart and in her head, I often ponder these existential questions about the philosophy of information itself – about what information is deemed to be safe enough for public consumption and what not and whether what is hidden or denied is really that dangerous.

Who ultimately policed, oversaw or ruled the new rulers of information? It isn't a thought I enjoy thinking about much in this brave *New Corporate Edwardian* world of men accomplished in the Arts of Illusion that is often in reality just ordinary wee grey mice-men who hid behind smoky mirrors. Hickory Trickery Dock which mice- men now control the media-technology-energy clock? For this clock was also running way too fast, unnatural in its rates and timings and ruling over a rapidly over populated globe that maybe couldnae cope with burdens.

Have arrived at Shetland thankfully. Insurers will pay 4 shop fitting. Hope all well XX Flora n Mac. Flora's text interrupts Alison's writing. Good timing as she's been wondering how her faithful pal had been getting on. Flora and Mac had gone on a different kind of time out holiday-strike, a recoup your losses and sob your guts out break to Shetland to try and recover from what had happened. Alison had passed the shelled out wreck of the shop many times, hoping that they'd have the courage to start again. To start a business is one thing, to maintain and run it quite another but to lose it so suddenly, through no fault of one's own, was surely another kind of savage blow. And after Lady Hyde's practical ministry by phone line she doubted if Grandma Gribble would ever be quite the same woman again. There'd been a stunned silence as her well-spoken friend had politely butted out of the conversation and Brett Gribble had at first threatened to report the incident to the UK police or US security, citing 'nut jobs listening in on a private call'.

But his panic subsided and he'd promised to have words with his new lady carer, Alison Mode as she was a bit eccentric it was true but she was well meaning. *We will get to the bottom of it together my son, like we always do when we stand together*, is what Betsy Gribble said, sounding privately doubtful and wobbly despite the familiar robust defiant tone. How dare any Scotch lady tell her how to live her life and poke her snooty nose in when it wasn't wanted. Alison hoped the evenings events would not come back to haunt either of them, they'd meant only good. Putting the whole day and her headdress to bed then, Alison collapses into sleep having recounted the entire day's happening to Spock. Lady Hyde was due for a sleep over shift at the homeless shelter but no doubt they'd speak soon. But what to do about the ongoing nightmare of Sinclair though, this was the challenge she'd pitched to herself, hoping that dream incubation might shed light on the issue

As an extra precaution, she'd daubed her forehead with olive oil, long convinced of the sacred oil's divining qualities of discernment. *Cast your problem or question to the universe with a good intention and all that and then wait a while, wait and see.* And sure enough, in the dead of that waning Gibbous moon-of-a-night, Alison is woken mysteriously by a very real sensation of someone, some hand to be specific, tapping her on the shoulder. She is drawn inexplicably to the front room where she watches a ghostly white hand appear through a wall. *Wood Sneeze, wood sneeze* the hand writes again and again, with the aid of the burnt end of the *Kwik Stix.* Then it disappears back into the wall leaving the odd scrawled writing. She has no idea what it can possibly mean, but she'd clearly recognised the elderly withered hand as being that of Barbara Mode's. It was almost as if the divining stick was actually supposed to get burnt.

Quibblon Alternative Dictionary

***GMS,* acronym. Gated Mind Syndrome.** The phenomena of the closed off self-righteous mind found anywhere and everywhere that always thinks it alone knows what's right and is never prepared to compromise, which in the end, may be the virtue or principle that humanises and saves.

***P.C*, acronym. Political correctness.** The beauty of the British language is such that one can appear to be politically correct, fair and decent if one uses 'correct' inclusive language. But language used often enough comes to be believed, it's all part of the mythology of Britain's green and pleasant fair land. According to *The Quibblon* terrible economic and ecological injustices prevail even if the language used seems polite. P.C can be slickly deceitful in a culture that values smooth appearances and ordered performances above anything else.

The Quibblon Song of Wrongs

The awful thing about PC
Invented way before BC
Is that it so often lies
Buried in words and disguised
And what seems polite and correct
Actually helps us to forget
The ever more yawning divides.

And the other PCs
They make it so easy
Those things with the mice
Which entice with quick vice
Or biased advice
So blurring the boundaries, the ability to see
The fine lines between PC and TLC.

So it is with this round Art of Blah
That the narrowing of gaps never gets very far.

17

Sweet Fags

Fife, April, 1962. *An early bird catches the worm*

Gladys Frances Sinclair sprays, laqueurs and backcombs her huge stash of hair into a towering pointy beehive, almost as spiked as the conical bra she's wearing. But rather than attracting her husband further, the new trappings and adornments seem to drive a deeper wedge between them. No glad rags lost here then. Not that he, William Sinclair Senior, ever comments on her appearance these days – no, he believes in keeping women in an uncertain kind of place that not even his dead clients have to put up with. Stewart Campbell who works at the local pub appreciates her though – and not just the way she looks either. It had started last summer; the affair. Gladys dared not just turn up in the pub as folk would talk but she made a successful excuse by going in to buy cigarettes a couple of times and the artful ruse worked well. She didn't want to start a ding dong on the side, it's only in stealthy retaliation for what she's caught hubby up to. Once she followed him, her husband, into Edinburgh on the sly and saw him walk up to some house in Morningside where this woman opened the door, her face lighting up like some artificial Christmas tree.

She'd kept mum about it, like a good responsible mother should. Bide your time, Glad. Read him the riot act when the time is right or just ask for a divorce. Six year-old Sinclair Junior is getting ready for school and is lacing up his boots, he's turning out just like his da, so much so that Gladys sometimes has problems looking at her own son in the eye and not slapping him aboot. No, she mustn't do that for if she did her fate would be sealed and she would be labelled, perhaps forever, as a *bad mum. Good mum, bad mum. Gladys Frances Sinclair has always found this paradoxical stifling contradiction too much to handle, she'd only ever just jiggled along finding her own way the best she could as a parent. Would she ever be good enough? Probably not. All these endless magazines about being a good housewife and hostess, they seem to be growing in number at the local newsagents and in the centre of the town too. There's a worm at the bottom of the garden and his name is wiggly woo.*

"Ma, what did you mean when you said da was as slippery as some kind of worm out the back the other day?"

Sinclair asks the question watching his mother's face carefully for anything hidden. Lord above, the wee man is so sharp these days, Glad thinks – he doesnae miss a trick does he? Must be all those carrots she's feeding him with the mashed tatties. New hip wall papering adorns the small detached house in Dunfermline, a lot of people had died in Fife in the last year and trade was good but there was no covering up of the cracks in the marriage. The flaws started to show when their son was three or so and the wee man's da had become bored with being a father. She lights up a quick ciggie before starting the morning walk to school, she'd woken extra early for some reason and seen the small bottle of perfume he'd slipped into his briefcase while he was having his usual bath. How strange, she'd kind of sensed beforehand that she might find a clue in his work case. *Have to look after the living body I've got, don't I?*

Otherwise I'm no use to the dead or the taxman, is what he'd said but somehow his glib too easy charm and the soapy suds couldn't wash away the ugly smell of deceit. He didnae like her smoking in the house but tough.

"Well son I just meant to say that really he, your father, could help me out in the garden a wee bit more as I do all the work planting and cutting. And just because I smoke cigarettes doesn't mean that you can, too, you know. You stole one didn't you when I left them in the kitchen earlier. If your father or I catch you smoking one of them here or at school, you'll be sorry. I won't have lies from you or your father. And what's this I hear about you having a girlfriend, Nora something is it."

Sinclair blushes slightly, remembering the makeshift card and love hearts sweet he'd given Nora a few weeks back when he found out it was her birthday. *Sweetie* was the single word on the pale pink sweet and Nora had popped it into her mouth, looking chuffed. She didn't really understand where babies came from, Sinclair seemed so clever on that front, but she knew boys had special friends that were girls and so did grown ups. Glad stubs out her fag, glancing at the kitchen wall clock. Just what she'd do with her day once the boy was dropped off she didn't know. But she'd had enough of this life, sitting decoratively around catchin' flies. She only hoped this wasnae having an effect on the wee man. Her secret life of hell and nobody knew about it. Kill a few hours shopping maybe, deciding what the two men will eat for their tea. Were there other wives and women really living lives like this in this miraculous *Year of the Pill* which supposedly freed half the human race?

"Nora is my friend but Miss Byrne says she's a tom boy who climbs trees. I don't mind. Can I have extra pocket money if I help you in the garden, ma? Oh please. Our Willie from The Broons says gardening is for pansys, what does that mean?"

But Gladys is zipping her son into his coat and walking him to school briskly in the spring sunshine, gracefully fending off the questions. The school is only fifteen minutes away; they'll pass a few shops on the way. Maybe slip in some shopping on the way back for a bit of variety. Fronts have to be preserved to make things palatable, Glad thinks bitterly approaching the school gates. Her stiletto heels are murdering her feet and freedom slowly but surely. She waves goodbye to her only son, avoiding chat with other mums. Now that's an art she's mastered very well.

"Sinclair have you got any more of those sweeties that look like cigarettes? You can see my pants if you like, I'll not tell. But if you tell on me I'll say about the faggie you smoked in the bush. I saw you. Why doesn't your mum stop and talk to the other mums? My da says you are a wee blackmailer, a bad influence only saying you'll play with me if you choose the game. That's no fair and kind."

Nora looks very minx like but earlier she'd called Sinclair a *minging midden* and that'd stung him as bad as any wasp she'd seen. She'd stuck her tongue out at him and hissed that she wanted more trails of love heart sweeties or else she'd tell about the rude words and sign *our willy* Sinclair had chalked on the playground next to the Broons character. She craved a sweet fag; she knew Sinclair hid things in pockets: marbles, gum, fags, and coins, dried up slugs in match boxes. But he ignores her, tuning her voice out and thinking about the programme he'd watched on TV about America and Cuba. There was this man on TV with a black beard; he smoked a fat brown cigarette which looked cool. Much better than the thin little cigarettes his ma had. Da said the man was a mad rebel who was not to be trusted but anybody who fought the big Americans must be very brave or crazy.

Sinclair knew the Red Indians smoked peace pipes but that *was* just too silly. It's quite windy even though it's warm and Nora wants the sweets and his attention too much so he knows she'll dare not tell. If it's boring liver again for lunch, he'll sneak something away in his trousers. Three days ago he'd heard his da swearing at his ma saying he would not be some *frigging fag* for her, wearing womanly shirts and looking daft. He didn't know what da meant but he could find out if he was clever. It was all about watching for a chance and timing and knowing that people had secrets. If Nora bugged him too much he'd wave the dead slug under her nose. That will keep her quiet. Thinking about bugs, he'd wanted to catch a green flying beetle that ate roses, having learnt about them in school – but he couldn't remember if ma said they had roses in the garden and if it was the right time of year. At any rate, hearing about the wee wings on the creepy crawly sleekit beastie made Sinclair Junior hanker bitterly after all things that flew. For the ability to fly meant being omnipotent and supreme. And if you couldnae have it or be it then at least you could eat it.

18

Fall Out

Early September and already wild black berries growing on some parts of the Restalrig estate are beginning to slowly blacken up in late summer. Though wild and unkempt looking, the residents on the estate had fought tooth and nail to save the row of bushes and shrubs arguing that birds and bees used them and that the extra green feature broke up boring shared flat greens. And good on them, these local resident associations and co-operatives who defended wee patches literally and metaphorically against the Council or corporates who only sometimes sang from the same *glocal* hymn sheet. Alison's just returned from yet another visit to a newly discovered launderette which is a hell of a lot nearer than the shadowy spin shop she'd had that encounter with Sinclair in. Dumping the clean bags of clothing on the front room floor, she thinks again about buying Spock a wee tartan shirt for his birthday which she'd decided would be the same as hers: late September. She's interrupted reading her star sign forecast for the month by a new text from Flora. *Weather berry lovely here. Police may visit about assault and vandalism soon. Hope ok, gave them ur details. XXX P.S Be careful, Al. Luv u.*

Amazingly, Alison had also got a text from Noel MacArthur about ten days ago saying that he'd put two and two together and having read of the horror of the murdered shop animals in the paper, he'd felt compelled to bus it down to Leith, paying a visit to a shell-shocked Flora and Mac before they'd gone on their trip. The shop had been named in the press and Noel vowed to them over the shop's clamjamphrie and rubble that he'd return when everything was ship shape as he was looking to acquire another cat perhaps along with his long lost French lover. But nothing more had been said and Alison deduced that, Noel didn't know that she knew Flora. *Sheer co-incidence.* Thankfully, Flora hadn't yet resorted to the strange narcissistic incandescence of the 'selfie' – it seemed there were some people out there in this mad burning insecure world who still valued quiet emotional privacy though that, too, was becoming harder and harder to find and conserve.

But after that infamous rooftop interception by Lady Hyde on the phone a few weeks back there'd been a lot of explaining and apologising to do to both Brett Gribble and his esteemed grandma – somehow both had come to the conclusion that there was truth in the sayings about the eccentric Brits. At one point Alison and Lady Katherine had thought that incident might even provoke another international diplomatic crisis about surveillance and privacy laws so incensed were the Gribbles. Special relationships, personal or otherwise were worth going the distance for they both concluded.

Ruddy huge bowl of glacé cherries, pal. I have become a raving hypocrite, haven't I – just like all the others, no better than anybody else at the end of the day. *On the one hand I complain about my personal space and noise bubble being invaded, about state surveillance cameras and a sense of profound anxious self-consciousness – a kind of living zeitgeist or restless spirit of the times – yet on the other I presume it's alright to allow a pal to eavesdrop on someone's private conversation!* And Alison mouths all of this to herself into the new hallway mirror, a gift from a grateful Lady Hyde, who, since knowing Alison Mode, had discovered new heights literally and metaphorically within herself. Her work at *Extra Rib* seems to be going well by all accounts, she wants Alison to incorporate new street cred-lingo in *The Quibblon.* But how to fully re-conciliate her with The Gribbles would require more serious thought. Spock's on his mad half hour or so scurrying around the flat, after some peanuts that Alison has sprinkled around to motivate him. He's still extra jumpy as if he somehow senses the presence of some evil energy within the flat. Maybe she really would have to resort to hocus pocus and space clearing feng shui – yes, and the good book had a section on wind chimes, mirrors and bowls of water. Sinclair's still at large in the city and seemingly unstoppable too.

Walking by many shops in Edinburgh these days it seemed to Alison that there were ever growing markets for DIY complimentary therapies, psycho-spiritual personal development techniques and the like but all this sat very oddly with harsh economic, political and scientific facts. An unresolved dichotomy or split in cultural consciousness, the left sphere of the mind not joined with the right. And she recognised the split in her mind too; she was not immune to it. It was as if the old familiar comforting armchairs allocated to specific rooms called 'reason' and 'belief' had got mixed up. But then maybe there always were hybrids and fluidity, people believed in abstract 'markets' as intensely as they followed redeemers and saviours. Evidently, the demise of some markets seemed to create a surge in demand for others as uncertainty and instability in all its manifestations created markets and jobs too.

And there'd been those two strange silent phone 'calls' too – to her landline … on both occasions Alison's message on the answer phone was obviously heard, but after a few seconds of silent air time somebody or some machine had hung up. Alison had seen the way Spock froze when the phone rang and the way he sat stock still for a while under the hatch-portal in the hall as if he knew it was a gateway to another dimension in space that defied the normal rules of gravity. *Animals have feelings too pal, you sadistic fucked up bastard Sinclai*r, she'd cried out when hearing about the horror of the decapitated animals in Flora and Mac's shop. She experienced great difficulty containing an intense violent rage when she heard about or personally endured cruelty, bullying, evil, or deceit so much so that she was now contemplating buying a mini punch bag and boxing gloves to vent her fury on.

In her mind she beat the crap out of Sinclair and all the tormentors she'd ever endured to a bloody pulp over and over again. She tried hard for her dead mother's sake to forget the school bullies and the terrible destructive vain sickness in the world which greedily devoured and burnt whole forests, peoples, the atmosphere, innocent creatures with no thought for tomorrow or the harm and sorrow inflicted on other living things. But it *was* hard and joining the massed inferno of hatred wasn't really an answer either. Not in the bigger scheme of things. And now, on top of everything else, she was trying to process the extra ordinary sight of seeing her mother's ghostly hand emerge and disappear in to her front room wall.

Some form of life-consciousness continued after 'death'. So rather overwhelmed, Alison sat on *The Sneezewood* instead for hours, contemplating human nature, and the daily reproduction of consciousness until she found a way to come to terms with and balance the dark destructive forces that also, she realised, resided within her. Perhaps they too might be useful, if used wisely and fairly. *I'm just not cut out to be a saint, ma – what can I do? You don't want to know ma what I'm capable of doing to some folk. Bet you know already, huh?* She cried often but tears and rubbing the metal coat hangers focused the agile wandering awareness between her mind's different zones and Domains.

Her very own Domain I and its realms. Now if she could access Domain I, II *and* III she really would be dangerously different, it would be an awful towering responsibility. She could literally make or destroy people and the world; she could become a new phenomenon, a female global dictator, whose currency was fear, greed and paranoia. She wasn't sure she really wanted to know the contents of the minds of others anyway, that was their business after all, to mind their own mind so to speak. But a degree of telepathy and empathy, if used in the right way, had to be a good thing Alison thought, stepping then into her weekly bath soak.

There was already way too much emphasis and fixation on seeing and measuring things in supposedly rational isolation or separation, sometimes used as an expensive excuse to defer addressing wider issues, for things have always existed both in separation and isolation as well as in connection to each other, in the wider milieu. Maybe I really should have gone to university, she thinks checking out her toes in the bath water for fresh corns. She had small but wide feet very different in size and it was always a hassle finding things that fit well. *Try to turn a disability or ailment or condition into a positive, the universe needed it, even if was not said or appreciated enough.*

There must be millions of other street philosophers out there, she concluded, drying herself off. She wondered if on her death, she should become a kind of legend of walks far woman. But the answers always did come if she just sat patiently, waiting on wisdom, if not on *The Sneezewood*, tapping the truly timeless inner Domain. An eternal place where science, physics and logic met consciousness, religion, and feeling. A Domain both abstract and real where thought and sound vibration resonated above more earthy sounds. The hatch in her hall offered a different kind of release and potential escape too, it was another magnetic black hole maybe, for when certain words were uttered, Alison discovered, the metal grill's spokes widened and a powerful sucking vacuum sound could be seen and heard. White power, higher empower.

She was yet to discover whether the hatch in itself could also function as a Domain III portal from her mind to Sinclair's mind. She could try and find out of course but she suspected her current predicament was already way too fragile and vulnerable. Maybe he'd even take a final swipe at her soon, so she had to act decisively. Enough of this navel – space and toe gazing for now. But if she really could transport *The Sneezewood* through the air vent, travelling through ceilings, plaster, roofs and over geographical space – then maybe there might be other possibilities, too.

She'd worked her way methodically through *The Quibblon* discovering trigger words and placing small objects under the hatch before she'd taken the eventful rides alone and with Lady Katherine. It had been trial and error but *pucker and large it up and away* seemed to be the winning strap lines. And perhaps it is also universally true about human nature that a lot of folk wherever they are from, tend to see the 'mad', the weird, the unusual or even the cruel, hypocritical and deceitful in any number of others but certainly not residing in one's own self. At least Alison reflected honestly upon herself and looked equally at the strengths and weaknesses.

At least Alison also took personal responsibility for her failings and didn't puff herself up or try to dish dirt on others – rejecting as she did the ubiquitous *don't look at me, guvnor, the nothing to do with little old me syndrome.* It was unfortunate that super bright student Brett, who'd only recently been studying Bentham's utilitarian utopia and the horrors of the panoptican, couldn't see the extent to which he also was tarred and feathered by assumptions, paranoia and mistrust as to Lady Hyde's real identity and motives. But then again, who really, nowadays, escapes the all mighty presence of the panoptican which prohibits seeing the wider societal view, the perspective beyond the immediate and sometime indulgent concern with self?

Try to remain focused this month, Libra, and remember to balance your heart with your head as both have important messages for you. A little bit of what you fancy does you good but don't reach too far too fast as you may become the burnt out star. How long have you known this woman Lady Hyde, Alison? Is what Brett had insisted upon knowing. *Does she make a habit of freaking out and spying on people, sticking her nose in other people's business or is she some kind of select people's champion*? It had been hard work convincing Brett and Grandma Gribble that all was well and that Lady Hyde had only kind honourable intentions.

Call it a kind of divine intervention if you want is what Lady Hyde had said, keeping her word and following up with her own private phone call to Betsy in Boston who took it in the closet on her mobile with the aid of Maria who'd held a flashlight. There had been intense anger and fear initially, it had taken everything Brett had to convince his grandma not to call the FBI, CIA or MI5 or all those other mistrusted apparatus of the sometime interfering states which she nevertheless relied upon in a time of crisis. Years spent sitting in the walk in wardrobe hiding away did not mean that Betsy Gribble was now any less of a walking paradox.

August 28th

Dear Alison,

I didn't like to say anything before about the headdress that you wear because I try not to discriminate but somehow Betsy recalled this fact that I mentioned casually to her about you and now she wants proper assurances, understandable I think, that you or Lady Hyde aren't members of an international extremist organisation. Although I see your intentions were good never the less the fact remains that you invaded our privacy and I really expect a written apology from you both. I will not be writing to complain about you to Help Is At Hand agency because I know you to be an honest hard worker who made a genuine mistake and we all make mistakes. Any note from you and your friend will be duly sent on to Boston. I think you can appreciate that, given these very unusual circumstances; I will have to ask you to stop your duties as carer for me at this time which I genuinely regret as I have appreciated your company. I wish you all the best for the future, Alison.

I must also say I found it highly insensitive of you and your friend to pull off a stunt like this given the nervous nature and personal history of my grandma and the stress and discomfort I, too, am under-studying here in Scotland. There is a time and place for every little thing and being spoken to in a patronising or even matronising manner has surely achieved a back lash and nothing more. Please think about what I have written. You said that you despised dishonesty and political double speak so here I am talking to you straight. And maybe ultimately that of God or good can be found both on our left and right if you will excuse the pun even now – that's what studying political philosophy does to your head you understand.

I have come to realise, especially after all this brouhaha business, that there's a philosophy of information too and that we are all ultimately comprised of mixed natures: progressive, traditionalist and reactionary in some shape or form. This explains the hotch-potch botch of much political and economic policy: one step forwards to centre left, another step backwards and to the right, now one to the side and then repeat. A continuous search for equilibrium, sometimes expensive and dangerous. This may be true in theory and everyday practise – but plain good manners, sense and integrity endure.

Sincerely,
Brett Gribble

Alison re-read Brett's note feeling like a guilty accomplice, but then she'd just let the whole episode go in her mind. All she'd been trying to do after all was to step outside her comfort zone and assist a likable young man who seemed to be suffering in some form and who evidently was addicted to late night Internet chat rooms. Lady Hyde had come round again last night to visit and to offer profound apologies to Alison for her 'severe error of judgement' – saying she'd been blind and selfish actually in not seeing that her friend's employment could now well be in jeopardy; and all due to her behaving like a complete humpty, a loose cannon at large who could say whatever she liked to anybody.

Even I do not have complete liberty, Alison, even though I can clearly afford to have a rant in the House of Commons and hire an expensive lawyer or pay any bail, is what Lady Katherine had said, her eyes full of thought and remorse. *Clearly, there are different notions of affordability as I think you may have tried telling me.* Alison had tried reassuring her friend that she was equally to blame for their roof top escapades – she could have intervened and said no, but didn't in the end. They'd face any possible nasty consequences together. Lady Hyde had been reassured by the note Alison had shown her from Brett.

As a kind of consolation prize and to appease her sense of guilt she'd given Alison a magnificent oval gilded eighteenth century mirror which had belonged to one of her many ancestors. Hovering on the doorstep, she'd also thrust a rather unusual looking red fruit into Alison's hand which looked like a cross between a pear and an apple. She said jokingly that it was another damn American hybrid import, a sign of how small the world had become, how far food flew. But equally, the term 'pear shaped' should be reclaimed as denoting things and events that were sometimes innovative, compassionate and daring and not just messy cock-ups.

She'd not said much about Lord Edward other than that he was staying put in a wealth rich but cash poor friend's Regency pad, spending most of his time swimming around an indoor heated swimming pool complete with autumnal leaves and all under the impassive gaze of a bust of Venus. The penny had definitely dropped with his wife but not the apple recently and she whispered to Alison that she was thinking about rescuing him from his 'U' turn. Alison doubted whether Lady Hyde had completely forgotten the bruisings she'd been given – who could? But he missed her more than she did him. Some unspoken things were just not written into any marriage contract. *Hard times, my friend. Dismal indeed. We are all tested in some way or other in this shared hurdy gurdy of a life.*

What was more worrying than upsetting a client though was the dry throaty laughter she'd heard yet again when showing a freshly shampooed Spock just how cute he looked in the newly acquired mirror. He'd seemed indifferent to seeing his own reflection close up and she'd hung it in the hallway, hoping it would bounce and reflect light. But it seemed it wasn't enough to dispel Sinclair's evil predatory essence visiting her own home. Putting Spock gently in his hutch, a horrifying thought occurs to her. Perhaps he wanted her dead after taking her money and terrorising her. He'd gone over to the dark side long ago. The end game. She doubted very much that Sinclair would have told anybody about seeing *The Sneezewood* in action – he'd keep such valuable information to himself.

Most probably he is coveting the stool right now as well as her money, sanity, dignity and her poor pet's flesh. It would never be enough. She didn't like to think too deeply about any verbal threats or dark arts the rent-pimp road-kill king might be practising in private. *Wood Sneeze.* Now *those* words, the repeated smudgy ethereal letters written by Barbara Mode's ghostly hand that still remained on the living room walls, they must *mean* something. Her mother was surely trying to tell her something. She'd not washed the walls for this reason.

Quibblon Alternative Dictionary
A poem by Alison Mode

Sleep

Unwittingly we drift into a selfless slumber,
It is midnight and Peace lays her brow heavily upon pillows.

The years fall away, all conscious order now defunct

Toes curl, our ankles have grown wings

We step into the looking glass world
The land where unicorns are born and roam.

Gusts toss at curtains, we fall and turn
Back into ourselves, the moon a guide

For final reckonings and confrontation with the hidden.
I am light, my body now stirs:

Surely it is an art to recall one's night time thoughts
And sliding with trust into the abyss

We weave images out of thin air
A lonesome owl hoots, a fitful moth flies

Into the blackness
The self-mastery now complete

To carry then the fruits of insight
Into the waking act.

Leaves sway gently, a whispered message
Dreams contain truth, listen to the silence.

19

Brothers Grim

"She doesnae look very braw, da. Do you think her ma shrunk her in the wash, like?" the nasty question is followed by guffaws and the lighting up of cigarettes. Smoke quickly fills the room.

"Sshh, Dougie. Dinnae be rude, she's only next door and maybe she can hear you. The wee wuhman has come direct from the agency *Help Is At Hand* and they are all vetted and qualified carers. The fact is, what with you two horizontal layabout sons and me having throat cancer and dodgy veins, well I cannae manage on my own anymore."

Derek McGhee's bright red hair contrasts vividly with his pale freckly skin. A large man with a rumbustious laugh and appetite to match, he'd passed on his colouring and swinging emotional moods to his two red-haired sons. Upbeat, down beat, highs, subterranean depths. Sometimes the moods took him unawares. Father and son are standing by the open hatch in the kitchen, trying to keep their voices down in the presence of the visitor who'd just arrived. Thankfully Shirker, their big greasy Alsatian, had not gone berserk when he'd heard the doorbell. Derek's locked him strategically in the upstairs bedroom for the time being. The stench of ciggie smoke, dogs and dampness and maybe something else fills the entire house as does unsightly piles of unwashed clothes, mouldy food and general clutter.

"Ah know, da. But you only collapsed for an hour in the road the other day didn't you, it wasnae like it was the end of the world was it? Wee diddy men in the ambulance or the men in white coats didn't come and whisk you away from your best beloved sons did they? And I did walk Shirker yesterday even though he shat all over the park ruining ma best trainers I should add making me look like a total prat."

"Now, son. Where on earth did you get such cheek? Certainly not from me. Probably your dear departed ma who cannae keep her knickers on for long. Try to be polite when you come back out and look her in the eye. Her name's Ms. Mode for your information and the lass cannae help it if she's 'unnaturally' short now can she? Ah'll need help getting my medication and my legs massaged. Well, I can't rely on you or your brother can I? Your brother Don is more interested in getting out of his heid regularly on mortal trip pills. They look more like sherbet refreshers to me son, but I'll take your word for it about them. Now let's finish up the fags and go out. Been quite a while since we've had any manner of wuman in this house right enough."

They re-join Alison who has been waiting patiently in the front room with a cup of tea, wondering what all the male sheepish looks had been about. Douglas tries hard not to stare but seeing a dwarf in front of him puts him out of his comfort zone. A lad well used to living in a zoned off part of the city had become overly accustomed to seeing the same community of folk day in and day out. But they'd all lived together like this, two twin sons with a father, crammed into the modern Pilton two up two downer for years. Three men, a dog and a wild unkempt garden. A mattress and dumped cooker out the front which had been left abandoned since the day Carol McGraw had upped and left without warning, preferring to do paid work in a twenty-four hour Botox and hairdressing clinic, rather than do unpaid house work. That had been over five years now but it had hit Derek McGhee very badly, devastating him.

He'd tried hard to be a kind and loving husband but in the end Carol grew bored with her lot in life and the housebound duties expected of her – she craved the world of work and maiden independence and in the end this was more important to her than the three men or the pooch in her life.

And right or wrong, Derek had mutated into a house husband and father as a consequence, falling into a deep depressive pit to such an extent that he was fired from his work as a painter and decorator. His hardy stoical boss was totally unsympathetic and really thought Derek should just 'pull himself together' through very tough times single handedly raising two cocky lazy sons who were just approaching the dreaded teenage years mumless. And this on shameful state benefits which seemed to shrink ever further every year no matter who was in power. The state and government and indeed local community had done such a great job of stigmatising dependency, poverty or even emotional vulnerability that over a whole year had passed before Derek had plucked up the courage to 'sign on' – but even then it was only as a last resort as savings had run out and they had begun to suffer from a lack of decent heating in winter. His twin sons Donald and Douglas both had asthma, and at first it had been a cruel stark choice between eat or heat – no joke in January or February.

It was a tough area of Edinburgh and life had been a relentless struggle both financially and emotionally for the McGhees – even when they had been together as a couple there had been that many factors to get stressed and argue about. For money and dignity can be sucked or beaten out of whole areas as well as people – raw market forces as cruel as brute muscle. Since she'd become a trained carer Alison had not so far visited poorer parts of the city but she'd not forgotten what it was like to struggle for money. The banking and credit crisis had hit them and this neighbourhood very harshly, exacerbating already existing emotional strains in the family. And this was the harsh reality within the home walls alone and not looking beyond at something obtuse called the *Scottish Diaspora* which some politicians, Scottish and otherwise, mentioned rather too liberally on TV when talking about defending Scottish interests. Such flowery language didn't always help appease more immediate concerns about bills, costs, jobs, alien-foreign invasions, instead it alienated some folk further. Scotland, it seemed, tried to retain a distinct mix of fair minded liberalism and social conservatism but some Scots still saw Scots from other homeland regions as *interlopers*, this despite globalisation.

Austerity cuts, imposed by largely wealthy London *ConDems,* a nebulous new tribe uncertain of its direction and ethos, certainly condemned Edinburgh's already poor and vulnerable to further insecurity, humiliation and fear. The area was zoned off and the identified *stated* focus was on social inclusion, perhaps a euphemism in reality for exclusions and differentiation – for though some in wealthier parts of Edinburgh had a rough idea as to how others lived the fact remained that geographical areas remained highly stratified. Thus the rhetoric of political correctness stayed mostly on policy pages, whether or not this was intended. Tales from very different parts of the city were rarely swapped or shared even in designated public open spaces – that is how culturally and spiritually impoverished the whole city had actually become. And it was neither fair nor really sustainable in terms of the range and costs of ailments, disorders, social and financial costs. High burn out society running on and for coffee, desire, profit, competition and oil.

Cash rich but time poor, cash poor time rich or cash *and* time poor – these were the living conditions the vast majority endured and who in their right minds or hearts could really say this was deserved? Few had or made the time to connect with those they'd not 'normally' fraternise with, for even energy and time, those ultimate further commodities in the all-consuming market, even these were sometimes robbed and stripped from the affluent. And even 'the rich' didn't really escape the paradoxical sickness. Discrete low key giving and donations to charities and churches might well have made the city's Victorian dead nod their bony heads in graves, in recognition of so much that actually remains unchanged. Derek came from a grafting solid working class family which constituted a big section of the perceived 'deserving' and working poor –as opposed to the non-working and 'undeserving' poor and this often meant that Derek's family had difficulty in either understanding or empathising with the long term jobless and workless.

And if these unchanging divisions, hierarchies and judgements were predictable just within the one segment of Edinburgh's society deemed 'working class' – then consider the attitudes and assumptions of the city's more affluent and secure to those who, for whatever reason, cannot or will not work. A foreigner visiting Scotland and Britain might well find a society steeped in suspicion, hostility and derision when it came to claims made upon the public purse. No such hostility or resentment however hovered around tax free private pensions which relied upon and were ultimately subsidized by this same public purse.

It was all curiously as if there were *two* public purses with separate rules designed to keep society highly stratified, despite years of political rhetoric claiming otherwise. And the beauty of all of this was that each isolated group remained pitted in ignorance against other groups so that even if the two horse voting system didnae throw a spoke in the wheel then real people would. So savage inequality would in this way remain a permanent cultural feature, its blight forever unresolvable because of cowardice, inertia, greed and the root ambiguity in the two underlying, rivalrous, political philosophies which always endured. Derek thought all politicians of all colours were giant apes competing over who scoffed which bit of cake – for this reason he hadn't voted for years. For maybe there are different kinds of disenchantment, political and otherwise. What was the point in it if all ultimately preserved the status quo and nobody did anything different? He hadn't turned in to a pillar of salt had he all because he couldnae be bothered with those up themselves pillars of The Establishment. Had anything changed in over a hundred years? Derek thought that in many regards the answer was 'no, not a sausage.'

But the wife leaving him was what cracked Derek, pushing him totally over the edge into black despair. He looked back at his track record and blamed himself. Over the last few years, Derek's family had slowly ostracised him in ways subtle and crude: guilt was always an ace card to play. He was a 'bad' father or parent who was too weak to cope. Derek had established that Ms. Mode infinitely preferred to be called Alison by her clients, and just as well because son Douglas had spotted her walking down the street towards the house and had harangued his da by the upstairs bedroom by continually asking "*what's that, what's that?*" a peculiarly Scottish habit when faced with someone who looked a bit different.

Talking about looking different, prior to catching a bus out to Pilton, Alison had seen the following in one twelve ten-minute walk or so in Princes Street: a young black man in a kilt, a girl with calves wrapped in plastic bags and a manky flea-ridden squirrel drinking from a puddle which nevertheless attracted the admiration of two hobos who were asking 'why more humans couldn't have such humility or gentleness?' Ah, Scotland in the throes of a long running identity crisis. Modern Edinburgh, now home of all sorts. Still, that was one tree rat that had survived and escaped the likes of Sinclair and his kind's rapacious cruel appetites. Sitting in the McGhee's poorly lit front room Alison realises her tea has gone cold.

"Ah'll only be needing home help and care for aboot a month, Ms. Mode if you understand me. I do hope *Help Is At Hand* made that clear to you when you got booked out. After years of being unemployed I've finally managed to get an interview for a job I'd actually like to do. Drains, Ms. Mode. There will always be a need for good drainage and the fitting and installing of unglamorous but necessary grills in roads floats my particular boat so I'm off to see the big boss at *McLuckie Drains* of Dalry. Anyway, my two boys are not the best helpers round the house as you can probably see but they say they are trying to find work though I cannae police them and tag them now can I?"

Alison thought it best to remain silent on the point about tagging sons. Upstairs, Shirker could be heard whining and scratching at the door. Lucky she wasnae afraid of dogs but she was wondering if he would be let out at some point – the sooner the better really. She expected she'd meet the other twin son Donald in due course. Derek McGhee had made it clear that his sons were perhaps incurably lazy and were simply not prepared to walk the fifteen minutes or so to the local chemists to fetch inhalers and medication.

Alison didn't want to join in the condemnatory chorus of blaming and shaming the less well-off and ignorant but she did think the behaviour of the sons selfish. Maybe she should tentatively suggest to their father that they help clear out their home and give it a clean? But if, from the sounds of things, Donald was addicted to *Mortal Kombat* tablets and other tabs that fizzled then Douglas must be hooked on video games or some other kind of screen as he has a perpetually spaced out empty look about the eyes, as if no amount of clicking, trolling and lurid flashing colours would ever fill the gaps. Derek had simply said *tabs* and *out of it like* and Alison put two and two together.

Maybe he was another of these walking avatar-husk beings that just got off on trolling and being trolled? No doubt she'd find out. There was a lot of this burning glazed eye syndrome about; Brett Gribble was just the tip of the melting iceberg. Many geeks, Alison suspected, never even ventured out briefly to confront the world warts and all. Another possible entry under 'w' in the *Quibblon* for *Wumps encountered* unless of course the twin sons could turn their behaviour around in some way.

"Look Mr. McGhee, I'm grateful for the work and I'm happy to buy medication and shopping. Sounds like you've sprained an ankle badly. Got any witch hazel in the house? Cold flannels are always good too you know. Try not to inflict excess weight on it. Have you tried raising the foot and ankle after soaking it to encourage circulation? I'll show you what I mean tomorrow. Drink at least three glasses of water a day."

Douglas looks at her, seemingly perking up at this display of common sense and initiative.

"Do you cook at home a lot? The reason I ask is that I'm thinking, just thinking about becoming a chef as da here is always going on about training this, skills that, job markets. Are you one of those people who won't eat dairy products and such like, I bet you are. I read somewhere that women don't need as much protein as men – what do you live off then if you don't eat meat – nuts and nettle soup? Not that I'm saying that you don't need as much meat because of *your size* or anything like that and not that I've got anything against *them – people like that,* short people or vegans I think you call them don't you? Yes, that's right da you need not look at me like that, I don't spend the whole day in front of a screen upstairs FYI for your information."

Douglas has a nice line in sneering sarcasm and innuendo but it takes everything Alison has, every ounce of moral fibre within, not to tell this young potential *wump* in the making to take some hike somewhere up his own backside or to stick with his brother to easy recipes like lightly tossed grass salads. Despite Doug's strenuous efforts to try and avoid appearing offensive, snide or discriminatory, he's actually managing to do all three. Poor Doug McGhee enjoyed winding people up and baiting them for sport, he didn't really have a lot going on in his life and it was as much about his tone of voice as it was his assumptions and presumptions about her. *People like that.* Here Alison was, trying her level best not to write *him* off as morally dubious, weak and bovine. And she of all people knew what it was to be labelled on the basis of her appearance, nevertheless all the extra qualifying indicators of *wumpdom* were there – the denial of responsibility to others, vanity, narcissism, cruelty and indulgence and the sometime blindness or refusal to see the effects of one's words or attitudes on others.

And wumpdom was by no means confined to one section of society, not by any means. No, wumps unthinkingly followed the herds, trends, and crowds and posted or sent cheap opinions and 'selfies' for instant gratification and self-glorification. Opinions were plentiful but who could say they really had time to listen anymore? Many politicians, amongst the more affluent were also Wumps, as Alison saw it, in that they were often obliged to follow a party's 'line' on something even if they as individuals passionately believed it to be wrong.

It was yet another peverse irony in an otherwise highly individualstic culture. A kind of insular cult of me, wumpdom was, a follow the herd mentality leading ultimately to a terrible different kind of poverty, a poverty of the spirit. For few could even afford quality time to connect or listen, everything had to be done quickly as attention spans had shrunk as rapidly as rain forests had done over the last forty years. Still, it was encouraging to see him taking an interest in *something;* she thinks walking away down the gravelly path and noticing three magpies chattering on an overhanging tree branch.

*

Partisan bread making, my giddy Aunt. Alison never thought she'd be asked to make that kind of bread for the workers yet that's what Derek McGhee is asking for help with in a local Pilton Community Centre Food Co-operative. It's not Derek that's doing the baking mind you while he's recovering from a seizure and a twisted ankle – it's the cocky son Douglas who needs to 'man right up', put on an apron and try and rustle up some new kind of food pronto if the McGhees are serious about unblocking arteries, losing weight, taking responsibility, eating healthily and attracting women back into their forgotten and neglected lives.

And cupboard love was at least better than no affection or interest in anything. Shortly after that very first visit when Dougie had treated Alison to a dose of his own brand of spite, she'd had to read all three men the riot act and then threatened to go on strike. It was then that she'd furtively started to slip little drops of *Twilight Dew* into their tea, hoping that the accumulated effects in the bloodstream would not be bamboozled by alcohol or fags. Grace, humility, respect and honesty were lacking in this home big time – but these virtues were not necessarily a given in more well off homes either. Far from it.

Societal rot and thoughtlessness and plain old fashioned rudeness were everywhere in fact. A symptom of these uber fraught and intense times. Alison wasn't even sure if there'd actually be a living working earth very soon to wake up in so busy were humans competing, bickering, posing, reproducing and acquiring. Alison had to *do* something to survive this job, call on some inner resource as she'd endured cat calling and hissing sounds from newly appeared twin Donald who appeared to be every bit as spiteful as his brother. Even Shirker had attempted to bite her. She would not back down though. One afternoon, when massaging Mr, McGhee's troublesome ankle, she'd overheard Donald deliberately trying to test her tolerance levels by telling his brother loudly within her earshot that he still visited *puntersandfunsters.com* to score-a-whore. That was a wind up too far and Alison walked out of the house abruptly despite Mr. McGhee giving his son a hell of a telling off.

She'd dodged the gob on the ground, dog hair, spit, shit and trash on the pavements, thinking she'd call the agency to report this house as unfit to hire home help staff. Did the taking advantage of and the undermining mocking ever end with some people? She knew she was just another lowly paid woman with zilch employee legal rights, stuck on the casualised bread line with sweet F. A's chance of getting a decent pension but she had pride and respect in herself and in her work. And nobody could take that away from her. She'd practised what she'd say to Mr. McGhee in front of the hall way mirror; if the ultimatum didn't work then she'd quit and report them. Let them go to the dogs if she couldnae help with the dinners. It was now two weeks into the contract and on her third visit she'd let him have it.

On the day in question which would go down forever in the household as 'Butterscotch Monday' the McGhee's anti-smoking drive was still not working, the whole house stank of tobacco and even the dog was coughing up something nasty. Time to spill the beans. She'd almost become lost in their lampooning judgements, not so much lost in translation for they all spoke Old Reekie and knew the lingo. She had to have a rant to re-claim her unique female sense of self in that macho household and she'd stood in the middle of the kitchen wielding a knife mid flow from chopping carrots, a vegetable rarely seen in that dire home. But this was more than posturing, this time it was the real deal. Bugger protecting some men from seeing their arrogance or vulnerability, instead *chop them off!* For testicles, the same as carrots, could re-sprout and grow.

"Look pals, you may think I'm not exactly a glamour puss, that I'm thick and easily taken advantage of. Maybe you think I'm a freak or charity case – who knows. I'm sure you've all seen dwarves before, people in wheelchairs and so on? If not then get over it, quickly like. I'm prepared to help you Mr. McGhee with getting your medication, treating your ankle, cleaning and now your son wanting to learn how to bake bread and do basics. Well alright, seeing as it's still classed as a kind of home help duty. I really don't mind my hands getting dirty. So far so good, all fair and square. And if you want my assistance clearing this whole house out big time as to be honest it smells and looks awful, then I'm even prepared to do that.

I'm actually quite physically strong you know – but mean verbal abuse and snide put downs from you I will not take. I'm not paid enough to take that kind of shit from anybody, I value my sanity and myself as a member of the human race too much to be insulted and humiliated. Yes, I need the work and the money for I am poor just like you, just like a lot of Edinburgh's and the world's population in fact – but I don't need the money so much that you have some right to walk all over my dignity and self-respect. No way."

Alison's outburst had the desired effect and she was offered buttered bread and ample supplies of scotch. They'd got pished together and shared their troubles and now, a week later, she finds herself scolding Douglas for over baking a raison and apple *Pilton Slab*, a cake Alison had invented just for the lucky McGhee's which was a cross between a small fruit cake and flapjack. Over the last week she'd persuaded both Derek and Donald to get off their backsides and get gardening outside into the small back garden which was an overgrown mess. Derek's ankle is recovering well, so much so that his new focus for anxiety is his impending job interview which he'd built up in his mind until it had become a vast obstacle to overcome.

He'd been out of the work loop for so long he'd begun to question his sanity, identity and ability, a triple whammy indeed. Alison, being a kind soul, tried to bolster him up as best she could, realising that his strutting displays of manhood actually hid deep doubts. It hadn't been easy showing father and sons the ropes and the bulbs and what to do with them as Shirker was one possessive Alsatian.

Eventually the dog accepted her too, and even began to wag a limp tail when she arrived every week, usually with great bags of leafy vegetables. It was just as well, as Alison, having tried and failed at the brusque, one-line, brush off approach with him, had then thought more seriously about shock treatment, maybe a good *smalting* with punky, blue dye would whip the aggression out of the hound? But there was no need in the end, for the beast, like his owners, was bristly for show, more than anything else. When both pet and owners had calmed down sufficiently,

Alison discovered she could ride all *on the snaffle.* Big grown up Donald had screamed at the sight of an earth worm, but she'd put him right about composting and the hidden wonders of soil churning worms. As a girl Alison had loved gardening with her mother out in their tiny ground floor front garden.

Shirker began to allow himself to be showered every two weeks which went some way to reducing the stench in the house and constituted a minor canine miracle. Fresh smells of baking bread fill the house as Alison's's been busy teaching Douglas how to expand his baking range. They'd covered stews, soups, pies and a huge pile of unwanted furniture and nick knacks had been piled in the front garden area, testament to a massive overdue clutter clear out. Undiscovered cloots, lying in cupboards were used for the first time since they were bought years ago, the sons were shoogly enough with the cloth action to begin with but she'd not really meant to fleg them with tales of dust induced asthma. Three lost adult men, grown wild, blind and vain in their crass indulgent living habits, teetering on the wider local brink of sexual, financial, ecological and political chaos. Work would not necessarily provide salvation or respect from others but it might help these abandoned souls regain some grain of self-respect and greater purpose. Edinburgh's forgotten, destitute and desperate, often grouped and fenced in patronising zones called 'schemies' – left to wither and swither, many of them couthy right enough but not sodie heid. And this diaspora replicated across the whole UK, if not the world. Occasionally politicians of all colours briefly visited these areas, voicing concerns over human rot, crime and empty housing yet it continued over decades.

After the ultimatum the other day Alison doubted whether she'd hear any more derision or crude wind ups but she wondered if she'd discretely ask Mr. McGhee for an extra cash payment for her work seeing as she was now dishing out what effectively amounted to business advice, counselling, home clearances, stress management, gardening, dog washing *and* grooming. For the great unwashed and well-heeled wherever they be. Talk about great added value the agency and the McGhees were getting for their money! She didnae want to join the depleted ranks of the disheartened, dispossessed or depressed husks like Noel, she wasnae a slave for love nor money nor anyone. Okay, so she went the extra mile for The Wipers, the Hydes and the Gribbles – but somehow her dignity as a human had been under threat what with the extra dollops of McGhee snide and she wasnae some trash can. Respect mattered above all else, but she'd have to watch how her tongue phrased it especially if she wanted the work.

Difficult, knowing which side your bread is buttered on but having to still tactfully bite the hand that feeds you, albeit in the name of common decency and dignity. She's holding a rolling pin in her hand as Donald steps into the kitchen, his hands dirty with good clean soil this time. His jiggery-pokery at any rate seems to have been productive as he's tackled the art of deep root dandelions. But there was *so* much accumulated muck and shit in this household, both tangible and unspoken, Alison simply had to confront the grim residues of reality.

"Some people don't even have a garden to speak of – instead they share drying greens. Me being one of them pals. Having *any* kind of small green peaceful space for yourself is worth its wait in gold and frankly, active regular gardening will help you lose weight and take your mind of endless fags, stodge, bickering or hot lasses you'd like to kerfuffle with."

Donald's eyes light up at the sound of hot lassies never mind the looks of them, but he puts his trowel down on the kitchen table and does sit and listen to his credit, perhaps realising that he had no real meaningful relations with any female. Where was there room these days for any real and ordinary flesh and blood woman if all were cast and framed as nymphos, witches, bitches, angels, ball breakers,

Goddesses – certainly not in the afore mentioned front rooms. Equally, whatever happened to the voices of calm reasoned men, fathers and sons exposed to this ill culture in different ways? Was it becoming ever harder to be human, fair and compassionate? Some people it seemed only wanted high resolution digitilaria, quick fix IT convenience, comfort, cheap credit and lots of TV channels not awkward ugly cultural truths. Douglas is slowly weaning himself off tabs and reefers, instead of getting out of his head, Alison's trying to get him to use his loaf.

"Could you see this bread actually selling, Alison? If we take it down to the Community Centre Co-operative – won't all the other numptys think we've become bumbling girly galoots? I dinnae mind if the lads think I'm a wag, cad, dandy or even what you'd call a '*wump*' – but weak, dependent and effeminate is the ultimate insult for many Scottish men, a dirty shameful secret. It's as bad as being a poof or pansy, like. And what do you mean by 'partisan' bread? Do you mean cheap working class bread, or bread that's only eaten by you know, *that* lot who say they are in the squeezed organic middle? Trouble is, these days most feel squeezed so it's hard to know. I know quite a few well paid lasses in top jobs up the toon who say they are squeezed, too, but not often enough by their husbands necessarily. If you take my meaning. In other words, lots of people make lots of claims about things and sometimes these claims have a grain of truth. Come on, Alison you must know what I'm talking about here, you hinted at your previous clients. Yummy mummies and eco babes brigade and blokes on bicycles with beards and sandals even in the winter – is that who this is going to appeal to?"

Alison ignores the potentially inflammable verbal vitriol, instead choosing to concentrate on giving the man honest polite advice. For even fair advice could be a sought after after commodity in Edinburgh, given that vested interests often lay in claims. She did have a paltry bank account to speak of but because she'd taken a long time to recover from her mother's death. She'd not worked for years, instead relying upon the savings that were left to her. Right or wrong, the Credit Union in Restalrig had looked at her as if she belonged in an asylum when she'd plucked up the courage to open an account. But maybe the real asylum was actually modern Britain with all its contradictions. She'd not said any of this to the advisor though; she'd put up and shut up knowing that complaining wouldn't win any sympathy at all. Know your place. Keep mum, she's not so dumb in the eerily familiar Corporate Edwardian Empire. Presume nothing, be watchful and grateful. Try to get a good night's sleep if you can.

"Look what you're offering is homemade produce, made in Scotland and with no chemicals. Au Natural and ultra-entrepreneurial – who is to fault this self-sufficiency? The government loves people like you; maybe you have a fledging business here. And okay, if I'm honest with you I can see this type of product appealing to the squeezed middle as you put it. Why don't you just try and take them to the Centre and make a small start. See how it sells, what the interest is. I must say it would be good to cut the nasty language out please. You may well be selling to people whose shoes you don't like – frankly, you are in no position to lord it over opinions. These days, opinions are cheap and plentiful but often not considered, everyone does them, you know that. I've told you lot already what *wumps* and *glunks* are in my book – make sure you keep this under your hat and become the latter not the former. Above all use words and language sparingly at times, be judicious with your tongue on some occasions but nevertheless defend yourself and your patch for no one else will at the end of the day."

"Aye, a small business that sounds like me. Not having to answer to some eejit boss. Well, you can only try. Thanks, Alison. Looks like Da is on the road to recovery. Shirker will miss you I know."

The two red-headed twins grin at each other knowingly. A small *ker-ching* had registered in Douglas's mind, the sound of a small whirring cash register. Blessed are the weak, the feckless and the unassuming. Duties over for today, Alison's given the entire house more than enough to think about and act upon. The future was in their hands. And all the while this conversation had been happening three magpies had again been chattering away outside on a branch overlooking the McGhee's front garden. At the lowest point in this assignment, she'd virtually thought directed whole packets of sugar and salt out from the filthy cupboards and out through a never used cat flap

Afraid she'd be caught smuggling the deadly white grains out in her bag or coat pockets, she'd had to tele transport objects ingeniously. Just because Shirker had mauled a pet cat to death a few years ago, didnae mean that the cat flap couldnae be used for something else. It had been hearing the gawkit sons boast about meow meow tablets that had given her the idea. *Higher Power, higher white power! Remove these crystals at this very hour!* She'd chanted in a trance at home whilst sitting on The Sneezewood and holding the *Kwik Stix* in the left hand. She'd lifted the packets and boxes way into the air and sprinkled the contents all over neighbouring flowers and plants. Nobody the wiser either. Too much sweet or sour was just not right after all, but she'd felt like a modern Goldilocks daring to challenge the ingrained eating habits of the three unbearables.

Next week will be her last week with them; perhaps there would be changes in the house from now on. Good for them. They were still trying to work out how she got the sugar and salt out the house, bless them. Let them wonder on. But talk about the pot calling the kettle black! To hear the early self-righteous complaints of these men who hated the judgements of others and yet were so sneering and contemptuous in their attitudes themselves. Alison feels grateful again she's invented her own language as a guide through the reactionary deceitful moral maze. For language itself, be it political, religious, financial or psychological had become a philosophical minefield often designed to obfuscate, confuse, divide, enrage, deceive. And on the very last day, a shy card of thanks and some chocolates is given to her, giving her fresh optimism for the human race.

Just then, as she walks down the path, taking pleasure in several jobs done very well, a magpie drops something just in front of her. Two other magpies protest loudly, maybe they are the same three from a few days back. A coin, it looks like. An old sixpence. 1638. REGNO.CHRISTO. AVSPICE. Turning the coin over, Alison deciphers the word CAROLVS. Where on earth did the magpie find this? Maybe it had been thrown up by some other gardener, though she doubted it had been unearthed in the McGhee's back yard. Finders, keepers.

*

"Ms. Alison Mode? Sorry to disturb you at this hour, we did try and leave a message on your mobile a couple of times but then we became concerned that it wasn't your number at all and that we'd made a mistake. Flora Macintyre gave us your contact details; a friend I gather?"

"That's right, Ms. Mode, we'd really like to ask you a few questions about a break in and vandalism. I gather from my colleague's report that not long ago you were also burgled. Is now a convenient time, please?"

The police officers standing at Alison's door have friendly, respectful expressions as if they really didn't relish haranguing people for information or arriving unexpectedly on the sanctity of someone's doormat. But a job's a job. Though startled initially, Alison sighs and lets them into her front room where one officer whips out a leather bound notebook and pen. Spock rustles about in his generous sized hutch. She thinks about offering them tea but then decides not to. She's done quite enough attending to men's needs for today, thank you.

"Is that a Russian hamster? My pal at work says you can get these mega hairy foreign hamsters which are about three times the size of the typical British one. Is that one there? Wow. My daughter would love a pet like that. Do you let it out?"

The polite jokey banter is designed to put her at ease; you could tell the officer has done this many times. Find an ice breaker, a conversation starter of some kind. Alison crosses her legs and smiles politely at them. It's a long haired guinea pig, she explains. His name is Spock. She tries to normalise things given that she'd had a few unpleasant encounters with some police when she was younger, when she'd been questioned rather too forcefully and for nae good reason. But these two seemed alright and not punch drunk on power.

"Look, Flora probably told you about my break in back in the spring, my neighbour did report it and the police did come round and I said I thought I knew who it was but there were no fingerprints of course. And I bet there were none left at Flora's shop either. And probably she told you about his, I mean a bald man called William Sinclair, beating and stalking me too. I still have very faint bruises but I didn't report it. Sorry officers, perhaps I should have done but the attack's savagery really got to me. I do have some pride you know. Being a short person, I'm not sure I'd not be mocked and ridiculed at some station too. It's been an issue before for me. How do I know it's the same person? I just know. He has a long term grudge with me over some imaginary rent he thinks I owe him and er, other things which shall remain nameless."

"Flora said you used to rent off a man called William Sinclair and that he has business interests and fingers in lots of pies, some of them very unsavoury I gather. So this is one and the same man?"

The officer writing the notes looks up from his notepad to watch Alison's face. Usually the expression on the interviewee's face told many tales and he's good at spotting a liar. He's interviewed folk from all walks of life but never a dwarf before and he doesn't want to stare at this lady who seems to be both sharp as a tack but down to earth too.

"Yes, his name is Sinclair; he's bald and must be in his fifties now. He has an eejit side kick called Davey who drives an old Vauxhall. Always has a strange vacant expression too as if he's the living dead. Both men are walking nightmares I have come to believe. Sinclair collects rent for people who I think he doesn't ever get to meet – maybe high up rich international property developers I wouldn't be surprised. I have over heard bits of conversation over the years in his back room office just down the road; he'd often say he wanted answers in English not Arabic or Russian. I say 'office' but he rents a back room in this launderette not very far from here. *Squeaky Kleen* is its name. But who knows how wide and far up this laundering web goes. He's too obvious and blunt in his manner to ever really get to the top of his shitty little pile so he does the dirty rough work for others. Whatever this may be as well: extracting rent, finding and recruiting hookers, selling drugs on. Bullying and interrogation are his calling cards. Oh and eating small animals live."

Both officers look at Alison, the horrors of this list sinking in. They hadn't blinked an eye at her headdress to their credit. She must be a hell of a woman both men privately think, somebody of real integrity and substance. Neither of the officers thought they could have endured half as much without cracking up completely. But it really did take all sorts. *Squeaky Kleen.* A trace of amusement flicked across the officer's face. You had to be kidding right enough pal. They explain they may need to contact her again and ask when she tends to be in. Clearly they had enough information for now. Spock's due a nightly run around, sometimes she lets him have the freedom of the whole flat all night, only to discover him the next morning in a tight little ball somewhere unexpected. She shows them the door and then realises she's running out of *Twilight Dew* and must replenish stocks. She notices the small bottle's nearly empty but it or her or both seemed to have worked an earthly kind of spell on the McGhees.

She didn't really mind folk calling her a white witch, some obviously had a need to label and corner her as a something, often losing sight of the fact she was human at the end of the day. And maybe she'd forage for wild mint, fresh dew or nettles when next she wanted to visit her mother's grave. Drifting off to sleep, her mind again turns over the enigmatic coin she found earlier. 1638. She'd put it on her bedside table for the now, as she had the tiny money spider she'd seen crawling away on her pillow. Now *those* kinds of webs she thought really were magical and spotting the money spider had reminded her of the seventeenth century silvery looking coin she'd put in her duffle coat pocket. *Is this a sign for me, mother?* What were the chances of this happening? And in Alison Mode's fitful dream that same night, she recalled a strong girlhood premonition she'd had of the panoptican, a chilling, alienating, dystopic building designed to instil fear, division, and submission. Her mother wrenched her away from its magnetic walls as she'd screamed for her very Baba Yaga's soul's survival. Then, in the dreaming mind's curious selective logic, time jumped and Barbara Mode was calling her and giving Alison a kiss on the cheek. Something is whispered in her ear but she cannot decipher the message, her mother's voice is too faint.

But in the still morning light that follows Alison spots the words, ripped deliberately from a local newspaper lying neatly arranged on the sitting room floor. *Send HIM back.* At first she's puzzled but then in a kind of storm of recognition, she realises what it means. And in that instant, a different kind of coin or penny drops in her mind. *Of course, she must try and send Sinclair back.* That was the meaning of *Sneezewood* spelt backwards over and over, the ghostly writing on the wall. Then the seventeenth century coin and now these odd printed words, no doubt assembled by Barbara's spirit hand. *Wood Sneeze.* Sinclair obviously belongs or belonged there, back at that time but not in this time. Or maybe both but *this* time was up for him. Strange but true. Just why she had to do this she didn't quite know yet but she must be obedient to her calling and transport him back to the year 1638 using *The Sneezewood.* Perhaps then she could live out the rest of her life free from constant fear and intimidation. It was surely worth a try.

Wood Sneeze
Born of Trees
Let time unfreeze
To set this free

Quibblon Alternative Dictionary

Glunk, adj. A new kind of clumsy gentleman hunk.

Snaffle, **v**. Figurative language, for example to ride someone on the snaffle. Alternatively, to steal, appropriate or seize.

Smalt, **n.** Glass coloured blue with cobalt or pigment made by pulverising this. In Quibblon, though, Alison uses the word to mean to show off or to gloat.

20

The Payoff

Davey bites into a warm skirlie burger, savouring the onions and fried vegetables. Tab sales have slacked off over the last few weeks but powders, particularly quick fixers, have been on the up and up. They get into the city with cars as it's far safer than boats or planes. Davey's got a couple of discrete collection and pay off points. But there's no denying it, sales of Smoky Joe and Blue Dragon Fly were so down that he was beginning to think about contacting his pal in Sighthill about branching out into driving an ice cream van just to keep the readies coming in. *What the hell's that? Wha's like us, eh lassie*, Davey had said to the girly who claimed she'd invented the skirlie burger selling chips from a street stall near Junction Road. She'd said that she had three kids and a bank manager to please. He's sitting in *Squeaky Kleen's* gloomy back room office, peering at a silent flickering screen which shows a televised debate between Sturgeon, Salmon and this smooth looking politico-civil servant from Westminster.

Little blocks of dialogue and speech appear at the screen's bottom, chopping and changing in an instant but nevertheless revealing just how difficult it is to have a polite and fair discussion about dwindling fish stocks, Scottish fishermen, EU rules and London policy. *I'm not calling you a liar Mr. Eaten but what I am saying is that your figures sound distorted to me – what are your sources?* The Salmon senses faltering in his English opponent and drives his point home but already Davey's attention levels have flicked back to food and the boss. Sinclair's turned the TV volume down as he's busy pouring over accounts on his lap top. A call has just come through from Moscow, a property tycoon who wants to buy up the business, rebrand it as *City Lettings* as it has a more cosmopolitan, international sounding name. Sinclair has to email the big boss in the New Town who answers ultimately to some other unknown man, Sinclair thinks it's in the Cayman Islands but he cannae be sure. For even he doesnae know it all and never will do as the reason he's employed and used at all is that he's learnt not to ask clever questions.

The police had visited the launderette earlier, before he'd got in, Davey told him all about it. *Did he know anybody called William Sinclair and did he work here? When would Mr. Sinclair be back on the premises please?* Davey said that there was a man of that name who used to work here but that he'd moved down south. No contact details were left unfortunately. But the officers' disbelief and doubt lingered badly in the air even when they'd left. Sinclair knows they'll be back but he also calculates that neither Flora nor Alison have a photograph of him to aid the process of identification. Now, surely, would be good time to disappear for a while, grow and dye one's hair. Might pop across to Dublin or Amsterdam.

I'll email the boss the details, then it's up to him. He doubted he'd lose his job whatever happened, *he* was safe pal as he was just too good at what he did and word got round. Later this morning he has to write up the blurb used to sell and rent out properties, the boss will update the relevant websites, he had fingers in loads of companies. The market in half-baked truisms, the art of sweet talking up. *A'hm alright jock* in this great game of winners and losers.

His own mortgage on the uber trendy harbour front pad's been sorted anyway – he got that taken care of as part of his pay deal years ago. No routing around in garbage cans, signing on, enduring peanuts pay or taking smelly public buses for him thank you very much. Driving about in Davey's car, he witnessed daily the shuffling beggars and scuttling manic misfit crawlers emerging from grimy holes like lice and earwigs. Little people with small minds, often run over and stamped on in the competitive food chain. And business chains not necessarily safe either, not in the current climate. Oh no. Several pubs and clubs he'd known sucked down into the pit too. Suddenly, and without warning. Sometimes mysteriously too.

Pity about the dwarf though, unfinished business that, but he would finish what he'd started. The freak will pay with interest and he'll take what he's owed. Couldn't really slot her in as a quirky call girl now, as somebody's gone official. *Long term game plan, stealth mover me.* Wear the victim down with nervous exhaustion. A kind of emotional taxation, as fatal as other kinds. Drinking up his eighth cup of tea that morning, Sinclair fingers his wee gold hoop earring. Having an ear pierced was his first obvious act of rebellion when he'd moved himself across the water over from the Kingdom.

Ah'm turning into a proper poofy tea jenny in ma golden years, he'd grinned at Davey. As bad as some lassies, using the toilet every ten meenits. They're both badly hung over as last night they'd had an excellent round of *Point The Finger* over bevies with the lads. A great newly invented board game that was, everything was for sale – you could even buy up and blackmail other players. All legit and above and on the board. An extreme version of monopoly with threadbare rules, total wipe-out, moderation be damned. They'd all laughed heartily together at Sinclair's pad with fine views of Leith Harbour and sea front, drinking and playing late into the night, smart manoeuvring lads bragging about their dodgy deals, sly revenge porn and outdoor fucks galore. Opportunists anonymous, a big brotherhood club not formally registered at Companies House or anywhere else for that matter but the hidden codes and sub language always the same no matter the time or place. Recalling these endlessly interesting tales, Sinclair remembers he's to meet Samantha at two later in Princes Street Gardens. *That* wuhman again. What an absolute downer. Unfortunately, there was no little tick box disclaimer he could sign and tick to be instantly or legally rid of her. Could get there early though, kill a few hours. The camera's in his drawer, could make use of that with a few shots.

*

"You settling in at your mither's hoose then? Sounds like you are right enough; you look well on it. You said you were working in a restaurant. In your text I mean."

Sinclair's sips at his McFluffle milk shake in the late September sun near the shadow of a large plane tree. They are sitting at a coffee and ice cream kiosk's outdoor table near the famous brassy looking Victorian Ross Fountainhead, resplendent with some woman's shapely nineteenth century backside. He'd thought about buying himself a small piece of boxed jerk chicken from a takeaway before meeting her but the breasts looked too greasy and small for him – and anyway there was still the aftermath of the alcohol to recover from. Samantha actually looks exhausted, there are big circles under her eyes, but of course he'll not say that to her. The fact is he does lies better than he does small talk. A shiny new tram rings tings by, but for whom those bells tolled seemed reserved only for some baying gulls as there are few pedestrians or passengers this afternoon.

"What's it to you, pal? Since when have you been interested in my well-being? You stink to high heaven; it's those Cuban cigars again isn't it. Just hand the money over, please and I'll stay quiet. It's what you wanted after all isn't it? For me just to go quietly with no fuss and saying nothing. So you keep your city hard man reputation intact.

My da and brother are raging Sinclair I warn you and ma's not exactly singing your praises."

Another very tense pause as she uses a spoon to scrape the last remaining trace of froth from her coffee cup. The bitterness is palpable; no amount of sugar or syrup can disguise it. Gazing up at the blue sky with white puffy clouds, Sinclair thinks he has a small epiphany moment recognising the mighty Scottish saltire flag carved into the heavens by passing aeroplane exhaust. *Keep cool, man. Play it out.* Thinking about exhaust, he reckons half of Edinburgh's stalwart residents are suffering from some kind of semi-permanent exhaustive-depressive cycle, for nobody's out 'man' with fighting walk. Just then a couple of young Italian girls pause at the fountain head's flower gardens taking snaps. *That's really what I should be doing now too* he thinks*; I should be offering to take their photo, giving a bit of chat, recruiting new bods.*

Either that or taking photographs of unsuspecting women and girls resting, reading papers, bending over a shopping bag or eating. Sometimes they saw him do it and shook a fist or threw shopping but he just laughed, giving them the finger. *This is a free country, nothing illegal here, pal. Joke's on you, doll. Too late now! Gotcha, birdy.* But oh the shame of it; when sallow-skinned darkies and the bloody English started invading little Scotland, soiling the language and creed and settling here permanently, often breeding, too. Maybe Scottish independence would mean tougher border controls with unique Gaelic passports and that had to be a good thing man. He unzips the brief case and hands her the large envelope with cash.

"I didnae tell them about the miscarriage, that was my choice but you give me any more hassle of any kind and I'll tell all. And you'll not be able to do a thing about it. I've got your phone records showing who you dialled, the police aren't stupid. I hope you're really happy now, Sinclair? Now that you got what you wanted never mind the fucking pain, misery and cost you cause. How much is here then? I asked for two thousand up front. It really better be here as well. Not that it will last me that long these days. I want another two thousand next month and that's it; providing you keep your side of the deal that is."

He looked at her grudgingly, reluctantly admiring her courage in a fierce man's world though never saying so of course. *What was it with some wuhmen, eh*? He reckoned it was all to do with their hormones; their feelings did the thinking for them. He nods at her, signalling silent agreement. Offering to get her something to eat, another coffee or something, he notices her warily looking at the money under the table. He shudders a bit in his thin canvas jacket, though the sun's out there's quite a chilly breeze too, hinting at changing seasons. He wouldn't miss her, let's face it. But then he'd never really missed any woman come to think of it. But she's having none of it anymore, none of his nonsense and grief. Satisfied seemingly with what's she's got packed in her bag she abruptly walks off not bothering with goodbye as that's just too good for him.

I expect you to call me next month is all she shouts out, startling an elderly couple. Then she's gone. To where and what he didnae know, but he had a rough idea as to where her ma stays. He watches her coat disappear impassively, not feeling anything. *See you later, Samantha.* Or just: *later, Samantha. How many times had he said those words to her over the last couple of years, giving her the indifferent brush off and not really giving a shit about whether he would see her later or not, other than her tits of course, now those bits of her he did like to see as long as they were passive, decorative and undemanding boobs, like some flashy appliance to be switched on and off when he liked. Once, back in Fife during his young buck years he'd hung some red slag pants on a railing outside a youth club he used to frequent briefly before he was banned.*

*

A seagull spots a scrap of discarded croissant near the table just then and he kicks at it, swearing. Pests they are.

Should be shot. He remembered seeing a swan's dying death throes as a child; it had been run over and its wings beat frantically, fighting for life. But struggles and pain, love and loss mean nothing if you are Razzle King. It's Mid October now, two weeks since the meeting with Samantha and the goodbye. He walks on then to the top of Leith Walk, home ward bound. There'd be something new to squeeze but he must have a break soon for even he feels faint under the incessant pressure of running his underground network. He stops suddenly, feeling dizzy but putting it down to more booze, late night and coffee.

Moving on again then and nearly at a cough and a pech, he has the oddest sensation of walking in the here and now but also walking in some distant there and then. *But then again I really am some here and there kind of man anyway, aren't I? A man for all seasons and many parts, especially some body parts*, he grins inanely to himself. He wasn't sure about all that karma stuff. He'd heard about a posh gang-bang party up in Stockbridge last night, lots of up – for-it uni students, but had just been too knackered out. Now that Alison Mode woman – if you can call her that. Plenty of men would pay good money to piss on her, see her dance, shit or vomit even. Sad but true. Put her in a cage, a travelling freak-fanny show, and rake in the readies.

He just had to own that flying stool Alison Mode had appeared on in The Banshee Cave, he wanted a stab at poking down the moon. He'd dreamt about it every night, it gave him no peace but now he'd have to watch and wait. A good Irish connection of his in Dublin has got this great chill out place overlooking the Liffy. Drastic action needed, change of scene; throw the police off the scent. Take the laptop, go for two weeks maybe. Nice little mid-October break, why not? He worked hard enough, pal. Got that right. Live off Chinese takeaways and tepid Guiness. Climbing the stone steps to his prime studio flat overlooking the harbour front, he notices what looks like a substantial matted ball of hair, maybe even human hair in a landing corner. Strange that, given that the block's cleaner is very thorough. I'm not touching *that,* pal.

I'm no mug, he mutters, but stepping into the minimalist décor the queasy dizzy feeling returns and he has to lie on the white shag pile rug in the front room to get over the disorientation. Recently, he'd been trying to do a bit of Pilates and transcendental meditation, like. *I am Aum in ma room; I am the total sum and invincible sun*. Move the small fat gut up, DIY style. He'd even tried astrally projecting images of his body as a means of kinky rent control for pliable international young tenants but he wasnae sure it worked. New Age stuff, man. Why the fuck should women only cash in on it.

Everyone does 'spirit' these days anyway too. Shops call hair products spiritual for fuck's sake, using words like *re-jueventating, uplifting, transforming, and healing.* Probably all the stuff was bottled in Slough or Stirling. Once he even saw some 'special' ladies' tights with Samantha in this hideous shopping mall which claimed to have skin replenishing oil in its fabric, wear them and the life and youth giving fluids were released, as if by some magic. Yeah, right. Pull the other one. Remote viewing, out-of-body? No, *in* the body experiences me, pal. I much prefer a bit of meat in the mouth or hand, none of this tantric sex business. Old hat game that magic crap that. But even hardened William Sinclair, the ubiquitous man of many parts, had been stunned by that flying stool contraption.

The dwarf really must have some kind of power. Maybe there really were hidden codes and spells tucked away in that antiquated book he'd seen in her tip of a flat. In the early hours he wakes and staggers to the kitchen for a glass of tap water only to be startled by the hypnotic moon light shining between the metal slats of the blind he has in the kitchenette. A lunar beam follows him, playing mischief on his face, making Sinclair toss and turn on the rug, giving him no rest. A few days after a full autumnal moon but still the pull is powerful. Laziness or sheer exhaustion prevents him from crashing into his own bed of his own making. And throughout the long fraught night he increasingly feels drained and there's a frightening vivid sense of being pulled almost magnetically through the floor.

21

Walk On Some Wild Side

Maria Gonzalez stood in the hallway, incredulous at the sight before her. A short woman from the Philippines who is nevertheless long in her wisdom teeth. And she has to be frankly, dealing with the likes of the Gribble family dramas for years on end. The decades spent trying to encourage, coax or tempt Betsy Gribble, out of that damned closet and now her employer has packed herself a little lunch in her travel bag, determined to venture further forth to Boston's city centre. For something has gradually happened to Betsy since the events of August, it's like she's shed some layer of skin and in the misty half-light of the morning she stood, her eyes staring off into some unknown space. Those fierce but tender Gribble eyes that have cried many real tears over the years, intimate tracks which have proved sometimes to be watery pathways leading to a better place.

"Betsy Gribble, do you value your life, ma'am, or what? Okay, so you are now stepping right out of the cursed closet on a regular basis and I'm real glad of that Mrs. Gribble, believe me I am. It must be what, coming up for two months now – you re-discovering the house you've lived in all your life and actually stepping over the doorstep too. To be honest with you there have been way too many dark nights of the soul spent in that enclosed space but, Mrs. Gribble it's now mid-October and fall's arrived and there's a windy bite in the air. I just swept a whole ton of leaves away from the mail box; this was after picking up the mail again from Brett. You gotta wrap up warm, my honey. Going out in just that tea shirt in this weather seems like a real life crazy stepping out of the closet and I'm sure not convinced that you're a total nut job. Not that I like that expression, having worked in a mental institution down south and seeing the way the staff were more often crazier than the patients. But you know what I mean, Mrs. G."

Mid October in Boston can be cold certainly but stoical Betsy, child of the stark twenties and thirties, still thinks she can cut it out there in a thin little twinset and cotton jacket. August and September were long and intense, Maria had to increase the hours spent in and out of that old musty dusty red brick house in a neighbourhood called Popes Hill in the Eastern part of the city just keeping on top of sweaty laundry and chucking out sell by date dairies from the refrigerator – food that Betsy turned her stubby nose up at despite Maria faithfully plodding up the stairs several times day and night with food, candles, torch batteries to keep her keeper alive of sorts. Betsy said nothing in return, determined though to go on her own freedom trail. She turned on her feet and walked away from her house and house-keeper. After hearing that old posh Scottish aristocrat's outburst, Betsy complained directly to Brett demanding both Alison's and Lady Hyde's contact numbers. She'd nearly bust a blood vessel, citing houses of correction for fallen deviants.

The utter shock of being lectured to, listened into, patronised and contradicted by a foreign stranger didn't sit well with her or her stomach and she'd refused food for a few days before becoming so incensed with fury during one stormy evening that she'd stomped loudly out of the house, not giving a damn whether she got soaked or not. It had been a strange freakish night, full of cracks everywhere as Maria had to retrieve her employer from a garden shed's small covered porch.

And then there'd been the letters, the angry lines sent to Brett demanding that Alison Mode be disciplined, fired, and struck off some care register. Maria had never seen her employer so animated but at least she'd been flushed out of a kind of depressive grief at long last. Betsy had then fallen into a strange prolonged period of silence and starvation for a few days after the Edinburgh epiphany moment but then incredibly and miraculously she'd become interested in food and the stuff of life beyond the closet. She began to hear voices and her conscience attacked her again and again, but it was a mental condition and state of mind that neither a happy pill or Maria could help her with. Her life of socially anaesthetised isolation, though comfortable and easy, was not conducive to happiness, growth or fulfilment.

Those two eccentric Scotch biddies must have cared enough about Brett and me to eavesdrop like that. I have to admit not many folks are that altruistic and daring, The World has become more savage, crowded and competitive, it reminds me of how I used to be all those years ago when I helped Ma and Pa and later Alfred out in the soup kitchens for the poor, unemployed and homeless.

Then one eventful day in late August, after suffering a minor panic attack in the front room and weeping over torn old photos of her married days, Betsy actually managed to leave the house and make the journey again down to the Mystic River just like she'd done all those years ago when that kind African-American man had seen some kind of terrible emotional blight in her and had given her a simple Samaritan lift home. She'd been wobbly on her feet at first, walking down the sidewalk out past the mail box and out down the street and Maria thought her employer might need to return to an emergency inhaler she kept in the washroom. *I'm gonna walk all the way down there to that darned river, Maria and make my ancestors proud of me again jist like my ma and pa would have wanted me to. I gotta be cleansed and wash my hands and life anew.*

Maria knew on some deep level that the river's waters would offer some kind of partial consolation and comfort or baptism but she also knew that Betsy would now never stop looking for something. Whether she'd find what was missing, a kind of happiness maybe or a lost noble cause was anybody's business. But Betsy had been sensible enough to take enough coinage for a bus in case she got bored of walking or it had gotten all too late. Maria had followed her discretely from a distance; a strong duty of care compelled her to do so.

On a whim Betsy bought a white tea shirt from a store seeing as it was so very hot that day. *Planet Boston People & Star Gazers Trust*, it said and it had got her thinking about the wider beauty of the cosmos, about the merits of seeing some greater picture than what was immediately before her. She'd bent down by the river edge in her tea shirt and had dabbed her forehead, uttering a kind of silent mantra and all the while those words she'd heard on the telephone kept flooding back from a few weeks previous. It had been an extraordinarily dark night of the soul, but it had shed some light on the too close a special relationship between herself and Brett.

Now my dear Grandmother Gribble, you little piece of grey lined dynamite you! This is the voice of your grandson's well-meaning Scottish guardian angel-carers tuning in with their humble but wise little penny's worth of kind good sense. Is it not a fair thing to say that we are all biased human beings to an extent? In that each of us follows our own self-interests first and foremost, this is no crime or sin. And yet each of us is also dependent whether we know it or like it or not.

She'd glanced up then at some houses near to the river bank and wondered if these same houses would be haplessly washed away if it rained hard enough for long enough and the water levels rose beyond control, flooding everything and sucking all and sundry out to the Atlantic. Of course that could be a real possibility even here in the US of A what with some folk talking about burning oil and driving cars. Maria often listened to the radio at night; Betsy could hear her even from upstairs behind the closet's sliding doors and news items quite often referred to claims, scares and inevitable denials over global warming and rising sea levels. Maria said, bringing up warm milk one night recently, that some people couldn't bear to face down badness or greed either within or without. She'd been shocked and moved greatly at the way people of colour had been neglected after Hurricane Erasmus, TV coverage hadn't edited out pictures of decimated homes and bloated floating carcasses.

If it isn't financial sharks preying on the poor then it would be real deal crocodiles gorging on the bodies of the world's flooded out poor, so help me remain calm in these coming cruel reckonings. She couldn't face taking a bus back though it *had* got late. Walking back down to the house she'd lived in for over forty years she recalled then her ma mentioning the Boston suffragettes. Betsy had always been a fighter, like her ma. Women had to be, whatever frontiers they were in. They had to work harder to get noticed and appreciated. How easy it was to forget small and large struggles for justice and respect, she mutters eyeing the unpacked grocery bags on the kitchen table with healthy interest. Maria's upstairs hoovering, even at this later hour. Maria's own son is hoping to go to Wallace College south of the Common next year so she's putting in the extra hours, practically living part time now at Betsy Gribble Senior's house. Working and grinding away it seemed for 24-hours, day and night, care work overdrive to pay for college fees.

For Maria's existence was also compromised and tenuous, she and her son were deemed 'poor' in the eyes of the US state but not sufficiently poor and talented enough to qualify for scholarships. Munching on a peanut butter-choc Hersheys, she considers again the pile of letters from son Brett. A small steady pile is growing on the carpet ever since he flew across the pond, documenting his trials, tribulations and clashes with professors over grades. *Was it even worth going to university or college nowadays though – knowing how scarce real jobs were everywhere never mind Micky Mouse ones. Having the bit of paper didn't mean as much as it used to, out there in the market place and money it seemed was now the new social class. And would she still need her hand gun in her final remaining years* she wondered, bedding herself down gingerly on a mattress outside the closet. She owned a rifle and a hand gun and had kept the revolver close by her just in case. You just never knew when you might need it. Never mind *three strikes and you're out*, it could just be one fatal steak out – freak out within the sanctity of one's hard earned home.

Then kiss goodbye to all you hold dear for it could be taken away instantly and savagely in just one moment beyond your control. And all because some chose or were desperate or ill enough to take laws into their own hands. But scars and trauma, be they psychological or geological could never be erased completely, she just didn't know if she could handle revisiting Ground Zero. That would be total melt down. It could be opening up a whole new Pandora's Box. Maria thought it a 'good thing' that Betsy had begun to befriend a neighbour's pet tortoise over the summer which had the audacity to scrape slowly beneath the dividing fence. *Little Alfred* she called him, feeding him fruit and carrots as she'd slowly faltered out into the back yard, gradually gaining confidence and not wanting any kind of assistance, whether this was Maria's or society's.

*

Fall leaves, rusty and gold, lie strewn across a misty Boston Common. Betsy Gribble, all five foot three of her, stood by the Parkman Bandstand. She'd been walking along The Freedom Trail in her bottle green velvet jacket, her multi-coloured, long, hand-knitted scarf she's had for donkeys' years and the same smart purple shoes she'd owned since the fifties. Good lasting friends they'd been those shoes, never letting her down when the only thing she could be sure of for years was the ground beneath her feet. Love, recessions, seasons, booms, money – they all came and went endlessly. It was just in the permanent and yet repeating nature of things. For some reason she finds herself thinking about the Scotch dwarf woman again, Brett had described how small a space she took up, too. Holy moly, what a dame *that* was making out like some Houdini-freak doing acrobatic rope tricks on Scottish roofs. Of course, she didn't believe this really weird shit about flying women with special powers. Brett must have made a mistake when he said there was no guttering or pipes to climb up.

There had to be a nearby roof they could jump from, right? Yet Brett said that he could recall hearing a loud thump, scrapings and semi deranged laughter above him just before the fateful transatlantic phone call. He'd put it down to folks staying in the landlady's flat. What were they anyway – self-help nuts or community pay-back avengers? The midget woman and her posh crackpot side kick used ropes and ladders not smoke and mirrors to get right up there on her grandson's apartment. Freaky deaky, now she'd seen it all. Maybe she really should make like Little Alfred right now and be hibernating too, back there in the clutches of the closet, isolated but alive of sorts.

She'd started out – pioneer like – from near Park Street station having sampled some fresh ground coffee and rocky road cookies at Marcos. *Are you excited about syrups*? The young Italian buck had asked, offering a bewildering range of powders and toppings. Too much choice! Just a plain old fashioned coffee she wanted – what happened to them over the last ten years? Then she'd taken a peek and a wander at Emerson College, having heard about the art exhibitions there. The campus had been an interesting experience, a magical mystery tour. Amazingly, nobody questioned her right to walk around the campus grounds, she wasn't issued with a dinky plastic visitor pass but the college security men drew the line at letting her enter the library. Normally she felt critical of liberal free self-expression because, frankly, one wasn't entirely free to say and behave as you like – it wasn't an indulgent free-for-all – and no matter what technology or advertising claimed to liberate – there were rules, obligations, costs, rights and property law. The way she saw it, being a plodding pragmatist formerly in business after all, was that financial and legal under currents carried more weight, value and influence than mere passing intellectual ideas, fashions, or the idea of any mystical and intangible flows of consciousness or altered states.

Abstract intellectual visions, though inspiring and no doubt noble in intention, had to be earthed in the here and now of messy reality. Brett's letters had been full of fire and Scottish brimstone when he'd first landed in Edinburgh, over there and over confident. His fascination with chasing mirage like words and arguments had irritated her puritan Republican heart, but he was her only grandson and she'd melted, learning to tolerate his quests for meaning and identity in a mad cruel world.

Law and money, aside from constituting new kinds of overarching global classes, were stealthily acquiring the spaces previously left for free-at-the-point-of-access religions. Having personally experienced horror, turbulence and loss and having seen growing permissiveness and the apparent emancipation of women, all political beliefs that now represented order, tradition and comforting authoritarianism felt like a blessed relief. That's why she'd mutated into being a Republican after a brief flirtation with the Democrats. *Hey missy, are you alive man?* The young black art student had said, offering her warm pastrami on rye couched as he was in a make shift student accommodation erected in a corner of one of the art spaces. About five or six tents had been put up around The Art Pieces and students were angry at cut backs to funding, courses and bursaries, increased workloads for lecturers and the bullying undemocratic diktat from the college management team. *A'int no sacred cows left anymore mam*, he'd said, saying his name was Warren and pointing to a paper maché multi coloured cow, its eyes wide open and terrorised by what the world had now become. *So come check out the whole city hip hop scene, I'm a part time master DJ* he'd grinned. As he was so friendly Betsy just sat down and ate with the students who just accepted her, no intrusive questions asked.

One girl wearing a tie dye artist's smock who couldn't have been more than twenty or so complimented Betsy on her shoes and she'd felt a teary warm flush of gratitude. *Had she been too harsh and set in her ways in that damned closet that she now couldn't really connect with another human being even though she may well have reservations or disagree?* For Christ's sake, she was an old lady now but the burning rage, grief and sorrow she'd felt for so long had extracted their price on her life. There was just nothing you could do about the existence of human frailties, you couldn't legislate away cruelty, deceit, arrogance, jealousy, evil or greed. *They would always occur, Betsy, no matter who was in power in The White House* she realised, feeling incredibly humbled and stupid at suddenly seeing the wider universal milieu and her own tiny anonymous yet significant role in it.

What had she been doing for all these years? Watering that awful plant of stasis and desolation until it had grown so huge and overpowering that it's sucking creepers threatened a kind of living death. Terrifying, phantasmagorical and many other words besides. It was painful to look at and acknowledge but she just couldn't spend any more time in closet re-hab. Life couldn't really reach you or touch you in there. The girl then said, dipping rye into a pot of humus, that she was taking a gap year out in Africa to work on an animal enclosure, helping to save elephants from ivory poachers by at least recording deaths and sightings. *I just have to DO something, you know in my life*, the girl said. *It's no good just passively hearing about awful disgusting things, moaning about your own life but not using your outrage and passion in some way,*

I *have* to do this, the girl said, because she'd been moved to furious tears at seeing the tusk-less, bloody carcasses of the innocent creatures that some say never forget. *Yeah I know, Betsy, the world is still run by men for profit and human life, stripped down to the basics now, is just a bunch of large avaricious alpha male monkeys carving up a big resource cake. You want an image? Well, being an art student that's how ugly it is. Next up with the carving knife is the arctic and everything in it,* the girl then said; saying her name was Melissa and that she was real sorry for dumping so much bitterness and negativity on Betsy but that she had grown tired of endless debate and political obfuscation and wished for the immediacy of action.

It's Hamlet's dilemma I guess Melissa said, but there has to be some doing *and* being in the end, in the final analysis. And Betsy had slowly stood back on to her world weary feet, smiling and nodding and making polite excuses about her Filipino home help who was probably stalking her from a distance in a kind caring way even as they spoke but that it was real interesting nevertheless hearing them talk and wishing them well with their studies and adventures. Walking wobbily away, her head in a spin, Betsy felt as if her thoughts were hobbling on the brink of madness, a cliff edge.

She'd practically stumbled onto the Boston Common again despite the encroaching mist. It was the oldest city park in the USA and it had been years since she'd last been there, recalling that she'd been married off in a church near the foot of Beacon Hill. Married off but not signed away for life, doomed to the darkest recesses of some mental closeting, if not to a real actual closet. *How are you keeping, Betsy? There's home coming apple pie waiting here for you. There's a Silverline bus at down town crossing. Maria.* A long text from Maria, showing that she cared when it mattered. Hearing the students talk had affected her deeply, maybe she really should now wear a placard and march up and down Washington Street and in the theatre district, screaming at people to wake up and engage in something. Maybe one front placard could say: who are you really? She passed the infamous spot where witches had been hung from a tree back in the seventeenth century feeling sickened and depressed by what had not changed in the human condition.

I am a caring conservative, that's what I am. Brett said that the Scotch dwarf carer woman, Alison what's her name, had been called a freak, a weirdo and a sorceress in abusive sinister terms in Scotland. Jeez and there Betsy was thinking this scapegoating and bullying just happened in the disunited states of America, past and present. Mudslinging, denigration and humiliation. She recalled watching the McCarthy TV trials of the 1950s, the red baiting which sometimes got aggressive and ungracious.

Always the same primitive fear and envy of the unknown different and threatening other, Brett had pontificated, citing necessary protective processes of 'othering' in both psychoanalytical and sociological theory. Yes, she knew it was a kind of contradiction in her, a paradox – her yearning for order, safety and stability yet her despising of the cowardice of some people who just slavishly conformed and followed crowds or herds no more than living papier mâché cows. Maybe it really was high time she weaned herself off her guns, she could hold her own in a man's world by defending the wild too. She had quite a bit stashed away in savings accounts and had never ventured beyond America, but maybe now, in her golden years, she could do a stint saving wild beasts on the African plains. She'd over heard some news item about the plight of elephants not long ago in fact as Maria had been ironing while she listened to the radio. Passing by the central burying grounds within the Common, Betsy realised she must take drastic action if she were not to throw her life away and become one of the living dead – all husk and mask but no tusk or teeth.

And then for some unknown reason she found herself being drawn, as if by some mysterious magnetic force, to Boston's Haymarket Square. It's bang on three o'clock in the afternoon and she's standing by some railings when she feels herself being pushed on to a wooden stool which appears out of nowhere, only to be pulled up through a hole in the overhanging mists. *Whooosh!* Up, up and away and she's clinging on to *The Sneezewood* stool for dear life in a kind of mortal ascension of a modern day grandmother.

Blink and you may miss it. Betsy Gribble had never ridden on an aeroplane and like a lot of Americans she'd never left the USA's shores, though she'd often been curious about the way other cultures operated. Quite where this piece of furniture is heading she wouldn't like to say but Maria's apple pie would sure get cold now. Some beady-eyed Boston residents stand transfixed on a nearby sidewalk, as they witness the elegantly dressed old lady pucker up her face as she gets sucked and larged up by some force so high and so ferocious that she soon disappears into clouds, her scarf preceding her like some exotic antennae. *Pucker up your face, then large it right up, pal.*

22

A.O.B – Anticipation of Other Business

In loving memory of uncle who loved sitting on this bench
It's not about what you've got
It's about what you keep
Dear uncle you never stopped believing

"What's your game plan then, Alison? Come on, I know you've got some secret card up your sleeve. Spit it out, better out than in. You say Brett Gribble's written to you a couple of times and even left a message saying Betsy Gribble seems to have turned some psychological corner back home in Boston. Well praise be and as you know I'm not a person who's organised religiously. Maybe we aren't so bad after all, huh Alison in the eyes of the yanks? You'll have to excuse me referring to the Gribbles as yanks – it's a generational thing I will admit. I meant to say Americans of course. It's probably too much to hope for though that either of them hasn't blown your freewheeling high chair antics all over social media sites let alone terrestrial neighbourhoods. It's a risk we took, huh? But maybe they still haven't figured out how we got onto that roof."

Alison stares off into space, considering the two letters and the text she'd got from Brett who, in the anxiety over his grandmother's welfare and her wild reported walkabouts, had focused less on his own bandage predicament and as a result had actually gotten through some of August with less dressings – though admittedly he'd not managed to fully face the sun's light as both his skin and emotions were way too raw. Lady Katherine and Alison are sitting on a bench in Seafield Cemetry and catching up with each other, if not trying to put the world to rights. In the most recent letter Brett said he felt as if he was peeling back layers of past parental bondage and he wasn't sure what would happen to him if he were to live with his skin fully exposed just yet. The doctors warned against it but the heat in the city had been too much so he'd partly removed some bandages from his legs and arms to allow breathing space. His major end of term exams had gone well but he couldn't quite believe that Betsy had finally left the walk in closet. He decided he'd stay in Edinburgh over the autumn, waiting until the new January term began but he really felt as if he and his grandma had benefitted in some mysterious way from being eaves dropped and intercepted.

"Look it's really about damage limitation I think at this point. If the world's media or even just Scotland's media were that up on my flying stool tricks and sticks and my knowledge of medicinal herbs they'd have beaten a path to my humble door by now. And Brett knows my postal address if he'd have been that freaked by anything. I suspect his own heid has been full of anxiety about getting through the exams and his ongoing skin condition. That and his grandma will have eaten up his entire head space. Most likely he's not stopped to think about how we got up there or technically how we gate crashed his conversation. *Pucker and large bowl of Scottish raspberries my posh pal* – why on earth do I have to be a talented magician, a modern day suffragist of the light and philosopher plus dwarf animal lover? My burdens over whelm me yet somehow I must multi task. Katherine, I see it as my lot in life to confront, overcome and expose evil – I cannot be a wump not after what happened to my poor mither. I accept that the capacity for evil exists in all humans but passive observation and tolerance is not enough for me sometimes. Not when it comes to bullying, killing, abuse, deceit, greed, squalor and arrogance. Evil and injustice prospers and grows like some diseased mushroom whenever enough people do nothing. And here I stand, all three foot six inches of me, a politician's delight in that I'm taking on more than my fair share of personal responsibility aren't I? This newly evolved voracious world which spins on the ever faster consumption of oil, technology, nature, and the cheap labour of women. But *Subucus Subucni*, the trick is not let the savage inhuman forces suck you dry leaving you a mere shell. Know your limit and your limitations but still do what you can, eh? Doing nothing is not an option."

Lady Katherine Hyde is looking very dapper in tweeds, jodhpurs and green wellington boots as both she and Alison sit drinking tepid coffee on the bench – coffee on the go au naturel. They've also come to pay their joint respects to Barbara Mode, catch up and plan and maybe pick a few wild blackberries. Wild garlic grew in the cemetery's grounds, Alison might suggest they pick some together to fortify the blood and strengthen resolve. Lady Hyde suspected her friend was planning something daring and admired her greatly for it. Alison Mode is a walking living example of a kind of *maximin* principle – maximise your assets, virtues and qualities for greatest effect but at least possible personal cost.

And she'd been shocked and disgusted, like Flora, Mac, and no doubt half of Edinburgh and The World by the anonymous postings of bloody photographs on *Flatter,* graphic in their depictions of Sinclair's animal slaughter and suffering. Alison, not being an Internet user at all, had found out by proxy via her friend and couldn't escape the lurid photograph in the newspaper.

So incensed and concerned was Lady Hyde that she'd been worried about the psychological effects on both Alison and the MacIntyres. But no amount of polite persuasion it seemed could encourage her small friend to engage with or utilise *shemail*, *Flatter* or even *AGOG* a new overseas based search engine accused in the media, that other two faced Janus, of being the puppets of several national security forces. Being a bit of an organic philosopher herself, she's used to her friend's existential explorations.

But despite her social class and privilege Lady Katherine was ashamed to see how many of her former social circles lived behind their very own veils of ignorance about the very human fall out and hardship endured by large chunks of the population. Hear no evil; see no evil or injustice, defend the status quo as at least it *appears* stable. Before sitting down they'd walked and talked for a while visiting Barbara's grave. Chrysanthemums were Barbara Mode's favourite flower Lady Hyde had discovered and so she'd bought a magnificent bunch to be placed as a mark of respect. It's a fine mellow day in early October, full of golden sunshine and warm mists rising from piles of sodden leaves.

Give it another month or so and this mist, given the right conditions, could turn to a kind of return of the 1950s toxic smog as Edinburgh, like many other UK cities continued to have an intense but bitter love affair with cars and driving. Some kinds of atmospheric conditions seemed to exacerbate toxic fumes. Seafield Cemetery is near sewage works and the Firth of Forth; Lady Hyde had travelled along Salamander Street to get here, concerned to be with her friend at her hour of need. *Salamander faith in true friends in the namesake street*, she'd quipped, ever witty even in times of dire straits. Alison had allowed Lady Hyde to say as little or as much as she felt comfortable with in regard to Lord Hyde.

It seemed they were on speaking terms but that he now had serious doubts about over reliance on chemicals in farming – so much so that he'd quit the parliamentary cross party committee he'd sat on but had done so gracefully without mudslinging. He was deeply and totally ashamed about his behaviour and managed to text her to offer the word *sorry,* which in Britain usefully serves as a catch all-save your pigs' ear-bacon politics with face and grace platitude. But without actually saying so directly it seemed to Alison that her friend cared more for her husband now, from a safely discovered distance that was, than maybe she ever did. Lady Hyde believed in calling a spade a spade after all – wherever possible that is – and she respected him more now that he re-joined the rest of humanity who spent a lot of their lives actually living in places of uncertainty, doubt, and frailty.

And this despite the looming presence of technology and economospeak which was no more able to know, predict or guarantee the future than mere humble mortals. When dealing coherently with unknown forces of darkness one needed careful plans and loyal friends. Poor Spock has constipation so Alison had the bright idea to feed him mint which she knew grew wild in some parts of the cemetery, so alongside visiting the grave they were on a surreptitious mint and wild black berry chase too while they were catching up on news and plans.

Alison had mentioned the extraordinary seventeenth century ring one of the magpies had dropped as if on purpose, on the pathway to the McGhee's house. 1638. Surely the date was another kind of message from Domain 2, otherwise known as another person's consciousness even if 'dead'; for the incredible thing about Domains 2 and 3 Alison was realising was that dead people could send mail, information and noise though the time and space of Domain 3 just like the living could. Though she hated the analogy, she was coming to the conclusion that maybe the universe was another kind of all prevailing computer in which knowledge once thought or expressed in information remained forever 'encoded' in the elements, in the stratosphere – to be transmitted, received or remembered by the living and the dead. Lady Katherine had likewise been intrigued by the ring and its possible meaning. It would appear that both time and consciousness could be spliced like a tape recording. She'd put the ring away in a jewellery box, reluctant to report it to any authority though it looked like it was made of real silver and certainly felt heavy enough. *Three for a girl,* the saying went and Alison felt she was being given some kind of message. There were three magpies that had pretty much circled and re-visited the McGhee's house all the time she'd worked there, a couple of times she'd spotted all three sitting in a tree in their front garden.

It had been a scary kind of aftershock to realise that the birds had actually been watching her. *But which girl and why the coin and that date? And why this girl anyway?* Maybe it was all just a happy coincidence but she wasnae sure. For one thing she'd not heard her mother's voice on or from another Domain during this particular visit to the cemetery and Alison concluded that this was because the mystical thinning of the layer between the living and the departed was only porous and truly mediumistic when there was a full or new moon. It had taken her a while, several decades in fact, but she'd come to this conclusion or rather she felt she'd been directed to and shown this conclusion.

Lady Hyde pours herself another cup of coffee in the flask's cup. It will get dark soon, they've been talking away intensely on the bench for some time engrossed in catch up – so much so that neither of them have really read and digested the poignant engraving inscribed behind them to some dead anonymous uncle who apparently never stopped believing. Who was he when he was alive? They'd never know now for he was one of the vast armies of dead and alive worker ants who, it turned out, were far more effective at processing information than the ubiquitous presence of any Internet search engine.

It wasn't intentional neglect or callousness that made them unaware of the inscribed dedication, though these qualities did seem all prevalent nowadays in the two very different worlds the two friends originally came from. No, it was just the sheer intensity and extraordinary developments of their lives that stopped them from noticing what it was they were sitting on let alone any 'squeezed middle' space between them both. A kind of time and energy poverty crisis or *life over engagement fatigue*, a close relation of compassion fatigue.

After all, it's not every day that ordinary subjects-citizens get to fly on weird and wonderful objects and tune into transatlantic phone conversations – normally this is the preserve and unquestioned right of national security forces across the globe. And this right also often abused and exploited alongside all the other types of misuse, frauds and deceits that were visibly and invisibly polluting and corroding the whole moral, financial and natural fabric of the world from dodgy accounting, tax avoidance to asset stripping, political manipulation of stats and that old predictable safe favourite, benefit fraud.

A chill breeze descends on Seafield Cemetery then, shaking the still developing conkers on old chestnut trees but not blasting away the terrible contagious sickness in the world. So far Alison had got through the year with no coughs or sneezes but Lady Hyde's nose is sounding suspiciously blocked. Looking at her friend-in-arms now, Alison hopes she'll be fit enough for the task she has in mind. She's on the brink of spilling the beans she calculates, noting with irony the brand name on the plush plastic bag Lady Katherine's used to carry a foil-wrapped picnic for them both in. *BEG, the finest Angora knitwear in the world.* And all this stylish and prudent eco- self-sufficiency from a member of the landed aristocracy who volunteered at a homeless drop in centre.

"You'll not be needing to collect any more *Twilight Dew* then, Alison, on this visit then? No doubt your supplies are in order. Maybe you'll need some dew to deal with your new colleagues at *The Harbours* though, huh? You say you're to begin working there next week, a private care home rather than just a private home. You sure you can deal with this Alison? I mean the awful association with your mother and all. Do call if it all gets too much. But I guess you know when you are ready.

Let me know how you get on won't you – if I can help you deal somehow with that piece of scum Sinclair please let me know Alison or I'll never forgive you really I won't. Have a roll, please do. I packed the lunch especially. Your good name is spreading across the city you know. Never mind *Flatter* or *AGOG*, we can deal with those if it gets really nasty. You say you got sent a birthday card and cake from The Wipers via *Help Is At Hand*. How nice that they must have remembered from you mentioning it to them way back in January. Hope you are enjoying the mirror I gave you too?"

"Yes, very much so thanks. It looks like it's an antique but not quite as old as the coin I found. And yes, Katherine, I do feel in some strange way that the magpie that dropped the coin was some kind of a spirit messenger from some known and yet unknown Domain – though the more logical, rational part of my mind is still, would you believe after many decades of moon gazing, incredulous and disbelieving. There's lots happening right now on many life levels – I'll be starting work at a care home called *The Harbours* in Marchmont next week and I'm a bit nervous and shy as who knows what the staff or cared for are actually like, eh? It's a risk you always take. So hopefully no alternative truth drug like *Twilight Dew* will be needed but never say never. Did I mention that Flora's nearly got the shop refurbished completely now, she and Mac are having to stay over in a B&B along London Road near Meadowbank stadium?

But I'm still wary Katherine, very uneasy like, as long as that arse wipe Sinclair is at large. I've got plans and I'll text you or ring you about that. Speaking of texts, I don't think I told you either about the totally bizarre three-page text I got from Noel, a former client telling me that French lover Laurence has returned to the fold and that the two of them are building a ginormous concrete statue of me in their front garden in artistic protest at the lack of statues of influential women in Edinburgh. They've got as far as the big toe of the left foot but were unable to continue without me sending over my body measurements.

Strange but true but I'm still afraid Katherine, terrified actually if I'm honest, as though our House of Commons stunt didnae leak out on a large scale – I still sense that knives could be out for you or I. You say Lord Edward, to avoid embarrassment and to save his political reputation, didn't tell many about what happened. Well, maybe – but hacks and journos are just great at sniffing out any whiff of scandal and given the level of hostility and abuse levelled at any female who dares to challenge power and archetypes I'm just doubly frightened right now."

The two friends nod at each other in quiet mutual understanding as they walk away from the bench with the inscription. A light drizzle appears from the sky, if not out of the blue then out of the grey. Autumn in Old Reekie had really begun, the nights were gradually starting to draw in the Western hemisphere but to what exactly Alison didnae like to think. They would never know *who* the uncle was and what it was exactly that gave him the tenacious capacity to believe but maybe there had been a less populated, busy and pressurised time when people really did have the time to connect with the dead or living – if only just imaginatively.

Both Lord and Lady Hyde were literary, well-educated and super bright but it did seem to Lady Katherine at least that E.M. Forster's famous call to 'only connect' with others was no longer an innocent simple task when American and English state apparatus was so actively participating in prying into these daily connections people made with each other all over the world. And that wasnae even accounting for the added connections – empowering, dubious or sinister that the growth of social media facilitated. Was the world 'just connecting' for its own sake on the latest app, phone, website, and device?

Lady Katherine was one of an old dying out gentle species called One Nation Conservatives who didn't believe in vilifying the NHS or casting the state as some parasitic wasteful entity stifling private finance or initiative – but even she was horrified at how cheap opinions, connections and sound bites had become. And not only this – the active encouragement to connect by nation states and private companies as a kind of tacky, placatory and distracting compensation prize for face to face relating, robbing the tax payer's purse, keeping the poor poor and the ultra-rich living in another transnational paper free glad rag land of the tax free-*blog-o'haven.*

Opinions and status updates were cheap but they did little to change deeply entrenched socio-economic conditions – that was one thing technology couldn't, interestingly enough, shift despite claims of efficiency and information as power. But then, just where power and freedom really resided these days was itself nebulous for both seemed overly controlled yet accountable to none so that it would be very hard for an individual to know who ultimately they could sue.

Perhaps democracy itself was just another illusion or chimera making impossible, unsustainable and untrue claims about safety, justice and stability. Only earlier that day Lady Katherine Hyde had read of a real life story on the uber powerful International Global News and Views Informational conglomerate website or *IGNVI* which featured lone pioneer American, a Mr. Jake Showdown former CIA intelligence agent who had dared to tell the world's citizen-subjects all about how unfree they really were in the free West. The world had become a dangerous, unequal, secretive, corrupt, snooping place where freedom, let alone responsible freedom of expression was increasingly forbidden in the establishment's relentless defence of unwinnable wars on terror and capital. A mad world indeed both friends had actually privately thought, sure that there must be billions of others who had at some point in their lives, thought exactly the same thing. *IGNVI.* Even the media conglomerate's letters conjured up some Imperial Neo Roman World Empire which brutally enforced savage campaigns of divide and conquer while appearing to inform. Both Lady Katherine and Alison doubted whether politicians, states or the church could really counter the new omnipresent corporate global elite. Indeed, both women had noticed language schools in Edinburgh now offering a new elusive language set for those in the know alongside the bog standard usual: *Corporate Edwardian.*

They part company then, glad to have shared and aired views, experiences and sandwiches the tried, tested and trusted way. Very soon Alison will resort to wearing her exotic looking Eastern headdress again, she'd taken a wee break from wearing it throughout September after the whole Brett Gribble's chimney affair as it had become majorly greasy but on reflection maybe she *was* going through a mini process of projective identification in that she understood, to a degree, what it was like to get emotionally attached to a piece of material that acted as a type of clothing. Okay, so she didnae feel or have the need to cover big chunks of her body with bandages but still, a potentially seditious headdress that looked different and foreign had at times caused Alison to attract further suspicion and hostility. As if female dwarfs should be silently gracious and mild mannered, grateful to have any kind of a job at all thank you very much.

And that was still the Edwardian ideal of femininity which still lingered oppressively in the UK, despite being given the vote. *You're asking for it aren't you? Think you're somebody special do you, who do you think you are, the Queen of Fucking Sheba – Has Bins?* had all been thrown at her as another form of snide denigrating, mocking and rubbishing.

Now a sustained campaign of nasty blighty might have pushed a person over the edge or on to pills as it was surely designed to do but Alison clung tenaciously on to Spock, on to the memory of her mother's love and on to her own self-belief, sure in the knowledge that her mother's death had not been in vain and that at least she had some kind of deep purpose in her life, the care of others. Barbara Mode had been carefully watching the entire conversation on the bench hovering as she was in the atmosphere and proud of her courageous only daughter's friendship with an equally brave member of the aristocracy – so an unlikely a two – but Barbara hadn't the heart to highlight the different ends of society the friends actually came from.

For in doing so the priceless hard-earned qualities of trust, integrity and understanding – another kind of fuel that lubricated and held together the underlying fabric of social capital – those tenuous threads so often decimated and under threat everywhere – could be irreparably damaged in the intolerant and inflammatory times Barbara was seeing. And this balanced wisdom and reason from the dead but so often not demonstrated by the living. One had to start somewhere after all; pragmatically speaking you had to start from where you were at and hope that honest shared intentions would by definition create common ideals and goals. And to have some kind of faith or belief in *something* – if not in a political party or religious creed as such – then in an overarching vision of the common good – this was what the world badly needed both friends had concluded, ironically way before meeting each other.

*

The caterpillar wriggles across the desk in an agonisingly slow fashion, perhaps it's heading for a peace lily plant which Ruth O'Connor, Manageress of *The Harbours* private care home, has placed in a saucer. Alison sits across from her now, the imposing desk signalling another vast power divide employee and employer. She's a woman in her mid-fifties who's worked hard all her life, the many professional certificates and diplomas which cover the wall behind her are testament to this. *It's a green one but a rather late in the year* Alison thinks, watching the caterpillar on its journey and wondering if this forth coming late metamorphosis is yet another indicator of a warmed unstable climate. A tasteful gold carriage clock sits and ticks loudly on a mantel piece which is behind Ms. O'Connor's desk. On the right of the desk there's a glass paper weight with what looks like a miniature model of Calton Hill and the Observatory.

Eyeing Alison's headdress with a look of mild bemusement, Ms. O'Connor looks at the printed out covering letter and CV that Evelina at the agency office had emailed over. The natural light in this ground floor office is not great but still Alison can discern Edwardian looking wall paper with large curling leaves and a rather magnificent monkey tree through a window to the right of the mantelpiece.

"Ms. Mode, an unusual name it seems. Look, this isn't an interview, you are already hired as you know and you start work today please. I'm happy with your references but I have to say I am curious. I like to get to know the people I'm working with seeing as you'll be here. Your SVQ and work history seem in order though I am noticing a few gaps in your employment history prior to you training as a carer. I'm satisfied that you have the necessary skills and you have glowing recommendations from former clients in Edinburgh but I'm wondering what the reasons are for the quite big gaps in your work record prior to training. You seem to have had a series of casual jobs after leaving school. Could you elaborate?"

Alison tries to avoid glaring at Ruth, choosing also to ignore the patronising tone. *You have to work with this one somehow, try not to be intimidated and see the better side of Ms. O'Connor's nature if you can. She must have some positive qualities somewhere.*

"Well actually Ms. O' Connor or Ruth if I can call you that as I too like to know who I'm dealing with – I don't quite know how to phrase this but I do believe in being candid and honest wherever possible. My mother died in pretty dubious circumstances and I had a kind of nervous breakdown due to grief. Okay I'll just say it out clearly: I got stuck in depression for years. Doing magic tricks and making others happy made me happy, it was one way out but. I'm not on anti-depressants and never was. Nor do I have 'mental health issues'. I didn't feel able to work for quite a while nor did I want to work or be around other people. It took me a long time to get over the loss of my mother. It's not an exaggeration to say that my esteem and confidence was decimated. On top of this I endured awful bullying at school. It's not something I share with everybody and I trust what I have shared with you will not travel beyond these walls. You say you have five residents here, two of them male. I think I met Fred Branch in the hallway just now. It's good you have a balance of men and women I must say."

A slight smirt of rain has started up outside, silvery drops fall from the monkey tree's primeval looking branches. First day at *The Harbours* for another six months, maybe longer, and it's now mid-October. The nature of contract work. All Saints Eve in two weeks, a night when the dead rose again and spoke to those who could hear. Earlier it had been clear skied and sunny but then the cloud had moved in unexpectedly changing the atmosphere. But then Edinburgh, apart from being a city of many different classes of gutters and minds, was also a city of ever changing lights.

"That's right. Fred is very friendly. A bit too friendly sometimes shall we say with the girls but he's okay. I put it down to years of not getting his end away. As if libido stops conveniently at fifty for people, huh? Well, I appreciate your honesty Alison about your loss and depression. A lot of people don't like to talk about such things, yet they are widespread. You are very forthright and should get along with the other staff fine in this respect. You'll need humour, that's for sure. This is just a clocking in chat I guess. Here's a locker key and timetable. You're starting off upstairs with Karen."

Ruth O' Connor hands her a pair of keys and laminated schedule. Alison's just about to leave the back office but is stopped in her tracks. The expression is arch but perhaps not completely unsympathetic.

"You are a trained up magician as well, your CV says. Well, a few card tricks might be appreciated by the residents."

A half smile almost reaches Ruth's mouth but dies a death, never quite making it. Alison hated cruel archetypes that stifled men *or* women in fact but Ruth O' Connor was beginning to resemble that other stock character, the one of the older, uptight matriarch. She didn't like herself for having this thought, perhaps she'd be proved wrong about the management style. *Still, at least she'd not been openly hostile* Alison thinks, walking up *The Harbour's* stairs. The care home, once a private home, is a real tasteful slice of *Edwardiana*, replete with original ceiling mouldings. Frighteningly, she'd again heard a man's coughing and a voice in her flat a few days ago and not only that but the enigmatic sixteenth century coin she'd found at the McGhee's had been taken out from a jewellery box that belonged to her mother. It had been left provocatively on the coffee table in the front room and when Alison saw it she knew it couldn't have been placed there by herself.

She'd never walked in her sleep in her life; she'd always dealt with worries and stress in other ways, even as a girl. Seeing it on the glass topped coffee table was a real slap in the face yet somebody or somet*hing,* some bodiless entity had surely moved it. For it seemed the thoughts of the dead must still have electrical power in some way for they could impact on objects and be accessed by some living minds. And it was not long after seeing the moved coin that Alison had heard what sounded like a young woman speaking in an archaic tongue.

Three for a girl. It sounded like olde worlde Scottish but the man's voice had certainly been Sinclair, no question. She'd used garlic, chants, the *Kwik Stix* and bowls of water to drive the bodiless entities out but who knows when they'd return? *Pucker and large it right away, pal.* These ethereal visitors didnae make an appointment with you or usually leave some calling card when they dropped in. And Sinclair was somewhere at large still, the stakes had been upped, his very presence in the city spelled danger for Alison and maybe a disappearance or a death. It was always in the back of her mind, lurking like some corrosive dis-ease.

Throughout the cosy introductory chat with Ruth, there'd been the sounds of loud conversations going on upstairs peculating through the ceiling. Fred Branch, randy English World War Two veteran is having his back scrubbed by staff member Michelle. The chat is rude and salty but Alison's knows better than to just to steam in uninvited. On the way to the home, before the rain had arrived, she'd walked up Leith Walk, trailing behind this pretty young woman who'd been wearing high heeled gold shoes and a leather skirt that left nothing to the imagination. A better class of hooker maybe but who really knew at the end of the day. A huge rotating advertising screen had beamed continual high resolution images of products and services, including rather surreally, a vast image of a pizza complete with pineapple, apple, mozzarella and apricot chunks and enticing customers to 'woman up' and eat some pizza. Alison wondered what the 'man up' version looked like.

And at the top of The Walk, she'd passed by a sculpture of an outstretched hand with palm facing upwards, it was unclear whether it was begging in submission, grabbing at something or assuming some religious attitude of humility and acceptance. Maybe a bit of all three jostling and interchanging positions got you accepted but you just had to keep moving on in this life, just picking your way forward no matter what the challenge. Then walking through the Old Town she'd admired the agility of a large seagull, gracefully stepping up old steps with webbed orange feet.

Glancing behind her, she'd had another fearful moment when she became convinced she was being stalked by a man she'd seen before in *Squeaky Kleen.* She was sure she'd seen him a few times over the years when Sinclair had come round to collect rent at her old flat near the waterfront. Davey. *That* was his name, she recalled. Sinclair's wee sidekick for a number of years. Michelle calls her for assistance in lifting Fred out the bath then so her flow of thought is temporarily interrupted.

The Quibblon Song of Wrong

The so called politics of envy
That lazy turgid old excuse
Designed to enrage, drive into a frenzy
So true divides remain obtuse.

And the day and night time robbers
Well versed in nick-strip tricks
Always give the same people an extra clobber
So to those wee expendables, great pin pricks.

Oh, to be more like proportional politics of the fair
Less savage to those further down
Seeing value in acts of reasoned share
In city, village and in town.

Quibblon Alternative Dictionary.

***n.* Corporate Edwardian Empire.**

Also known, somewhat ironically, as CEE. Ironic and paradoxical term because a) a lot of people don't appear to want to see just how truly Edwardian the divides now are between the rich and poor and b) the contrast between the rigid archaic lack of social mobility and the hyper mobility and fluidity of corporate credit and capital more widely helps to create a kind of schizoid sense of reality in which the rhetoric of politicians and the media becomes more and more estranged from actual lived lives. Mind the gap. Evidently, some kinds of freedoms are valued more highly than others. Observe the growth of two distinct new classes mirroring societal trends: the precariat and the commentariat.

Adj. **Trickle Down Effect.** Can also refer to demonstrated behaviours of elected representatives, Captains of Industry and such like in that just as it is true that *some* created wealth does drip down reaching the masses, so it is also true that the behaviours of the elite and influential also trickles down, quite often setting terrible hypocritical examples. As above, so below.

23

Across and Backwards

"Flora, if you stand over there near Spock's hutch you'll just make him nervous and I can see he's twitching a fair bit already poor old chap. In fairness he probably knows you better than me, that's if guinea pigs can remember faces *or* smells. Maybe standing over there in that corner by the window would be better. We've still got enough candlelight for about two hours I think so we should be fine. Let's just both keep our eyes peeled on the clock, it's coming up for quarter to eight and Alison said she'd ring once she gets there. At about ten to eight I think we should move out into the hall just to prepare, okay? I take it you've got the coat hangers then from the wardrobe. She said metal conductors help the mind to conduct, having a single point of concentration and all that to focus on in a busy noisy world.

Lucky Edward can't see me now, huh Flora? Or indeed my London set or my staff from the estate. They'd think her Ladyship bonkers, though for some time now Edward has shown mild interest in Eastern meditation. He'd read an article about its uses in healthcare in the FT. Oh, and by the way I'm sure I'm not as sophisticated and clever as Alison's no doubt described me. She's such a generous soul and brings out the best in people, don't you think, yo?"

A creesie looking Spock runs riot around Alison Mode's front room on some mad trail of crackers. A few hours ago, he'd thrown a massive guinea pig raj refusing to leave his hutch and eyeing the three assembled women cautiously. Alison left about an hour and a half ago, leaving Flora and Lady Katherine to take care of operations at this end. It's dark; they've had a wee tipple in nervous anxiety not sure if the forth coming thought experiment will work. *The Sneezwood's* been placed underneath the ventilation hatch in the hall, both women will need to have their metal coat hangers at the ready. Sprigs of lucky white heather adorn the hall's floor. *To focus your thoughts* Alison had said to them, winking as she left.

Trust me, it should work if we all say the mantra, do the same task and visualise. The combined powers of three synchronised minds was at stake, Alison had given both her friends a talk and lesson on the Domains and her discoveries earlier that day over lunch and they'd been willing to try in the name of a good cause. Flora tries not to laugh out loud at Lady Katherine's Edinburgh posh version of L.A rap street talk which still sprinkled her speech. The holiday in Shetland had been helpful in providing a brief respite from the horrors of what happened to the shop.

Conveniently, it was the evil English down south who'd always excelled in the arts of violent plunder, slavery and profit. And now the potentially savage forces of globalisation had not spared Scotland either, no nation great or small was completely immune from the neoliberal ubiquitous double edged city lights, planted in Edinburgh's streets, parks and squares, blinding and yet exposing, reifying the winners and spotlighting the scummy weak losers – pitting all against each other in open arenas so that actually smiling at someone, daring to offer something with no thought for getting anything in return had now become a socially revolutionary act. But at least *online* Flora and Mac could both share some of their real life story with a few select identified friends round the world. *Flatter* could be useful if used sparingly. Here Mac managed to open up a bit more emotionally; it was safer for some, it seemed, to express themselves from a distance when the other person couldnae see your face or what you may be hiding. That said, neither Flora or Mac were happy or comfortable about offering up their *entire* life story and history for global inspection and consumption, the beauty of *Flatter* was that you could dip in when and how you chose to; with no pressure from the Internet provider, one didnae have to compete conspicuously with endless status updates. The Macintyres used their account sparingly, with discretion and privacy which was why it was so shocking to see the way Sinclair had misused the same software in the act of some warped idea that some may wish to see pictures of dead animals.

And the acts of consumption, whether visual or economic, had reached new absurd intensified levels, never mind the male lazy gaze, the world was now over gazed upon by both men and women alike. *Full stop.* And that was just one disturbing modern day phenomena, had large sections of the world's population become addicted to passive gazing and observation only, frightened, pacified and too seduced to fight for or believe in anything anymore beyond the comfort of one's own home? They'd received the insurance payment in full for the damage to the shop which was rightly due to them for having the entire place re-furbished. It had been indescribably difficult and traumatic burying all those decapitated animals – everything from rabbits, mice, guinea pigs, kittens, fish and even a puppy.

Awful. Gruelling. Not exactly character building, for the Macintyres were already kind, honest and hardworking but their story, like many other every day lived tales of the gutter never reached the press. And those often overused adjectives, exploited ruthlessly by politicos with their own high moral ground agendas that invariably failed to first consider the genders delivering the woman-ifestos. Because politics of course, whether sexual or geo-political, has also always been about what's not discussed as well as what is. And maybe that was a good thing as there was certainly enough hysteria, hot air and moral outrage knocking around anyway never mind the daily reproduction of this by the shadowy media with sometimes mixed intentions. Small doses of true-isms and reality were not seditious and therefore were allowed by mainstream media.

Some of Sinclair's victims had clearly had their heads bitten straight off – but it had been horrific finding a bloodied knife which must have been utilised. He hadn't hung about then clearly after taking the photos as they'd been uploaded on to *Flatter* just a day later. Cocky or just plain stupid? Maybe he'd framed a pal by uploading from a different computer, anticipating a possible police investigation. Mac had tried to persuade Flora to report it on top of the killing and vandalism but as it happened another city resident had and the offending computer couldnae be traced. Then, after a week the photos were taken down by someone but the damage had been done.

Sinclair had really wanted to reach, hurt and undermine Alison through her best friend, killing if not two lady-birds with one stone, then killing them off psychologically and spiritually. Tar, feather, slur, slander. Attack property, the actual person or their reputation, undermine credibility. Slash, burn, and consume everything as quickly as possible for gratification or profit: whole rain forests, pristine ice wilderness, someone's mental or physical health, somebody's job or livelihood. This kind of predatory, selfish and narcisstic behaviour was rife.

"Why on earth did I have to start up my own business with my husband, Katherine? First there was the long wait for the trams which nearly went *do-ally tap* and had us going fairly *pealy wally* what with the hype and scare stories. As if the costs of running a business and surviving in the current climate weren't high and risky enough but I guess there's anticipated risk and then the unexpected. Some things you cannae predict, there is the unknown factor after all and maybe it's not even called X. Maybe just go back to working in a broken biscuit factory outlet for ten pence an hour. Sorry, must be the whisky talking. You say you have the mobile on? Good. But I think it's going to be hard to focus on the task in hand with Spock running around! Let's round him up quickly if we can."

*

Alison walks along the Grassmarket, by the seedy strip clubs and the antiquarian book shops. Thankfully there's no sign on the pavements of any congealed fat extracted from sewers as there was in London. Now *that* sight was just as awe inspiring as seeing Barbara's ghostly hand write out of thin air. It's dark, a bit windy and rainy but the Haymarket area will be well lit. The Kwik Stix's' in her duffle jacket pocket, she can feel it almost tingling with the electricity she'd directed to it. Use the power of the synchronised place names. *Haymarket.* She's deep in thought, wondering if the brain's Domains or modes of consciousness could be co-ordinated successfully.

The momentary suspension of the phenomena and experience called 'reality'. Thought or a frame of mind which might be termed oceanic or attuned, the induced blurring of boundaries between self and other, the living and dead. So far she'd not tested the speed with which the three modes of consciousness could be tapped, sure she'd sent clients thoughts and suggestions on the airwaves via Domain III but how quickly could Grandma Gribble be reached across the pond?

More to the point, would the good lady be able to receive the three messages at once and be sufficiently open to allow herself to be tele transported? Her receptivity to them would determine both sender and receiver's ability to then move the lady and *The Sneezewood* to Boston using Domain III. *Oi, hen. Show us yer wee fanny then. You'll not be needing a big broom handle? You an Arab sympathiser then. What's under neath the headdress? Fucking Jewish freak.* Ignoring the wolf whistles, abuse and dog yelps of the passing patrons, she turns into a small metro supermarket feeling hungry. Seven thirty pm. Last night she'd had another weird dream that she'd been playing chess again with Brett Gribble on this huge chess board which was also a tiled floor. Though Brett's bandages were off, both of them were inexplicably turned into life sized wooden pawns at the sound of a woman's shriek. The shriek was followed by childlike sobbing. Waking in the early hours, Alison discovered an unknown hairpin on her pillow. Wandering round the supermarket aisles, she hoped Flora and Katherine were seeing eye-to-eye and that Spock was behaving himself better than the human louts outside.

She'd often heard women complaining about the behaviour of some men, but she'd also seen women haranguing and being lewd and aggressive to both men and women. Sometimes it wasnae always obvious that the leering innuendo actually meant you were genuinely liked, respected or desired. The Brits it seemed liked to insult and denigrate, it was easier than expressing your vulnerability, your care or your real self. *The State Held To Ransom* (by greedy opportunist benefit claimants, illegal immigrants and reactionary pressure groups), *Abolish the State* (it's too costly for taxpayers), *The State Is Watching* (so watch yourself, your freedom is being infringed upon), *Look at the State of Her* (thank goodness we have Royal representatives of our proud nation who epitomise decency and grace.)

The varied headlines and soundbite stories in the newspaper section never changed and revealed ongoing ambivalences about the entity called 'state'- and indeed any institution or person perceived as dependent – paradoxes which perhaps could never be maturely resolved as there was too much vested interest in the commercial selling of papers and accompanying mudslinging. The art of saying nothing really new, the industry of regurgitation only. *The State Is Watching* story though detailed the rise of super conglomerate search engine *AGOG* which was rapidly swallowing up other competing search engines in a bid for global domination of information flows. A public demonstration was planned in the city in two weeks, further details to be announced. Swallowing the last of a sandwich,

Alison stands stock still in front of the Haymarket train station in the midst of commuters. It had been hard keeping this a secret from Brett who was just too clever for his own good. She'd worried for some time that Brett would sabotage or spoil the experiment and so far it seemed he remained ignorant in this department. Alison had not heard from him for over a month. People rushing past her are so engrossed in their own lives; they don't really notice the small figure standing in the wind and rain. Somewhere behind the dense cloud is a full moon.

Wood Sneeze,
Born of trees
Set this lady free
We command thee!

Oh white lucky power
Of the heather flower
Reach high
To help Grandma Gribble fly!

"Katherine, I'm feeling something, I'm sure of it! A slight tingling in the spine and in the fingers. The coat hanger's getting warm. Wait a minute! Gosheronee, Katherine look. *The Sneezewood's* wobbling. It's rocking now quite violently. Open your eyes!"

Lady Katherine and Flora stand stock still in the hall, coat hangers in hand full of breathy anticipation. They'd doused the entire hall floor with flour as well, needing the power of white in this very domestic war they were fighting. Full moon tonight, chosen specifically. Strong magnetic beams, conducive to movement. Let the men of the world build their monstrous databases and horrific weapons, here the ladies were fighting back giving the special relationship between the UK and the USA new added ingredients. After in depth consultation between the three women, when the dismal closeted years had become shared knowledge, they'd decided it would do Betsy

Gribble no end of good to see how other folk lived and to take a trip of a lifetime.

For before trying to save Africa's last remaining elephants, it was becoming clear that Grandma Gribble's faith and vitality needed saving first and they'd heard enough via Brett to know that the elderly lady's fighting pioneer spirit needed re-kindling. Or else what was life worth living for? They knew she'd relish a new life challenge. Spock in the end had to be blackmailed with chocolate biscuits in order to prize him into the hutch as the special hour drew near. Flora is unable to contain her excitement or keep her eyes shut through the uttered mantra. But Lady Katherine refuses to open her eyes fearing the magic will be broken if she does so and wanting to see this whole damn experiment through, no matter what.

"Flora, you were quite clearly asked to observe the rules set down by Alison and I think it jolly rotten of you not to play ball now, now at our neediest hour, in this shared process. Buck up girl. Or should I say *yo sister.* A lot of the homeless people I work with slide into transatlantic slang. Courage and duty under fire and all that."

Flora is shamed into submission and just as she shuts her eyes a tremendous cracking, rushing and roaring sound can be heard as the hall's air vent's cover is blown off and *The Sneezewood* is sucked up into some unknown orbit. Tense moments pass, then, a stupendous crash and loud coughing. The two ladies stare in rapt amazement at the dust covered pint sized woman in front of them who is standing defiant on *The Sneezewood.*

"Say, could someone please tell me jist where the hell I am?"

Betsy Gribble unwinds her long knitted scarf from her neck, her face and clothes flecked with dust and sea water. The scarf's gotten a bit damp and clingy in the journey.

"Why Betsy Gribble I do believe. How *awfully* nice to meet you at long last. Splendid. Welcome to Edinburgh and

Scotland. We've heard so much about you, all very good commendable and marvellous things too. You've spoken to my pal here Alison Mode briefly after *that* conversation of course. Good to see you arrived safely. I suppose you'll be wanting some tea then?"

*

"You actually live in this pile all by yourself? I guess you really must be true blue British blood, sorry old Scottish blood. Whoops – I know Scotch identity is a sensitive issue right now. I'm actually very sympathetic – who doesn't want more independence anyhow. Anyway, you've sold me the idea of teletransportation and maybe telepathy too. My ride over here was incredible, a couple of points mid Atlantic I almost lost my grip on the stool, but it was all over very quickly. Fast as the speed of travelling light. Are these what you call scones, I'm eating right now? Great. So tell me more about this Sinclair guy and how I can help you. You know I'm still stunned and amazed by what's happened don't you? It's taking everything I've got not to call Brett and Maria up right now."

Lady Katherine, Alison and Flora are sitting down to evening tea with welcome guest Betsy Gribble in Number 38 India Street's drawing room.

"And how is your grandson doing with his studies? I do hope he's not quite so enthralled by late night chat rooms as he used to be. It's a growing social problem you know – Internet addiction. Edward, my part time house husband currently not in residence, tells me there's some kind of parliamentary inquiry going on into levels of excessive use and its effects on health – another round of misspent money spent on research which to most people is just common sense. And quite how you restrain or restrict the use of technology is impossible – the call of the libertines is too strong.

I'm all for freedom of expression – but not at any cost. I do email sparingly but can't be doing with social media sites at all. It's all too quick and instant gratification for me; I've always valued things which grow naturally over time, the tried and trusted. And yes, they're home baked scones you are tucking into, courtesy of my home help. Do help yourself to some raspberry jam; they're made from the finest estate raspberries. In fact, Neesha's just returned with her husband from a weekend of picking and freezing them. She's a multi-talented wonder. I'm lucky to have her as a staff member."

Alison notices the way Lady Katherine avoids using the actual word 'servant', as if changing the noun somehow either glorifies or denies the continued existence of such jobs. The old British Empire had gone sure enough, only to be replaced by a covert new one. She wonders what Betsy makes of it all but then recalls that she has a Filipino home help back in Boston. *And I'm just another of this new unnamed global class of unsung low paid female carers and domestics, we are everywhere irrespective of skin colour or geography,* she thinks with some irony, biting into a sandwich, acutely aware of how absurd and cruel all these hierarchies and facades are which obscured and distorted real human connections, vision and understanding as badly as any archetype. Nevertheless, it's still odd to see a modern Pakistani servant in blue jeans and white pinafore – an unsettling mix of centuries. Katherine, Flora, Alison and Betsy Gribble are sitting comfortably on floral covered sofas surrounded by richly embroidered curtains and eighteenth century plaster mouldings. Spock's skulking around for scraps near the armchair Alison sits in as he'd been packed earlier into a cat basket and bought along to this indoor picnic as an honoured guest. Luckily Neesha had not screamed at the sight of him as he'd run up and down the steps at number 38, causing much hilarity and much needed laughter.

The last few days have been a mini whirlwind of sightseeing around Edinburgh right enough. Betsy particularly enjoyed the Botanic Gardens and the views from Arthur's Seat and last night, deducing how much

Betsy Gribble liked and needed star gazing after so many years hidden away in darkness, Lady Katherine had given Betsy a fine Victorian brass telescope which had been in the family for about a hundred years. They'd visited the refurbished *Creatures of Habit* store and Betsy had heard and shared the horrors of 911, massacre of the innocents, the power of the focused mind, the *Quibblon*, the three mind-time-space Domains and Sinclair's bullying reign of terror and abuse.

Alison had stopped short, no pun intended, at telling Betsy about the old coin dated 1638 as she felt this extra bit of the extra ordinary might be a bit much at this stage, even for a seasoned veteran pioneer like Betsy. Her flying visit must be kept a secret from Brett who couldnae be trusted not to blurt about it on the Internet. The cross Atlantic journey on the stool in the twinkling of three pairs of ladies' eyes and the amazing tales of what her new found Scottish friends had gotten up to in Edinburgh and London was enough for now, the significance of the coin and its date would become apparent tomorrow when they'd try experiment part two. On a lighter note, Betsy's taken a firm liking to Spock and to all of them and it was as if she'd had crammed ten years of life in two or three days. A new joyful glow burned in her eyes and cheeks.

"You say Brett's taken off some of his bandages in the last few weeks and actually managed to venture outdoors a bit. I'm so glad, that must have taken real courage. Is it a genuine skin allergy to light or do you think it's partly psychological? I know that before I met and married Mac I often panicked about going out at all, I easily got overwhelmed as it's sensory overload these days. And I never would have had the courage to start up a business by myself.

Now of course it's the opposite, I'm the more outgoing talkative one! It's interesting isn't it that Brett should make these changes just as he's hearing more about you daring to venture out more. Facing your fears really will set you free, if not suddenly then gradually, it really is true. But I take it

Alison's explained why we felt we needed to 'call' you, long distance wave so to speak, not only because we thought you'd relish the challenge and needed a new experience but also because we weren't sure if three brains would be enough for what we have in mind."

Alison winks at Flora then, warning her not to say anything more for fear of scaring Betsy. But it's way too late for that, the cat's slipped out the proverbial bag. Outside, October strengthens its chilly grip on the city, hinting at what's to come.

"And what is it exactly that you have in mind, you crazy Scotch ladies? If you want me to smoke a line of dope or go perform summersaults in public I'm afraid I'm just not up for it. Is it anything real unsafe? I'm hoping it isn't because I'm sure beginning to regret not bringing my rifle."

And then, realising that Betsy would find out soon anyway, Alison changes her tack.

"Time travel, Betsy. That's what we have in mind. Summoning Sinclair just the way we called on you only to send him back to where he belongs. Don't ask me why as I don't know it all yet. It's as if Sinclair's missing from this earlier time for some reason, as if he has to go back to fulfil some unknown purpose. You see I think I've been given some kind of message from someone in the past I've not yet met. A cry for help if you like and as you probably know by now, and these two certainly do, I have felt for some time now an over powering desire for justice in defence of the innocent and vulnerable."

*

William Sinclair Junior hasn't felt this light headed and weightless since he got stoned soon after he came over from the Kingdom, a Fife settler to Edinburgh come to carve out his grisly reputation. Lunatic, moonatic. Incredible, really. How time passes. He'd walked and stalked round the city's streets, knife in pocket trying to get a job, a roof over his head. People had looked at him as though he were a mad or desperate convict it and it infuriated him. The deep grudge was born then, burnt into his skin and psyche like a cattle branding. Shaving his hair off was a habit he'd acquired around then as a way of refusing to completely fit in. *But look at me now* he felt like saying, *I'm far cleverer and grittier than a lot of you.*

Edinburgh could be a closed but pretty city, shut off to outsiders, well defended against foreign invaders and opportunists – people who were different or threatening. His fight for respectful acceptance had been a long one, won in blood, bullying, fucking over and extortion. Now down through the floor his mind travels, through the shag pile rug and where the mind goes the body surely can sometimes follow. He's dimly aware of the moonbeam on his face and a familiar picture on the wall in the half-light but then all goes black.

The thought occurs to him that he's having some kind of near death experience or that maybe he's experiencing a weird out of body adventure – just without the drugs. He'd seen a TV programme once on near death experiences or NDEs as they were known as and people described seeing a white light or figures in white beckoning them on, whispering messages of support at pivotal life moments. Unconscious patients undergoing critical surgery at hospital recounted detailed conversations held between medical operating staff as if the mind and consciousness did exist beyond the mere physical brain.

Now there's a kind of curious hissing and rushing sound past his ears and he's aware of moving horizontally through the chilly night sky over roof tops away from Leith and towards the New Town and all the while the insidious whisperings of female voices can be heard. Now he knew what it felt like to be sucked up, helpless into some kind of powerful vacuum as for years he'd sucked spiders and insects of all sorts into the hoover when doing housework, unable to tolerate even the mildest form of crawling irritation. *Domain one and Domain three, send him back in hist-or-y! Kwik Stix, kwik hook, but first please send us this evil crook.*

An almighty, violent thud and female shrieks follow, and Sinclair finds himself forcefully pushed down on to that bloody dwarf's stool he's coveted secretly for so long, *The Sneezewood.* He's sitting upright as if amidst some private inquisition, surrounded by four peering curious women. Blinking rapidly, Sinclair takes in the cream and pink coloured period eighteenth century room. A bright side lamp has been adjusted so that its beams capture the exact spot where he now sits. *How the Christ did he get here? Is this his day of final reckoning? Chintz hell fire maybe*. He notices the tarts knickers curtains at the windows, he bets the classy fannies are highly buttered up here alright. His legs feel horribly numb, as if it would be dangerous to stand up or walk out or even give any of these ladies a good kicking. Recognising Alison Mode and her friend Flora from the pet shop job massacre, he shifts slightly on the hard wood of the stool – but quite who the other two ladies are he hasnae a clue. Both are elderly, one is chewing gum and wears a long knitted colourful scarf, the other looks posh in pearls, twinset and pinz nez glasses. *What a bunch of odd bods,* and Alison in her customary urban turban. *Women should never have gained the right to vote. Give them a bit of independence and look what happens to them.*

"Alison, you weren't over staring at the lampshade during that last mantra were you? It's creaking ominously. It's a family heir loom, worth *silly money.* Yes, I know the expression is revealing and I can't take the damn thing with me when I leave this earth but I do hope to leave the house and estate is suitable conditions for future generations. And from what you've told me the staff at *The Assembly Rooms* in George Street are still recovering from your experiments with their chandelier last winter. Lucky I'm insured. Quickly, Betsy! He's regaining his balance and bearings. He's making a lunge for freedom!"

Lady Katherine Hyde sprinkles some *Twilight Dew* into Sinclair's face, momentarily startling him while Betsy Gribble, brave woman of many frontiers, tackles Sinclair by throwing herself at him, binding his legs to *The Sneezewood* with Flora's help using her very long scarf. It's taken years to trap and snare him, Alison's sure not going to let him go now and looking closely at his face she resists a strong urge to spit at him.

"Take that you jerk ball and total waste of space! Heard all about you from my Scotch friends here and little Alison Mode who may be small physically but morally she towers over you. Chuck some more of that water at him Katherine – it might just get him to confess and own up in a rare moment of grace. Has been known."

Betsy Gribble may be over eighty but there's still strength and steely guts in her, she knows a bad thing when she sees one. She holds Sinclair's writhing legs still as Alison issues her ultimatum.

"Sinclair, you are a complete git and total misery guts who causes nothing but fear and rage. You bullied me for years, accusing me of owing you money when I don't. And the beatings you gave me and no doubt others let alone the extortion rents and savagery inflicted on those animals which happened to be Flora's livelihood … I really don't know what motivates you but your reign in this life is over. We have decided that you really don't belong here at all and seeing as murder isnae really an option for us we are going to send you where you belong."

And with these transforming words Alison waves the *Kwik Stix* and flicks a few drops of the collected precious dew in his face knowing that it, along with the repeated mantras and the combined power of group directed thought, will make Sinclair more receptive and pliable to being permanently transported through Domain III. *Pucker him up completely, this total sucker. Pucker and suck him large up right away white thought power, send forever and a day. Domain one, we have just begun. Domain two, we attune to you. And so, waning power of the mystical moon, let's be rid of this cruel buffoon!"*

And so it was for the third time that fateful day that the once seemingly omnipotent William Sinclair Junior feels himself mysteriously sucked and lifted through time and space, back, back to some great as yet unknown. For we still don't know what time and consciousness really are and how these relate to space within or without. His current reign of terror over however, who knows what he must now face. For is there recycled karma and the debt and lessons of souls to be paid and learned? We have been asking ourselves what 'soul consciousness' is anyway for thousands of years and maybe now more than ever it might be possible for humans as a species to consider their fellow humans as more than just consumers or just a demographic group with more or less buying power in the market. But how to persuade people of this other form of value, equally as important? But neither profit nor well-being is what these firm friends are thinking about just now. No, these four women from very different backgrounds all believed firmly that there is more to life than meets the eye and at the end of the day, it is surely the power of true belief that often surpasses mere fact or intellectual theory.

Something as intangible as faith and will can really move mountains, the apathetic, cynical and uncaring, whole chandeliers and sometimes whole human bodies let alone bodies of knowledge. Sinclair's floating around now in a place and space full of particles, thought waves and infinite light, where science meets art, and past meets present and future in some eternal suspension along with clouds and brave daring sea birds. The feeling of being so free and yet at the mercy of something greater than his mere little self terrifies him, the 'going with the flow' of the universe's energies a new humbling experience.

Alarmed, he glances down at his heavy bother boots only to see them mutate slowly before his very eyes into some earlier unrecognisable form of footwear – boots that are obviously strips of skin sewn crudely together forming a very different kind of servitude. Those old boots! He'd worn them for years, stomping up and down on old landlord city playgrounds, up and down his familiar haunts, building reputations. Once past master to most, now servant to some, he's again deposited roughly on what looks and smells like a large pile of pig shit.

24

1638

Harvest grips the land like English Protestant doctrine holds the hot unwilling souls of free thinking Scots who try to believe and worship their own way. She's been raking the hay in all day in the intense heat, at lunch there was ale, a hunk of bread and luxury of luxuries, a small piece of salted fish. Herring. Carted up from Newhaven. Mary Urquhart's a hard worker and she stops to look at the neat piles to be fed to pigs and cows or baked into bread. The sky's pure blue is dotted with the sound and sight of whistling swifts, swooping and swirling around the cropped stubble and haystacks of the fields. In the distance, mirage like, lies the shimmering big house with its grand newly built brick chimneys. Despite political and religious chaos, some family crests and wealth were still respected in these parts imbuing some form of stability, employment. An inherited and fought for right to rule over lands still intact and unquestioned, though the divine claims and right of Kings to feed and control the minds of the masses a liberty too far for many.

He'd left her at it for hours, out on the far edge of the Wauchope estate and farmlands, promising to return at lunch, hopefully not drunk this time. But Rum Tum Butler had traipsed soberly over the rich brown soil of Niddrie fields in his new dyed pig skin boots bypassing the mill to bring her some sustenance. He'd had the boots made for him from the pigs he regularly feeds and slaughters for Sir John Wauchope. Mary's white cotton cap is sodden through, testament to the honest sweat of her brow. Eating the simple lunch, she'd dreamt of the next time she could steal a turn at that fine ivory chess set that lived behind the carved wooden screen in the great hall of mirrors. Bishop's move, check mate. She'd played herself well; to date nobody had spied out her little servant secret. If she could but invent a move or rule herself it would keep her mind occupied, she might be respected and leave a recognised mark on a history. For the creation and recording of history, including religious testament and the reading of books seemed to Mary to be yet another elite game played by wealthy men. The rebellious idea turned endlessly in her mind.

Despite the fecund tranquillity of village life there is talk and speculation over violent reform everywhere, Mary heard there were recent riots in the town centre with people hung as disloyal traitors to the English crown. Protestants, Catholics, covenanters. Always these questions of faith, independence, identity. News had swept through the countryside and villages surrounding Edinburgh like some unstoppable plague. But if it was not religious deviancy that cost you your life these days then it was female difference, sexual independence or even owning a form of knowledge.

There was a frightening day last week when they'd ridden into town to stock up on supplies of sugar, salt and spices from a merchant's house in the Old Town. Butler and two other servants had left her briefly in the cart's front seat attending to the horses when a beggar started screaming at her, accusing her of putting a spell on his family worn down with the pox. Soon a small crowd gathered round the cart, she'd used her wits to gracefully answer charges, saying that being a serving dwarf or living alone without a husband did not mean she was a devil's daughter who had less right to live than any other creature. *No, I do not go to church or have improper relations with men. I do not own a cat but my employer and his staff can vouch for my steady trustworthiness and thrift.* She'd handed the demanding beggar a smile and some sweet meats and this seemed to appease his hysteria.

But she had been much afeared, well aware that women were strung up quite regularly in some kind of purging anxious whim, accused of witchcraft, of upsetting apple carts, daring to question and just not fitting in and being 'normal'. The sun turns red-gold in the late afternoon; soon Rum Tum will lead the small parade of carts on the daily round up of hay and servants working in the estate's other fields. *Enjoy the riches of the outdoors while you can Mary* she says to herself, allowing her eyes to shut for a brief rest.

Soon her duties will be house bound enough, attending to laundry, embroidery, mending and plucking again at shot pheasants, deer and pigeons until hands became sore and numb. For hundreds of years the surrounding woods and fields had supplied earlier occupants of similar houses with plenty of game and rabbits, Rum Tum Butler had even had one little hoolit and two rabbits stuffed, copying the Wauchopes who hung stuffed hunted stag and deer heads over doorways in the house to remind themselves to be grateful and humble both in victory and abundance.

*

Knight's move, pawn's move. Then a counter attack from a white castle maybe and it could be whites to win. Move the pieces with stealth, undetected. The game could be over in another ten moves or so, all a matter of probabilities not certainties. Was the sly playing of chess, uninvited, really the playing at above one's station in life? Sitting behind the ornately carved screen in Niddrie House's great hall of mirrors, Mary Urquhart dares to drink some water from a metal goblet that's been left out from last night's revelries and dances. She'd been working at the big house since last year, starting just after it had been built. She was an orphan dwarf born just outside the city and discovered in a Lothian field but taken in and nursed despite her being an ugly foundling baby. Nobody knew who her parents were, nobody claimed her. She'd been spawned however and grew up the best way she could on a farm, forever mindful and then later looking for work with plenty of domestic maid experience, she'd said and Sir John Wauchope and his wife took pity on her, being charitable nobility. But Rum Tum Butler, with his small gold earring and clipped pirate like beard, so nicknamed because of his rumoured smuggling of rum and his liking for smoking clay pipes, rich foods, rough language and women, was not to be trifled with, the other servants warned.

Stand your ground with him and he'll not bother you. The trouble was of course that, being a little person, Mary Urquhart didn't have as much ground space to occupy as Rum and besides he was the kind of man she could see that didn't appreciate being answered back to. She'd seen him scowl at other maids who were tart back with him. The servant quarters were up at the very top of the house, up a separate stone stairway.

Last winter though, in some horrible test of grit, Rum Tum Butler, Mary's immediate superior, left a moulding of a frozen ice hand in the ice house when she'd been asked to fetch ices for creamed fruits. He'd watched her walking through the bare woodland trees in her hooded red embroidered cloak and laughed at her as she shrieked in horror thinking it was some spirit come to avenge her. Then this spring he'd shocked her again by openly urinating on her Ladyship's roses. *You tell anyone, dwarf, and I'll have you skinned alive like a rebel,* he'd leered. Some of the other maids said he used whores in the underground rum taverns around Niddry Street in town. The hall's striking black and white tiles reminded Mary of a giant chess set used by people far richer and taller than her and the entire hall is mounted with rectangular gilt framed mirrors, which further puffed up illusions of height, status and beauty sometimes where there maybe were none Mary thought, watching as she had the elaborate ritualised fan waving and flirting that had gone on by massed candlelight.

In such settings people could watch themselves and others master and flounder at the arts of appearing to say something knowledgeable, a vanity hall of mirrors that you could easily lose a sense of yourself in if you were susceptible. Last night she'd sneaked behind the screen and saw the ladies' courtly voulez vous wooden shoes encrusted with velvet and jewels, flashing tantalisingly along with powdered bosoms and ample ringlets. Hide and seek-peek.

There had been dancing, jesting, conversation, live music and much drinking of wine. Finishing the chess for today, her feet take her around the hall, delicately picking out the tiles. *One tile forward in any direction then one tile diagonal, in any direction* bloody brilliant. *Dwarf's Move.* That's what she'd call it. In time maybe she could share her very own invention. It was compatible with other established pieces and their moves too, it could really work. Her reverie of wonder is rudely shattered.

"Prithee what are ye doing with yerself now Mary Urquhart? You are nothing but pocket sized mischief me thinks. The other day you complain of a mob turning on you in town, a likely story. Then yesterday I catch you tarrying on and day dreaming and falling asleep while gathering hay – and now you have the nerve to stand stock still in the middle of the hall of mirrors, almost as if you are playing at life sized chess. Hardly an appropriate pastime for a mere servant don't you think? Ah, I see. You really have been taking liberties with this chess set. Trying to be a bit clever were we? I'm not sure I like that. You'd better watch yerself or I'll be telling Lord John or her Ladyship about this. My word against yours."

Thirty reflections of a drunk Rum Butler swaggering about in the hall of mirrors would be enough to frighten anyone and wee canny Mary Urquhart sweats as she realises her secret chess playing habit has been discovered. It is late in the evening, their graces have retired to bed and the hall is dimly lit. Shadows flicker ominously in the hall as his voice echoes. Her only real pleasure along with sewing and gazing at a particularly old statuesque fir tree which stood in the house grounds. That and being oddly drawn to metal objects. She swore the gently swaying tree almost whispered to her when she'd first arrived at Niddrie House, warning her to watch her tongue. What could she now do? She could say a silent prayer but where was God when evil looks you in the face? She wasnae sure she believed in the same sense that many were supposed to anyway; she kept her beliefs private.

But it was hardly as if she'd been caught stealing something was it? Growing up in green fields outside Edinburgh she remembered as a child seeing farm workers and labourers humiliated and screwed into village stocks for crimes such as stealing sheep or making a girl pregnant, but if the authorities discovered *reported* theft on the other hand then these offenses could mean a flogging, hanging or forced labour. Brave him out, Mary thinks. Maybe he's full of bravado. And for pity's sake don't tell him she's just invented a new chess player and accompanying move: *dwarf's move*. It could revolutionise chess and open it up. The man would just mock you relentlessly. It's not a female's place to think, let alone a small unmanly servant.

"I'm just figuring out the next move when I play chess with myself Rum Butler. I hardly think it offensive or strange that I find pleasures in such things, there are worse acts of sedition and disobedience. It keeps me busy. Prithee don't go telling tales to Lord Wauchope or her ladyship will you? Their good opinion means a lot to me."

Mary Urquhart instantly regrets saying these last words, but they'd just poured out of her in fear. Now Rum Butler knew she was really rattled. Moving too close to her, he whispers an obscenity in her ear making her jump and almost enough to deave her ears. Then he walks off with a glazed look in his eye and it's only then that she notices an odd, irritating pain on her arm and discovers a cattle tick sucking at her blood.

The cries of the corbies and wild jackdaws in the surrounding fields and woods could be heard well before the house bell summoned the servants to their daily morning duties. Further off, in still denser forests, some servants said they'd glimpsed a grey lone wolf and wild boar sniffing out truffles, mushrooms and new territory. Nine servants piled down the stone steps to take a meal and drink in the basement kitchen. They clutter down, their faces half clarty and in need of a wash. Sitting around the table in the August light are the maids, cooks, blacksmith and stable staff. Rum Butler sits at the head, clattering his metal dish and speaking in a low serious tone for dramatic emphasis. Even in the summer months, oats and water were eaten. Another week or so and all the hay will be in, they have enlisted the help of men from a local village who were keen for free food and seasonal work.

"*Someone*, I cannae say *who* exactly as I dinnae know yet, let the pigs out overnight and I woke this morning at just past five to discover a load of them munching through the kitchen garden vegetables, their snouts right down into the roots and earth. All that work that cook and Elizabeth put into watering, growing, and tending. To no avail. The gate to their enclosure had been left open deliberately. I spent over an hour rounding them up safely, but not after cranking out my old weary bones completely. Worse than this, a few of them have trampled on and eaten her Ladyship's flowers. Whoever did this awful horrific thing will be found out, what idea possessed them I just don't know. Now we all know the rightful time honoured laws of pannage in Scotland and allowing pigs to roam and forage freely for acorns and nuts and such like on common land but this is taking liberties and the consequences will be severe. Cook or Elizabeth, did you hear nothing last night or this morning? It's a mystery to me."

The servants sit mutely shaking their heads in silent wonder. Who ever heard of such a thing? Some sitting round the table suspected Rum Butler and his good companion drink to be the culprits but fear makes cowards of a lot of people. Mary thinks it wise to say nothing, managing to avoid eye contact. *He's trying to cast me and blame me, just wait and see,* a little voice in her head said. *He wants to be rid of me here, surely but I just cannot prove it. He'll start up a little nasty gossip mongering and whispers amongst the staff.*

Slowly, the breakfast plates are cleared and put away and Mary, walking out into the pig enclosure felt a sick feeling overcome her as she heard the tread of someone behind her. Though it's cool now, she senses the immanent heat. Opening the gate, she glances back along on the short path but she saw nobody. But as she entered the smelly shed full of squealing hungry pigs, she felt his presence and turning round quickly to ask why Rum was following her she was silenced by him grabbing her throat. He fumbles in his pocket and produces a knife which he slices quickly across her neck.

Feeling dizzy and overcome poor Mary Urquhart fell where she stood, knowing she was dying. *Pig in a poke, you filthy pig in a poke that's all you ever were dwarf witch! Unnatural and not fit for this earth,* he snarls, poking her dying body with a cattle prod. *Oh would someone please hear my silent death throes of agony and pain, if not now then sometime in the future? Somebody help me please. Avenge my cruel murder, some sympathetic like soul who can hear,* thinks Mary Urquhart. *Dree yer ain weird.* He drags her limp body across the shed floor, stamping his feet to ward off the pigs who, given half a chance, would eat her flesh even though they'd gotten to know her and sensed her gentle spirit. Lifting her up, Rum Butler bundles her on to a shelf. Later, when it's safe and dark he will burn the body and then bury her. He begins to concoct the story of her confession, guilt and subsequent disappearance in readiness for the inevitable questions. Tossing grain and seed out to the running pigs who have been let out into their enclosure, he marvels at how easy human butchery is.

Quibblon-Scottish

Dree yer ain weird, adage. Forge your own destiny, create your own fate. Use of metal conductors optional in this process.

25

The Harbours

Fred, an elderly resident of *The Harbours* care home in Edinburgh's Marchmont, loves dookin' apples at this time of year. All Souls night, start of late autumn proper. Piles of moist leaves have accumulated outside in streets, parks. Bob in straight away, sink your teeth in. Think like a tank. He'd seen service in North Africa during the war and still has an eye for the ladies, though not for starchy Manageress Ruth O'Connor who had only agreed to the revelries on condition that all five residents didn't stay up too late. Alison Mode, newest staff member, has got Spock and the *Kwik Stix* hidden up her sleeves; she's planning to treat the residents to some fun juggling acts with her furry sidekick. It'd been a task and a half smuggling both into the house using her bag as Spock had wriggled around a bit, struggling to get at air holes. But Ruth clocked off duty quite early in the evening, and Alison, having foreknowledge of this, had been prepared.

For pucker and large it right up, pal – the residents are mega depressed in this care home but they've not sneered or stared at me because of my height or my headdress. On the contrary the residents have just accepted me, grateful for help and the company. What an attitude of gratitude. She was counting on nobody blowing her cover over Spock; she'd try some receptive empathetic magic. If nobody actually saw her wave the *Kwik Stix* or say a mantra, then really it was just Spock that could be reported. This is what Alison thinks, helping Stewart, another wheelchair bound resident, to his fair share of the fruity game. Earlier Fred's false teeth had plopped out into the water, an unsettling sight. Stewart communicates with the aid of a device which looks like a typewriter on his lap, *a speak-a-metre,* Alison had joked to a stony faced Ruth. *What's yer problem hen?* She'd felt like saying to her but didn't.

Two weeks into the job, maybe she's trying too hard to impress and be liked. Purely as a precaution, she'd sprinkled very light amounts of cinnamon powder and twilight dew in various corners of the building, sending silent thought blessings to all who lived and worked there, hoping that her arrival at *The Harbours* might signal a new dignified approach taken to the acts of care, both given and received. She hoped the dew drops would facilitate the residents feeling less afraid to voice their needs and feelings and Ruth being a bit less of a possessive control freak. Something was missing from Ruth's carefully ordered life, but her façade, like the house itself, looked impressive enough.

It's another full moon this evening, time for new beginnings. In his time Fred claimed he'd seen the underside of several African moons, he knew its magnetic disorientating effects on the animals and people who lived on the plains. Hyenas barked and stared manically, lions were unable to hunt and tribe shamen refrained from hocus pocus knowing these nights were rife with the dead's activities. And his mentioning of that continent got Alison thinking about Grandma Betsy Gribble's immanent trip to Kenya to protect last remaining wild elephants from being shot at. She'd called shortly after flying successfully back to Boston on *The Sneezewood* but once landing over there in Betsy's home, the three Scottish friends encountered great difficulty summoning the pesky stubborn stool back again to Alison's flat. It took everything Grandma Gribble had to keep her visit to Edinburgh a secret from a curious Brett.

But then horrors! The truth had spilt out somehow in a phone conversation between them and now Brett had only gone and posted pictures of his adventurous grandma, various stools and a life-like drawing of Alison Mode on a social networking site – *Flatte*r – attracting huge numbers of devoted followers keen to know what #User Brett_Underscore1990's former carer actually looked like. And only two days ago Flora had called too, letting Alison know that there was now a price bidding war over obtaining photographs of the famously courageous Edinburgh dwarf carer called Alison Mode. Thankfully there were no hungry hordes, media or otherwise, lurking around with cameras, with never ending insatiable appetites for 'real' celebrity.

Brett knew Alison's home address but hopefully he wouldn't stoop that low would he? Nevertheless, Alison spoke to Brett asking him to please not release any further information which he promised he'd stick to, wrapped up as he now was – not so much in bandages these days but as a new fully fledged *Child of Liberty* founder member and campaigner, devoted to organising pressure group protest sit in occupations over the corrupt relationship between state security forces and the commercial search engine *AGOG*.

Apparently, three students had been suspended from university because they'd dared to question an *AGOG* executive who'd been lecturing on the impartiality of the Internet. *There'll be protests in the next few days in central Edinburgh*, Flora warned, leaving Alison wondering how on earth Brett thought alleged state intrusion was too much whilst still thinking it entirely okay to privately post revealing images and text of another individual whose permission he'd not sought. And besides all these musings, there was of course, the crème de la crème recent event of Sinclair being sent back to where Alison guessed he belonged – to fulfil or relive something. She wondered if Davey, Sinclair's side kick, would have realised that something was wrong by now. She'd always been a believer in past lives, knowing that human consciousness lives on. *But I guess I also have these contradictions in me, I resent labels and archetypes but I capitalise on them to survive* she reflected, juggling four oranges in the air.

"Wow, where did you learn to juggle like that, Alison? Can you handle five or six oranges, do you think? Don't try with eggs, though, in case of accidents. We'd never get stains out of carpets."

Alice, a resident who was a retired barrister in her time is singularly impressed by Alison's nous.

"Alice, I'm sure you'll get a chance to have a go at the apples after Fred's stopped his daffin' about. Karen, be careful he doesn't start to grope you what with all that fruity punch down him. We sneaked some mulled wine in with Big Marg's help."

Michelle, one of the young care staff at *The Harbours* along with Karen, tries to reassure Alice. Orange paper lanterns swing slightly on the large monkey tree in the back garden. Though it's not cold it's slightly breezy and glancing out through the Edwardian back window, Alison thinks it's fine flying conditions for the living or dead. Eerie. Big bowls of nuts, satsumas, sausage rolls and smiling pumpkins have been placed on a table, the residents wear party hats – another rebellious act not agreed to by Ruth. Last night Grandma Gribble had called again to just say how much she'd enjoyed the visit and 'the Scottish experiment'. But Sinclair's final come-uppance in the world and through Domains – both literally and metaphorically – that had been the highlight of recent events.

"Alison, my God! Is that a guinea pig that just poked its nose out from your sleeve? You'd bloody better be careful about smells and droppings-doo dars as Ruth will go mad. As it is she can just about tolerate the neighbour's tabby popping to say hello and get a dish of milk."

Spock dives out of Alison's sleeve and runs around the dookin' bowl which has been placed on a small table, delighting the residents though Alice's bookish cleverness means she rarely loses composure. This winds Fred up a lot in who is more the practical retired man of action rather than a woman of the mind. *Go on you meanies, give the poor blighter a bit of apple* Fred says, roaring with laughter, his speech a little slurred due to the Halloween punch. Michelle quickly moves to shut the kitchen door as she knows Big Marg, cook at *The Harbours*, will scream the place down if she catches sight of Spock. Having done this, a sudden doubtful look sweeps across her face and reaching behind one of the full length front room curtains she pulls out an artist's sketch pad which had been discretely leaning against a wall and shows it to Alison. It's a skilful drawing done with pastels on black paper. In the centre of what looks like woodland is a small enigmatic figure in a red hooded cloak.

"I didnae like to say anything to you before Alison 'case I gave you a fleg right enough. My aunt's a bit tapped you know, she hears and sees spirits and is a bit clairvoyant. I mentioned you'd started work at *The Harbours* and how much I admired the fact that you insisted upon being treated like any other member of staff though you are a dwarf. Kathleen, that's my aunt, said just the other day that she'd read something about you and flying stools on *Flatter*. *I have a message for this woman, Michelle I'm sure of it as these last couple of days I have seen this figure walking around Hunter's Hall Park across the road. I'm not sure but I think this person I have been seeing is also a little person.* I swear that's what my aunt Kathleen said. She lives out in Niddrie and would like to give you a reading."

The evening's festivities are disrupted by the unexpected arrival of Ruth who is silently furious at the pandemonium before her. Alice is feeding Spock a bit of an orange that Alison had been juggling with, while Fred, Stewart and Rose giggle and joke away, pished as three deranged human bats. Big Marg told Alison later that Ruth had actually been spying on them through a small high set window in the front room.

*

The demonstration against the shady relationship between the government and *AGOG* had reached almost frenzied proportions by St. Giles Cathedral in the Royal Mile. About seventy people had set up tents near the Heart of Midlothian, having made makeshift banners and declaring the area *Occupied Here, No Notice Order* which had been duly shortened to *OHNO* by some wit. Hundreds of angry frightened city residents stood out in the dark evening, not caring about the cold November night's air. They banged on drums, chanted and drank cans of beer. *We are tired of being lied to and robbed* one woman chanted. *Who surveys the surveyors?* another asked. Illicit violence lurked in the atmosphere, threatening civil disobedience or worse.

Edinburgh's residents had never tolerated fools or asses be they politicos or laws and if they were ignored repeatedly the formerly silent majority could mutate into modern day mobs. Sacred fools, of course, were another matter, certainly Alison had felt like one for a long time. Somebody had lit a make shift camper fire and people huddled around it in gloves and thick overcoats, carrying candles and straining to hear a crisp young speaker who identified himself only as Tam MacWhirter, the ready salted student rep who'd fought a few battles in his twenty-two years. Every now and then another man blew on a whistle to rally the crowds into silence.

With a shock, Alison recognised Brett Gribble as the other man but without most of his bandages. She'd been walking past, the brisk walk making her pech. She was still recovering from Ruth O'Connor's stern disciplining over Halloween and had been given a verbal caution at this stage. Spock's appearance or any magic tricks in the future had to be run by her first. Did she realise she was lucky to get off with a mere verbal caution? Alison politely and bravely fought her corner, arguing that the residents didnae seem engaged or stimulated. *The Harbour's* television set was on constantly but there were no interesting books to read or conversations to be had. She'd phrased it diplomatically but Ruth had gotten the implied criticism of her management and Alison sensed trouble brewing.

But she just couldnae help it, she wasn't prepared to suppress her personality completely in order to fit in. Though it's cold, Alison's curious to hear what leader MacWhirter says. Standing close to MacWhirter and Brett is one academic looking elderly gentleman wearing a sandwich board with the words *The Age of The Panoptican* on it. He'd had actually built a small model of Bentham's famous creation out of papier mâché shouting in a hoarse voice that he'd *burn the bugger later.* The MacWhirter coughs for attention down the megaphone he's holding.

"Friends, residents, fellow students and tax payers! I do declare we are now living in the age of The Living Panoptican, the crowning achievement of the new Corporate Edwardian Global Empire! The time for action and vision has come, hot air and rhetoric has been done to death. This peaceful public protest is about the right to redefine what we mean by the terms liberty and freedom, it's about the very real human right of all people, not just the more affluent, to define themselves in their own private space, it's about the right to own one's own identity and to disappear if one wants to and not to share everything about oneself in full view of some ultimately unaccountable database. We are concerned about the erosion of fairness, accountability, human dignity and privacy.

Yes, I'm fully aware of the double edged sword irony of social networking media – we, as Children of Liberty, used new site Flattter to organise this demo relatively quickly yet we are also angry at the way AGOG is passing info about us to state governments and corporates. We privately admire Flatter's new monopoly in status updates as it suits us nicely, thank you, but other types of monopoly we are not comfortable with. But it's the abuse and misuse of power that we are most concerned about here. Yes, I also know some individuals choose to behave rudely and abusively to others on Flatter – but that too is a kind of abuse of personal power. And what's deemed 'private' can be deeply political too. Here, there is a case for the state to intervene and protect the sanity, freedom and dignity of individuals if there are threats on life or extremely undermining personal attacks designed to destroy esteem and reputations. But that fine line between genuinely defending the well-being and interests of citizen-subjects and actually invading privacy has been crossed.

We've always had an ambivalent relationship with governments, be this with Westminster or Holyrood and both The Salmon, The Sturgeon and The Eaten-nites in Scotland and England seem silent on this issue of continued state surveillance and the erosion of liberty. But if there really are terrors to be faced then can we trust either government or corporates to always tell us truthfully what they are? For at the end of the day, despite claims of paternalistic neutrality, they also have their agendas – and some of them not always altruistic. The problem of course is that there never has been just one definition of justice and freedom- both terms are contested continuously.

Yet I do believe in my heart of hearts, standing near the shared ground of the Heart of Midlothian too here, that there could be the political will to achieve broad agreements about the big issues that face not just Scotland but the world. And it goes right to the heart of the relationship between what is deemed private interest and what is public. It seems government departments, big corporates and technology giants are given no end of freedoms: freedoms to lift up shop, scarper off and avoid paying fair shares of taxes, freedoms to pay what they like to staff and pollute what they like and all this free behaviour impacts crudely and subtly on the freedoms and justice of others.

Lack of common tax revenue means less spending on public projects and the lack of maintenance for parks, for example. Excess liberty and non-regulation in one sphere of society's capital and credit – and here I mean casino banking, stock markets and predatory venture capitalism – can actually restrict the generation and freedom of other types of credit and capital – be they social or environmental capital or credit used to lend to business or home owners. And both types of credit and all types of capital should and could ultimately be contained in and accountable to the one sphere that includes all of us – bankers, politicians or otherwise – that sphere called 'society'.

Can there really be different spheres and principles of justice within the one greater sphere called Society? Maybe, as justice for the individual is not necessarily a just outcome for the majority or the collective – this is the problem of contested and competing rights. But equally, surely we cannot say that one set of rules about fairness and obligation applies to states, the media technology giants and financial sector and another rule applies to the rest of us. It's an irony isn't it – for in some ways we have over emphasis on individual rights so much so that we are now blinded to the way this can inflict on others. But there are collective rights and common human rights. And this is another of our concerns – that the socio-economic purposes of both types of capital and credit, and of technology itself, has been sacrificed and critically reduced to a narrow definition of market purpose only – and more specifically to a neo-liberal type of market. Is it just a matter of time before society and the environment we all share completely implodes and is this a fairly functional and democratic way to live I have to ask myself?

I argue that it is a world that only appears functional and efficient but at what cost? Even the term efficiency is contested – efficient for who? The poor's freedoms and choices have never been as highly valued as others and the way the new Corporate Edwardian Empire actually reduces choices, freedoms and justice for some is by actually imposing savagely harsh cuts in public assistance or welfare. And this is inflicted on those who are most vulnerable, who are least able to defend themselves with expensive lawyers. They have the weakest voice so the Elite get away with it. What an irony, my friends, that welfare policy so often produces the very opposite of stated intentions because of unconscious continued ambivalence towards anyone deemed in need, vulnerable or dependent. That and good old fashioned greed.

Yet who are the real parasites here, who is not pulling their weight financially? Recall the appearance of food banks in modern Scotland. We think we live in a globalised democracy friends, but I'm not so sure. There are new Elites. We are passing around a petition and donations box and we ask that tempers are kept, private property respected. If the police arrive or the military, then we stand far more chance of winning arguments and being listened to if we practice what we preach and remain polite and tolerant of others no matter what may be hurled at us by the media or anyone else. Nevertheless, the time for polite letter writing only is over and people crave something more immediate and visible. We shall stay as long as we can."

The startling sound of two circling army helicopters drowns out MacWhirter's speech which infuriates some of the crowd who throw rotten vegetables to the chants of *how did you know we were here? We have a spy-mole in our midsts! Who are you really protecting? My son's addicted to AGOG! Always plenty of public money to spy on innocents yet the age of austerity deems the bedroom tax necessary!* The crowd surges forward, protecting those in tents and then, as if it wasn't extraordinary enough seeing Brett Gribble shorn of bandages blowing loudly on his whistle – Alison spots The Wipers of all people carrying baskets of cakes. And more incredible than this odd strange sight was the fact that Mrs. Wiper wears a kitchen colander on her head. The domestic battleground had clearly shifted to the wider social milieu and noticing Alison on the outskirts, Mrs. Wiper manages to steam her way through the angry chanting hordes.

"Well, I'll be! Alison Mode, carer extraordinaire. How lovely to see you again. You see we have baked cakes for the masses believing they deserve it. Shame about the aborted speech though, huh? As you know we don't do the Internet at all but we heard about this demonstration through our local church. We are compassionate Conservatives with a small c but we also are worried about many of the issues identified. And so we find we have the most unlikely of allies! Simon has befriended some students you see. But you are looking at my kitchen colander strangely. Well, it's partly to protect my head from missiles but I'm also cross about the way large companies see Britain as an easy tax target. It's symbolic.

I've heard about the extent of tax evasion and ridiculous Executive pay levels in the companies Simon and I hold shares in and I thought the symbol of a colander summed Britain up extremely well in that hardly any tax revenue is retained. As shareholders we feel helpless and usually I'm very *ARP* you know even in this showy ostentatious recession. And no, I don't mean Alright Presently, that good old war time favourite but instead *Always Really Prepared.* All in all, it's like trying to catch water with a sieve and so says this well-heeled lady too in the New Corporate Edwardian Empire. What are you doing here? No doubt whisking up your sweet magic on some new couple. You cooked up some romance and passion back into our marriage you know – and for that we will always be grateful."

Alison tried to suppress a naughty giggle seeing the way the colander wobbled precariously on Mrs. Wiper's head. Clearly Mrs. Wiper hadn't quite got over her fear of being attacked – be this by a flying missile or even a seagull. She wondered if Mrs. Wiper wore any other kitchen utensils in bed or around the house but quickly dismissed the thought. But it took the saucy phrase pussy whisked-whipped to a whole new level. A very quiet kind of revolution or private trench warfare seems to have affected her. But she shouldn't laugh, the former client looked flushed and earnest in her glowing admiration. I should cocoa. Mrs. Wiper, though a traditionalist of a kind, was also kind, honest and fair and those qualities would always matter and endure. Making polite excuses, Alison leaves the riotous demo and heads off for home, the quota for weird and wonderful happenings having excelled itself for now.

Large flocks of grey and black jackdaws sit perched on trees, Alison had never seen so many assembled but then the bus ride out to Niddrie had felt like she was actually leaving the city behind her. Niddrie had been a village on the outskirts of the town for hundreds of years and even now it had a semi-rural feel in some parts. The birds' colourings match the dull November sky, full of oppressive dark clouds. They call and rustle their feathers, disturbing last remaining leaves as they watch the traffic and people below. Soon it will be winter but there is cloying dampness already, Alison can't believe how quickly the year is passing by. Christmas next month too. There had been quite a few arrests after the Royal Mile riot but no names were released in the press. Predictably enough though the university had been quick to distance itself from what it saw as deviant militants. Strong pungent smells of farm fertiliser puncture the air. Michelle at work had said Kathleen Kennedy lived along the Niddrie Mains Road, opposite a green parkland area.

She'd been given the address and she walks on tentatively, remembering what Michelle had said about her aunt being clairaudient as well as clairvoyant. *I have a message for this woman, Michelle, I'm sure of it, as these last couple of days I have seen this cloaked figure walking around Hunter's Hall Park behind the Jack Kane Centre. I'm not sure but I think this person I have been seeing is also a troubled little person, somebody from the past who lived nearby.* Looking across the long winding road, she sees the green parkland area Michelle described. Old bare trees stood tall around a flowing burn and glancing at a raised area of land she sensed, she wasnae really sure how, that a fine house once stood there. In her mind's eye she saw a terrible fire filling the sky with black smoke. Reaching the right house then, Alison rings on the door. A long haired blond woman in her fifties appears, smiling a wide smile.

"Ah, Alison Mode? Michelle's told me all about you. I've been expecting you. Please come in."

She notices the unusual looking ring Kathleen wears, a black stone with a greenish tinge set in silver. The ring, combined with a full length coat gives Kathleen an eccentric appearance. Why wear a thick coat indoors?

"Ah, I see you looking at my ring. It's a falcon's eye. When I receive universal messages I go all goose pimply and cold and the ring, well it actually flashes at me, telling me I must pay attention. A bit like traffic lights. We all have our different ways of working don't we, us sensitive types. Yes, the house burned down in a fire. Suspicious circumstances."

With a shock Alison realises that Kathleen is actually telepathic, too. Her thoughts are being read and she wasnae sure she liked it, it's unnerving. Before coming out to visit Kathleen, Alison had swallowed some *Twilight Dew* and done a meditation with the white higher power to protect herself. The *Kwik Stix's* in her coat pocket if things got really hairy and she felt unsafe. For never mind the political abuse of power, what about spiritual misuse of insight and influence? She's shown down a gloomy hall way and into a front room which has what can only be described as a kind of alter in one corner. Star and moon paper mobiles hang in the window, lit candles on the mantelpiece. Was this woman for real or another case of smoke and mirrors? An antique iron, dating from the last century, was evidently still in use as it has been left on an ironing board with some item of clothing. Bizarre. The bodies of seven dried and flattened frogs are mounted on a wall behind a glass casing.

In the middle of the room two chairs sit in opposition to each other round a small round table. A clear glass bowl full of water and a drinking glass are on the table. Shelves of books line the room's alcoves; on one is a vase full of unnaturally bright blue chrysanthemums sitting in water which is an equally lurid blue.

"Please sit down opposite me. I was doing a spot of ironing before you arrived, nothing like negative hot ions helping to release spiritual phenomena into the atmosphere as every physicist or spiritualist worth their salt will tell you. Excuse the pun on iron, it's a common woman's prerogative to pun, one of the few ways she can still influence and be heard. There's no need to be afraid but I see you also have gifts of the sight, my dear. I use bowls of water in my sittings and not crystal balls, contrary to what the locals round here think. I saw your face in this bowl of water months ago. If you drink this water from the same bowl, it aids the connection we have, and this helps me go into a trance-like state.

One is all and all is one. Here, use this glass. Sometimes I'm under for ten minutes, at others twenty but I will re-emerge. If you cannae get through to me after half an hour pinch me or please kick me awake. All things being *eeksie peeksie*, I should not be out for that long. My eyes get a glazed look just before and after a reading; it's the Irish descendent blood. I used to live in a mobile home not far from here for years. Maybe you saw a collection of traveller caravans coming here?"

Alison drinks from the glass, quietly watchful. She wasnae sure what this woman would come out with next. The water tastes strange as if it's been flavoured with coconut. *Maybe this woman colours and dyes water for special effects?* And if so, are these not theatrical props of a kind? Alison thinks. *I prefer nature's own, thanks very much. If she genuinely has powers, then why rely upon such things?* But she sits patiently, listening. And as she's been doing just that Alison's been aware of a tiny little flash of light in the room but has been unable to pinpoint its source.

Kathleen Kennedy's eyes look distant, her voice altered. But the ring she wears! The falcon's eye stone was pulsating with greenish light. She'd not noticed it before but Kathleen's eyes are slightly different shades of brown which clash violently with the hair that's quite obviously been peroxided to look younger.

"Beware the home manageress; she's watching you as she's very jealous. She wants something, an object you often carry in your pocket. She knows about you and about Spock, the powers and juggling. You are clever and independent and she doesn't like it; cover your back at all times. I can see a man buying a small puppy from a lady friend who owns a pet shop. *I need your help, Alison Mode. I was horribly murdered hundreds of years ago though I worked hard as a dwarf servant. You sent him back here, his soul and a new body but now he torments me all over again. Once was enough when I was one of the living. He lives in the Hall of Mirrors and has no shame in life or death, deceiving all with his vanity and brutality. I had to come, you see. He used me like a pawn in his game and they never found him out. Please avenge my death and clear my name."*

The full impact of the reading only increases as Alison Mode, carer, agitator, modern white witch and philosopher extraordinaire, makes her way back home. Feeling numb, she walks towards her block of flats, her heid still spinning and absorbing it all. Of course! *1638*. It all fitted perfectly with hindsight. *You sent him back here, his soul and a new body.* The spirit talking through the medium Kathleen Kennedy must have meant Sinclair, that the man Alison knew as Sinclair had also lived before and had been as cruel and tyrannical back then in 1638 as he'd been to her in this century. Flabbergasting. But then there will always be the evil Sinclairs of this world until they are stopped in their tracks now or back then. For evil, or the potential for it, resides in all individuals dead and alive as well as more widely in cultures and institutions, never suffering from social immobility.

And as such all humans wrestled with or denied this inner darkness and some who were courageous dared to confront its existence in the external world. But more to the point – who was the cloaked she-dwarf whose death needed to be avenged? It sounded as if she'd lived out in Niddrie. Tears pricked her eyes as she thought again of her poor mother's suspicious death and how vulnerable and innocent she'd been too. Feeling a renewed sense of moral duty, it seemed her powers would be needed in the past now too.

Alison hadn't really thought about the concept of twin souls before, but this message from this unknown woman felt like there was still some kind of necessary psychic connection. And then, just as she's about to enter her block, something primeval screeches and claws at her shoulder before flying off into the all-encompassing darkness. A falcon! She'd caught a snatched glimpse of pinky-brown feathers, fluttering paper and a black eye but it had been so quick. She's dropped her keys in fright and now stooping to pick them up, Alison notices the writing on a scroll of paper. *She's buried in the grounds of the house.*

26

The Sorceress

"How is Spock coping with his wee lead? What a curious laddie he is. Does he do a runner when he sees dogs but chase after female squirrels on heat? What a sight. Looks like he's taking you for a walk, Alison. Watch out, you nearly walked right into that bush. Are you feeling okay? You don't seem your usual self."

Flora and Alison are taking Spock for a stroll on a muddy Leith Links by a row of imposing houses which looked like they dated from the early nineteenth century or so. The Wipers live very nearby; Alison had wondered if they'd both got home unscathed after the Old Town antics. Silently austere but graceful windows seem to watch them as they walk on by, almost as if the houses took on the personality of those who once occupied them or who live in them still. Cautious and reserved, fearful of anything or anyone different. This was one side of Edinburgh old and new, the small city civilised mind set. But there was and is a violent, abusive and rough underbelly to the city as well – the two faces usually denying all knowledge of each other in some permanent Jackal and Hide enactment. Spock's stopped by a discarded ice cream cone, devouring the remains. Alison had bought a bag of nuts to trail before him and keep him on track but they'd run out. Alison likes the way Flora calls Spock a laddie, it amuses her. They were in a kind of solidarity with each other, Alison and Flora because they were both selfish childless females, yet another kind of social oddity and taboo.

"Flora, I have been feeling a bit disorientated and dizzy ever since that reading with the seer out in Niddrie over a week ago and being scratched on the back of my neck by what looked like a falcon. The strange message, too: *she's buried in the grounds*, I cannae rest until I get to the bottom of all this, and the thing is I don't think the tormented spirit can rest either. The amount of water I've been drinking, it's like I need the fluids to keep me standing upright. *I have been a pawn in his game*, the spirit said, through Kathleen. And the weird thing is, Flora, images of chess pieces and giant boards keep flashing up in my mind, it must be significant.

Brett Gribble plays a lot of chess; funnily enough he said he thought *I* was a chess player! Hardly. It's been a totally crazy year so far, Flora. A roller coaster. The journey and mission down to London with Lady Hyde, Spock being kidnapped, discovering *The Sneezewood*'s inate properties, expanding and developing my knowledge of the Domains. It's been far more exciting than watching Mr. Collywobbles's afternoon magic show as a wee lass I can tell you. Realising too that the three Domains in the mind that I keep talking about can be accessed regularly with focused concentrated thought and that, in some sense, the Domains within can be attuned to spaces outwith.

Then of course my mother's handwriting on the wall, describing my discoveries in my own *Quibblon* language. A flying visit from Betsy Gribble, realising that *The Sneezewood* could travel both across geographical space, but across time, too. Coming to terms with the fact that my persecutor has finally perhaps got his come-uppance, seeing a rejuvenated Mrs. Wiper traipsing about with a kitchen utensil on her head, being attacked by a bird of prey and now, finally, this – an extraordinary message from some spirit who needs my help."

"Can I see the coin again, Alison? Have you got it on you? When you told me about the magpies at the McGhee house hold I just struggled to believe it. You moving chandeliers, doing a spot of meditation and hearing your ma's voice was enough for me. Do you think the falcon's a message, too; from the seer?"

Alison fishes out the old coin from her duffel coat pocket and hands it to Flora. Earlier in the walk Flora had mentioned the fact that Lord Edward Hyde had been sent to visit *Creatures of Comfort*, on instructions from Lady Katherine to introduce himself to her and buy a suitable puppy. Lady Katherine had decided that her errant husband needed to get out more and start caring for another living thing. It also gave Lady Katherine an excuse to walk and talk with Alison more regularly.

She'd also gotten into the habit of rubbing metal coat hangers particularly at night, much to Lord Hyde's tolerance levels who was now living in number 38 India Street as a part time live in husband. She'd let him move back on condition that his political interests and commitments were somewhat reduced but not completely compromised. She said she'd forgotten what the man she married years ago really was; she'd lost sight of him and herself in the marriage. She would not budge on her new found passion for the dignity of all life forms though, making no promises that she'd not gate crash Westminster again.

You should have seen him, Alison! His manner was so apologetic and self-conscious, I had a difficult time trying to get him to relax a bit and just bond with the puppies. "How do I know which kind of personality it will have?" he asked. So I said just trust your instincts and that the owner can influence an animal's character, too. That seemed to do the job.

Flora and Mac had a couple of high tech security cameras installed outside the shop as a result of the attack and killings, the steel shutters they pulled down at night had triple reinforced strength. But she'd been as delighted as Alison at hearing the news that Sinclair had been permanently transported. Flora, now well aware of *The*

Sneezewood and Alison's marvellous powers, had nevertheless edited the fabulous full story for Mac, not wishing to fleg him. All Mac Macintyre knew was that Alison Mode was a bit of a dreamer space cadet who was into her own version of yoga mantras. As for Sinclair, well, Flora told him he'd been caught smuggling drugs abroad. Mac, being a canny soul, suspected there was more to the story than his wife was telling having seen the stories about Alison, The Gribbles and the adventures of the amazing flying stool on *Flatter.* Yet he was a discrete honourable man who believed in allowing folk to say or reveal as much or as little as they chose.

"Kathleen Kennedy said she was descended from Irish gypsies and that I should beware Ruth O' Connor who apparently envies something I carry a lot in my pocket. But I don't think it's the coin she's after, Flora. I think she may have overheard me whispering a spell in *The Harbours* with the *Kwik Stix."*

Fred Branch kisses Michelle, turning on his silver charm. It's afternoon in *The Harbours* and all five residents have had their lunch, an unimaginative mix of boiled vegetables, cold ham and crusty bread. Outside, seasonal mists had begun to encroach on the city, engulfing all street scapes in mystery, even the trail of multi coloured plaster cow sculptures that had long been trailed round the city centre and tolerated by the council as a kind of nod to the psychedelic, Bohemian undertones threatening to disrupt Edinburgh's genteel façade. Betsy Gribble, on her brief guided tour of the city courtesy of her four Scotch friends, had delighted in the city's cow sculptures, commenting on a similar one she'd stumbled across at some Boston college sit in. The newspapers were proclaiming the return of smog and wondered if Edinburgh would be inundated with gas masks and face masks, screaming that the city centre would be a *new kind of war zone. It's hard enough to escape aggressive chugger-beggers and deal with the fact that our military budget is being cut, now this assault on our health.*

But the press has always been good at conjuring, just as good as politicos in building mythology, misogyny, controversy.

Fred did his customary dinner table trick and slipped some cooked veg down his pants when Ruth or the other staff weren't looking. This made all the other residents laugh out loud until Alice choked and Joan Murdoch had to give her a firm thwack on the back. Scoff and danger over, now they are playing at *Grey Flutter*, an off shoot of Beggar My Neighbour, a card game both Fred and Stewart have perfected in their years spent in various care homes. Ruth's in her office and Alison knows she's not really forgiven her for the Halloween night antics. *This is the trouble with working with a collection of people not of your own choosing and in an enclosed space, all the petty jealousies and personality clashes were somehow inevitable* Alison thinks, joining in the game and trying to *KOKO* in a calm fashion but refusing to remove her headdress for work, seeing as it couldn't really be construed as a health and safety hazard could it?

Sooner or later she had to overcome her difficulty being around people for extended lengths of time, especially if she found them 'difficult' – but it was always a compromise, this final laying to rest of her poor mother's death by being the best carer the world had ever seen. She was determined to try and improve the residents' quality of life, inch by inch or by stealth. Hide your utter boredom, this was the trick. Appear to play by the rules, but commit secret acts of humanitarian kindness and espionage. Michelle's being very discrete about asking after Alison's visit to her Aunt out in Niddrie and all the better really as any more perceived disturbance or weird happening wouldn't be tolerated by Ruth.

"Alison, can you come into my office please. I think there's been a mix up over your shift times plus I'm concerned about punctuality and sloppiness. Fred, I'm sure you can spare her for a few minutes."

Ruth's tone of voice sounds ominous and following her into her office, Alison silently notes the way Ruth had no problem humiliating and insulting Alison in full ear shot of the other staff and residents. *Punctuality. Sloppiness.* How harsh and judgemental the shared British language is, yet privately how subversive and liberating. So many people in authority resorted to humiliation and mocking as a management tool. Some people evidently thought it clever. Tasteful flourishes of aspidistra patterned wallpaper line the hall way as well as well as Ruth's office, again throw backs to Edwardiana, that not so distant empire. This week Alison's been working the early shift and the effects of the very early rises tend to kick in around the afternoon. Sitting down, Alison politely stifles a yawn. *Whatever you do, don't let your fatigue show either*. Ruth looks stern in horn rimmed spectacles.

"Alison, I have to say I am greatly concerned about your lateness three days in row as well as your appearance at work which I think's unsettling the other residents and staff. At lunch I couldn't help noticing you swaying about and looking distinctly unsettled on your feet, so much so that when Alice had her coughing fit I thought you'd actually keel over. Now, seeing as you are a new staff member I'm trying not to be too harsh with you but I have to ask, Alison, are you on some form of medication? And just over the last week I've noticed you drinking large quantities of water. Now as a former trained nurse, this tells me your body is out of sync in some way. Are you getting enough vitamins down you and can you please reassure me that you possess a copy of your shift timetable for this month? I cannot afford lateness. As it is, to date I feel I've been very tolerant of your headdress and unusual manner, but live animals near residents is pushing the button."

"Ruth, look I get the odd headache from time to time and Spock's been ill which has upset me. That's all it is. When I get headaches I just need to drink more water, but it doesn't happen that frequently. And yes, I do have a timetable copy. Spock's been sick first thing in the morning, a different kind of morning sickness and I guess Spock's my replacement baby. So that's why I've been late. He's got some kind of bug and has trouble sleeping at night just now."

Alison gritted her teeth inwardly. *Pucker up your lips Alison, and definitely don't large it up this time. If anything, play things down and sweep firmly under the proverbial carpet.* She hated lying but sometimes it was a life line. Ruth O'Connor already thought her an eccentric oddball and she really didnae need to know more. Thankfully though, Alison had deduced that Ruth wasn't a *Flatter* user and so was ignorant of some of the recent wilder postings about her. It was becoming ever harder to be anonymous.

Bowing out of the office gracefully, Alison finishes the shift and heads towards her bus stop. It's just before the schools' finish, and there's only a few elderly people about. An old man asks her the time and glancing at her watch, she doesn't notice the falcon swooping and landing on the bus shelter roof, eyeing her. Blate awkward bird movements, but then it drops something from its beak onto the pavement and then takes off. Another message from the Niddrie seer! Bending down, Alison unfolds the piece of paper. *Her name is Mary Urquhart.*

*

The kitchen sink has never looked more huge and imposing and she's lost track of the number of hours she's been standing in it, swaying about in a trance. It was all these bloody bird messages; it makes her feel a true sodie heid herself. Alison, drawn strongly to anything metal, finds herself feeling wobbly, drained and yet quite mad. Hours ago, she'd popped out to get a pint of milk as you do when you run out of basics and she'd had the shock of her life. A familiar back and gait but strange crude black boots and short trousers ending at the calf. And that height and build! It couldn't be, surely not. *But it was.* Stepping out of the local shop and walking away in the opposite direction, Alison recognises Sinclair's familiar way of walking. Only this time he's dressed in what looks like seventeenth century clothes. Blinking her eyes, she looks again but then he's gone. Vanished into thin air. And yet returned to this time and plane briefly.

Who had sent him or called him back to this time? Certainly not her that was for sure. At last she'd thought Sinclair safely out of sight out of mind, but it'd taken years, months and close loyal friends to be rid of him. And that wasnae mentioning personal qualities like having the courage, faith and tenacity to confront a big bully boy. Alison had stood stock still in shock, taking it all in. But now, here she was standing in the kitchen sink stuck in a kind of metal stasis and it wasn't even a full moon or new moon – so she couldn't even blame it on that.

Something or someone had gotten possession of her mind and she no longer knew herself. Was her name Alison Mode? Earlier, she'd looked at Spock as if seeing him for the first time. Fancy owning a guinea pig, now who would do that? Her stomach finally signals its needs for food and she reluctantly steps out of the sink. Usually when she was receiving psychic messages from the dead or living she found herself lying down in her bed or staring off into space but this was a first.

"Spock! Do mind yerself won't you, pal. I nearly tripped over you. Is it your feeding time again, hmm? Well, give me a chance to get a cup of tea down. You're looking a bit frisky but let's hope we can both shake off this insomnia and strange drowsiness permanently."

Spock, in a momentary surge of energy, had scuttled up and down the hall several times before stopping to look at her in a watchful way, as if he half expected some ghostly hand, voice or an unexpected visitor to again waft down the air vent. After all, living with the likes of Alison Mode could hardly be called dull or humdrum.

Her name is Mary Urquhart. She's buried in the grounds. The falcon's two extraordinary messages that Alison couldn't forget. Michelle had given her the drawing of Kathleen's diminutive cloaked figure in red walking in some past wood; Alison had mounted it on to her bedroom wall. She kept everything that 'spoke' to her in a spiritual way in her bedroom, including the coin which she'd put under her pillow. And what was it Kathleen Kennedy had also said to her? *Something tells me your body is out of sync in some way.* Well, that bit of the reading was true enough as she'd felt the need to stand in a sink to somehow get in sync, and yes, she'd drunk enormous amounts of water. But surely Kathleen Kennedy hadn't placed some evil spell on her now?

She was the one who'd warned her about Ruth O'Connor as well, something else that Alison sensed right. Walking back to the kitchen to make Spock some food and herself some tea, she passes the antique mirror Lady Hyde had given her and glancing in the mirror, she's startled to see a man's face looking back at her, snarling. *Sinclair!* Only this time his hair was different, he'd grown a beard. Rooted to the spot, she watches the way half of Sinclair's face then dissolves into her own face, as if she and he were tied and bonded together in some eternal but damned dance of the predator-victim. Like for like, two faces of the same metaphorical coin, as if her many brushes with evil both without in others and within herself did not leave her untarnished in some way, as if she'd internalised the roles and parts of both the hunter and hunted.

Black and white. For of course it'd been some time ago that she realised she'd mutated into a modern urban predator, too, reclaiming the wild-id huntress part of her own psyche to fight the savagery well. Become the thing you hate and fear to ultimately overcome it. The principle worked in homeopathic treatment, that much she did know, when the body is given just the right amount of something it cannot tolerate or is allergic to 'teach' it to either accept it, incorporate it or develop new immune strategies to it.

Thus a little bit of what you find unacceptable or repulsive at first glance or taste could do you good. Black medicine, gradual exposure. The face in the antique mirror changes again, this time dissolving into an unknown woman's face who is mouthing words Alison cannae hear.

My name is Mary Urquhart, I was a caring innocent murdered, the mouth seems to be saying but then, just as Alison moves closer to the mirror, she's shown a different scene again. A bearded Sinclair draws a knife across the terrified woman's neck. *You filthy unnatural dwarf freak of a whore. Fishing for trouts in peculiar rivers, no doubt. Well, not if Rum Butler has anything to do with it.* Then Rum Tum's face again or is it Sinclair's in an old but new Edwardian top hat, Alison couldn't tell. Some things never change in human dramas.

An image of some chess piece then distant sounds of pigs squealing down the centuries, the top hat fades and there's nothing but Alison's face looking back at her. As if she'd just dreamed the whole encounter or had eaten some hallucinatory mushrooms. But what she'd just witnessed was real enough she thinks, giving Spock some bran flakes and celery sticks to chew on. Was she now reaching the higher levels of her abilities?

Some order was needed here, some sanity, a touch of the *TOTT* treatment when all else fails you. Think about the caffeine slow releasing in your mind might do the trick. In case you fear you're joining the drifting zombie *wump* armies, the people who have lost the capacity for courage or any truly independent thought. Drinking hot sweet tea, Alison mulls over what she's seen. She'd just popped out to her local shop not expecting half a pound of skeleton from her own closet. Sinclair in seventeenth century clothes! So time *could* be spliced and somehow 're-played' like with film recordings, if not in actual geographical places then also recollected, stored and played out in memory. It was as if people, their actions and feelings were remembered in the universe's thin air and waters. So what was then is still now and present in some sense.

The past is present somehow, the two times in the one. Spaces on the real physical earth could facilitate and thin out, accommodating the repeated 're-playings' of people and events and so such places became temporary worm holes or black holes, for the moment devoid of just the one time or gravity. No wonder there couldn't really be any final 'closure' of such phenomena when past lives and souls would always use receptive minds and places as conductive mediums. And now all this replayed like an exclusive private preview to Alison who knew in that precise moment drinking her tea, biting on a petticoat shortbread and reading a wish-you-were-here postcard from Grandma Gribble in Kenya; that she must also journey back in time on *The Sneezewood* to ultimately lay four souls to rest: Sinclair, Mary Urquhart, her mother and herself. Justice couldn't be buried and forgotten again. *Dwarf's move.*

*

"Alison, the statue looks just like you. Your very likeness, so why are being so coy about all of this? You're a natural star, don't hide your light under a bushel. Laurence and I think you are utterly divine darling, like some pint pot angel. What a struggle we had with the authorities though over planning permission to get this finally sorted. The press has already been and liked it, needless to say. So expect to be far more recognised on the streets in the future. Don't you think the statue a hit, Lady Katherine?"

Alison's former client Noel and his returned French lover Laurence, stand in Nicholson Square delighted with their achievement. A life size marble statue of Alison Mode, deep in ponderous thought with *The Quibblon* tucked under one arm and a wooden spoon under another, took pride of place within the centre of the square. *Faith in my left and right,* said the statue's diplomatic inscription below. The mist's cleared for a while, the clear blue sky had lended itself well to press flash photography. When she'd first arrived a small assembled crowd had begun to loudly sing a song. *So, no longer the unsung heroine, eh Alison?*

Lady Katherine joked, trying to put Alison's very visible unease at rest. But Alison hated being photographed and had just grimaced through it, valuing her friends. It was getting to the stage that she was often recognised in the street and she sincerely hoped she wouldnae become more famous. Now here they all stood, Alison, Lady Katherine, Noel and Laurence, taking in Noel's master work of art. She'd been 'launched', via the statue, into the minds if not hearts of the city's residents. The love labour's lost and found Laurence, being a man of action and not much spoken English, had playfully hung a string of onions and a scarf around the statue's neck, promptly amusing Lady Katherine who'd been invited, as a city dignitary and arts patron, to cut the statue's ribbon. Lady Katherine had met Noel at one of his private exhibitions in the New Town and they'd got talking as people did. He'd mentioned his sculpture and former carer, she'd put two and two together.

"Noel secretly battled for ages to get his creation erected, Alison. The statue's inscription was my idea, hope you don't mind Alison, as I know in your own way you care very much about politics and despair of the endless point scoring which achieves hardly anything. I thought it rather witty actually. We wanted to surprise you, Alison. Call it a spiffing late birthday present. I also shook and oiled a few wheels along with Noel to get this thing built so I will not have it soiled with seagull shit, pigeons or traffic cones.

The shame of waiting so long before a statue of any notable woman in this city is put up or commissioned is terribly revealing of what's hardly changed – but you, Alison, *modern suffragist*, have single handedly changed all this. And to quote somebody not very far from me, so much for all this sugary *puckering up to people and then a bit of largesse on the side, pal.* Lord Hyde sends his apologies but I have consigned him to the kitchen cooking with Neesha.I thought a spell wearing an apron feeding people would make a pleasant change from all the committee big wigs talk.

But you are all welcome back to number 38 for dinner. In fact, you are all expected. And speaking of unnecessary soiling, what in the world is that woman over there *doing*? I say, she's just nicked another plant from that bed and she's just brazenly putting into her bag, roots and all! Talk about nerve, but perhaps she thought nobody would spot her. She'd been pretending to tie a shoe lace, I see. I'd noticed her before, Alison, before the press gang got here. Sorry to say this I really am, but I think perhaps she's not quite the full shilling, yet she doesn't exactly look like a destitute bag lady. Do you know her at all, Alison? She keeps glancing in your direction. Oh, she's off now. Quick, do look and see."

Alison looks to where Lady Katherine is pointing and is startled to see Ruth O'Connor, certainly one of the living unhappy souls, walking quickly away. She must have followed her here, on her legitimate afternoon off from work. It's one thing being haunted by someone you loved or hated, quite another to be stalked by the delusional envious living. And from your supposed social superiors too, 'professional people with responsibility', whatever that meant these days. Like some ghoulish clone Ruth must have seen and watched all the proceedings, over nosy about what her employee got up to outside work, who she hung out with. With a sickening feeling in her gut, Alison realises there will be more trouble with Ruth. And as for the bizarre stealing of plants!

They easily overtake Ruth, rumbling along smoothly in Lady Katherine's chauffeur driven Bentley The car's been given a new lease of life recently and the Hydes had re-invested in a driver. *So that's why there are often trails of earth and dirt in Ruth's office and along The Harbour's hallway*, Alison deduces. She'd obviously done this before as a secret plant stealer. Perhaps it was the only real kicks and pleasure the woman got in her sad overly sheltered life. Still, it might give Alison some kind of ammunition should she need it. *White power, white heather's flower, I'll mark you with the Kwik Stix come Ruth's reckoning hour.*

Quibblon Alternative Dictionary:

***Acronym.*, KOKO. Aka. Keep On Keeping On.** Putting 'calm' in front of the word keeping is entirely a personal choice. And whether this calm keeping on also entails eating the ubiquitous 'cupcake' again is entirely up to the individual. Alison Mode always did prefer cake of a more traditional character without the fancy OTT toppings – for example the classic great Dundee Cake and the aforementioned Pilton Slab.

***Acronym.*, TOTT. Aka, Think of The Teabag**. If one is going to hark on about the merits of cupcakes which are an acquired taste after all, then it only seems right to give a nod and a mention to another classic British institution: the teabag. Round, square, pyramid – when in fatigue, confusion or turmoil drinking tea and visualising the humble tea bag slowly releasing calm, positive thoughts within your mind helps Alison Mode and could help you too. Keep the ritual simple and private; don't share with cynics or energy vampires.

27

The Hall Of Mirrors

November mists thicken over Edinburgh but not to the extent that Alison couldn't spot Davey's car parked outside her Restalrig flat. She'd noticed it one night but hadn't seen the owner and she'd not thought any more about it when the car disappeared during the day. Sighing despairingly, she peeks behind her bedroom curtain in the early hours of the morning, disturbed as she really thought that her days of being stalked, pestered and harassed by the living at least were over. But then it was back again, turning up again like a bad penny, the same car parked just outside two nights in a row, again with no sign of Davey the drug mule driver, Sinclair's old gang bang pal. And that had been just problem number one that cropped up out of the blue, as if dealing with Ruth O' Connor, her line manageress, spying on her and following her to the public opening of the statue in her honour was not enough.

Oh, and the other little forthcoming matter of travelling back in time and dealing once and for all with Sinclair or whoever he was called back in 1638 and avenging the murders of Mary Urquhart and her mother's death by proxy, too. She didn't know if an extra dose of ginger or spice would assist her mind in time-space travel, one way or other she'd have to prepare. An hour or so mediation then a mantra on *The Sneezwood,* which hopefully would play ball on a two-way ticket.

Why not take the bottle of Twilight Dew? You don't know what dangers you'll encounter and you'll need to protect yourself with honesty and purity of intent, she thinks, slipping on her bathrobe and unable to sleep. She hadn't planned on being away for long but then, what if something should go wrong? Spock didn't have a guinea sitter booked. Thankfully, her severe case of sink-o-citus and her cravings for excess water at least seem mysteriously to have vanished, as subtle and enigmatic as the movements of the moon itself.

And there had been no more encounters with the falcon or hearing of coughing within the flat at least. Spock was his usual curious, charming self and had eaten a ginormous quotient of wotsits earlier that evening but right now her one symptom had returned: insomnia. For goodness sake, she was still recovering from seeing that blast from the past plus a life size statue of herself, a working class dwarf woman in central Edinburgh. It was the most revolutionary statue the city had to date, seeing as the plans for Wojtek, the infamous war time bear, were taking so long.

Who'd have thought it, would it be denigrated and undervalued or would the tourists and residents who might revere it in times to come, ensure that she'd not be airbrushed from official establishment history as so many other inconvenient deviant subversives were? Pacing up and down, Alison considers what action she should take about Davey's intrusive car. Nipping out to the quiet misty street she waves the *Kwik Stix* three times, shrinking Davey's car down to the size of a match box.

Kwik Stix
Do the trick
This a persecution gone too far
So take away this pal's car.

For you can pick on little people
Only so far

And bullies really are cowards
Being weak even as they try to scar.

Hurrying back inside in case she was seen, Alison allowed herself a secret little smile. Job done well, and who knows how many tonnes of CO_2 she was saving the planet. Let the bugger think what he likes, he cannae prove a thing. If Davey tries to follow her, she'd use the trusty stick again. Would the world miss the likes of him? No, not really. But she didn't want to take anybody out, it wasnae her nature and dwarves didn't enjoy wanton killing or harming for its own sake. No. Any learnt or inherited powers must be used wisely and justly and death a very last resort only in defence. There were surveillance cameras further down the street, but not in this particular section and her block's security extended to a buzzer entry system only. Her invisible unrecorded act was surely no worse than more visible acts of cruelty.

*

"Oi, *Pal.* Is your name Alison Model and is it true you're a witch and you fly around on wooden stools? I thought witches flew on broomsticks myself but it must be a very small stool like, for you. You being so short like with a small …"

"Aye! It's her alright. I saw a picture of her on *Flatter.* Some post said she also sells herbs as well as being a lady of the night shall we say. She must be desperate, like."

Manic male laughter bordering on the frantic but the teenagers don't quite finish the sentences off with the words they really want to say. *Just ignore it, don't stoop to their level.* Shortly after arriving in Niddrie again on the bus, Flora had called on the mobile. Niddrie, Edinburgh's so called green quarter. The area had changed a lot since the 1970s when Alison was a wee girl and the area besieged with drugs, shoddy housing and unemployment.

Alison, I have to tell you firstly that Brett Gribble's posted some really provocative comments on Flatter about your special powers shall we say. He refers to the statue of you too and by the way well done for that. You are quite the toast of Edinburgh. Secondly though Brett's now been arrested for loitering with suspicious intent outside AGOG's satellite office. I'm calling Lady Katherine as she knows good lawyers. But anybody who does something different or outspoken is bound to attract the good, bad and ugly. The curious and the envious.

It seems that Brett got really fired up and drunk after that demo you told me about and went a bit do-ally tap online saying as a Child Of Liberty he had to tell The World and spread the word about Edinburgh's very own freedom fighter. The piece is admiring of you but does suggest that you love animals, hear voices from the other side, believe in UFOs, can fly, and can hear other's thoughts. No mentioning of Domains, you moving objects, your liking of metal or any sub language you've invented though.

Be grateful for small mercies I guess. And Alison, I'm afraid there's a close up photo of you this time. Looks like it was taken on the sly on a mobile at the actual demo too. At least it's not a nudie one of you in the buff, like some folk get. Be warned. If you can, laugh it off. Unfortunately, the law cannae do anything, not unless you are actually threatened. Thought I'd better tell you. Good luck, Alison. You know what with. I hope to hear from you soon. Never mind, eh? People will see through it, Alison. Dinnae you worry, hen. We'll vouch for you as friends. Nobody's posted your address or where you work or other family details of your past and hopefully it'll not come to that. I'll let you know ASAP if it gets worse, okay? If you lie low, the fuss will go down. Just as well you don't have a computer though. They want a response, a rise from you, so dinnae give it. Brett's an idiot because though he didn't mean harm himself, others will latch on and try and bait you. It seems words aren't sacred or private anymore. But what is, then? I promise you I'll not mention the Domains to anyone.

You just couldn't be anonymous any more it seemed, not if you were exceptionally brave or spirited. The Internet had changed things forever and made it more difficult to guard your private, dark regions of the soul. It felt strange being offered up for consumption and hearing about these virtual comments, made mostly by people she'd not even met. Ironically, the glamour of fame created distance and artifice when she'd struggled all her life to be true and real to herself, not to others. She's become an unwitting celebrity but most definitely not of her own choosing. What exactly was she for others? What function did she serve? She'd never know and it didn't really matter. You couldn't legislate for opinions or all human actions.

All she could do at the end of the day was live her truth, be authentic for herself. The gang of teenage boys move off, bored with her for now and more interested in their IPhone where you could display and strut virtually. *Wumps*. Closely related to trolls but sometimes there are hybrids. But whatever the name, some folk just loved this dignity stripping, anything for a fresh bit of smear, innuendo and sport. Ignore the arrogance and hostility sometimes hidden in the presumed familiarity of *pal*. Alison knew she used that word too, but she tried to avoid the biting sarcastic tone that it often seemed to be said in.

The journey out to Niddrie had been uneventful and despite frequent glances behind her, Alison didn't see Davey on her case. *Whatever you do, don't look back*. How many times were those wise words uttered in fairy tales of old, but no matter the Internet trolls had followed her nevertheless. Follow where the golden ball of thread took you instead. She wasn't that surprised hearing Flora talk about the postings online, wondering again at what seemed to her the inner emptiness of some that they had nothing better to do with their time. It didn't seem right, though, that in the living world of humans, *wump-trolls* could freely exercise their right to abuse and smear and too often do this anonymously and undetected.

Brett is a kind of hypocrite she thinks again, fuming about the over watchfulness of the state on the one hand but invading the privacy of someone he knew as an individual. But then, with a start, she remembered the way she and Lady Hyde had eavesdropped on Brett's roof, listening to a private overseas conversation between him and his hermit grandma. Maybe everyone was ultimately implicated in these major or minor acts of surveillance and neighbour watch, but it was another kind of blunting savagery this semi-perpetual self-conscious watching of others and the self – as corrosive and dehumanising as gross inequality. But so many insidious images, screens and gadgets to distract and anesthetise from this basic awful truth.

Deep mist surrounds the modern housing estate as Alison Mode boldly walks on, humble but brave in her duffel coat like a timeless small heroine of old. *Why Mr. Wolf what big paws and eyes you have. All the better for finding flesh.* She put her spirit of adventure down to Star Trek, Mr. Collywobbles's magic show and her mother. Conker season again, everything shades of brown, red and rust. The year had flown by, in both senses of the word. And this she hadn't seen coming though she sensed her psychic powers were becoming ever stronger and couldn't be ignored. *Do you realise there's a parallel universe, hens? The veil between the living and dead is so thin,* she felt like saying to some passing young mums pushing babies in prams. *Do you know everyday miracles can happen, if not in the simple everyday things like the value of a smile and a kind thought, then in the visitings and messages from other Domains. We only use some of our minds.* Seen in this sense, money was just something that circulated around with its own energy, coming and going like the seasons but with the awesome potential to both free and imprison if not on the earth's practical plane then in the torments of the inner mind. Sometimes it felt like a curse hearing other's secret thoughts whether living or dead. Finding a hairy peppermint in her pocket, Alison pops it into her mouth partly to appease the nerves. Driving a stake through Sinclair or his likeness's heart was not really her style but she did wonder if on this trip she'd need garlic to ward off anything that sucked at her intention or energy. *Incubus Succubus*.

All her life it seemed she'd been busy either protecting herself or warding off evil forces which lived on in people who were not really aware of themselves and in some sense were not integrated wholes. Walking on towards the site of old Niddrie House then, she's amazed to see a flying grey object in the mist changing its shape gracefully like some air borne jellyfish as it skims across the road. Blink and you'll miss it. *What on earth had she seen?* It looked as if it belonged to the spirit world but it wasn't human in shape. Was it some kind of fly-by-day-and-night guardian spirit of the place? She'd heard about such phenomena before.

Just as she's having this thought, the fly-by-day-and-night entity or whatever it is flies back across the road again, this time squealing like a stuck pig. Alison prided herself on her open mindedness but this really took the biscuit. At first sight she thought it a plastic bag – but there was no wind or gust to make it move so. No doubt the meaning of what she'd seen would be revealed but then, with a sudden vision of the past's truth, she recalls what she'd seen and heard in the mirror Lady Hyde gave her. The terrible visions!

That knife, the agonising pleas for help, the unknown woman's face and in the background the maddening porcine squeals. And Alison knew then that Mary Urquhart had been killed near pigs, in some shed or field. Niddrie House must have had farm animals and labourers and servants working tending both. Had Mary's body been dumped in a ditch somewhere or was she tossed in some crude pit as the animal carcasses were? The truth had to be faced and unearthed no matter how awful or there never would be any rest. A car drives by slowly, cautious in the thick mist and closely followed by two young lads on roaring bikes, impervious to the dangers of driving in such conditions. Squadrophenia. No more peppermints this time and she cannot really sing for toffee. *Pucker yourself right up, girl. Koko with a kind pat on the back.*

An impressive looking fir tree, majestic in its height, stood before her after turning a corner. No, not everybody liked what Alison Mode made people see about themselves, but no matter as searching for balanced light has always been dangerous. The tree had an ancient feel, as if it once stood in the grounds of an even earlier version of Niddrie House and glancing up at the tree's top branches Alison's taken a back to see a hooded red cloak hanging in the mist. *Of course.* The small cloaked figure in the drawing Michelle had given her in *The Harbours,* the drawing Kathleen Kennedy had done clairvoyantly and from memory.

The drawing of a wandering Mary Urquhart. How on earth to get the cloak down, the branches didn't look strong enough to withstand her weight. She'll conjure it down with the handy *Kwik Stix* that's what she'll do. Taking it out of her pocket, a whispered voice emanates from inside the tree: *take this cloak it belonged to her.* The voice of Barbara Mode. But before any time or space travel or the wearing of cloaks can be attempted *The Sneezewood* of course must be summoned, her sitting stead. It looks quiet enough for a Saturday afternoon, no sign of anyone immediately about. Move quickly. But then the sounds of a fast approaching ice cream van spur her mantra on.

Woodsneeze, born of trees
Help me again if you please.
Travel back in time for me
Helping the innocents in history.

Whhooosh! In the blinking of a city bat's eye the wooden stool appears before Alison Mode and about time too as she's just conjured the red cloak down when the ice cream van turns into the street she's in. Holy moly, quick! The mist and fog should obscure the driver's vision she's hoping, putting on the cloak which fits perfectly while uttering another white power spell. But bad luck, the driver's spotted her and nearly crashes the chiming van into the tree. Ding, dong. *You are my sunshine, my only sunshine!* Quite who would want ice cream on a foggy November day was anybody's guess but horses for courses. Up, up and away she rises through the misty portal … until her body feels strangely light and weightless. She must be above the clouds by now she thinks, closing her eyes for fear of what she may see. Alison had not travelled this high or far back in time before. It was a risk but then being an independent white witch cum carer-philosopher was bound to be.

Part of the job spec after all. Top hats float by as do various kitchen utensils and other old unclaimed pieces of clothing, no doubt remnants of other past stolen empires or maybe even future unknown ones. A golden jewelled crown appears; its true origin, rightful estate and Kingdom, unclear in these mists of suspended time. Scottish, English or British? Alison tries to snatch at the hats but they dart away like frightened fish. It's almost as if she's falling asleep but then, jerking her eyes open she's again … falling … slowly, down through time and mist until she hits the ground with some force. A ground that has black and white check floor tiles to be precise. And shock of landing over, Alison sees that *The Sneezewood* has now moved of its own accord to another part of what appears to be a large hall. *Dwarf moving, check mate.*

The hall is vast, mounted with long mirrors on every wall. Her ears pop abruptly adjusting to the landing. Alison senses something burning and taking her hands away from her face she sees candles in tall ornate stands and rich coloured cloth. Spun maidens, unicorns, wild bears in strange unknown lands feature in large hanging tapestries, competing for space with the mirrors which reflect light. Rich floor length curtains are drawn back beside mullioned windows. It is daytime, weak sunlight penetrates the hall. At the far end of the hall is a carved wooden screen, an imposing dining table and high backed chairs placed nearby.

Her feet feel tingly, and feeling the urge to walk all of a sudden, she finds her crude cut shoes are oddly compelled to trace out the same movements on the chequered floor over and over. *Count one square forward in any direction, then one square diagonal in any direction.* Was this some remnant of a forgotten seventeenth century courtly dance she was psychically picking up on? Intrigued by the discipline of the highly regulated steps, Alison's senses are for the moment entranced by all that she sees. Then as she travels across the hall she becomes aware of lowered voices behind the screen. Freezing on the spot she carefully picks her way to a long velvet drape she can hide behind. Through the small lead-paned windows she thinks she can trace the distinct upper branches of the fir tree she'd just found the cloak in, but maybe it was just her imagination. Craning her ears, she tries to catch the whispers.

"You see my Lord, Elizabeth the serving maid has an unbecoming mark upon her body that she showed me and 'tis a sign of devilry and witchcraft I am sure of it. I looked away at first but she insisted that she show me her thigh just the other day before bedding down. 'Tis an odd mark, sire, and the milk from the cows has been sour these last few days. Something's upsetting the animals. Cook said she saw Elizabeth being over familiar with the cows, talking to them as if the beasts were people, sire. Then just the other night, Elizabeth happened to leave for bed very early and becoming suspicious and concerned for the welfare of the servants and your good selves, I confess I followed her upstairs where I discovered a goat's skull and what looked like blood spots in her bedroom cupboard. As you know, she shares a chamber with cook and I don't want to alarm the other servants. I think Mary Urquhart's disappearance has something to with Elizabeth, sire, and I seek your permission at this stage to continue to gather evidence and facts for your consideration."

Alison shudders behind the curtain, the man's voice sounds horribly familiar. Just then a corbie calls loudly outside from within the grounds startling what sounds like two men in surreptitious plotting.

"What's that sound, Rum Butler? Oh, 'tis just a corbie. But we must keep our voices down, Butler, so's not to frighten anyone. Mary's leaving in such an unexplained way and now this. 'Tis unfortunate timing, Lady Wauchope being pregnant and weak with child. Do you think the house is marked out in some way or is there a curse upon it put on us by those who do not like my rejection of the covenanters and sympathy for the English? We live in dangerous times and I know some in Edinburgh mistrust me. I heard some noblemen in town say that there are spies in the countryside, looking to assemble anti parliament troops. Talk of treason and men and women loyal to Charles and the new ways of worship found dead. I fear for Lady Wauchope, yet I have tried to be a tolerant fair master, holding my tongue on my private views. Is it possible Elizabeth's a devil's witch or spy? We must endeavour to watch her. A toast of ale Butler, to your loyal service which has been noted and thanks indeed."

"There are many secret cavorters with the devil, some Scottish, some English, sire. Those who do not like any form of organised prayer who prefer ignorance, savagery and raw meat. We must be on our guard."

A sound of metal chinking as the men drink. Alison's getting pins and needles in her legs with muscle tension. She wants to scream bloody murderer, liar, traitor, panjandrum, sycophant but has to content herself with feeling the *Kwik Stix* in her pocket.

"Now, Butler, tell me this truthfully. Is it true, as the other servants say, that you have found out a new secret chess move? I do not mind if you wish to play upon this board here. But you must tell me the move so I can win with guests. What is the new player called by the way?"

Just then and without warning, *The Sneezewood* rocks back and forth violently as if in vehement protest. Lord Wauchope gasps, and both men dash out in front of the screen to see what had made the sudden noise. The Lord is a tall man with commanding features, his wide velvet doublet revealing a hunter's athletic frame.

"That stool, Butler! See the way it's moving as if by some invisible hand. I do not recognise it as belonging to the household. Where did it appear from, it wasn't here earlier today? It looks like a ducking stool for nagging scolds or witches. Look how it's stopped moving. I do not like it, Butler. Especially after what you've told me about Elizabeth. Go and touch it Butler. Is it hot on the touch? Maybe we need an exorcism from a man of the church. It's a sign of some kind. I have an ominous feeling about it. But I must see how Lady Wauchope is in her bedchamber. We will speak later."

A frightened looking Lord Wauchope hurries out of the hall, leaving Rum Tum Butler alone. Rum Tum walks up to the stool, somehow recognising its shape. Alison watches him carefully from behind the curtain and then seeing an opportunity, she steps out with *Kwik Stix* at the ready. It's the strangest sensation staring at a man you'd known before yet at some later time but the features were the same despite the clipped beard. Yet there he was, staring right back at her and looking like he was seeing a ghost. Sinclair in an earlier life.

"Ye Gods! It's Mary Urquhart come back from the grave to haunt me. Or are you a mere spectre a figment of my mind? Either way, Mary, I will deal with the lies of your tongue again then."

Butler Sinclair pulls out a knife from his doublet which he holds out in front of him, his eyes fierce. But Alison's ready.

"Don't you dare touch that stool, Rum Sinclair, that's my familiar friend and stool and not yours. We have met before alright, before at another later time. If that makes any sense to you. But that's another story. I know what you did to Mary Urquhart, you scum. For I'm not her though I may look similar. No, I'm another dwarf you terrorised and humiliated over four hundred years from now. You framed Mary and slaughtered her in cold blood, no better than a farmyard animal. I thought I'd dealt with you for good by sending you back in time but it seems you're carrying on with your malicious lies, cruelty and womanising unpunished.

No wonder poor Mary Urquhart's soul cannot rest. So now most reluctantly I might add I resort to my most severe treatment yet. No, I am not Mary you idiot, come back for justice. As I said I am a dwarf lady from another future time, a victim your soul likeness tormented centuries later. But then or now, you are no more! So be gone!"

And waving the *Kwik Stix* at him, plucky Alison Mode casts her fatal spell. It might be pie-in-the sky thinking but she had to change him into something fitting for the enduring corruption and rot on this common man was as insidious as any to be found on the sly men of influence or politiks of any age. For some truths endure, no matter the times and you can't teach old similar dogs new tricks.

Half a pound of tuppeny rice
Half a tonne of treason
Mix them together with old lies and spice
And whoosh! Up and out goes this sly weasel's reasons

Rum Butler-Sinclair is spun round and round mercilessly by the *Kwik Stix's* jabbing gesticulations, at a pace so fast and furious that he drops his knife, becoming a blur on the edge of histories. A mere blot, to be erased permanently. Alison had thought about chucking a few drops of *Twilight Dew* on to him to get him to confess but he now looked so stewed in his own juice it wasn't really worth it. It was a powerful damning curse; she'd been reluctant to name the white power on this occasion.

"Where's the pig shed, you bastard? That's where you killed her isn't it? No matter, I'll find it and Mary's sorry bones too no doubt. Seeing as your behaviour is so boor-ish I turn you into an invisible flying pig herder, condemned forever to round up the spirits of dead pigs in the ethers! They may need help crossing roads safely."

And sure enough the man known then as the notorious Rum Tum Butler and later as William Sinclair junior, was dissolved into a fine powder, filtered through the panelled ceiling and scattered out of the universe's memory for good, more efficiently than any computer record. He'd been sent up to a place where his butchered pigs ran and shat, somewhere invisible to the naked eye but there nevertheless in another eternal Domain, accessible to those in-the-know with knowhow. Never again would he trouble or torment anybody for the charm was non reversible and indelible. Now she just had to find the bones and walking towards two heavy oak doors at the far end she knew somehow that it was poor but clever Mary Urquhart who'd invented the new chess piece and move. *Dwarf's move.* Brett Gribble would just love it she was sure.

Formal clipped looking hedges are easy on the eye yet Alison cannot see a way out through the grand house's gardens which are laid out in a series of squares. Roses, marigolds, lavender and small fish ponds provide dots of colour and interest in amongst the green. Pushing the Hall's great double doors to the outside grounds had been a job in itself but she'd never been one to give up on things easily. She'd have to move fast and try and find Mary's bones before someone who stopped and questioned her realised that Rum Butler had mysteriously disappeared without trace. Feeling hungry, she bites into an apple she'd seen in a bowl in the Great Hall of Mirrors and managed to stuff into a pocket. It's a big sweet red one, rather like the specimen Snow White, a fictional friend of dwarf people, had fatally bitten into.

How was Spock doing back in 2014? Or rather fast forward to that year. He was okay by himself for a few hours but he was a sociable wee thing and became withdrawn when he was alone for too long. The sun is high in the cloudless sky and looking up Alison spots the graceful fluttering of a kestrel. *The kestrel again.* Bearer and carrier of messages. Surely it was no coincidence. Did the bird really belong to this time she was in now or had it been sent travelling? Maybe she should follow its movements and trace where it lands, it might provide help finding the bones. Perhaps Kathleen Kennedy was sending more guidance.

She watches the bird glide on some fine high air currents before it swoops quite dramatically down near a cluster of stone built farm buildings. It lands on a roof and waits for something, a mouse, a frog or perhaps even her. Cows graze and plod in a field beyond the gardens, clearly oblivious to all treachery and black and white magic. Alison heads towards one stone building, realising rapidly from the smell and grunts that it's where the pigs are kept. Clumps of weeds grow round the side of the building, but judging from the terrible stench and the sight of trotters and bits of pig half covered by burnt soil, this was where some butchered pigs ended up.

There was a fair chance that Mary Urquhart was just dumped here. Gingerly kicking some soil away, Alison offers up a silent white power mantra prayer. She needs all the help she can get locating the grisly remains in this heap. Yet the task must be accomplished somehow, there was no turning back. She picks up a woven sack that's been left beside a wall, preparing herself for gore and maggots. *It is still summer now, here in 1638 isn't it*, she thinks, so presumably Mary hadn't been that long dead. Bodies didn't take that long to rot did they? But if flesh was burnt first of course then any remains would disintegrate that much quicker.

But Alison's gut feeling about the falcon proves right and just as she's about to give up searching by the pig house, she spies the bird again, this time perching on an ornamental sundial back in the garden enclosure. Was it possible Rum Butler buried her there thinking it would be least obvious? The falcon eyes her beadily as she carries the sack over to the metal sundial which had been mounted on a stone plinth. It doesn't move or bat an eye as she scrapes at the earth around the plinth. The soil feels loose and moist as if it's been recently disturbed and then her trembling fingers close in on something hard: a small human thigh bone. *Horrors*.

Just then she hears the sounds of women talking in the gardens nearby so she ducks down, crouching behind a bush. Maybe the Lady of the house. Danger over, she keeps on digging and finds a skull, the fractured remains of a backbone and arm bones. The blackish tinged bones have been burnt, too. But how exactly? Her enquiring mind had to know. Then, just as she's putting away an upper arm bone, Alison gingerly pulls what looks like a big magnifying slab of glass from the earth.

Rum Tum Butler obviously knew how to harness the rays of the sun with paper and glass which could stoke a fire. He could have used a lit candle of course but the manner of the burning had all the hallmarks of some black magic ritual, when rays of light are used to cement cruelty and not to enlighten. Hastily putting the bones in the sack, she hurries back towards the Hall of Mirrors, hoping nobody had seen *The Sneezewood* or moved it to another room thinking it belonged there. Approaching the grand Niddrie House was daunting, who knew how many rooms and chambers were tucked away under those vast stone chimneys? Searching for a humble stool could take several months. Then just as she's about to go inside, passing under a stone gateway, another whispered voice.

Beware the sorceress, too, Alison; she's not what she appears to be. Only those who truly know themselves will survive the Hall of Mirrors. Whatever you do, don't lose yourself in her! Don't look into the eyes! Listen to your own voice above all else.

Not the falcon delivering a message this time but another uttering from her deceased mother. *If people only knew what it was like being super receptive to Domains and energy for not everything's rational or measurable* she thinks, cautiously pushing the Hall's oak doors open. Alison creeps back into the Hall, alarmed to see a white capped maid sitting on *The Sneezewood* with her back towards Alison. Worse still, the maids appear to have heard her come in.

"Margaret, is that you just come in? I have had trouble threading the needles this afternoon gone but the mending's done."

The maid laughs an odd little laugh and spinning round on the stool, Alison sees that it's actually Kathleen Kennedy who proceeds to fix Alison with her eyes. *Don't look into the eyes.*

"You stupid little fool! Did you honestly think I'd let you find the precious bones and continue practising your own brand of warped dwarf magic? Don't you understand, Alison? I know everything there is to know about you. I possess your whole life. I know your mother died in suspicious circumstances, I have seen the years spent battling Sinclair. I watch you at night in bed, too, there's no escape. Look at me, Alison. I own your very identity, I read your thoughts. I own your soul; you obey my commands. Your sorry episode in the kitchen sink? Yes, I must confess I was surprised you made so quick a recovery. Your mind and soul is mine alone because I now own the film of your life."

Alison doesn't understand what's being said, and Kathleen Kennedy's long blonde hair looks matted and full of knots as she walks towards her, almost spitting out the words. Though she's terrified, Alison knows she's got to defend herself. Her fingers close in on the *Kwik Stix in her pocket.* Her secret weapon.

"It's no use, Alison Mode. I see you then, now and what you will be. And it will be me who owns *The Sneezewood* and the *Kwik Stix*, repeat after me. For I am Kathleen Kennedy, Queen of all she surveys! Listen to the voices now Alison! They know best, midget. The voices from the mirrors of life and your past and present! They know what's best for you; look at the mirrors, Alison. They will help and guide you."

Loud whispers echo through the Hall of Mirrors, and daring to glance at three mirrors nearby, Alison's amazed to sees the reflections of people from her past and present in them. Though it's still daylight, the candles give the ghostly talking and gesticulating reflections an ultra-bright glow. *Look at us, Alison! Hear us! We are your future and your now. All the people you've ever met in your life who have formed impressions of you, true to life or no. For we are you and we know you better than you know yourself. So come closer and hand over our rightful powers! Step right this way for we need you to be a passive thing or any little thing for us. Who can resist the desire and need to leave a good impression after all? Good impressions are everything Alison, for image and illusion rules.* A smiling fourteen-year-old Leonard and Mr. Wiper stand reflected in two mirrors, whilst in another Flora's image beckons her over, reassuring Alison that she can safely hand over the *Kwik Stix.* Realising the trickery, Alison pulls out the *Kwik Stix* and the *Twilight Dew* as an afterthought. Some intense magnetic, hypnotic force is emanating from the mirrors and Kathleen's eyes, its suction over powering but with an effort of will she looks away.

Only those who truly know themselves will survive the Hall of Mirrors. Whatever you do, don't lose yourself in her. Don't get lost in the mirrors or the reflected opinions of others. Remember who you really are inside, Alison.

Her mother's voice! This is a severe case of a combination spell, using mesmerism, hypnotism and magnetism combined – not to mention a dose of added delirium, as Kathleen Kennedy almost shrieks above the whispering voices to be heard. Alison had never seen these forms of energy used so potently in one go.

"You're wondering how I know all of this, Alison Mode? Well, just look at me. I have an advantage you see. That and the tiny hidden camera I have implanted in my chest. I took a secret picture of your eyes, you fool. And the eyes of others are the windows for *my* soul. They are my way in. For I eat own and recycle the souls and minds of others and all I need is an essence, an impression, a thread of hair or drop of saliva and I can own and unlock the minds of others. The act of eating is a kind of owning you see. And consumption, just like quick impressions, are what really only counts these days. The imperfect and different ambiguities can no longer be tolerated. Nothing lasts long in these demanding days and thirsts are strong by necessity. And we must have demands and never ending vacuous cravings, for these give purpose and value in the impossible quests for happiness no less, otherwise known as the key to life itself which will be owned and patented soon too. I have watched you in your flat using that wooden power stick and the stool will be useful for my purposes and plans for expansion. You are on my records, stored away forever, Alison. Now, hand over the Stix to me."

Then more horrors still, for turning her head this way and that, there's a terrible rasping sound as Kathleen Kennedy brushes her hair away from her face to reveal not one but two *other* pairs of eyes on either side of her head. And all six eyes are now staring at Alison, the menacing transfixing power intensified. A spider woman, weaving and spinning evil with deceit and flattery, petrifying and stunning her victims first to then extract and store the soul-essence later. Uber creepy. Alison realises with a jolt that she's probably been doing this energy hosting on others for years, undetected.

"Yes, you naïve, shrunken idiot I have eight eyes, one pair at the back, too, that sees what's gone. You're wondering who I really am no doubt! Well, I work for myself but am 'contracted out' at times. That's one way of putting it. My back is always covered and I can store people's memories and struggles, I know their strengths and fears so I cut and slice time *through them,* using the Domains in other's minds. For I am a super conductor, a ravenous hungry shell, whose emptiness can only be filled by using and manipulating others. *Informational abuse* I call it, the cynical but glorious misuses of personal information for gain. *I* do not need metal objects to access my powers either.

"But it's far too late for the likes of you Alison Mode, you're becoming too good at what you do. Way too content for your own good! How dare you manufacture your own well-being and language. So Ms. Goody two shoes, here your identity and ownership of your life ends. From here on, I control the script of your life, I run the programme. Sinclair-Rum Butler was an artful projection on my part don't you think? I own him then and now, too. For a moment you doubted your sanity and there are some who are willing to pay handsomely for such personal detail, believe me. New markets for watching information are always opening up to those who are resourceful. For some it's the only way they feel alive. *Infomania,* a new dis-ease, closely related to *Informania.* Fear of exposure and disclosure has never been so socially potent as now. People pay to hide and secrets are a luxury that costs. Look into me, Alison. I can help you steer your life the way you want."

Alison knew she had to act fast and use the highest invocation of the white power to deal with the likes of Kathleen Kennedy, a seasoned sorceress. Kathleen looked as if she was uttering a secret mantra-spell under her breath and was quite possibly about to duplicate herself into many copies making it impossible to be rid of her. *Double my double, multiply the trouble*. And all the while the reflected people from Alison's past and present, a cast both known and not, murmur and move in the Hall's many mirrors, voicing their approval and endorsement of Kathleen Kennedy, until Alison Mode stamps her feet in furious revolt throwing drops of the dew at the mirrors and silencing the wagging tongues. *Shut up the lot of you! I know my own mind and always did! None of you will distract me, I know this is some kind of test of my resolve.* Brandishing the *Kwik Stix* in one hand and the bottle of Twilight Dew which has flour dissolved in it, Alison stands defiant and alone. Stand up and be counted when facing an abyss.

White Power combined with twilight flour,
This hour I call upon your pure power
For let the one with wicked intent
Be powerless, her powers spent
As she uses minds to manipulate
And it's cruel not to love or liberate.
Shrink this woman down to such a size
So she'll no longer play at deadly eye-spy.

Alison hurls the dew drops at Kathleen with passionate conviction, causing her to sizzle out hot smoke. Holding her flushed face and screeching with shock, the sorceress of the ultimate abyss scrabbles towards a jug of water left on the dinner table. She throws the water over her face, looking furious at this blatant rebellion. The dew, whether drunk or absorbed on the skin, detected lies, helped to sweat out untruths and compelled the afflicted one to speak honestly. As she repeats the fixing spell three times, Alison waves the *Kwik Stix*, and something extraordinary begins to happen as Kathleen Kennedy, who'd looked so infallible and invincible just a few minutes ago, begins to shrink down, groaning in her down size treatment … until – she's firstly Alison's height … then the size of a small dog.

But I have the tapes, the recordings on file, you cannot destroy me! I am the future's key! Humans must keep regressing backwards whilst only appearing to go forwards. Simple easy convenience is what is wanted at any price.

Kathleen tries one last desperate attempt at reasoning with her small victor but the come-uppance or downance or whatever you wish to call it, doesn't end here and very soon she's the size of a large bumble bee, whereupon Alison promptly puts her in a match box she kept in her pocket in case of the odd emergency. The word was *gumption*, that's what her mum said she had. Alison will think of a way to deal more permanently with the sorceress of the abyss later but not right now as she can hear the footsteps and shouts of servants who'd obviously heard Kathleen's screech and had raised the alarm no doubt. Commanding *The Sneezewood* to travel forwards, Alison sits tight, waiting for the familiar *whooshing* sound and momentary dizziness. *What a pity we didn't give those self-important politicos the full dew dosage in the House of Commons*, she thinks during lift off – and just in time, too.

Quibblon Alternative Dictionary

n, *Infomania.* The obsession with the random over collecting, storing and measuring of information, often banal personal trivia, as if these accrued acts bestow some supreme unquestioned authority on the collector. Sometimes permission is sought transparently for data, at other times not. Then there are one off splurges of information collecting to be contrasted with ongoing tracking.

n. *Informania*. Another modern pathological disorder, closely related to the above condition in that collectors and controllers of information then see it as an automatic right to report allegedly suspect individuals or groups to companies or state forces. Spying, snooping or surveillance might be other words to describe these activities. The problem is that the power balances and justice can be heavily loaded against certain individuals. *Informania* could be seen as a possible reaction to a growing sense of actual political and economic powerlessness for example, claims about personal empowerment and representation. Governments get in on their own brand of *Informania*, by sometimes relishing the over presentation of data, surveys, facts and measurements to Joe and Jane public, while making claims about being democratic and participative as if the continued showering of people with sometimes *too* much information compensates for and distracts attention away from continued raw inequality and from the disproportionate power and influence of the new political-financial elites. Much emphasis is placed on *appearing* efficient, participative and transparent (whatever this term really means) while producing such information. And, of course, too much information can overwhelm, stun and confuse the recipient. Sometimes whistle blowers are useful but they are also at risk of being discarded and discredited once used.

Rum Butler's Lament

Oh, this is me then
A muddy wretch
Dragged as if from the seabed herself
To spend my last days counting pig-clouds.
How much I'd rather make that my bed of rest
Than here in these rumbustious skies.
But to hang, like a piece of cloth in the wind
A grisly reminder to the landlubbers
O' how the devil got himself
Inside Rum Tum Butler
And tossed him about like a cork in a bottle.

28

And Pigs Can Fly

Tiny scuffling sounds are coming from the matchbox by Alison Mode's bedside. In the grey December gloom of her bedroom, Alison glances down at it, still deciding what Kathleen Kennedy's ultimate fate will be. What would be a fitting punishment for practising this kind of abuse of her undoubted powers? She's got a couple of ideas stewing around in her mind. The journey back from 1638 had been a bit hair raising and she'd very nearly not made it back at all as several of the Niddrie House servants had dashed into the front room just as take-off occurred, giving said staff the frights of their domestic lives.

But Mary Urquhart's bones were safely transported, that was the third major accomplishment of the journey back in time though. They're contained safely within a sack and Alison is waiting, she realises, for the possibility of some kind of guiding message as to what to do with them too. Another small joy was having at long last discovered her Polish neighbour's name – Tomasz. She'd hand delivered a thank you note through his letter box. The kindness of 'strangers' who live nearby. Lying in bed on a Sunday morning is a luxury she can still afford as Alison's used to living on a small budget. *It's a minor miracle of engineering in its own right, isn't it Spock* she mutters to him.

For it is another truth rarely universally acknowledged that a single, female, working class dwarf will almost certainly be in want of a decent income. But Spock's scrabbled his way up the duvet and he sits on the bed looking at her, his dark eyes full of intelligent curiosity. So Kathleen Kennedy had been another one on the snaffle for her prized *Sneezewood* and *Kwik Stix* alongside Ruth O'Connor. Ruth's obvious dislike of Alison was becoming more and more obvious, so much so that other staff at *The Harbours* warned Alison to watch her back as instant sackings were not unknown to this woman. Those old chestnuts of envy and resentment. It was another glorious perk to be had from being a modern *precariat* worker without rights. Alison's mobile phone vibrates into life. It's Lady Hyde, her voice slightly breathless. They'd spoken once on the phone since the presentation of Alison's statue and Lady Hyde knew most of what Alison had encountered on her time travel but not about the shrunken captive in the matchbox. That surreal sniblet could wait for a rainy day but she wasn't surprised to hear about Brett's arrest.

"Brett's out of jail, the bail wasn't high but now there's no separating these two from playing chess! Talk about brothers in arms, straight up, yo. Edwards's slightly in awe of Brett's idealism I think and wants to know all about the *Children of Liberty* Movement. Apparently they have members in the USA too as Brett has contacts. *AGOG's* lawyers cited defamation of their commercial reputation as well as state security would you believe. But according to Brett and his pals, they were peacefully protesting and gathering signatures outside *AGOG's* satellite office and *AGOG* have cynically exploited the news exposure. Lucky Edward knows a few good lawyers. He says helping me in London and now Brett is his nemesis or long term conditional rehabilitation back into our marriage. They're upstairs right now, figuring out the chess moves and I cannot get a word out of Brett about the demonstration, they are both so enthralled.

I told Brett about dwarf's move, sorry Alison, as it was just all too exciting and I'm sure the chess world will never be the same again. They both want specially made chess pieces and are trying your invention out for size, so to speak. Whatever next, eh? The reserved establishment member playing an American liberal protestor, though I'm gathering from Brett that the word liberal has many interpretations. But never get into conversation with a heavy duty philosopher; it's like wading through heavy treacle. This is a bit of a gushing on from me, isn't it? Well, how are *you*, Alison, and what have you decided to do with the bones?"

"Lady Katherine, I have a couple of ideas and I'll let you know. I had a strong feeling that you'd call this morning. I'm sure I could use your and Flora's help again. You didn't tell Brett about *The Sneezewood's* time travel capacity did you? Brett still doesn't know about Mary either. It's enough that he's deduced that *The Sneezewood* flies through current time and space. As far as I know he knows nothing of the *Kwik Stix* or the Domains, though he does know the odd word of *Quibblon* of course. When he was my client I taught him a few words to try and shift his depressive mood but now look at him. Do you know if he's posted anything on *Flatter* about dwarf's move?"

"Not to my knowledge, Alison. But if I become aware of anything of course I'll keep you posted. Yo, my sister in arms. Extra Rib's been holding rap and karaoke evening classes and I've been overseeing them. So, excuse the slang. Oh, and by the way, very best of luck with the sticky situation at work. It sounds like the residents or other staff don't think much of her care regime either. Try to keep on her right side but don't grovel. Difficult, eh? Especially when it's your boss. Toddle peep for now. The wee hound is gagging for a walk so I'll take him round the gardens, I have a key. Hope to see you on The Links soon though or you can come over here of course. Could be a long day and they were up all night, too."

Alison notices that Lady Hyde's conversational tone and style still slips into a kind of street L.A mockney, or the Edinburgh rap version of this every now and then. But it's as she's shuffling into the kitchen for breakfast, closely trailed by a hungry Spock, that Alison has another brainwave. Of course! A fitting reminder, a souvenir or trophy. In her mind's eye she visualises the glass paperweight on Ruth O'Connor's desk with the mini scenic view of Calton Hill. She summons the object in to the kitchen with the aid of the *Kwik Stix* and fetches the matchbox. She who petrified others and stole souls and identities will now suffer the same fate. Carefully opening the matchbox, her fingers close in on the struggling Kathleen Kennedy who looks as helpless and exposed as a maggot. *I banish you forever into this frozen glass world, be gone! Your powers are redundant.* And with those words, Kathleen Kennedy is implanted within the paperweight, forever a static curio within glass. Doomed to be stared at, turned upside down and overlooked.

*

"Can you please explain to me Alison how it is that Fred was found wandering near my office study door which was left open? I'm sorry to have to say this but a number of items appear to have been stolen or moved from my desk which is not a nice feeling. Of course I'm not blaming you Alison, I just want to know if you have seen or heard anything at all. You can tell me in confidence. I always thought we had high levels of trust in *The Harbours* and that disagreements and secret resentments were dealt with in an open honest manner."

"I think Fred's medication was given to him too early and he'd drunk too much tea and wanted to use the downstairs toilet. I don't know anything about your office door being unlocked but I think Fred's not agreeing with his mood stabiliser tablets. He's been restless and irritable ever since staff upped the dosage."

Alison was very careful to avoid directly accusing and blaming Ruth for giving the ultimate order on raising the medication dose on the visiting GP's request. Ruth could always, of course, refuse or question the GP's opinion, being a trained nurse herself with knowledge of medication and drugs. The longer she sits under Ruth's scrutiny, the more Alison can feel her headdress begin to itch at her skin. She began to realise how Brett might have felt, wrestling for years with irritable skin. Her eyes drift off outside through the window again to the macabre monkey tree in the back garden whose wild tendrils sway gently in the cold wind.

A primitive looking tree, maybe the species graced the planet the same time as the dinosaurs. Ruth's fountain pen scratches down all the details of the formal yet informal chat with Alison; in the background the familiar clock ticked, that probably pre-dated Ruth, too, and was here before her ascension. Management seemed all about form filling and accounting for yourself and Alison vowed that, should she ever manage a home like she dreamed she would one day, then her style would be purposefully different. There must be real quality relationships with all residents, decent amounts of time to care and not just ticky boxes and undervalued staff. Christmas soon again! Alison couldn't believe that the residents were baking puddings and mince pies already; the crashing of baking regalia can be heard from the kitchen.

But the tree outside is still definitely green in a world that's rapidly becoming stark grey-black. Somehow it manages to be both ugly and beautiful at once in the shifting sky light. Its obvious state of health contrasts dramatically with the peace lily on Ms. O'Connor's desk which looks as if it's dying of thirst. Curious ambiguity everywhere. It was a shame Ruth didn't have a sense of humour and couldn't find the funniness in Alison trying to cheer the residents up with an animal and some juggling tricks. Looking at Ruth then filling out yet another incident form and entering this latest scandal into the home journal, she almost felt pity. But not quite. This was the same woman who stole plants from public places and had the nerve to track and follow Alison. She sensed Ruth was privately delighted that the paperweight had gone missing as this would give her an opportunity to frame and scapegoat her. The longer she spent working at *The Harbours,* the more Alison felt the heavy depressive air of the home and its management regime. She was reminded of poor Barbara Mode's home and treatment and it wasn't good.

She was due to visit her mother's grave soon in Seafield Cemetery and lay flowers and maybe do some weeding. Some new moon night soon. Alison still felt stunned by the power of the spirit world, she was still learning things and just how her mother's ghost had guided her and watched over her even back in 1638 was phenomena which defied conventional science. But then, what exactly was reality and experience made of? Nobody really could make ultimate judgements and evaluations as human experience and the mind's capacity was so diverse and wide. Ruth's cough shakes her from reverie.

"If you're helping Marg out in the kitchen perhaps you would be so good as to send Michelle in next so I can interview her. I'll question Fred tomorrow. Thank you, that will be all for now."

Alison feels she's on borrowed time and that if she slips up again then she'll kiss goodbye to her contract and have to call *Help Is At Hand* again, giving some polite covering line to Evelina. It was so unjust but as a temporary agency worker, she couldn't do anything about it. Knowing that there were many others in the city and no doubt the UK too in the same boat wasn't really consolation.

"You want to help the pudding army then I take it?"

Fred grins at Alison who can't help smiling at the terrible mess he's making of the icing sugar. A small white lake is rapidly being absorbed by the cake mix; he's not listened to instructions. Big Marg meanwhile is doing her best with Alice and Joan, two other residents who are dutifully rolling out puff pastry. Piles of dried mixed peel are scattered on the table top alongside rolls of greaseproof paper and little plastic models of robins and reindeers. Michelle looks anxious as she walks off to see Ruth.

"Get a bollocking from the nasty witch about stolen goods? I don't think she likes you, Alison. You or your headdress or anything about you. Never mind, eh. But your head gear reminds me of North Africa, I rather like it. I bet your pet hamster would like this dried fruit, shall I save some for him do you think? Never mind, the residents like you though don't you girls?"

Joan tries to hush up Fred who may or may not have been having tots of cooking brandy on the sly. But it was too late, the blasphemous creature was out of the bag and Marg had heard all. Not sure where Big Marg's loyalty ultimately lies, Alison casts a furtive glance at her and sees she is actually trying hard to hide her sympathy. As a large lady herself, she knew what is was to be targeted and blamed. The feckless and lazy seemed to some quite often poor *and* fat after all.

"That's not a polite way to talk about Ruth now is it Fred? And talking of witches, I've been called one myself you know, but as an insult not because anyone thought me enchanting. Fred, what on earth are you doing with that icing sugar? It's way too runny and will not set. You messed up the ingredients, so we'll have to start again. Joan, please don't over roll that pastry as it'll be too thin. We can't have any explosions in the oven. Didn't they teach you *any* basic cookery in the army Fred?"

Big Marg tries to restore a modicum of order and politeness to what otherwise threatens to become culinary anarchy. *But I have the tapes, the recordings on file, you cannot destroy me! I am the key!* And it's as Alison's rolling out her dough duties, that Kathleen Kennedy's words come back to haunt her. *Tapes, recordings*. It sounded as if Kathleen kept programmes on a computer somewhere, maybe at her home. Tapings, footage, photos that were just sitting there. But in the wrong hands, who knows and chances were there are other victims. As if an individual's unique experience and identity were no longer private and mysterious property. But how to find these recordings, could she risk visiting Niddrie again and doing a quick break in? She caught herself laughing at the hilarity of this but the mirth's replaced quickly with a wee gasp as she considers the possibility of a remote visit. Maybe she could complete a job from a distance. It would be another test of her powers.

Dishing out spaghetti strands to Spock has always been particularly rewarding and funny as his wee teeth and claws invariably get tied up and covered in sauce. Alison had discovered quite soon after first getting Spock that he had a weakness for all types of pasta. But the wee beastie deserved a good nuggle for at least trying to tackle long strings of spaghetti. The cookery session at *The Harbours* a few days ago was saved by Big Marg's intervention, and as a result a few batches of only slightly burnt and over spiced Christmas fare was bunged strategically in the freezer. The mystery of the depleted cooking sherry and brandy stocks in the kitchen remained an enigma, as unaccounted for as the missing paperweight, and though separately these objects and incidents were small and trifling, the sum total of these disappearances cast a distinctly unseasonal atmosphere in the home.

There was anxiety and fear when there should have been mounting cheer. Life in the city is again becoming noticeably icy, so much so that Alison's experiencing trouble getting a good flow of hot water from her bath tap.

She's been pleased with the way Spock's taken a liking to Lady Hyde's puppy who'd been named Pit, the yelper. She'd given Spock a bath and mild shampoo in a plastic tub earlier, but his distressed squeals always told her he didn't like the water, so she kept it to two baths a year. But she always found lying in water before a meditation very inducing to other states of consciousness. In her life she'd travelled many times in her mind and viewed places and people from on high but she'd never actually set herself a specific mission to enter a property or to purposefully destroy something by proxy, virtually almost and from a geographical distance. But who knew what the Mind's Eye could really achieve? The views above Calton Hill, The Pentlands and the Old College building in Nicholson Street had been especially thrilling over the years. Travels on the stool, of course, had been a bonus.

But would this bold, new experiment she was about to conduct in the safety of her bedroom be more effective if she visualised herself on *The Sneezewood?* Probably it would, as long as she didn't utter any audible command to it. She'd just have to trust the untapped subterranean depths that she sensed were there. One audible command though might have it up and running. Finally, after a banging with a heavy duty hammer, the hot water tap spurts and clangs back into life and Alison thinks about intentions and outcomes like any good modern day mystic yogi or magician-philosopher should. Lit candles and soft lighting help her to focus in the process and stepping out into the half lit front room; she's startled to hear scratching taps at a window. There aren't any trees directly over looking her flat but tentatively she goes across to the window, pausing before pulling back a curtain. She'd seen horror films as a teenager which featured flying vampires, and nasty blood sucking ghoulies but surely there wasn't some undiscovered colony of bats nearby?

Oh, pucker and large up some ounce of courage, woman, you who faced down and dealt with the great KK and Rum Butler singlehandedly didn't you, where previous dwarfs may have feared to tread.

Since training as a carer, working and earning some kind of wage, Alison's given herself more self-help pep talks. All these brushes with evil and darkness had strengthened her. Pulling back the curtain in a fit of impatience, Alison's surprised to see the falcon again perched precariously on the window ledge; the one that she's convinced belonged to Kathleen Kennedy.

Another message, surely. How timely. On instinct, she opens the window fully allowing it to fly into the front room. It lands on top of the TV with a cry, knocking the aerial clean off. It must have followed her home, somehow tracking the bus. Incredible really. She's heard of pigeons' homing instinct but this was a whole new level. Somehow it must know that KK is no more and that it's no longer at her beck and call. The falcon swivels its head round suddenly, watching Spock keenly. *Oh no, how stupid of me. Of course guinea pigs would be a potential meal.*

Alison cusses her stupidity under her breath, but then an incredible sight unfolds as the falcon seems to call to Spock ducking its head up and down three times, as if giving a signal. It flies down to Spock, who, though riveted to the spot, seems unafraid. Alison takes a deep breath fearing the worst but the bird just starts grooming Spock, combing his hair with its curved beak, as if looking for fleas or mites. Then she knew at that moment that all this was supposed to happen, it was preordained and that quite possibly something even more magical was about to manifest.

There's an odd moment when the bird stares intensely into Spock's eyes, and then, as if hypnotised or drugged, the trusty guinea pig sways itself across the front room carpet in slow motion. It's as if the falcon itself has passed some message on, using another animal as a carrier-medium. After a few long minutes Spock makes it to the bedroom and practically drags himself in front of the enigmatic portrait of Mary Urquhart in the wood which Alison's propped up against one wall. It's as she's following him into the bedroom that Alison hears the voice, a new unknown female one speaking in old Scottish. *Oh thank you, Alison Mode! You heard my cry for help and the bastard we both knew is being punished in the heavens. Please bury me on the Island, on Inchkeith near where the puffins nest and rest. There's hallowed blessed ground there, I will be at peace at last. Bring the sacred dew that you carry, cover me with white heather. Do this one last thing for me and I'll trouble you no more. I'm standing by your mither and she's a fine woman like you.*

Alison could swear that the voice seemed to emanate from the picture and as soon as the ethereal broadcast is over, Spock curls himself up into a furry ball and promptly falls asleep. Hearing about Barbara Mode brought tears to her eyes but she knew her mother approved of all that she did. Well, she hadnae planned on getting another pet but it looks like the falcon has rather chosen Alison as a new keeper-mistress and it would need some form of meat at some point. If she shuts the bedroom door the bird cannot fly in and disturb her remote break in.

Lying down on the bed, she shuts her eyes trying to cast this most recent message from the dead out of her mind. So there really is an eternal third Domain, a space-place where spirits or consciousness still exists and where time and memory as we know it is really suspended and recorded. It functions as a kind of portal in itself, a gateway just as parts of the mind can operate as receptive doors given awareness, training and the right conditions. Disciplining her mind, Alison Mode attempts the crème de la crème of all experiments withdrawing her awareness of the bed and pillow she's lying on in the here and now and instead visualises the house in Niddrie where Kathleen Kennedy lived.

Approaching the house, she's disturbed to see two men in smart grey suits lock the front door and walk quickly down the front path. They look nervous and carry suitcases. Who are they and why do they have a key to her front door? Are they government agents? Casting a potent third X ray eye into the suitcases, she sees thousands of computer records on disks which contain both trivial and highly personal information about people's religious experiences, political beliefs, DNA and genetic information, sexual relationships, physical and mental health, employment history, shopping habits, travels abroad, income, wealth and postcodes. Government or Corporate records, they must be. How dare they operate in this covert way. Whole lives and identities coded and summed up in a few banal lines. She felt sure much of this information was stolen, mined, extracted by stealth and without permission and all done in the name of efficiency or security most probably.

What the devil did they plan to do with all this information anyway – lock it away in some policed ivory or glass panoptican tower? If Lord Hyde could only see this going on, he might be more sceptical about the supposed paternal impartiality of the establishment. And the Gribbles, too, would be outraged, both grandma and grandson. And who knew how many similar violations of trust were going on in the name of democracy, power and the welfare of the ruled over? But the principles of neutrality and justice could not be left just to the state's definition, there must be independent rules of law in place but where had they gone? Had they been eaten away, sold and sacrificed to the highest bidder in sacrosanct markets or starved of funds, too?

The men climb into a car with darkened windows that's parked nearby and Alison knew she absolutely had to do something. Doing nothing was not an option not when liberty, privacy and freedom were at stake. Either big business or Government or both had been using Kathleen Kennedy as a data supply stooge, maybe money changed hands too. She'd heard of the police using psychics and mediums to uncover victims and murderers but this felt more sinister. Whispering a spell under her breath, she warps and shrinks the disks down to a miniscule size but watching the car drive away, she knows she must also do a house search. Did those people call themselves public servants? And climbing the dark stairs in the house then, Alison's sixth sense and vision is drawn to a small back room filled with what looks like a flashing server and filing cabinets.

Well pucker and large it up, pal – maybe the evil KK had been emailing some anonymous office with this stuff. Unplugging what she can first, she cuts through wires with scissors and then pulls open the cabinet drawers, shocked to find hundreds of life- film rolls, CDs and photographs. Running a boiling hot bath in the bathroom, she chucks the whole damn lot in, appalled at how long this had been inflicted on others undetected. As long as Kathleen Kennedy owned these images of people, both fixed and moving, she could tune in and access the minds of others. Destroying the images meant no access to people's minds.

A kind of mental rape and appropriation of identity. Job done, Alison again allows her mind to sink back into her immediate bedroom environment, focusing on the steady rhythms of her breath and heartbeat. Om, I am, it is all one. From third Domain back to first Domain, and no cynical prostituting, exploitation or misusing of the second Domains – or the minds of others, unlike KK. She remembers she has ham in the fridge, left overs from when Flora had been to tea just a few days ago. Stuff it, the bird can have that. Brett or the newspapers musn't know about this, she'd get no rest at all or might be discovered dead in some gutter. Maybe keeping some secrets was necessary.

*

"Flora, will you be alright operating the engine over there alone? You said you've operated one before when you and Mac were on holiday so I'm trusting that you'll deliver us safely. How you can steer a speed boat in darkness I just don't know but at least you have a torch and there's a lighthouse we can aim for."

Lady Hyde sits in one end of the boat alongside Alison who's carrying the all-important sack of bones to be buried. It's a bitterly cold clear night and all three huddle themselves as best they can in thick coats. In the distance a string of glittering lights illuminates the Fife coastline. The Kingdom just across the water that spawned Edinburgh's hunter. Alison's decided Mary Urquhart's final send off must be carried out under the covers of darkness and a full moon and there was an end to it. Crammond beach is quiet all for the sound of gently lapping waves and high above the loyal friends' heads transparent wisps of white clouds waft out to sea, *higgledy piggledy.*

"Shh, Alison! Did you not hear a man groan and a pig squeal just now? It sounded quite far away but I'm sure the squeal part *was* a pig. And look up you two at that cloud that's just moved past the moon. It looks like an animal."

"I'm not surprised Lady Katherine. It's the spirits of Rum Butler and the butchered pigs that were fond of Mary Urquhart. I condemned him to be forever rounding up the beasts in the afterlife above so he must now follow where the dead beasts trot. So every two weeks when there's a full moon Rum Tum will be up there somewhere, forever driving the pigs over to Inchkeith Island and back again. And seeing as the dead pigs wish to say goodbye, too, in their own way to their former lady keeper, we should expect more noises from up there."

"You really must consider getting your face on a stamp, my dear Alison. After everything you have been through. I feel the statue is not enough and that carers more generally need more recognition so please allow us to help you. Edward and I think it a fine idea. But really odd isn't it, the manner of Ruth O'Connor's death? Are you sure you didn't have some dealing with that too?"

Alison reassures her friend as the boat speeds out across to the Island. She hadn't needed to 'deal' with Ruth in the end for the woman had mysteriously self-combusted seemingly with a toxic mixture of jealousy and bitterness. Only her shoes and part of her legs had been found in her office. Everyone had been deeply shocked, the governing board of the home, residents and staff alike but the containing of the story had been the real challenge. If the fee paying relatives knew too much they might threaten to withdraw the residents so once again, the truth had to be carefully covered up. But then again, there *was* now a vacancy for a manageress and Alison had felt destiny calling. Some clouds did have a silvery lining. Carrying the bones safely to a spot she knew would be both blessed and safe; Alison starts to dig with the aid of a spade and torch.

Her two beloved friends wait patiently in the boat knowing this is something she must do alone.

Deed done, Alison Mode looks out towards the open sea. There's a chilly wind blowing in from somewhere, a breeze that signals more doses of the all prevailing over populated Corporate Edwardian Global Empire. And with this all-consuming doctrine of the market which almost felt like a religion to Alison, with it came the accompanying *wafflelopocae* and *wumps* – the army of chatterers and commentariats profiting in their self-perpetuating creation of endless hot air on the one end of the spectrum. On the other end were those who either completely opted out of socio-politics or who developed their unique individual moral codes in the ever shrinking pockets of private time-space that were not surveyed or gobbled up by the overpowering machinations of the media. Slaves' new world.

For those who resisted and thought for themselves there was one type of informal social contract they could still rely on, the one called friendship underpinned by *values* which transcended petty dualistic divide and conquer power games. And in the end, Alison mused – this could be one of the ingredients or components that saved humankind and the earth that species lived on. Not just the rhetoric of supposed financial efficiency which was so limited and soul destroying for all of creation, but instead kindness, honesty and knowledge of the interplay of the ever changing Domains within consciousness. Blue, green and red sky thinking. Now telepathy, moving objects with magic sticks, wish-full thinking and time travel could not by itself re-humanise or educate people of course but it could help some who'd forgotten how to feel, imagine, relax or even dream about the power of words.

To re-connect and re-charge within one's wild pure soul taking fresh vision, energy and integrity out into the universe. But where did this wind come from, America or Europe? Who knew in the end for Scotland, unsure of her destiny, still remained geographically part of the disunited

British, and the British have always been unsure as to which continent they are more like. Had anything changed since the eighteenth century Alison asked herself, gazing out on the watery horizon.

Yet despite her depression, terrible loss and poverty, Alison Mode had minimised claims on the state's finances, she endured debilitating taboos enough without the extra shame of officially being dependent on benefits. For she'd lived for a time on other types of old fashioned social capital: trust and co-operation which often flourish well when folk have nothing to lose. *I have climbed out of the vale of shadows, a kind of human endangered species as precious, soulful and deserving as the innocent African elephants that are shamelessly massacred for profit and greed. I have been attacked with insults and words so I grew my own language. Invention is truly the mother of necessity. And my damage and hurt became my gift; I would not be the woman I am without the black trials within or without – that is the value of the existential dark matter and the beauty of living your whole deep self. I reflected, survived and fought back on my own terms, believing in the dignity and sanctity of grace and courage under fire even when nobody else did. I would not be stripped or sold, no matter what. For I never was just a fawning pawn. Now rest good gentle Mary Urquhart and you, too, Barbara Mode.*

I will not easily forget the lot of those who care, of those who protect what's vulnerable, precious and has no voice. I have fought for the right to define who I am in my own private space, something I hold dear. For love and imagination endure, along with the memory of these. With these quiet words, Alison Mode walks down towards the beach and her waiting friends, the private burial on the Island known to the three alone. She would apply for the job of manageress for *The Harbours*, seized by a boldness irrespective of her fame. How ironic though, to become feted and celebrated for just being herself. But then the world, despite its ever more intense production of images, technology, goods and its huge disparities in wealth and health actually remained a lost and primeval hungry place searching for what felt real.

A lot of the time it appeared to run only on oil and envy and how anybody could retain their humanity and soul in such a climate was a kind of small miracle. It was a hidden painful truth, a paradox sometimes called 'progress'. But at least nobody watched or judged her here; it was a last unregulated stronghold. Here you didn't have to pretend that all people are the same with no differences; that very perverse ongoing game of denial of differences while celebrating individuality the Brits always exceeded at. *And that's really where it's at after all isn't it,* thinks Alison. We honest friends holding our own as best we can in another much greater secretive and savage little Isle called Britain. This story of the dwarf's true backbones, of the essence within the island of the isolated brave heart.

Quibblon Alternative Dictionary.
***V.* Nuggle,** a cross between a hug and a cuddle.

Dwarf Queen of the Mer

I am sure she is Queen of the Mer
I am sure
She hears
With ancient conch ears
The songs of the waters
With her knowledge of the moons
And the whispering sighs.
And she breathes and she sees
This primeval creature of the seas
Walking on sands
In deep golden lands
The humble wise female in the seaweed cloak
Her long held belief pearls
In the white-mother cave.

Disclaimer

This is the end of "A Dwarf's Tale" but hopefully not the end of imaginative visions or African elephants and rhinos that are hunted ruthlessly for their tusks and horns. Never underestimate the power of individuals (or the power of positive thought and action) to make differences. Now that's a never ending story.